OCTAVIAN NOTHING

VOLUME II

The

ASTONISHING

LIFE

of

OCTAVIAN NOTHING

TRAITOR TO THE NATION

TAKEN FROM ACCOUNTS BY HIS OWN HAND

AND OTHER SUNDRY SOURCES

COLLECTED BY

MR. M. T. ANDERSON

OF BOSTON

VOLUME II

THE KINGDOM ON THE WAVES

PRINTED AT THE SIGN OF THE BEAR AND FLAME
BY CANDLEWICK PRESS
99 DOVER STREET
SOMERVILLE, MASSACHUSETTS
MMVIII

To N.

Copyright © 2008 by M. T. Anderson
Map illustrations copyright © 2008 by Pier Gustafson

First paperback edition 2009

The Library of Congress has cataloged the hardcover edition as follows:

Anderson, M. T.
The astonishing life of Octavian Nothing, traitor to the nation. v. #2 The kingdom on the waves / taken from accounts by his own hand and other sundry sources ; collected by Mr. M. T. Anderson of Boston. — 1st ed.
p. cm.
Summary: After escaping a death sentence in the summer of 1775, Octavian and his tutor find shelter but no safe harbor in British-occupied Boston and, persuaded by Lord Dunmore's proclamation offering freedom to slaves who join his counterrevolutionary Royal Ethiopian Regiment, Octavian and his friends soon find themselves engaged in naval raids on the Virginia coastline as the Revolutionary War breaks out in full force.
ISBN 978-0-7636-2950-2 (hardcover)
[1. African Americans — Juvenile fiction. 2. African Americans — Fiction.
3. Freedom — Fiction. 4. Slavery — Fiction. 5. United States — History —
Revolution, 1775–1783 — Naval operations, British — Juvenile Fiction.
6. United States — History — Revolution, 1775–1783 — Naval operations, British —
Fiction. 7. Virginia — History — Revolution, 1775–1783 — Fiction.] I. Title.
PZ7.A54395 Asu 2008
[Fic] — dc22   2008929919

ISBN 978-0-7636-4626-4 (first paperback edition)
ISBN 978-0-7636-5377-4 (second paperback edition)

10 11 12 13 14 15 RRC 10 9 8 7 6 5 4 3 2 1

Printed in Crawfordsville, IN, U.S.A.

This book was typeset in Caslon and Archetype.

Candlewick Press
99 Dover Street
Somerville, Massachusetts 02144

visit us at www.candlewick.com

[TABLE OF CONTENTS]

ARGUMENT

—. OF THE .—

FIRST VOLUME

THE BOY OCTAVIAN IS RAISED IN A GAUNT HOUSE by men engaged in mysterious pursuits. ❦ It is revealed that the men of the house are philosophers pursuing subtle knowledge of the arts and sciences, calling themselves *The Novanglian College of Lucidity: Novanglian,* for the house is located in the New England Colonies, in the town of *Boston; Lucidity,* for it is an age when Enlightenment illumines every corner of the unknown. ❦ The eccentricities of that College are many; the boy Octavian's mother will not tell him of why he must live there, or why she is constrained as often she is. ❦ The reader is made acquainted with two of Octavian's friends, a slave named Pro Bono and Octavian's tutor, Dr. Trefusis. ❦ Through hints by these savant gentlemen and examination of his circumstances, Octavian realizes the nature of his situation: He is the subject of a great experiment, in which the scholars of the College of Lucidity seek to determine whether the capacities of the *African* are equal to those of the *European.* ❦ Accordingly, Octavian has received instruction in all of the gentle arts, in the deepest sciences, and is an excellent Latinist. ✲ The College of Lucidity having suffered some financial embarrassment, Pro Bono is given to a potential investor as a gift. ✲ As the Colonies resist taxation by the Crown, the tumults of war press themselves upon the College. ✲ Adding to the distresses of the age, the smallpox threatens the beleaguered city. ✲ Fearing disease, a revolt by the slaves, and a myriad of other destructive eventualities, the scholars of the College flee Boston and establish quarantine in the countryside, where they inoculate all of their party against the pox. ✲ Something goes amiss with the inoculation, and several members of the party suffer the full agonies of the disease. ✲ The disease proves fatal to Octavian's mother. ✲ Dumbfounded by the scene of horror he discovers when he seeks to pay his last respects to her, Octavian flees the College of Lucidity. ✲ He takes refuge with the rebels, aiding in the fortification of the countryside as Boston, now a fastness for the King's Army, is besieged by the Patriots. ✲ One of the Patriots, without knowledge, betrays our hero to an agent of the College of Lucidity, and the boy is again captured. ✲ Taken back to the house in the countryside, he defies his former masters. ✲ With the aid of his tutor, Dr. Trefusis, he escapes, leaving the masters of the College drugged and insensate. ✲ Dr. Trefusis and Octavian, now under fear of a sentence of death, flee towards the city and the King's camp, where they might find safety. ✲ Octavian muses on who — the King's forces or the rebels' — offers the greater hope of freedom to him and his fellow Africans, embonded in the New World.

[V.]

THE THEATER
OF WAR

drawn from the
Manuscript Testimony
of *Octavian Gitney*

Persona in Latin signifies the Disguise, or Outward Appearance
of a man, counterfeited on the Stage; and sometimes more
particularly that part of it, which disguiseth the face, as a
Mask or Visard. . . . So that a Person, is the same that an Actor
is, both on the Stage and in common Conversation; and to
Personate, is to Act, or Represent himself, or another.
— Thomas Hobbes, *Leviathan*, XVI

The rain poured from the heavens as we fled across the mud-flats, that scene of desolation; it soaked through our clothes and bit at the skin with its chill. It fell hard and ceaseless from the heavens as the deluge that had both inundated Deucalion and buoyed up Noah; and as with that deluge, we knew not whether it fell as an admonition for our sins or as the promise of a brighter, newly washed morning to come.

I left all that I knew behind me. Though the ways of the College of Lucidity were strange to the world and the habits of its academicians eccentric, they were familiar to me; and I traded them now for uncertainty and strife. Though I returned, indeed, to Boston, that town best known to me, its circumstances were changed, now that it was the seat of the King's Army and sat silent and brooding in the Bay. We knew not what we would find therein.

Dr. Trefusis and I stumbled across the ribbed sand. Treading through seaweed mounded in pools, we slithered and groped, that we might retain our footing; and on occasions, we fell, Dr. Trefusis's hands bleeding from the roughness of rock and incision of barnacles.

We wound through the meanders that led between stubbled mud-banks in no straight or seemly course. I pulled Dr. Trefusis out of the ditches where water still ran over the silt. We crawled over knolls usually submerged by the Bay. At some point, soaked, he shed his coat.

After a time, there was no feature but the sand, corrugated with the action of the tides. We made our way across a dismal plain, groping for detail, sight obscured.

But that morning I had been a prisoner, a metal mask upon my face, and my jowls larded with my own vomit, in a condition which could hardly have been more debased; but that morning I had watched the masters of my infancy and youth writhe upon the floor and fall into unpitied slumber, perhaps their bane. A sentence of death might already rest upon my head. The thought of this plagued me—the memory of those bodies on the floor, bound with silken kerchiefs—and I found I could not breathe, and wished to run faster, that I might recover my breath.

Tumbling through the darkness of those flats, revolving such thoughts amidst utter indistinctness, I feared I would never again find myself; all I knew was lost and sundered from me; I knew not anymore what actuated me. We ran on through the night, across the sand, and it was as Dr. Trefusis had always avowed in his sparkish philosophy, that there was no form nor matter, that we acted our lives in an emptiness decorated with an empty show of substance, and a darkness infinite behind it.

Forms and figures loomed out of the rain: boulders in our path, gruesome as ogres to my susceptible wits, hulking, pocked and eyed with limpets, shaggy with weeds.

We came upon a capsized dinghy in the mud, mostly rotted, and barrels half-sunk. My aged companion now leaned upon my shoulder as we walked, his breath heavy in his chest.

Once, I started with terror at a ratcheting upon my foot, to find a horseshoe crab trundling past in search of a pool, its saber-tail and lobed armor grotesque in the extreme. Dr. Trefusis, wheezing, greeted it, "Old friend."

His amiability to the crab, I feared, was merely a pretense to stop our running. He did not seem well.

We could no longer detect the city, the night was so black, so full of water and motion, so unsparing was the drench. Our senses disorganized, our frames trembling with cold, we calculated as best we could the direction of our town and made our way across that countryside of dream.

Once I was shown by the scholars of the College a rock, spherical in shape, which, when chiseled open, revealed a tiny cavern of crystal; and they told me that these blunt stones often held such glories; that though some were filled only with dust, others, when broke open, enwombed the skeletons of dragons or of fish, beaked like birds. Thus I felt in approaching my city; that place which seemed known stone, but which, when riven after its long gestation, might contain either wonders, or ash, or the death in infancy of some clawed terror.

We found ourselves at the brink of the returning tide. We walked through it without notice, so thick was the very air with water, until the flood reached Dr. Trefusis's knees, and there he halted, swaying. "I cannot continue," said he. "I will return to shore."

Thus his offer; but well did I know that he had no intention of returning to the bank and could not unassisted, did he wish to. I was aware that if I left him, he would sink to the ground and allow the waters to cover him.

I instructed him to climb upon my shoulders.

"I will drag you down, Octavian."

"You have risked your all for me, sir; and it is only right that I do the same for you."

He considered this, and at length, we now feeling the motion of the tide through our legs, said, "When I become burdensome, cast me off backwards."

I leaned down as best I could with the waters rising, and he clambered atop me, clawing at my head and neck for purchase. When he was situated, I stood again and began striding through the returning sea.

I know not whether we miscalculated the hour and season of the tides; whether we had stumbled too far out in the darkness; whether the mud-flats were less passable than they appeared from the shore, flat puddles actually concealing deeps; or whether, had we been able to see the topography of the mud-flats around us, we could have avoided this current by circumnavigation. There was no time to ponder the extremity and futility of our progress. I walked on, clutching the ankles of my shivering tutor.

The water soon was around my waist. The tails of my shirt were licked to the side. By such actions of the tide, at least, I determined the direction of the mouth of the Bay, whereby the water returned; and knowing this, I oriented myself so that we headed, as I figured it, near to due north, so we would intersect with the city, were we not swallowed up by the waves.

The waves came up around my elbows. They slapped at my chest. One beat as high as my neck, and I struggled to remain upon my feet, hitting at the water for balance.

"Saint Christopher carried the infant Christ upon his shoulders," murmured Dr. Trefusis above my head. "And now, the child carries me."

"You have carried me often enough, sir," said I. "Whenever you praised me to Mr. Sharpe, you held my head above the water. For that, I owe you my eternal gratitude."

"My boy," said Dr. Trefusis, weeping, and he slapped his hand, clammy and shaking, on my forehead.

[7]

This display of sentiment was interrupted by a detonation so loud I stumbled. It was, I perceived, summer lightning cutting through the storm, etching mud and spire.

"No worry," said Dr. Trefusis. "The most excellent place one could be in a lightning storm is stranded in the middle of a wide, featureless plain, chest-deep in water."

"The lightning has at least afforded us a glimpse of the city, sir. It is to our right."

"We will not reach it, Octavian. Throw me off and swim."

"I can do no such thing."

He sighed and tapped my arms. "I hope to meet Louis the Fourteenth again in Hell."

"Do not speak of that place, sir."

"I was but a child when introduced to him. I should like to ascertain if even in the flaming chasms of Tartarus, he wears high-heels."

"Please, sir." I stumbled onwards.

Again, the lightning rolled through the heavens. This time, I perceived something near to us — a dark shape upon the water but a few rods off. I believed it was a boat.

I stalked forwards, the water now risen fully to my chest. The drag upon my limbs was considerable. With difficulty did I make my way across the seaweed beds and barnacled rocks beneath us.

The boat rested upon the waves; and therein, slumped, was a single, cowled figure. There was a lantern before him, fixed to the seat, which illumination touched the edges of objects obscure in their outlines.

The water surged past my swaying frame, and I sought to remain tall as the wavelets teased me.

The cowled figure perhaps surveyed us, or perhaps was hunched in sleep or even death.

"Sirrah," said Dr. Trefusis. "You are in a boat, and we are out of one."

I reached out and seized upon the gunwale of the boat. "Sir," said I, "we must beg your mercy. Might we climb aboard?"

The figure, dimly seen in lamplight, pulled one oar free of the lock and suspended it above my hands, prepared to do violence to my grasping fingers.

"Gentle Charon," said Dr. Trefusis, "conveyancer of the dead, I have obols on my tongue."

The figure made to strike us with his oar.

Rapidly, I translated: "My master offers you money."

The figure regarded us. "Ye," said it, "are a strange kind of fish."

"Never has fish been so eager to be landed," said Dr. Trefusis. "Though not, perhaps, gutted."

"When this fish talks of 'money,' what does it mean?"

"Sums in excess of one crown for passage to the city."

"Describe the excess, sir."

"Two shillings. I offer you a crown and two shillings."

"In fish money. Surely that ain't good human money. Refigure. What d'ye call that in the money of men?"

"In human currency, I should think that an even pound."

"Y'art a good, talkative fish, but not strong in sums."

"Perhaps I mistook the exchange," said Dr. Trefusis. "A guinea."

"And two shillings more for not slitting ye and frying."

"Agreed," said Dr. Trefusis. He reached out to grasp the lip of the boat.

Our conductor said, "One other rule, sirs: Ye glimpse my face, and I cut your throats."

Dr. Trefusis climbed aboard. The water was now moving strongly against my chest. My weight being much greater than Dr. Trefusis's, there was some danger of my upsetting the craft as I clambered aboard. Both my tutor and our mysterious captain leaned out over the water opposite to me, that they might right the boat while I struggled over its gunwales. The boat was heavy laden with casks covered in a tarpaulin. I scrambled up, heaved by our captain's hand, and lay panting upon the boards.

Once we were settled, facing resolutely away from our host and his fatal visage, he commenced rowing.

Dr. Trefusis and I huddled side by side, our eyes fixed upon points in the darkness, that we might avoid any accidental glimpse of our captain's features. We heard only his rowing and felt the advancement afforded by his strokes upon the oars. We kept ourselves in silence, in obedience to his dictatorial will.

I know not what his errand, so hidden in obscurity, was that night. After a half an hour, we were approached by a whaleboat, also marked with a lantern upon her, and the two drifted without words until they were joined in comfortable parallel. Shadowed sailor confronted murky oarsman like a levee of the dead. "Gift for your mama," said our shrouded captain. Without further parley, he unloaded his wooden casks from beneath the tarpaulin, and they were received by two figures on the other vessel, which wraiths stowed them under a cloth and produced a purse that they proffered to our host. He took it, said only, "Keep them dry, boys," and began to row away.

The rain had lessened now. The returning Bay was fully in sweep around our prow. It was but fifteen minutes after that we approached the wharves of our interdicted city.

Our revenant rowed to the side of a dock and held it with one hand. "Two pound," he said.

Dr. Trefusis did not argue. He reached into his shirt, drew forth a money-bag, and paid out the sum.

We rose and stepped out of the boat.

We were come at last to the city.

Our spectral host lifted his hands from the dock, thus giving himself over to the directions and exhortations of the tide; and with that, he was swept away into the darkness.

Our mysterious ferryman having deposited us on a wharf off Essex Street, we made our way to South Street, where Dr. Trefusis recalled that there was an inn that might accommodate us. This found — the Graven Bull — we roused the innkeeper and begged a room.

It must be admitted that we presented an image little calculated to quell fears of the indigent and the beggar: a tall, gawky Negro boy in torn breeches and loose smock (and, as most certainly I was, wild-eyed with fatigue and the allure of the cook-fire within), and an aged man in tattered stockings and breeches so involved in mud that their color could no longer be descried. Though that very morning, Dr. Trefusis had been dressed in all the finery of leisure and the cut of fashion, now was he reduced to the appearance of one who had snatched his clothes from a rag-cart, being slashed from barnacles, bruised from falls on stone, wigless and almost hairless, a few wisps straggling down the side of his skull, dripping with rain as he shivered and coughed profoundly.

The innkeeper informed us that he had no rooms, the most of them being enjoyed by the King's officers, but that for a few shillings we might sleep by the kitchen fire, though he complained of entertaining such vagabonds. Notwithstanding the price was exorbitant for such hard accommodation, Dr. Trefusis nodded, which movement was imperceptible almost from the palsy of his chill, and we were admitted into the house.

We slept, therefore, upon benches next to paltry flames. The hearth smoked immoderately, given the dampness and warmth of the night. During the early hours of the morning, I stoked the fire more than perhaps I should have, attempting to warm my tutor, whose very life I feared for, so clutched was he by shivering and agues. I slept but little.

In the morning, with great anxiety I left Dr. Trefusis huddled upon the hearthstone and went forth to seek us more permanent lodgings.

Beneath gray skies, I wandered the streets, engaged not simply in my errand, but also in wonder at what was about me. By the light of day, I saw the changes wrought upon Boston by military rule. A great metamorphosis had come upon the city since last I had been there, the winter previous. The whole of that town was occupied in making preparations to repel the assaults of rebellion.

All that I saw struck me with the transports of wonder, for these habitual scenes were so greatly transformed, the familiar mingling so unreservedly with the confusions of combat, as to suggest the landscape of dream. Still could one mark the bustle of citizens with baskets, the cluck of drovers, their flocks reduced; still did one see the chaise and coach resting before houses; still did one hear the banter of livestock, the cry of the hawker, the tears of children, the exasperation of drays; but now, the hustle of commerce gave way in every corner to the demands of martial regularity and the irregularity of hasty defense.

Soldiers in red marched ranked down private avenues, muskets held at ready. At certain intersections were deposited mortars and cannon, a few idle powder-monkeys lying atop them to guard them, awaiting commands or playing cards in the shadow of these engines of destruction.

By the Common, the almshouse yard was thick that morning with Tory refugees fled to the city, groping now through the palings of the fence and clamoring for coin. Such an uproar and the sight of those pathetic faces could not but spur me on my errand, and impress upon me the necessity for swift accommodation and employment; for I had no wish to end my voyage incarcerated there.

The Common itself was little more than an encampment, the infantry having erected their tents in among the malls and grazing-fields. Many of the trees that had lined the gracious and pleasant walks of the Common were cut down, and the smoke of countless cook-fires hung heavily in the humid air upon those denuded slopes. The paths and lawns were turned to muck with exercises and evolutions.

The regulars marched upon the green in their formations as tiny men snapped orders.

The beacon-mast upon Beacon Hill had been removed, and replaced instead with a wooden turret; there was another fort stood opposite Carver Street, and a battery of guns atop Fox Hill. Flag-Staff Hill was dug up with entrenchments. Down at the bottom of the Common, where on sunny days in years of peace, the tanners had pursued their noxious trade in yards, and the clamor of tinsmiths shearing and riveting their goods with doors thrown wide had fallen upon the ear as harsh and lively as the tanners' art upon the nose, now doors were closed; the Marines were encamped along the road. Graves were dug for soldiers, some still open pits, others marked with wooden crosses.

There was, as I wandered through the streets, a continual popping and cracking as the guns on Copp's Hill fired, though I have no notion of what they might have aimed at.

At the first instances of shelling, my breath was arrested and my motions strangulated by the alarums of fear, lest at any moment return fire should be hurled back across the roofs and channel; but no such return was offered, and gradually I perceived that this dialogue of shot was empty of communication, its leaden utterance falling short, rebel and soldier gasconading as two libertines discoursing in their cups, lain on two sides of a ditch, their language full of gesture and epithet, but debating to no purpose, their subjects dissimilar, their logic a-ramble, their ears closed to suasion.

The populace went unimpeded about their business, little regarding the detonations, betraying no notice that invisible to sight, all about us on the streets and the green sward of the hillside were extended sweeping the dotted lines of ordnance calculation and the hovering directrix, focus, and vector of martial geometry.

The streets near the city gates were almost entirely evacuated, owners fearing too much the assaults of enemy artillery. To frustrate invasion, the avenue hard by had been torn up into trenches; fascines and abatis—bound together out of tree trunks stripped of bark and sharpened to fierce points—lay on the street before the empty houses of society dames and gentlemen of fashion. Stacks of cobbles, pulled up out of the dirt, were piled in yards.

Along the road there were mounds of furniture and clothing: stacks of headboards, gaming tables, stools, and Dutch *kasten;* these being the belongings of such as petitioned to be allowed to quit the city, but who had not yet received their exit pass, and so had been forced to tarry. Many of these chattels were on their way to ruin by the late rains, their veneer being invaded by the water and swelling so that the wood wrinkled and buckled. A soldier stood by to frustrate the designs of thieves.

For a time I regarded the picket-guards patrolling the gates of the city. I meditated upon the peculiar circumstance, that but a half mile away, across the Neck, my former companions—good Mr. G——g among them—glowered back from the fortifications at Roxbury.

Such was the state of the city at this time.

My search for accommodation did not go easily. Officers had laid claim to most of the rooms in likely inns; others were taken by the wealthier of Loyalists come in from the countryside.

I passed by the abandoned habitation of the College of Lucidity on Cambridge Street. Notwithstanding the hazard was too great for us to take refuge in that mansion, lest some agent of the

College return, I wished to see it now that my circumstances were so deeply changed.

I lingered before its gates. Guards in red coats with buff facings were stationed by the door. I made bold to approach them and, in the guise of a slave, make inquiries as to who dwellt there. They replied that the house had belonged to members of the rebel faction, and had been requisitioned as barracks for Clavering's Regiment, the 52nd. As they spoke, the doors opened, and several officers issued forth, laughing and tripping down the steps.

I bowed my thanks and walked on. I marveled at the strangeness of those rooms so well known to me—the moldings and wainscot, the herbs hung to dry on the back stairs—now echoing with the tread of martial boots and the shouts of command, the arcane experimental chambers, perhaps, housing the pallets of rank and file.

I left behind that scene and sought our accommodation further.

The difficulty lay not in finding vacant rooms—for there were whole houses vacant—but rather vacant rooms in houses where owners were present still to let out their property. At length, inquiring at an inn, I heard of a woman of some quality who wished to take on boarders and put them in her former bedroom, where her husband had died of an hectic fever in the most exquisite agonies some months before, the chamber being now loathsome to her, associated with the remembrance of pain and the tauntings of former felicity.

The price, given her distress, was such as would not soon be met with elsewhere. I told her therefore that likely my master— for so I called Dr. Trefusis, though he would have protested— would soon return with me and we would take up residence there.

Now I hurried through the streets beneath a new drizzle to the inn where we had stayed. Upon entering that house, I discovered a pathetic scene that moved my heart: The room now was filled with merrymakers and roustabouts upon the trestle-benches, calling toasts to one another. Slumped by the fire, in the midst of all of that shouting, was Dr. Trefusis, insensate, shivering though near flame, stubble upon his cheeks and chin, his scarce hair still clammy.

I woke him and told him that I had located a room for us in the North End, upon Staniford Street. He congratulated me, and asked that we might remove ourselves there instanter so he could sleep without being roused by Irish balladry and ensigns lifting their shirts to compare back-hair.

I helped him rise to his feet, though he was unsteady. He begged me find a hired chaise on which he could be conveyed to our new dwelling, to which I eagerly assented; we only then discovering that, while he had slept, his purse had been stolen.

We did not even have money sufficient to pay for our miserable night's stay at the inn.

The landlord, little inclined to believe our tale of distress, pointed out that he had seen our money the night before, and that we should make good on our promises now. We begged—we remonstrated—and, at last, he agreed to take Dr. Trefusis's silk waistcoat, ruined as it was, in payment.

So we walked the mile to our new lodging. Dr. Trefusis leaned upon me. I could feel the expansion and contraction of his ribs with each breath. He scarcely showed the spark of consciousness in his eyes. I am certain we looked to those we passed like a scene of utmost destitution and ruin; and indeed, perhaps we were:

myself, newly liberated into penury; and Dr. Trefusis, who had, just twenty-four hours previous, sat drinking tea in a country house, surrounded by all the trappings of luxury, waited upon by servants and bondsmen, now stripped to his shirt.

We arrived at our destination; where our hostess, seeing the state of my *quondam* master, refused us the room. I begged. She denied. I pled. She was hard as iron, saying that her nuptial chamber should not be subjected to the stench of the sea-bottom that accompanied this penniless wretch.

Dr. Trefusis, for his part, reached over and picked a white cushion off the chair and held it on top of his head.

I assumed he had gone deranged.

The cushion held to shield his balding pate, he said, "Madame, your servant."

The hostess regarded him first with disgust — then with fury — then with astonishment — then, finally, with abashment.

"Dr. Trefusis," she said. "Sir." She curtseyed. "I knew you not, without the wig. . . ."

"Indeed," he said. "I shall have to purchase another. But first, I have some need of sheets, a bolster, a fire, and, with an even greater show of celerity, Madame, a bucket into which I may vomit broth."

Mrs. Platt was a woman of some substance whose late husband had entertained Dr. Trefusis and Mr. Gitney upon occasion. The widow was trapped now within the city, so lost in her grief at the death of her spouse some months before that she had lacked all motivation to flee when General Gage declared military rule. Her servants had been dismissed, save three; and one of those three had died of the smallpox a sen'night previous. She now had a single maidservant, devoted to her since youth, and an aging manservant, Jacob, previously of the stables, who performed all heavy labor about the house.

Everything was in a state of disarray — sewing projects abandoned upon the spinnet, shutters drawn, dogs sleeping on the settee, dirty plates and platters still lain on the table, the food crusted to their rims. The neglect of the dishes, I discovered, was due to a curious impasse: Sally, the maid, now serving also as cook, refused to clean dishes, despising the lowly office of scullion. Madam Platt could not countenance this insubordination, but neither could she insist upon service when she could not pay a farthing in wages. Thus, the dignity of both women demanded that they never speak of dishes nor of swabbing. Mrs. Platt simply moved to a different seat at the dining table each night, was served there, and, without a word, left the plates for some future period. Thus, she distributed behind her, rotating through the room, a record of her meals, a calendar in rinds and cores.

We conducted Dr. Trefusis up to the bedroom and laid him in the bed in his shirt. He being settled and falling swiftly into a shivering sleep, I quitted the chamber and repaired downstairs. Amply did I render thanks to Mrs. Platt for the beneficence of her entertainment of my master.

"Pho, don't speak of it," she said. "But he does have coin? Upon his person? Because I cannot pay for so much as victuals now, the salt-meat is become so dear. We are starving. No person will extend us credit." She hugged herself, her arms wrapped hard around her stomacher. Her looks were drawn and pallid. "He is possessed of the money?"

I did not know how to answer her, being startled by her forwardness and unversed in the telling of lies.

My silence served the purpose.

She took it as a reproof, and held up a hand. "My apologies," said she, shaking her head. "Dr. Trefusis is a gentleman of quality. I do not doubt his word. You will forgive my anxiety. This strife and bombs have made me run distracted."

I bowed my head and indicated that we could not but be gratified at hospitality so seasonable and generosity of so open a character.

"Yes. Yes, yes. You are welcome to rest in this house until your master's work takes him onwards. Is he pursuing some philosophical theme?"

"He inquires always," I said, "into the nature of right and wrong; which is the issue in this present contest."

"Indeed," she said, but she was no longer listening, wiping dirt off a picture-frame with her finger.

I bowed again and set off. It was imperative that I swiftly find employment, having no coin nor credit nor property for barter. It appeared that not simply Dr. Trefusis and I, but also our new hostess, depended upon what work I might find.

I wandered the streets again. I walked by the side of the Mill Pond, which smelled of rotting weeds and fish, gulls clustering above it, screeching at the sea-winds, their cries punctuated by the detonation of artillery. I followed Hanover Street to Dock Square, musing upon strategems.

My plan for employ was simple, and was drawn from the lures of my former master, Mr. Sharpe, in his deceptions; as oft the trout may sup on the worm snatched away from the barbs of the hook dangled for his destruction.

Some weeks previous, Mr. Sharpe had told my friend Private G——g that I was in demand to play with the orchestra gathered for the diversion of the officers and the consolation of the besieged.

This position in the orchestra, but putative, conceived as a feint to draw me away from my fellows so that rogues might throw me in chains — this phantasm might now be conjured to solidity.

I stood before Faneuil Hall, observing the few men who passed in and out of its doors; all the while, my fancy painting the exhilaration of performance, the auditors delighted, the bows drawn in unison, the candles affixed to our music-stands, the ardent labor and delight of shaping melody, so much more grateful a work than the mounding up of fortifications and the crafting of ditch which had been my portion for so many months past.

I made a motion to enter the hall, but could not. My heart misgave; a sudden fear struck me. I hung back, and could in no wise continue.

I was a refugee, without instrument; I had not so much as touched a fiddle for weeks — and for months before that, had not played a violin worth the name — not since the dances at the Pox Party, now awful to recall. I was a Negro, a mere boy, a cricket with only youth and greenness to recommend me, demanding to be heard by gentlemen and ladies of the first quality. And I could already hear the sneers at my poor scrapings, the scorn at my childish vanity.

There was no employment I longed for so much as to play in a band of music — such was my thought; but the spirit accustomed to disparagement and humiliation, weaned upon castigation and contumely, relucts to believe itself capable of attainment — and relucts so in proportion to how much its aims are desired. The inward person doth shrink and hesitate before the daunting inception of active deeds, wishing that some discouraging voice should intervene and forbid, so that no hazard might be made.

Those accustomed to failure fear the novelty of success. Those taught the lessons of subordination are oft timid in the school of self-service. And those freed from a habit of bondage— bondage of the chain or the spirit—may feel as a man deposited in caverns without benefit of lantern and told he may range infinitely where he will: The word of his great latitude for motion is little consolation, when he might at any moment strike his head upon a ceiling he did not know dropped so low, or be precipitated into pits, and breathe his last broken on some umbrageous declivity.

So I did not allow myself to believe that I might offer my services where most I wished, but rather sought out other employment.

I turned from Faneuil Hall. With heavy heart, I made my way along the quays to inquire after positions. For several hours, I presented myself in shops, but none required help. The privates of the Army were in such desperate circumstances, their pay being so meager, that they worked at other trades than killing and dying to supplement their income. The city was glutted with them, and they looked upon a Negro who might labor for even less pay with jealousy and suspicion.

The gristmills were locked. Many docks were empty of ships. The smithies were out of blast.

At each disappointment, my spirits rose.

Had my route been witnessed by another, he might have noted that my inquiries wound their way back toward Faneuil Hall.

I repaired to the market to see if any might have need of someone who could tell sums and lift. A gloom had settled over the place, and the haggling was mercenary, sharp-tongued, and often shouted. There being few provisions for sale, the bustle of commerce had given way to the scurried agitations of scarcity and the angry chafferings of need.

I inquired of fishmongers, bakers, the officials who weighed the bread.

None required assistance.

Now, standing in the marketplace, engulfed in that invested town, that hive of my former masters' enemies, my eyes fell again upon Faneuil Hall. With relief, I recognized that I had escaped other employment only narrowly. Did I continue my pretense of seeking work elsewhere, I was in great danger that I might find it, cruelly disappointed by success; and I knew that my gifts, such as they were, might not be of inconsiderable interest to whatever impresario now organized these symphonies and dances.

I knocked upon the doors and was admitted; having made inquiries, I was told that Mr. William Turner, the music-master, was in the hall demonstrating fencing to young officers; but that if I could return within an hour, he should hear me out.

I returned at the time specified, and found him to be engaged still in lunging. A few of the officers dawdled after their lesson, enjoying Mr. Turner's foining and the free exchange of youthful braggadocio.

Waiting until they were gone, I was eventually greeted by Mr. Turner, to whom I humbly submitted that I hoped my small talents might prove useful to him, adding, with much stammering, that when I had played in Concert Hall a few years previous, my efforts had not been found unworthy of applause. He having heard my entreaty, Mr. Turner barely spake to me, but asked me to play him something upon my violin. When I owned that I did not have a violin, he looked at me with impatience, informing me that there were two articles very necessary to be a Negro violinist: to whit, pigment and a violin; and that without the latter article, I was not avowedly a Negro violinist, but a Negro, of which he had no definite want. I begged that if he might grant me an instrument and three minutes' audition, I hoped that he would not find his time poorly used. He left the room, where I stood anxiously for some moments, discomfited by our interview, gazing at the ranks of empty seats.

He returned with a violin, poorly tuned. I quickly adjusted it as he observed. I inquired what he wished me to play, indicating that I knew by heart sonatas by Corelli, Tartini, Locatelli, and such other venerable Italian masters as were most highly esteemed.

He requested I play "Poor Polly Is a Sad Slut."

Flustered, disheartened, I said I did not know the tune. He hummed it once for me. I played it back for him; I elaborated upon its melody as a fiddler would — exercising what I had learned of this art when playing tunes for the dances at the Pox Party — and played divisions upon the song — and, now warming after weeks without the welcome cordial of bow and strings, I introduced with a flourish my favorite among the Corelli sonatas — bursting into that beloved piece, so familiar to me and so gratifying an object to my senses — I then catching fire and playing with joy — motivated no longer by the dictates of necessity and the eye of censure, but rather by delight in my new freedom, bow skipping with the pleasant prospect of paid employ and new-found utility.

I came to a close, awakened abruptly to the shame of my display. I awaited his judgment.

As it transpired, this demonstration was, I believe, not distasteful to Mr. Turner; except insofar as its excesses suggested an overweening vanity, it made no unpleasant effect upon that versatile and incisive individual, and he agreed to let me play in the orchestra, providing that I could rein in my over-exuberant fantasy and unseemly pride.

Though chastened, I felt every nerve thrill to have braved scorn and demonstrated my worth.

Thus I was employed. He inquired as to my name; I did not know what to reply. I cast about.

"It is lovely," said he, "when a Negro has time in the day to deliberate even about what he is called. Perhaps, sir, you are newly at leisure?"

'Twas imperative I answer. My head thronged with names; but chief among them, my own. Thinking then of Cæsar Augustus, called Octavian until his majority, I replied that I was named Augustus.

"Augustus. Well chosen," said Mr. Turner. "It has an imperial ring." He instructed me to return the next day for our rehearsal and exhorted me to find clothes better suited to playing before the premier citizens in the Colony. I allowed that I had no money with which to purchase clothing. He informed me that though he wished ardently that he could help me, he was an impresario, not a Benevolent Society for Africo-Italian Virtuosi in Reduced Circumstances, and that I should "scuttle off" and steal myself some handsomer breeches.

As it transpired, this was precisely what I did.

The streets now displayed a kindlier aspect, for the sun had brazened the low clouds and shone past the weathervane atop the hall; the half-hearted artillery fire had ceased; merchants moved through the streets; there was the appearance of industry and health in the city; and I had an income.

I did not for a moment consider Mr. Turner's suggestion that I procure new clothes through theft, the habit of seemly, submissive, and orderly carriage being too great in me to admit of such a plan. Little knowing how to secure the requisite finery, and motivated now as much by pleasure in exploration as by utility, I passed up and down the town's byways, dreaming, as youth dreams, of Providence: that I should be suddenly supplied by a suit of clothes tossed into a garbage heap or lain in an alley, or that perhaps I should through some unexpected commerce with maid or char be heaped with a waistcoat hanging to dry which Master no longer desired. Though no such felicitous circumstance transpired, still I walked with light enough step. For the first time, I was free, and, better than free, employed; and now, unencumbered by the terrors of the night and pursuit, I was fully sensible of the exhilarating sensations of that liberty. My long *Adagio* was succeeded, thought I, by this new *Scherzo,* and I may even have endeavored to smile.

Well can it be imagined that my view of the city was rosy in hue. The sun fell golden and blue over the streets. Citizens laughed with soldiers.

And with every step, I rendered thanks to our Creator, who in His kindness had led me out of the house of bondage, out from under the scepter of Pharaoh, and across the dry sea-bottom to wanderings and liberty.

Though my heart dilated with my good fortune, still was I surrounded by perplexities. As I circled through the city, my thoughts, too, ran in circuits thus: The Widow Platt waited in expectation of payment; I could not obtain money without employment; I could not obtain employment without clothing; could not obtain clothing without money; but could not obtain money, alas, without that first employment; thus bringing me wheeling back to the original circumstance, as greatly vexatious predicaments often chew their own tails.

I had ever considered myself, up until that point, as possessed of a meticulous and even over-fastidious disposition. I was no man of action. Given such a snarled knot of cause and demand to untangle, I had sat and picked the ends with fingernails until the utmost hour, pursuing each strand in its involutions, little realizing that the knot might in one swift motion be cut, *Gordian*-like, with scimitar and the vigor of self-assurance.

So had I been; but in this hour, I became someone else.

It was my hands first knew my course.

As I passed down an obscure street, I felt spread through all my palms that tingling of the nerves that presages a great leap. I touched my fingers together, and found they sweated, as in the commission of some crime.

I bethought me suddenly upon the fact that I stood not thirty yards from the house where Mr. Gitney's nephew, Jonathan Gitney, Esq., had lived; the house where Bono's mother had served in bondage; and musing upon this house, I considered that the last time I had seen Jonathan Gitney, Esq., had been at the Pox Party in the spring; which would suggest that he had evacuated the town and had not, in all probability, returned since the outbreak of hostilities.

Abruptly, at this remembrance, I could not hear the clamor of passing carts. The street seemed tilted in my fancy, and vertiginous, and there was knowledge in my nerves and in the muscles of hand and leg that, having poisoned my master just one day previous, I now would steal from his family; and yet, from this thought, terrible to utter — for which the Lord may forgive me — I felt only giddiness where justice met with pleasure.

I being entailed as their rightful property, thought I, *it answers to the dictates of ownership as well as expediency that they should provide me with clothing. Such a solution is only meet.*

I suffered the shock of knowledge that this plan was lodged within me and I was indeed going to carry it out. Oft doth reason, enthroned in the pillowed *seraglio* of the brain, hang back; whereas the flesh, which must walk abroad in the streets, finds its own temerity. Oft do we act, and then inform the governing principles within us of our past action, and leave for them to write their reports and justifications as they will.

I thrilled, knowing my body would now commit this crime.

And at that, the commotion of the street poured in again upon me, and I heard sounds in all their particularity—the striking of hooves, the call of goodwives, the heaving of wood off a cart.

I stood before the door of the house, through which, when I had passed before, I had passed in train with others, and had then been bid to stand silent and serve unless spoken to. The windows were shuttered. I calculated my route into the empty mansion.

I made my way back through the alley to the side door, which led into the kitchen yard. This I found locked, as might be expected.

For a brief moment, I leaned against the door, my hands behind me, as if I lounged; thus situated, I ran my eyes across the windows of the house which stood upon the opposite side of the alley to confirm that they all were dark or shuttered. I steeled myself for activity.

No plunge into water chill with the rush of spring freshets could have administered more sharp a slap to the nerves than my plunge into the acrobatics of larceny: a heel upon the latch; hands grasping the top of the gate—and then me astraddle—and another leap—and I was in.

I crouched there where I had landed for some moments, hands spread upon the turf, reminding myself that I was stealing only from those who claimed to own me. My heart stilled. I was safe, and a thief.

How do we change—within moments, the whole form of our habits and dispositions may become alien to us, and we almost cannot remember what we were. So saith Heraclitus: *"The river where you set your foot just now is gone—giving way to this, now this.... Just as the river where I step is not the same, and is, so I am as I am not."*

I did not know who I was become; but I knew this person would be named Augustus, and would be habited in excellent array.

I rose and made my way across the little yard to the kitchen door. It was locked and could not be forced. I put my shoulder to the door, with the intention of bursting its hinges, when I spied an irregularity with one of the windows: A pane had been smashed, so that a hand might be inserted and swivel the catch.

Nothing held the bottom sash down. It was the work of a moment to lift it.

Now I was wary, however, having established proof that another had been here before on some similar errand of mischief. I crawled into the kitchen with great trepidation.

The chambers were dark, lit only by that light which might make its way through the slats of the shutters. Alert, I passed through the dining-room to the stairs and proceeded up to the bedchambers, walking carefully with my bare feet lain upon the extreme edges of the steps, so that they might not squeak.

Nothing, curiously, seemed to have been moved from the day when the house had been abandoned. Portraits still hung upon the walls, unmolested by thieves; no vandal had inscribed his name upon the walls; the cushions were pierced by no blade of jealous disdain; and the drawers were sound in their sockets.

I, then, was the first to rifle through Mr. Jonathan Gitney's possessions. Seizing upon several shirts and pair of breeches, I rolled them quickly into a bundle, to which I added three waistcoats, one of them fine silk for Dr. Trefusis. I found a wig, stockings — though the gentleman of the house had taken the finest, I presume, for the Pox Party — and cravats. I feared that the frock-coats would not fit Dr. Trefusis, but I rolled up two, shaking off the moth-powder. It was the work of but ten minutes; I then retired, scampering upon my bare feet, into the servants' chambers, where I sought out a suitable frock-coat for myself of some humbler cloth, ratteen or cherriderry. Finding a few articles suitable, the whole mess of apparel I wrapped around two pair of shoes, swaddling it all in the thickest of the coats and tying the arms about the parcel for easy carriage.

My theft complete, I descended the stairs as softly as I might and passed silently through the parlor towards the back of the house and escape.

I had got no further when I heard the scrum of shoes upon the floorboards of the kitchen.

Whoever the mysterious visitant was had smashed the pane to get at the latch — he had returned.

I knew not what to do. I could not move, so clamorous were my senses; I was fixed by panic. All my bravery abandoned me.

I heard the intruder move carefully, quietly across the kitchen floor. The broken glass clicked, ground, and splintered beneath his heel.

Suspended on the rounds of my feet, I glided to the sofa and slid beneath it. I had no opportunity to bring the parcel of clothing with me beneath the seat; for the intruder swung wide the door and entered. His calves were before me; and I waited in excruciation for discovery.

He paused near me; then crossed the room, at which corner I could see him from my hiding place: a youth of my years, perhaps, dressed as might befit an apprentice at some trade. He made his way cautiously through the chamber, then set off through the door to the hall. I heard him make a survey of the house, seeking something, perhaps, which he did not find.

Anxious with the passing minutes, I had almost determined to slide out and make a bid for the exit while he inspected the chambers upstairs; but no sooner had I purposed thus, than I heard him clambering down the steps, and he burst again into the room, giving me but a scant instant to conceal myself.

I lay in my hiding place, praying he might head for the kitchen window and egress.

Then he sat upon a chair.

The disorder of my senses might well be imagined; for long habituation had taught me to fear any infraction in the house of a Gitney; and added to this, there was uncertainty about the motives of this other thief, and whether he carried a dirk.

For some time, we remained like this, he sitting motionless and I Observant now, regarding the burlap weave on the bottom of the sofa, measuring my breath for silence.

He sighed; and there was another fumbling in the kitchen.

This clearly threw him into a state of confusion. His cheek flushed; he half rose; then sat; then rose again, straining to hear this new intruder.

He had no time, however, to effect any concealment—for another crossed the kitchen floor.

The first intruder sat upon his chair, which he clutched on either side. I closed my eyes, for there is some subtle magnetism in the gaze that nudges the lambent spirit in those viewed and draws attention to those who watch concealed.

Tensed for disaster, I heard the second intruder throw wide the door to the back hall. I could not forbear opening my eyes. Another youth stepped into the room. The first swiveled his head to view this new menace. He rose.

They looked upon each other, both reddening.

For a time, they stood in some embarrassment, unspeaking, immobile.

They came together in the center of the room.

Without further word, they clasped each other, their arms thrown around each other, bosom to bosom; they kissed, offering only, after some moments, a few endearments—as, "My darling." They whispered inquiries as to the other's safety. "I feared you was caught and dead," said one. They clasped again, and one of them hissed, "I have so much longed for . . ." He did not complete his sentiment, but grasped his friend's face and shook it.

I had heard of alliances of this stripe, a gentleman of the College having spent some years in Italy, enjoying the coarse blandishments of stevedores; hiding there, beneath the sofa, I did not condemn, but I wished ardently for the adoring prentices to gratify their Classical lusts above-stairs in the bedroom and quit the parlor, where, if they tarried, I would soon be noticed and undone.

They held each other, standing in the midst of the room. I lay my head upon the floor, praying that the enticements of Eros would prove more involving than the intelligences of the senses, as I was not well concealed, and the bundle rested beside the sofa.

Embracing cheek to cheek, they remained unmoving, clasped; I could hear each inhalation measured in that chamber; and each, I could see, drank in the breath of his friend, so dear in its emission; until one of them began to mock the other, exaggerating his respiration, panting in his ear, and they kicked at each other and laughed.

They wrestled, each plucking at and then casting off the other's bob-wig, one of which landed near me like some creature of the sea. The youths kissed and rubbed their bald heads together.

"Bedchamber?" said one.

"Oh la, sir," said the other. "My maiden blushes speak louder than words."

"Then here," said the first, "upon the couch?"

He sat in the neighborhood of my head. I closed my eyelids. He drew the other upon his lap, which weight made the sofa creak.

"Right here?" the upper one murmured.

"Aye," the other assented.

"But," said the first, "that might startle the Negro boy hiding under the cushions."

The room was still. In that silence, panic subsiding, the blood returned to its courses, my heart expanded once more to fill its wonted chamber; and I felt nothing but relief at my detection and gratitude for the laxity of their humor.

I spoke to the cushion. "I am beholden to you for your clemency," said I.

"'Tis nothing, sir," said one of the boys above me.

"'Clemency,' is it?" said the other. "He is exceeding genteel, for a sofa."

The first explained to me, "I beg pardon, sir. It weren't our aim to slap the wrist of any pilfering hand."

"Not for a thousand worlds," added his accomplice.

Said the first, "A man should never be embarrassed in the midst of pilfering."

"Almost as galling as being discovered in the midst of an embrace."

"'Tis, ain't it? That first embrace of thief and gettings. Delightful."

"A man trembles. Love at sight. Love at touch."

"That ain't our game. Thievery. Only we like a manse with a few fine whim-whams."

"I want the whims; he wants the whams." (Then followed scuffling and laughter.)

"Have you sacked the cellars?"

So disordered were my nerves from their romping *badinage* that I did not mark this question was addressed to me.

"Did the light-fingered gentleman ransack the cellars?" the other repeated. "I'll reckon they have a tearing fine collection of wines."

"The steps are by the pantry," I replied. "You will be pleased to find the wine around the back of the stairway, circling to the left."

"Many thanks."

"There is a crate of Malmsey supposed to be particularly fine."

"Very beholden to you."

"And the gentlemen may be pleased to enjoy the claret. Its owner spake of it highly."

"O most excellent sofa," said one to the cushion. "Most excellent and talkative sofa."

"I will remove myself immediately, sir," said I.

"And we will commence our game at tip-cat."

"Whackets."

"Hot cockles."

They rose and left the chamber, making their way to the kitchen. I heard their laughter; they descended into the cellars.

Finally at liberty, I pushed myself out from under the couch, took my bundle, and rose. I passed through to the kitchen; but then arrested my progress toward the window, and stepped quickly into Mr. Jonathan Gitney's study. I had it in my mind to remove some book with me, which volume might provide entertainment and improvement in my hours waiting upon Dr. Trefusis.

The young Mr. Gitney possessing a not inconsiderable shelf of books, I surveyed their titles for one which might engage me. With all the pleasure of old acquaintance, I seized upon the *Æneid*, delighted, I having been transported through its channels and rough bays in my childhood; but then I espied several volumes of the philosopher Locke, of whom my tutor had spoke with such approbation, and I lay down Virgil's epic, and took up those books instead. I weighed each volume in my hand, and wondered at which I should remove with me.

With timidity, I placed the three volumes of Locke upon the

heap of clothes, which little library rested there rocking atop the frock-coats and shirts. I considered the Virgil.

Mr. Gitney and his crew had demanded I read, and then had snatched all the books which gratified me from out my hands; I recalled Mr. Sharpe sitting in gloom, preaching of the impracticality of all Dr. Trefusis had taught me; speaking of my failure; admonishing me to succeed, and yet administering only cold fragments; sitting by while I performed and stumbled.

This was their constant study: They had taught me to adore; and then removed the object of that adoration and observed my discomfiture — as were I a beetle of interest, an eel to be stroked, a cur timed for drowning, or lightning itself.

And, this thought acknowledged, I began pulling books off the shelf and hurling them into my pile. I little regarded their titles or authors; it was a phrenzy.

Shakespeare; Congreve; Milton; Pope; the Stoics, the Skeptics, the old tragedians. Their covers slapped in congress on my pile. I was sensible of joy.

I had never known a pleasure equal to this pillage.

If you dare not give me an education, thought I, *I shall take it from you.*

The books were in a confusion on my bundle, far too many for me to carry. Having mounded them up, I shuffled through them, discarding some upon the floor. The others, I wrapped up in the midst of the garments.

Habit ruleth like a task-master returned from the grave; I could not leave the unneeded volumes in disorder. I stacked them neatly by the desk, lifted my pack, and sought the kitchen once more. Thus my walking library.

I could hear shouts from below, the delights of the grape. Bidding a silent farewell to the magnanimous Sodomists, I crawled out through the open window; opened the garden door; and fled down the alley, with my books and clothing held beneath my arm.

The plunder had been startlingly circumstanced, but its issue had been all I could have hoped. The bundle was large and contained everything that Dr. Trefusis and I would need to establish him as a gentleman and me as his servant.

So proceeded my own rebellion. First escape; then theft. In all things, we become acclimated; this is our strength in wartime, and also our weakness. What is a principle, if it alter with circumstance?

But what is a man, if he cannot change to meet changed times?

And if he can change to meet changed times, is he a man, or several in succession?

Whatever he was, this youth named Augustus, he appeared to be me; and he fled towards Madam Platt's house, secretly giddy not simply with the practical success of his assay, but with the good fortune of close escape and the petty delight of vengeance lightly taken.

When I returned to the house on Staniford Street, I entered by the back door and made my way up to the bedchamber; but was waylaid by Mrs. Platt, who lingered in the hall before Dr. Trefusis's door.

"I gave him some candles against the evening," she said. "A farthing apiece."

I bowed and said, "We are sensible, ma'am, of the kindness of your attentions towards us, and honored that you would with such assiduity regard even the most minute of our—"

"Is he an atheist?" she asked anxiously.

He was, and had been hounded from many of the gilded courts of Europe for his blasphemies; but I avowed he was the firmest Christian I had ever known; which was not, in its way, untrue.

Uneasily, she nodded, and continued along the thin corridor.

She having departed, I entered in and found the most beloved of tutors lying almost in a swoon, so distempered was he by fevers. I took his hands and asked him how he fared.

"The woman is watching me," he whispered. "I believe there is a little maggot in her brain whispers I don't have two farthings to clink."

I informed him of my employment at Fanueil Hall, and that it should result in a small sum sufficient to carry our rent, with, however, no excess. Still wary of censure, I further related to him my entry into Mr. Jonathan Gitney's house and my theft of clothing. He did, however, but praise me.

"Excellent!" he cried, laughing. "Excellent. Good boy. Nothing breeds fortune like a hat and jabot."

That night, Dr. Trefusis suffered greatly from his chill. He could not cease shaking, though he was heaped with blankets and it was high summer. The chamber was infernal in its heat and rank in its scent. I now held the pot for him when he urinated — he who, in my childhood, had been called upon to capture and weigh my water and fæces. Now distempered as he was, he yielded no solids.

He felt a discomfort in his very bones, as if they contracted so that they might struggle out of the mercenary peel of flesh and walk abroad. The ache in his marrow lashed him all the night, and he turned from side to side, seeking oblivion's solace. I slept on a straw mattress upon the floor, and I was often awakened by his pained tumblings.

I lay beside the bed, fearful for his health; determined he should recover; and conscious of a foreign satisfaction, perhaps even pleasure, that awaited a ripe moment to grow from bud to bloom.

I was, though still bound in law, free in practice; I would soon be receiving a small sum to play my music, I would pay for my own lodgings, and the kindest philosopher that ever the world saw was my mentor and remained at my side. And though we lay in a city starving; though we were surrounded by an implacable enemy; though we slept amidst the encampments of soldiers from afar, Scotsman and Mancunian, convict and younger son, all over-whelmed as we by the intimations of the coming strife when Boston should rouse itself and march; though the dark of the night was marked with the thousand cook-fires of rebels who would, if not checked, soon rise to overrun us; though I little knew what would come and little understood what had already transpired; still, I felt the motions of happiness perhaps for the first time since the Transit of Venus had passed over our heads and left behind it clouds and shadow.

In the midst of this chaos, I had found contentment.

The next day, arrayed in black satin breeches and my ill-gotten waistcoat, I made my way again to Faneuil Hall. The clothes were poorly fitted for my frame, being cut for one much stouter, and the breeches fairly flapped about my knees.

When I arrived, I found the orchestra arranging themselves on chairs; the strings being a collection of civilians, the brass drawn from the military band of the 64th Regiment, which famed consort gave a strict and louring aspect to the proceedings, their uniforms being black shot through with white lace and red. Apprehensive at the sight of these men, so stern in their demeanor, I hesitated by the door, unwilling to go further.

Mr. Turner caught sight of me, wincing at the sag of my stockings. He came to my side. "You still," he asked, "are in need of a violin?"

To this I assented; and he requested a boy fetch me a fiddle lain in another room. That battered instrument placed in my hands, Mr. Turner came again to my side and, observing how I held it to my ear and plucked its strings, he inquired of me, "Does it sound well?"

I gave a slight bow and replied, "To he who is parched for music, sir, and who swells with gratitude to one who so benevolently grants his desire, even the most ill-tuned string sounds with glorious—"

"Indeed. That instrument, my recent Augustus—that instrument belonged to your predecessor, an old Negro with about one tooth. He was excellent at playing an Irish jig and lively at the *allegros,* but he was, as it happened, spying for the rebels, so we hanged him for treason. He did a little dance with more vigor than regularity and died with his tongue out and piss on his britches. If the new Augustus will pardon for one moment a fond dancing-master's forwardness, might I inquire whether you too plan on conveying intelligence to rebels? Do you long for the domino and dagger?"

"No, sir."

"You are sure?"

"Yes, sir."

"Because there is nothing easier than plucking a Negro out of an orchestra and setting him to dance on high. Aye?"

"Yes, sir."

"Kicking a gavotte in Lady Hemp's embrace. I merely request you consider it; and if any rebel should approach you and ask for news of the Sixty-fourth or any other matter, I would be gratified if you informed them you are bespoke for the next several dances."

"Thank you, sir," said I, but he was already gone from my side. He left me wary.

It took no little time to shed these disagreeable impressions, even once the brilliancies of the symphony were cast up around me. Notwithstanding such anxious reflections, however, I was mollified by the exhilaration of playing in company—for it must be remembered that I had only very infrequently played with a full band of music previously, most of my instrumental turns being as part of a small consort, best suited, respectively, for the contradance or the *sonata a tre*.

To participate, then, in the pomp of the orchestra, in the full scintillation thereof, was in the highest degree thrilling. Is this not the image of the perfect republic—each instrument singing its wonted melody, endeavoring at once to express its part, and, in the same instance, to conform its voice to the conversation of the whole?

We prepared, as it transpired, for a concert to take place later in the week in benefit of the poor of the city, the officers of the army being much concerned that the citizens starved as the rebels blocked off all routes of trade save the sea-routes from the farthest destinations. We played several symphonies and a few arias which a soprano much admired by a lieutenant-colonel would sing; and there was to be a harpsichord concerto writ by a celebrated sapper of the Army Corps of Engineers, a man whose speciality was tunneling under walls and laying detonations, but who had enjoyed the fruits of gentler arts, and turned his nimble fingers to scribbling for the jacks and strings. I found the whole program of the greatest delight.

The rehearsal being complete, I packed my borrowed violin

in its ungainly box and set forth across the market square, little crediting that I now was at liberty to play upon that instrument dearest to my heart whenever I pleased, did Mrs. Platt allow it; and that I might play whatever my fancy suggested to me. I delighted in the thought.

Seagulls cried above the town dock and settled on the spars of ships just off the wharves; the heated air smelled deeply of sheep and tar.

As I made my way back to Mrs. Platt's house, I had a sudden notion to return by way of the College of Lucidity. I know not whether I was actuated by the desire for some phantom approval of my new situation or for defiant display, but I wished to pass its door; I wished to stand before it, to look and be done.

It was not a walk of any great distance to that gaunt house; and, that quickly accomplished, I halted, violin-case in hand, and regarded the place, examining both the familiarities of infant association and the novelties of occupation: the guard who stood beside the door; the Regimental colors hung from out Mr. Gitney's bed-chamber window; the cook-fire lit in the stable.

The last time I had gazed upon the house before the previous day, it had been December, the morning when Mr. Gitney had revolved the key in the lock of the great doors at last and we had evacuated the town in favor of the rural retreats of Canaan some months before the Pox Party. The carts had been heaped with our belongings; my mother had been alive.

In my memory, she darts back from the carriage, her arms slim, her hands volant, her smile vivid, her head inclined with all the graces of art, her neck, marked with lace *collier,* imperial in its attitude; a cap upon her hair. I see her run across the cobbles to the door.

"I have forgot my mantilla," she says.

"The door is locked," says Mr. Gitney.

"I will catch chills."

"You waited," says he, "only to delay us and so prove your sovereignty."

And yet she took the key from his hand; and smiling, unlocked the door, and flew up the stairs to fetch her scarf.

I have forgot my mantilla. Of such trivialities are moments made; and hours built; and years constructed; and ruins, finally, remain, with ornaments half-seen beneath the grasses.

She ran, an animal endowed with contraction and extension; she ran; *I have forgot my mantilla.* She stepped from the carriage, flesh envivified; her brain tricked out in schemes; *I have forgot my mantilla;* only this do I recall; she ran.

And then she returns with that whimsy wrapped around her shoulders, and is handed into the carriage; then we are gone upon the carts and equipages, our sojourn begun; and we are without the city gates; and the fields are about us, ice in the meanders of sloughs; and then a somber boy and his tutor tread the road the other way, gray with summer's dust, and it is eight months later, and she will not return.

This I know. We return, but she shall not.

I presume her body lies now in Canaan.

At her last, she did not appear to be human. She had abandoned species.

Staring at the house in the full heat of summer, it was scarcely credible that the world had so swiftly fallen into confusion. I looked at that manse, now a bedding-place for the Parliamentary Army, its interiors unknown to me after a life of confinement there. I did not know how to understand my changed state, nor that of the rugged world.

As I peered, I seemed to spy her at the windows, all of them equally, each window engraved with its own scene, its own revenant in cloak or sacque, each spirit passing a different way before my sight.

They lingered to regard me — she at sixteen or seventeen, when first I could recall her, telling tales of petal thrones and chariots hauled by panther-team; she at twenty, smiling and severe, gazing at me though surrounded by men; she at twenty-five, quiet and rueful, scarce attending to her embroidery upon its hoop as long evenings passed in silence.

In each pane of our abandoned house transformed, she watched me.

I pled with her — knowing not why I pled — "But I am free. I play my violin."

It was not enough; I saw the blank windows; and that was more terrible than the specters of memory with their piercing gaze; that absence; those sheets of glass that held no image but transmission.

"Please," I whispered to her. "Please let me feel this joy."

That night, I returned home, anticipating the felicitations of the most generous of tutors upon my first rehearsal, and anxious to minister to his health; but when I arrived, I found Mrs. Platt awaiting me, sitting upright without repose on an old *fauteuil*.

She instructed, "Tell Dr. Trefusis I find him uncommon rude."

I submitted that no thought could be further from Dr. Trefusis's intent than to incommode such an excellent hostess.

"He is indeed an atheist, is he not?"

I could not deny it; and yet endeavored to, when she demanded, "And the fine Dr. Trefusis don't have a grout to his name, does he?"

I offered, "We do have a scheme, however, that shall cover our expenses, madam."

"Capital," said Mrs. Platt. "We shall all starve." She walked from the room without dismissing me.

She returned a moment later to add, "Kindness is never repaid. I should have known no good would come of feeding a philosopher." She turned and frowned, framed in the door; behind her in the gloom, circuits of soiled plates glowed faintly like the lunar phases. "His death will leave the chamber haunted."

"I trust, madam," I said calmly, "that there is no reason to anticipate his death."

"He anticipates it constantly when you're abroad," she said. "He calculates." She demanded, "He shall not die in that chamber. Philosophers require a whole retinue of devils for their removal from this world. They are the grandees of the infernal kingdom." She turned and left me. "I may be sure of constant annoyance from red-eyed frogs."

I lingered some minutes, being unaccustomed to retiring from a chamber without permission or direction; but our hostess having disappeared, I passed above-stairs to see what strife had occasioned such an outburst.

Dr. Trefusis lay abed, staring into the darkness, the smell of his perspiration and urine thick in the chamber.

No sooner had I made polite inquiry as to the disagreement below, than he asked me, "Do you recall what words I spake to you this morning?"

I considered, and admitted that I did not recall any specific thing.

"Yet those might have been my final words," he said.

"Your health, I trust, is not declining, sir."

"Oh, I am most sickly," he said. "I must needs have blood let."

I remonstrated that we did not have funds sufficient to call doctor or surgeon.

"Open my vein," he said. He held out his arm. "We must flush the poison. I have been stirring helplessly all day."

"Mayhap, sir, you stir because you mend."

"Open my vein."

"That seems a perilous course, sir."

"I demand to be bled. My blood is hot."

"Sir, we have no skill in that art."

"My constitution is unbearably plethoric."

This debate went on for some minutes, me demurring, he requiring, until his demands became so violent I feared damage through apoplexy, and discerned that indeed, he perhaps would be aided by exsanguination; though it pleased me not at all to be administering that remedy myself, for I had never attempted it before, and so little was it a course I had considered, I trembled at my inexperience.

Still, I querulously assented, and, upon his order, went to seek a knife.

Sally was in the kitchen. "The Devil's in him today," she said. "I took him his broth and asked after his wellness, and he didna' give me no answer, so I asks him again, and still no answer, so I asks a third time, and he starts to rail and shout."

I looked at her with quizzical eye.

"Don't be asking me. He was all up about Nothing and the Void."

I returned with the knife to Dr. Trefusis's side. He raised himself up upon the bolster, and I slipped a pewter bowl beneath his arm. I lay the knife upon the skin.

"I do not know how deep to make the incision," I said. "We have no benefit of lancet or fleam."

"Light cuts," he said. "The blood will come."

I pressed one hand to his chest to restrain him, should he start when I pierced him. My teeth grit, I cut my tutor.

The blood flowed easily into the bowl. He groaned with relief at its exudation.

As we waited for the blood to pool, he said, "I spake to you this morning of the Void. I made a pretty speech regarding how all of what we know is but a small light space in the theater of matter; and that space is unfurled around us like a set piece upon a stage. I opined that nothing exists without us to perceive it."

"I recall it now, sir," said I.

"With me to remind you. If I had passed? Would you be able to publish my final words?"

"Those were not your final words, sir."

"Precisely!" he said, shaking the arm that bled. "Sally asked so many garrulous, probative questions that at ten this morning I was reduced to answering, 'I am sufficiently well, madam.' Which only a fool would offer as his last words."

"So, sir, you then repeated your original speech on matter."

"It was more exact in my memory at the time."

"Though she did not note it in detail."

He made a flat, dismissive noise. "One might sooner scrawl on granite with a lilac than impress rhetorical niceties upon that woman."

"You cannot anticipate your final removal in this way, sir."

"Bind up the vein, if you please," he said. "I am done with bleeding."

I lay the knife in the bowl and slid a rag beneath his arm. The blood would not stop its flowing, though I tied the rag tightly about the incision. He did not watch the process, but surveyed the ceiling as my fingers, slippery now with his gore, worked to tighten the tourniquet.

I grew fearful that we would not be able to staunch the flow. The blood now drenched the sheets; his elbow had tipped the bowl so that the blood I had already let also stained his side.

I worked at the knot, but my fingers were too wet.

Jogged by my exertions, he murmured, "We may so easily slip out of ourselves."

His looks were pallid and waxen.

I scrambled to find something else which might provide a tighter bond. Full of alarms, I surveyed the room. A woolen stocking presented itself to me upon the floor, and I pounced upon it, snatched it where it lay, and brought it to the patient's bed.

I tied it so tight as I could, fearful also of empurpling the forearm.

The new tourniquet complete, I surveyed my gory handiwork. He raised the hand and placed it on my head. He whispered, "'Do not weep: Heaven fashioned us of nothing; and we strive to bring ourselves to nothing.'"

With that, he removed the hand from my head, curled it against him, and closed his eyes.

"You must not sleep," said I, and called his name. "Dr. Trefusis," I pled, "you must not sleep. I fear I bled you too extremely."

He who had been my benefactor within the College of Lucidity now lay in his sheets looking as vulnerable as a child, blinking at me suddenly in fear; yet he did not speak.

"Are you alert?" said I.

He nodded gradually. I chafed his arms and rushed below-stairs for a basin of water with which to shock him. Upon my returning, I slapped at his face with the wet cloth as he snorted protests and held up his hands.

This I felt a sufficient proof of the continued activity of his vivid spirits. I was sensible in equal measure of relief at his delivery and shame at my incompetence. I wished to do or say something further, but he simply blinked and looked ruefully about the room.

I sat by him and watched the throb of his pulse in the wrist of the marked arm. Darkness was falling, and we could hear the sentries firing far off to mark the end of day.

Our hostess and Sally entered, and, seeing the blood upon the bed, were much disturbed, crying out to the good man upon the bed, urging his condition.

"Sir," said Mrs. Platt, "are you well?"

He would not respond to them.

"Would you wish some broth?" asked Sally.

They plied him with more questions.

He looked at me in supplication.

"Speak a word to us, sir," said Mrs. Platt.

He reached up and locked his mouth with his fingers.

"Oh, sweet mercy," said Sally. "It will be your final words again, is it?"

He shrugged and nodded.

We got no more word out of him, he stubbornly avoiding all inquiries but those which might be satisfied with affirmative or negative; and after a time of this, I began to be aware that he enjoyed this peculiar pantomime; and Sally began to smile. Notwithstanding the displeasure of our hostess, who spake dismissively of old men who act the part of little boys, we even laughed, and the doctor was forced himself into merriment; and at length, he even nodded to an offer of solid bread, which delicacy we could not, as it transpired, provide him, having none in the house.

That night, I listened with care to his breathing as he slept; and I thought on final words, and that he did not believe he had a soul that would survive his decease. It pained me beyond measure that this man, the most magnanimous of mentors, the shield and buckler of my childhood, should confront death as mere negation, and by so doing, perhaps forfeit his chance at eternal bliss.

I considered his last sentences, his atheistic unction, and lamented that in his sight, the human character was itself little more than a sentence spoken, a succession of sounds that acquired meaning only with accretion; but which was only to be a succession, a train of one thing following another, rather than a thought entire and whole, as the soul should be, cohering beyond our breath; and looking at my tutor, I feared for that moment when the final word might be said and done.

Those weeks in August were not easy ones for those of us besieged. The rebel blockade deprived the town of victuals. Rations among the Army were reduced to salt-pork, now rank with flies and greening. Hunger was become general in the city, and sickness too. There were few engagements with the enemy at that time—the rebels, we suspected, had little powder and less spirit—so the most numerous deaths were from distempers and disorders.

Sally often came back from the market without meat or vegetable, and we all fell to eating Dr. Trefusis's diet: biscuits and whatever broth could be won from the bone.

Mrs. Platt's circumnavigation of her supper table completed, she began to revolve around the parlor, the plates being lain on the mantelpiece or the gaming table. The fewer viands, the more dishes. Dr. Trefusis asked for daily reports on the progress of her table settings.

"Today," I would tell him heavily, "she ate upon her sewing table."

"I am impressed with her store of china," said Dr. Trefusis. "Prodigious. Is it still Canton porcelain?"

"She has passed out of the china, sir," I informed him. "She has descended to common redware."

"Ye gods. Humility at last."

I had little stomach for Dr. Trefusis's sparkishness. I feared for his life; I despaired that he should ever rise from his bed again; and I could not abide the hunger.

Many in the city were taken with the smallpox, not so much among the soldiery as among the remaining citizens. Red cloths were hung up upon their doors to mark their festering and convalescence. I saw mothers issuing out of doorways behind small coffins, screaming at the pall-bearers to return the dear corpse.

Though it was summer and the leaves heavy on the trees, people went about the streets coughing as if it were the catarrh season. The derelict bodies of the poor were found in abandoned houses, disfigured with disease's scabs, swaddled in table-clothes and all the refinements of shattered luxury. Society matrons who had fled to the sanctuary of the city when riots had broke out in the countryside now caught their deaths of fever, their eyes ringed with spectacles of corruption, their mouths bearded with sores.

The carts carried their bodies through the streets, finery stained with blood and the exudations of their scabbing.

These unfortunates were buried in silence. General Gage had ordered that no bells were to be rung for funerals, for fear the rebels should know how sickly lay the city. All solemnity, therefore, was silent, the peals muffled; and bodies went unheralded to their final rest; and we shoveled dirt atop the dead and watched their wooden vessels sink beneath the earth without a cry.

Mr. Turner had informed me of the pay per concert, which seemed adequate to my needs; but he had not disclosed that the concert season *per se* should not be well under way until the fall, when hostilities with the rebels were expected to taper off as both camps settled into siege and winter quarters — or by which season, as everyone buzzed and histled, the Redcoats should have issued forth from the city gates, laid waste to the countryside, dispersed the militia with a proud show of superior weaponry and tactics, reduced the pamphleteers to quivering, and hung high the few sneering Harvardians who had engineered the plot.

The other musicians supplemented their pay through various individual engagements, most of which were arranged by Mr. Turner, he taking some portion of our pay for the privilege of our hire. Through him, a few of the orchestra played at small dances held by officers and Tories, or accompanied suppers with chamber music. At first, having little to recommend me, I was not chosen for these grander occasions; but was equally gratified to be chosen, with two of my fellows, to play a few nights of the week at the Weary Pilgrim, a tavern on Fish Street. We fiddled dances, rounds, and catches, and the soldiers were glad enough of our company. Some would demand songs of their homeland which we did not know; and they would sing them for us, thinking of their beloved moors or the charcoal-pits of their youth, the wolds, the village churches, green with mold, ancient as the kings of legend; and we would oblige them, playing these songs back to them as they drank New England rum and wept for a country far over the sea.

Upon one day, the Negroes in the city were swept up into a general work-party, for which the pay was in no coin but stale dinner. It was our commission to clean the streets, so I spent some time in sweeping gutters, which was a profession too full of monotony and the despair of seeing one's work undone even as one did it. The defecation of horses clotted my broom.

The day after this Negro sweeping-bee, we were enjoined, such of us as wished employment, to lend our aid to the Army in erecting fortifications; which work I undertook with a fellow violinist from the orchestra—a fellow named Scipio and called Sip, a freeman and a father who spake always kindly to me in our rehearsals and observed my destitution was as great as his own.

The Army offered us rations, which gettings Sip and I could not refuse; and so we repaired to the city gates, where our fiddlers' fingers took to ruder labor.

Such lowly offices as I had performed for the rebels, I was now commissioned to perform for the King's Army: the work of mattock, spade, and shovel. 'Twas a curious reversal, and made no less singular by the fact that Bunker Hill, the rebel fortification to which I had lent my sinew some months previous, was now an Army outpost, stormed upon that fateful morning.

Our work-party was peopled entirely by Negroes. As we labored that day, half-naked, in the sun, binding together stakes to enhance the fortifications near the city gates, we heard shouts of alarm above us — followed by the smart crack of volleys — and then the cries of battle; and we who labored regarded the walls and our brethren in consternation.

"Steady, boys," called our overseer. "Eyes and hands to the work."

Frowning, we bound the stakes, our knots loose with inattention. Across the saltmarshes of the Neck, the blinds and redoubts, the flanks and faces of the bastions, the gates near us, armed with their anxious picket-guards, the reports of the conflict grew more insistent in their clamor — the rattle of musketry, the calling of commands. Then commenced the thunder of the howitzers.

Sip did not look at me as he spake; but low, he muttered to me, "Jesus God, them rebels crash through those gates, we's in a sorry state. It'll go mighty ill with us. They come through them gates, we is standing here tying together twigs without the least weapon. They take this city . . . Don't bear thinking on. Jesus God. I ain't going be taken for a slave and sold to the Indies. I got a wife and I got two babies. I ain't —"

"*Back!*" cried one of the overseers — "Back, back, back!"

Disturbed by the man's alarum, we looked up from our labor and found a detachment of Redcoats running in formation for the gates. We retreated from our work, leaving our frames half-bound and unmanned.

We huddled in the shadow of one of the half-completed breastworks, crouched in a ditch; and there situated, we watched the light infantry, alert with their danger, pass through to the outer fortifications.

While we stood, Sip muttered to the others, "News. News, boys."

"What's news?" asked one.

"News," said Sip. "From the Sixty-fourth. Hautboy player— what's they called? *Hautboyiste,* I reckon. This *hautboyiste* tells me that General Gage, he asks about whether slaves'll join the King's Army, gave the chance. It's an idea he has. An army of Negroes."

"When?"

"When he pleases."

"If he pleases," said another. "All of them are too affrighted." He spat and kicked at the spit with his heel.

Sip turned to me, and seeking intelligence, demanded, "Augustus, I hear you dug ditches for the rebs. I hear you dug out Bunker Hill."

Little did I wish to become an object of disesteem among my new colleagues; and I hastened to say, "The conflict was then in a very different moment, and my circumstances would not allow of—"

"How is they set for food and powder?"

I began to recount that of food, there seemed ample provision, but that they husbanded their powder; in which recollection I was interrupted by a man who said, "You couldn't serve with them, now. Couldn't join them. Couldn't carry arms."

I allowed I did not carry arms among the rebels, but dug among the artificers.

"Well, the rebels says we can't carry firelocks with their army. Heard this from a sutler. You hear this?"

"I ain't heard it," said Sip.

"Their general gets up here few weeks ago, gets to Cambridge —"

"What general?"

"The rebs' general. The Virginia slave-driver general."

"Washington."

"That general. There's a proclamation now, no Negroes can bear arms in the reb army. He don't like Africans carrying muskets. It's all . . ." The man held up his hand in a gesture I understood not.

This was a circumstance which could not be other than galling; for I still harbored a hope that the rebels would at length resolve to comply with the firm dictates of humanity and the soft graces of benevolence.

Without such a reprieve, we knew ourselves in constant danger if the city should be retaken. We many of us had escaped, and so, upon the town's falling, we would be conveyed to our former masters — at which thought, my spirits froze, thinking upon Mr. Sharpe and his devices.

The cannonade which had disturbed our labors being at an end, the corporal called to us to continue our binding of *chevaux de frise,* which labor we undertook again in silence.

Later that afternoon, a detachment returned through the gates with two of their number dead, arms sprawling, the hair on one a ruddy sop. The rebels had annoyed them with fire from the Roxbury lines; some contretemps had begun amidst the warehouses of the Neck; and, no ground won or lost, two had died.

We continued our solemn work of fortifying against invasion.

So we exchanged intelligence, and watched each other as we held our own silent deliberations, and considered which side might favor us with liberty. We worked at our dusty tasks beneath the summer sun; later, we played for tavern dances.

The British Army and Navy sang a rousing song called "Heart of Oak"; the rebels had writ one to counter it called "The Liberty Song." Both songs blustered of freedom; but both were sung to the same tune.

And we, to avoid offense, played the tune without words.

Thus, amidst uncertainties and temptations, arrived the autumn with its rains. One day, a packet-ship arriving from Nova Scotia with meat, thus alleviating the city's starvation, I purchased a salted ham-hock with Sally, and, by her side, stripped it for cooking. A small portion of the meat I took above-stairs for Dr. Trefusis, who, notwithstanding his frequent repetition of tags regarding vacancy and doom, improved tremendously.

He consumed the ham with considerable stomach, and, while licking his fingers, declared, "We devour meat, so that meat we may remain . . . though we hope to keep the spirit stuffed like herbs in the midst of it, for without that, the dish is simply flesh." He waited.

"Sir," said I, "final words are futile. You are not close to death."

"Unless you were to bludgeon me with the thigh-bone," he invited, smiling sweetly and batting his eyes.

I rose and took his plate, little entertained with jests on matters of such gravity.

"Augustus," said he, "what is happening in the world outside these walls?"

"We are better supplied with meat," I said.

"So I see."

"The Navy captured a rebel ship off the coast of New Haven, filled with sheep and beeves."

"Bravo."

"We have received supplies from Nova Scotia." I considered. "The officers are discussing where to erect the winter quarters for the soldiers."

"I see."

"Mrs. Platt has begun her third revolution of plates around the house, stacked one atop the other."

"Excellent," said Dr. Trefusis. "Anything further?"

"We are playing a suite by a sapper-composer."

He regarded me quizzically. "By 'sapper,' you mean of the siege-engineer species?"

"Yes, sir."

"Who tunnels under walls?"

"Yes, sir," said I. "He is of the Corps of Engineers. He is applauded for his ingenuity."

"As well he might be."

"I wish one could compose in darkness," said I. "And play music without others observing."

"Ah, yes. Fancy the effect upon his melodies, laboring with his muse there so much closer both to Hell and the ruddy forge of Vulcan."

"He must have a strong acquaintance with earth."

Dr. Trefusis looked at me with more seriousness, now. "What was it like," he asked, "when you dug ditches for the rebels?"

I did not meet his eye. "One might write a Symphony on the Four Strata," I said.

"I forget that you had a hand in constructing the fortifications on Bunker Hill."

I looked at my hands, which had grown harder over the summer. "It was difficult work," I answered. "I was not accustomed to the tools."

"We did not always serve thee well in your training," said Dr. Trefusis.

"You little anticipated I would be packing dirt in redoubts to combat His Majesty's Army."

"That was not our intention," said Dr. Trefusis.

And of a sudden, "What was?" I asked. "What did you wish to make of me?"

"Octavian," said he, stumbling and using my name, "we . . . we did not know. We would, I suppose, eventually have taken you to France. To present you at court there."

"Why France, sir?"

"The English would have showed admiration for us of the College; but the French would have shown adoration for you. Women would have built their hair into Negro Violinist coifs. They would have written indecencies to you upon their fans.

There would have been theories advanced as to what your excellences told young philosophers about the nobility of man."

I nodded. I knew not why, but even these meditations on my strengths filled me with sensations of exhaustion and discomfort.

I gazed upon my hands; upon the knuckles, and upon the palms.

"What," I asked Dr. Trefusis, "is color?"

"Epicurus maintains that everything we see, we see because a fine film of atomies is constantly shed by all matter, a sort of mist of particles which strikes the eye."

"So color, sir, is a shedding of the skin."

"I suppose, my boy, one might phrase it thus."

"Color is the loss of person. Dispersed into the air."

Dr. Trefusis smiled.

I said, "And in order for us to be seen, we must constantly be losing some part of our being."

"Indeed. We are ever diminishing," assented Dr. Trefusis. "Like a garment fretted by the moth."

"And in order for us to see, we must constantly be assaulted by what others shed."

"As surely, saith Descartes, as if we were struck in the face."

This I considered. "If one," I ventured, "were underground, in complete darkness . . . If one were a celebrated sapper-composer who had tunneled down deep into the bedrock, there to compose descriptive symphonies on the four strata . . . Would such a sapper-composer, engulfed in darkness, still be diminished?"

"You cannot stop the superficies of objects from evaporation," he said. "Light or dark, the particles still fly off the surfaces of things."

"And yet," said I, "beneath the surface of the earth, the sapper-composer would not constantly be exhausted by the particles strik-ing the eye. The eye would have rest. No longer would the face receive blows."

Dr. Trefusis took my arm and turned me to face him. "Octavian," he said, his look full of sobriety, "I hope thou shalt never retreat beneath the ground. The sun is thy inheritance. The sky is thy birthright. Stay here, my boy, and with the conversa-tion of mankind, rejoice in the light."

I could not but give thanks for the trill of emotion in his voice, which spake so sincerely of his regard and affection. Said I, "More last words?"

"No. First words." He held forth his arm. "Help me rise," he said. "I shall walk across the room."

"Are you feeling well, sir?" said I.

"In a world, Octavian, where composers tunnel beneath us and men kill men for sheep, too much transpires too quickly for one to lie long abed."

He smiled; and I suppose I smiled too.

I helped him rise. He was not firm on his legs, not having walked for several weeks. "I wish to make my way down the stairs," said he.

"That is inadvisable, sir," I answered.

"Augustus—support me, and I shall walk."

It was a difficult but triumphant descent. His mass hung upon my arm, for he supported but little of his own weight.

Mrs. Platt waited for us down in the foyer. "Dr. Trefusis," she said, "I am delighted to see you are mending."

"I am come down to see your third strata," he said, tottering and wincing. "We were speaking of geology."

"My strata?" said she.

"Your noble experiment in sedimentary cuisine," he said. "Fancy to yourself how invaluable the record might be someday of your past meals, as you dig your way down through a stack, with each ridge of dried gravy or leaf of salad speaking to your heart and your innermost parts of former days."

"I am sure," she said, "I do not like your mockery. Nor your speaking of the gut to a lady."

But she did not seem displeased by his recovery, and clapped when he reached the bottom step, and led him into the parlor, there to rest and take tea.

So Dr. Trefusis descended out of the obscurity of death through talk of the underworld, and rejoined the conversation of man.

The fever departed, and Dr. Trefusis now in health, he walked abroad, dressed in his stolen habiliment, swinging a cane like a beau of the first fashion.

"Yes, my boy," said he, "it is time I sought out powerful friends to better our poor lot. I am off to break bread with officers and impress upon them my age and sagacity. The company had best be elevated, mighty, and wreathed in the incense of Mars. Anything less than a lieutenant-colonel at the table and I shall not drink a sip of their tea. Never a bite shall I swallow, i'faith. I'll keep my cake under my tongue until I'm fair out the door, like a witch absconding with the Host, and if they complain, I'll spout out the mess on their pteryges."

I inquired if it was his pleasure I should attend him; but he said, "Certainly not. It is time your frail tutor contributed ought to our maintenance. I go out to publish forth word of your excellence, to hunt out engagements for you—suppers and dance lessons, assemblies, what have you. And to ensure that I am known as a resolute Tory."

I was surprised by this attestation, and I asked, "Sir, are you such?"

"Augustus," said he, digging between the cobbles with his cane, "there may come a time when those city gates fall, and houses burn, and the infantry flee in their battalions. When such a day arrives, I wish us to be aboard a ship; as otherwise, we may be sure of hanging. I go to procure friends who might, in that terrible hour, offer us passage."

My looks were perhaps expressive of anxiety; for gazing upon me, Dr. Trefusis said in tones mollifying and gentle, "You must consider it, my boy. This peculiar life we have these many weeks been leading is a dream: thy concerts and thy generous profits. A fancy. Thou art still a slave, and I am yet a poisoner."

"I wish," said I, uncertain, "our state here would not change."

"In a siege," said Dr. Trefusis, "time's passage is itself an event, and one of the keenest weapons of assault. You appear discountenanced."

"If we leave, when shall I be allowed again to play in an orchestra?"

"Perhaps in London." He placed his hand upon my wrist. "My boy, I would also liefer that we could remain here, but Fate oft . . ." He scratched at the flags with his cane, said, "But no matter. I am off to assure our fortune." Then he bowed to me, and took his leave.

I did not wish to think on leaving our present circumstances; I would they continued thus forever. But I knew, too, that the enemy waited without the gate, and shots were fired, and we subsisted here only by constant vigilance and show of arms; which *bravado* might at any moment give way, finally, to blows and the full fury of battle.

With delight, our orchestra played our first concert after the restitution of meat.

There is no sensation so sweet as the gratification of applause when one has hazarded embarrassment and humiliation before a crowd; no thrill so physical in its application nor so keen in its extension of the senses. Rare is it that the intellect and the dexterity, the activities of the mind and the strategies of the nerves—the body and the soul—are put to so supreme a challenge all at once; and having triumphed in that arena, with response immediate to one's exertions, one feels almost like a machine elevated to the status of a god. And how much more superior still the transports, when one is surrounded by a community of brethren who share in the success, whose efforts and collaboration brought about this triumph of mechanism and spirit, this apotheosis of the animal.

For the concert, we played symphonies by Monsieur Gossec, Herr Beck, and Dr. Boyce, as well as airs by Mr. Arne sung by an officer's mistress, all calculated to gratify the hearers with an impression of the rationality and graciousness of the human animal all too lacking in the months since the flight from Concord and the savagery of Bunker Hill.

The seats were full of officers in full dress and citizens of the city so stirred by the circumstances of the performance and the vivacity of execution that they often hooted and clapped to demand we play movements a second time through; some twenty of these loud gallants being friends of the musical sapper who had composed the harpsichord concerto, which giddy claque whistled and stomped vigorously, not ceasing until Mr. Turner stood and shouted that *he begged of the fine gentlemen that they would, as a demonstration of their benevolence, cork their bungs so we might have some Stamitz.* He promised that we would soon have a satire acted upon the rebels, writ by the notorious wit Major-General Burgoyne, with curtain-tunes and airs by this same excellent sapper to please the crowd. At this, there was an outburst of gaiety from all the assembled; and I was sensible that the delight of the evening enlivened my spirits as well as all of those seated around me. I could find no cause for anything but rejoicing.

The concert was soon concluded; alert and with the whole frame illuminated in success, I replaced my violin in its case and assisted in the removal of chairs against the wall; when a voice called my name — not *Augustus,* but *Octavian.*

I turned, startled, fearful of whom I might see.

[79]

There stood no stern academician—but my former music-master—Mr. 13-04, as I had most familiarly known him—who rushed forward and seized my hands, throwing my perceptions into confusion; so I scarce was sensible of what he meant when he said, "Octavian—I am so sorry . . ."

I stammered and could not speak, and it was some moments before he established that he had heard of my mother's passing from one of the Gitneys' servants, who had returned to the city in one of the periods of laxity in the siege to claim some furniture and clothing. Mr. 13-04 condoled with me on the death, so he said, of that blessed being, so accomplished in her conversation, so graceful in her carriage, and so charming in her person—once again, it taking me moments to recognize that he spake still of my mother—whom I saw before me as last she appeared, her skin brittle with sores, her tongue inanimate, her animal spirits in constant irritation from the depredations of the pox. I did not know whether I could bear to speak to one who would advert to her.

Mr. 13-04 had a thousand questions upon my well-being and the well-being of those of the College of Lucidity. I did not fully disclose my situation, but did say that Dr. Trefusis was in the city, too, and recovering from a long fever. This intelligence of Dr. Trefusis's presence and health filled Mr. 13-04 with delight, he harboring the warmest of regards for my tutor.

"Octavian—"

"Augustus, sir," said I.

He looked at me askance; then continued, "You must come to my apartments. I have in my possession something which, I trust, you will find interesting."

I inquired politely as to what it might be.

"Music," said he, "which I transcribed from the songs of your mother's country."

I was startled at this revelation. Though of course, I had known since childhood, as I have said, that in my infancy, she had assented to perform songs for his transcription —

But that they still existed — that I might play, myself, the music she recalled from her childhood —

The thought made me run almost frantic with suspense.

I heard her saying to me, in the candlelit darkness of my bed-chamber, "'*By the rivers of Babylon, we sat down and wept....On the willows there, we hung up our harps.... How can we sing the songs of the Lord in a foreign land?*'"

She laid her hand upon me.

"Mr. 13-04," I said, "I cannot disguise my anxiousness to see these melodies. It is in the highest degree —"

"Come with me," said he, plucking me by the coat. "Since I heard of her death, I have spent weeks staring at them."

I finished my work for Mr. Turner with all the speed I could, aiding in the extinguishing of candles and the stowing of chairs. When I had completed my tasks, Mr. 13-04 and I set out for his rooms.

He lived some ways away, in the shambles of Mount Whore-dom on the northwestern side of the city, an address somewhat inauspicious, it being a quarter of the city where one did not lightly walk alone at night; but I would have faced footpads and *banditti* with alacrity, armed only with my fists, to see the proffered documents; and so I repaired with him, though the dusk had long since fallen.

We went by way of Cambridge Street, and passed even the

Novanglian College of Lucidity; pausing, both, for a moment to regard it, where we had spent so many hours of my childhood together. Now 'twas lit with torches, and sentries stood outside the front doors, jealously protecting the officers who slept within.

As we walked onwards, Mr. 13-04 interrogated me about the denizens of the College and how they had fared in the few years since last he had been a visitor. His hostility to Mr. Sharpe, whose hatred of music still stung him, could not but put me more at my ease; though we should attempt generosity to all, even those who wrong us, recalling the Creator's hand in their construction, I could not bring myself to do other than despise this man who had so soured the headwaters of all that sweetened our household.

As we walked up the steep streets of Mount Whoredom, the crabbed houses hanging over the street, their walls uneven, the dirt of the road thick with rubbish, I recounted in as few words as I could my mother's final days and my escape.

His rooms were at the top of a boarding-house near an expansive puddle, which we skirted without entire success. We ascended the stairs, my pulse quickening with anticipation, and he unlocked his door.

He entered almost on tiptoe, suggesting to me that someone else was in the set of chambers, and, within, lit a tallow candle which shed but a very feeble light. It appeared that he had two rooms, a sitting-room and another, the door to which was closed; he slept on a pallet, clearly, in the sitting-room, next to his spinet.

He lifted the candle to the wall, and there I saw that he had tacked sheets of music all over the plaster, high and low, affixing other pages with paste. They were written in his hand — the which I recognized from our lessons — and, without close examination, I saw that they were the songs in question, notes scribbled hastily as my mother had sung, words written in some language unknown both to him and to me.

"Octavian," he whispered, clutching my shoulder, his eyes heavy with impendant tears, "I have wished for so long to show these to you." I could barely see the papers' brown scrawl, so precious as it was, in the faint light.

"She was perhaps fourteen when she sang them for me," he said, his voice unsteady. "Her voice was like a child's. In her eyes . . . I saw reflections . . ."

He held the candle close to the music again. "Hum it," he said. "I have been waiting so long. Hum the tunes."

I did not stop to think why he did not hum the music himself; I merely leaned close and picked out a few notes, murmuring them.

"Quietly," cautioned Mr. 13-04.

I had only murmured a few more when the inner door opened, and a Redcoat in his shirt, with his jacket hung about his shoulders, demanded, "We're sleeping."

The music-master explained to me, "My landlord has let out my room to soldiers."

"Who rise at dawn," said the soldier. "With the first light."

"Begging your pardon, sir," said the music-master. "We did not wish to disturb your tranquility."

"He's humming," said the soldier.

"He is singing me the songs his mother sang."

"He the one, then?" said the soldier. "With the mother?"

"Indeed," said the music-master.

The soldier did not return to his bed, but swore lazily and sat down with his back against the doorframe, observing us.

I turned back to the music. While the soldier and Mr. 13-04 conversed quietly of small things—cheese eaten which had to be replaced—I surveyed the pieces. Most were songs for one voice—though perhaps in their native land, they would have been sung by many. In a few, she had indicated some harmony, and in one, counterpoint. I could not thank Providence sufficiently for the trove here bestowed upon me. I sang a few more notes, giddy with anticipation, until I came upon a smudged symbol which I did not recognize.

I turned to the music-master. "What is this, sir?" I asked him.

He looked at me with expectation. "Yes?" said he.

"I cannot descry all of your marks," I explained.

He looked at me with some confusion; he examined the wall. "That," he said, "yes, that symbol. She made, do you recall, a scratched noise—a noise in her throat?"

I regarded him with bewilderment.

"It brought the note . . ." He did not finish.

I awaited explanation.

"You recall," he urged.

Ignorant of his meaning, I hesitated.

"This is why my desire has been so great for you to see these sheets," he said. "You shall be able to interpret for me all of these marks . . . recalling the songs." He smiled at me; and it was a smile of slowly growing desperation. "I could not record what she sang; there was no notation for it, all the peculiar . . ." He moved his hand fishily in the air, unable to describe what he imagined. "It was not . . . there were not symbols enough to depict what she sang. The tuning was too alien in its accents . . . so deliciously strange . . . and there was no key as I could understand it to many of the songs. So I made marks ... but later ... I could not recall what they signified. There were so many marks ... ambiguously drawn. ... And later, when I asked her, she would deny all knowledge of the music. ... So you, knowing the songs, may tell me ... what ..."

He ceased speaking.

"She never," I said, and hesitated. "Sir, she never sang these songs to me, in my memory. I was an infant. You are the only one who heard them."

Stricken, he took in the pages on the wall, their cryptic lines drawn to depict oscillations in the voice, cries and dips lost to both of us. "You must recall," he demanded. "Perhaps by your bedside? She ... ?"

"Sirs," came a cry from the other room, "we are sleeping."

"They're sleeping," said the soldier crouched by the door.

Ardently, I believed that could I but read these tunes, I would hear her again. Her voice should speak, and I have proof of lullaby and tenderness.

With fervent desperation, I scanned them, seeking one firm melody; only too sensible that my mother's voice inhered in these pieces, strung between these notes, frayed to the point of snapping—could I only find the line of it, and grasp it—her mouth, her throat, her lungs, her teeth, her tongue—all of these frozen in concert in the crude lines before me—

Vainly, I cast my eye over the sheets; but like the first, I saw that they were rife with equivocations and parentheses, notes that Mr. 13-04 had made in ignorance, attempting to capture turns of melody and vocal tricks that could not be rendered. One song was written clearly in harmony, runs of thirds; but she had also beat a rhythm which he had assayed to reproduce, and this was nothing but scratchings and clumsy scribblings, revisions he had not ever returned to review and apply methodically. Many were scarcely legible. The words of none had been set down with care.

One of the soldiers called, "Did you tell the fiddler, 'twas us nimmed his cheese?"

"Aye," said the soldier leaning against the door, and to Mr. 13-04: "We'll buy one for you new."

From the dark, a voice explained, "We et rarebit."

With frantic eye, I sought my cradle-songs, the songs of comfort she might sing for me again, dandling me in her arms. My gaze leaped from bleary note to blotted slur, none yielding music, none quitting me of clamor.

"Does any of you have a powder tester?" asked one of the soldiers. "I'll need one tomorrow in the forenoon."

"Hughes has one. The handle's off, though. Almost. So wear a mitt."

I could not apply myself fully with their speaking; I lifted my hands to my ears and pressed my fingers in.

"Does any of you have a mitt?" the soldier asked.

I could not block their chatter; all awake, now, as they were ("Robbins burnt his thumb purple on Hughes's gadget"); and sobbing once, I pressed my hands to the paper—seeking in these scraps, some memory that might have snagged—as strung therein were all the secrets of my childhood erased, that life I might have lived: ceremonies and dances, what women wailed for in the marketplace, the sweep of ancient grasses; and I fancied that if they would simply let me sing, I would hear the voices of my forebears; I would hear their tales, which they wished still to tell me; I would smell the hides of beasts of burden, twitching from the flies; taste the savors of my family's confections; and I might see the lips of those who had sung these songs to my mother in her infancy: a grandfather, his hair an unimagined white; a grandmother, sitting in a grove and laughing. I considered, scarcely daring to entertain the prospect, a father might hold me swaddled in his arms, and raise me to his sister's lips.

"*'If I forget thee,'*" she had hissed to her invisible homeland, "*'if I do not remember thee, let my tongue cleave to the roof of my mouth; if I prefer not my nation to my chief joy....'*"

But when I looked upon the music, it did not sing for me; my tongue did not move; for it was not my past. It signified nothing. These tunes were silent. I knew only the graces and mordents of Europe.

"It is all lost," said Mr. 13-04. "Is it not?"

I turned to him. "Most," I said. And added, at long last, "Sir."

"I shall make you copies."

I nodded; knowing that the copies would be even further from these scribbled originals which hung upon the wall.

The soldiers, sensible, perhaps, of my anguish, did not speak.

"I shall walk you to your dwelling," said Mr. 13-04.

"You needn't, sir," said I, desiring no conversation. "I do not wish to trouble you."

"It is after the curfew. A Negro will be detained by the watch," he said.

He spake the truth. I thanked him and bowed my assent. We took our leave of the soldiers, who with some warmth indicated the pleasure they had in making my acquaintance, so much having been recounted about myself and my mother in previous months.

Mr. 13-04 and I made our way through the darksome streets. At one moment he could not restrain himself from declaring, "I loved her"; which news could not but inspire weariness and indifference.

He never wrote out fair copies of these jottings for me, fugitive as were the marks and impossible of interpretation. I never returned to the rooms on Mount Whoredom — or did walk by the door, one afternoon, but could not bring myself to knock and be once again confronted by the vaguaries of those imperfect staves, those ballads without text.

I was sensible even that night of the folly of my expectations — that notes on a page might restore her voice to me. *What is the voice*, I meditated, *but an expulsion of air, a few vapors scented with the curdled decoctions of the stomach, vegetables mulching and pulverized beef? What is a song, but an instant evaporation?*

It is as futile to seek the past there as in a refuse of dishes encircling a table, each with its own crust of gravy, its own tale of bone and crackling. One might as well weep over Mrs. Platt's dry orts, thinking they might restore what was lost, what had been swallowed, all that had, in times of feasting, been cut away and devoured.

Conformable to Mr. Turner's announcement, we were engaged in rehearsing the airs and curtain-tunes for the satire upon the siege called *The Blockade of Boston,* penned by Major-General Burgoyne, famous for a notorious dandy and foppish blade, which play the officers themselves would present in Faneuil Hall come the end of October; the suite of music for this piece being supplied by the Corps of Engineers' sapper-composer, whose previous efforts in the concert hall had met with such prodigious success, his fame, as it were, tunneling so broad a swath with so assiduous an effort through the dross of obscurity, and propped now securely against all assaults, that no detonation of critic or carper could knock him into disarray.

We played through his overture and sighing airs, his rowdy hornpipes for inebriate barbers-general; and yet, there were days when every scene which opened itself to our view as we walked about the streets seemed a coarse satire upon the siege. 'Twas not acted upon a stage, but upon the Common, upon Marlborough Street. We played comical songs for lieutenants regarding bombardment, and then issued forth to discover that, on Frog Lane, cannonballs and shells lobbed from Roxbury had tackled wooden walls and burst them through, or plowed strips in the slates of a roof, and citizens stood about, looking wonderingly at the progress of shot through wood.

These are such sights as greet the view of those who suffer siege in cities: the anxiety of violence mingled with the antics of incongruity.

I saw military washerwomen dressed in fine silk waistcoats for men, brocaded with water-stains and grime. I saw a child dead of the pox buried in a pie-cabinet. Passing through Cornhill Street alone on a misty morning, I heard a voice calling out commands in the square, with none to obey. There was no ghostly regiment, responded to those orders; just the gray stone, the blue mist, and an officer alone, hanger raised, bawling formations.

I saw Old North Meeting House pulled down for fuel. I saw Old South Meeting House stripped of its furniture and transformed into a riding-school for the cavalry so as to chagrin the rebels, who had oft let loose their rhetoric there; now gravel was strewn over its floor, the pews hauled out to make pig-troughs; and dragoons rode fierce circuits through the sanctuary, roused on by an officer screaming in the pulpit while ladies in the balcony whisked themselves with fans.

I saw men whipped for complaint or desertion; I saw men hanged, their bodies freshly at a dangle.

When it was ordered that the soldiers should bathe in salt-water twice daily to fend off disease, I saw a regiment walk into the sea at dawn.

The ocean was ruddy, as were they, and some passed into the sea from the shingle, and others rose from the sea and waded to shore. They came forth dripping, shivering, naked, and made for the land, lit by the first sun, as if the Creator had determined to make a new race of men from the foam, this one perfected, gentle, and dandled by light.

Believing the siege of long continuance, and impatient of news, I wished greatly for another interview with fellow members of my race, that we might discuss how best to secure our indefeasible rights, so cruelly taken from us. I was soon to receive both interview and news.

One night I played at a ball held for privates, petty officers, and their camp followers in a factory once devoted to the rendering of fish-oil. The hall was dark and briny, the couples smeared with soot and joy. A great vat was overturned, and our little band of music stood upon it as upon a stage, our instruments accompanied by the unison tread of the company assembled.

From that vantage, the line-dances of these men who might tomorrow march in rows into battle had a look of impossible complexity: ranked arms interwoven, circles formed and broken, bodies filing in curious design, confrontations met and swept aside. And those of us who stood atop the fish-tub received the jolts of their ecstatic rhythm through our feet—and we played the more wildly for the dancing of these men beneath us—filling the solemnity of their hours of watch and sally with last dances, last embraces, a final chance, mayhap, to feel the world spinning beneath them before it stopped and swallowed them whole.

There being a call for a halt to the music, so that a collation might be laid out and eaten, my fellows and I retired from our instruments and sat upon our tub, articulating our tired fingers.

That we might become better acquainted, I inquired of Sip whether his children were as musical as he; for he was prodigiously knowledgeable, acquainted with the tunes of five nations.

He replied *six nations,* for he knew a China tune, brought back by the Jesuits from the palace at Peking, which lilting melody he then fiddled for me; that song, he explained proudly, bringing his national tally up to six. He ate some bread, and said, "My girls, they do like to dance. Little one, Shirley, she going to dance like a courtier when she's grown. The big one, she wants the graces." Wreathed in the smiles of paternity, he related, "She mainly buffet Shirley around in circles and step on her toes like a rummy dragoon."

I inquired if he played for them, which he answered gratefully that he did, he had that pleasure; I inquired whether he knew any tunes of Africa, and he said, no, saving a few his grandfather tried to remember; and I inquired whether he might play them for me; and thus we would have continued, had not the two other members of our little band—who were white, and of the 64th — approached us and requested the honor of speaking to us outside the hall.

At the severity of their countenances, I felt a chill.

Sip excused us, saying, "Sirs, we is enjoying some bread."

With looks of veiled significance, our two white companions bade us follow.

Follow we did, anticipating some disaster. Sip and I exchanged glances of no little concern. We made our way out the door.

After such an eve, the crush and dance, utterly awesome was the silence of streets abandoned by all.

Our breath issued forth in steam. We stood, abeyant, ready to receive what shock fate should administer.

The bassoonist, a man of sallow and heavy cast, said, "You carry tales."

Both Sip and I were silent, knowing we both had conveyed rumors to our fellows in the Negro work-parties. I was fetched up by terror, and surveyed the street for escape, did this encounter become a beating.

"I says a thing," the bassoonist accused softly, "and you report it to others of your race."

"We heard —" said the flautist.

"We hear a great many things," said the bassoonist.

"Sirs," said Sip, in tones confident of his lie, "sirs, I know not what you's aiming at."

The two looked at each other, as if embarking on some dangerous course; and the bassoonist said, "We hear news from the South, might be of interest."

"To the others," said the flute.

"If you wish to repeat it."

The flute nodded, and leaning toward us with look of sharp conspiracy, said, "Lord Dunmore."

"As is Governor of Virginia," explained the bassoon.

"He's writ a letter says he's been hounded from his own palace by the rebels."

"Fled."

"Onto a ship. They chased him off the shore. And here's this: He threats manumission for all loyal slaves."

"He don't dare land. He's trapped out in some bay. The entire Virginia Colony —"

"It's in a monstrous uproar."

"Chaos."

"Rebels running through the streets of the capital."

"So he says he'll free whosoever joins him. I says, says I, if he issues that decree, every Virginian of property is going to throw in against the King's right, see? Every Virginian of property. They'll enlist in the militia."

"But we says to each other, *Them Negro violinists in the orchestra should know*. Because if Lord Dunmore frees them in Virginia, General Howe might too, up this way."

"A body can't play a symphony next to a man, without compassionating with his woes."

"As soon as ever we heard word, we says, *We'll tell them violinists*."

The bassoonist asked us, "Where do you boys reckon the Negroes will put their loyalty?"

I was much distracted at this news; I knew not what to say,

for my thoughts were engaged wholly in considering this story and the name of Dunmore, which appellation was not unfamiliar to my ears.

Sip did not answer their question; saying only, blankly, "I's already a free man."

At some length, I responded, "If you are asked, you may relate that most of our numbers shall swear fealty to whoever offers emancipation with the greatest celerity."

"The rebels, they don't want you. You heard? They don't."

Said I, "You shall find, sir, that whoever takes such a measure and releases us from bondage will be amply rewarded with the most zealous of followers."

The men appeared anxious; Sip was not wholly pleased with my frankness and probity. The white men nodded, and we peered about in the dark and the cold, the white men still nodding; and then, there being nothing more to discuss, returned within to play more dances for the troops.

We played for an hour; but as may be imagined, my faculties were not wholly trained upon my part, but rather in reflection upon what I had heard; for I had been informed, during my late period of incarceration, that Pro Bono was like to have fled to Dunmore's palace, and I pictured him now, standing upon the prow of a ship, serving, perhaps, as valet to the Royal Governor of Virginia.

The coming days would confirm our fellow musicians' report that Lord Dunmore had indeed abandoned his capital and now governed from a ship harbored in Chesapeake Bay; and that Governor Martin of North Carolina was in like wise fled his palace; and that both of them drifted up and down the rivers of their colonies, disrupting the shipping, threatening violence. It was then said that Dunmore harbored slaves who fled to him, and our musical companions were not alone in believing that Dunmore should soon issue a general emancipation to all Negroes as would join him.

In the moment, I knew no particulars beyond what they had spoken. But still, I was transported, envisioning ranks upon ranks of men of my Africk nation, marching forth from ships, armed and disciplined, halloed from plantations, met with rejoicing, as streaks of liberation spread like verdigris across this tarnished colonial sky.

I stumbled on my part, too lost in reverie, and the flautist fixed me with a look most vexed.

Late that night, as, back at Staniford Street, I unloaded my pockets of biscuits and treats for the delight of my tutor, he asked me how had gone the dance, and I told him of Lord Dunmore's rumored ire and his thought of clemency for loyal slaves, and I recalled to Dr. Trefusis that Pro Bono was thought fled to His Lordship's side.

Said I, "We are an army that but waits to be mustered. We shall join whosoever doth free us first."

Dr. Trefusis paused in his enjoyment of a rusk. "Oh, my dear boy. Hope as you will. I fear, however—I greatly fear—that on this side, General Howe and his minions are too much affrighted at the wrath of the wealthy to cut the shackles; and on the other, the rebel Congress in Philadelphia is full, leech to luff, of slave-owners who have no earthly enticement or incentive to free their servants and beggar themselves. Their estates would fall to ruin."

I slowly laid out sweets upon our little table, disheartened by so glum a prognostication. To Dr. Trefusis, I delivered scraps of turkey pulled from a carcass. He approached the flesh with relish, pinning it to his rusk with a thumb and devouring it.

Outside, there was a racket of crows, startled by some passerby in the street. They bickered, and we heard them retreat over the roofs.

I asked my tutor, "Sir, was Mr. Sharpe right? Is everything done for self-interest or profit?"

Dr. Trefusis shrank back, eyed me cannily, and ceased to chew.

I renewed my inquiries. "Sir?"

"The inimitable Locke," he answered, "saith that mankind is engaged in perpetual uneasiness, and that it is lack which motivates us forward. In our desires, we resemble the action of a two-legged table."

I watched him eat the heel of his bread. I urged, "You yourself are proof of the selfless benevolence of man. You have submitted yourself to ruin so that you might save me. Surely you are an example of kindness without profit?"

He frowned his thin lips and his lined cheeks. He lay down his bread. He reached out a hand and pushed away the cakes on the table. His water he left idle.

With a harshness of accent not usually his, he said, "I shall relate a fable." He rearranged himself on his chair, and began: "Let us imagine that there is a man," said he, "who, when young, traveled about the Continent, enjoying numerous *petits amours* with young ladies with whom ... he was not always ... entirely forward with all aspects of the truth, regarding the length of his stay — nor of anything else, i'faith. . . . Let us note in passing: Voltaire, in his *Philosophical Dictionary*, maintains that self-love is like the penis: It is necessary; it is dear to us; it gives us pleasure; mankind could not continue without it; and yet things proceed more agreeably, with less of shrieking, when it is stowed.

"Now fancy for thyself that hadst thou asked this youth, 'Sir, do you love these chambermaids, these milliners' girls?' — if thou hadst asked, 'Do you love your hot-breathed country nuns, smelling of their cattle?' — he would have vowed upon his honor he loved them indeed ... and would have swore truthfully that he thought of them often — with noble melancholy — as he slipped away at noon and rode from them forever.

"Let us figure for ourselves that this man, this young libertine, engaged daily in concocting a philosophy of Eros and in visiting the great courts of Europe, heard occasional rumors that the previous year's late dalliances of a few weeks had borne fruit ... and that, were he to return west to scenes of earlier pleasure, he would find himself a father several times over. And so, hearing of his paternity, he rode further east — first to Prussia, and later, into the forests of the Magyar.

"Then imagine that youth passed, and manhood, and he crossed the seas, fleeing from court to court, and he came to the end of his years, and discovered he had been loved by none, though his grandchildren, it was not impossible, were spread as thick as Abraham's through the hovels of Christendom. Imagine that he faced his own dissolution. Imagine that waiting for him on the other side of the grim portal were neither the shrieks of the damned nor the harp *glissandi* of the saved, but rather the stone chill of a vacuum, the failure of a machine. An instant, and the self ceased.

"Then you might imagine how he longed for one who depended upon him, who said, 'I shall remember you as one who gave me life.' Imagine how he might yearn for one whom he might use as a grandchild."

Hearing his tale, my heart swelled with pity, and I put my hand upon his wrist; but he shook it off. He stood and walked to his bed.

"Altruism," he concluded, "is the kind of pie best eaten with a lot of gravy and little inspection of the kind of kidney it's stuffed with."

The air grew colder. Fuel being scarce, and the Staniford Street house being draughty, I offered my services to a work crew in exchange for wood. The soldiers were similarly in need; my work-detail was given orders to assist them in pulling down rows of houses and wharves in the South End, where these structures should be replaced by a line of defensive works.

Demolishment was an excellent sport for me; I welcomed the savagery of axe and beetle. The peril of being trapped within the city, without hope of change until some calamity, weighed heavily upon me. I thought drearily on the clamoring of rebels in the streets of Williamsburg, the flight of royal authority from that beleaguered capital; I thought on the rebels who surrounded us, baying for liberty and offering none themselves; and I, rehearsing the indignities suffered by my people of Africk hue; the tortures; recalling the ships still plying the waves with more of us in their holds; the howling of rebels anxious to see us bound; their brutal Congress, full of men who spake of vaunted reason; examining the need, the anger, the infant wail and grasping which allowed them to cast aside logic and enthymeme, the valid and the true—I was full of fury.

Destruction, therefore, was apt divertissement; and with each blow of the hammer upon the beams, I forgot further my former years and my present predicaments, and rather occupied myself in calculations of stress and impact, and how I might best avoid nails.

I was sensible of a new excitement. I had waited and hid, and what I had ever feared was conflict: first, in the rebel camp, dreading the issuing forth of the Royal Army to destroy us; then, enchained, anticipating some dire fate in the College of Lucidity; and finally, here, surrounded in this city invested by rebels with no action taken, awaiting the summation of this siege—always constrained—always inert—but now I desired justice eruptive.

I now imagined violence—the bayonet-thrust, the detonation—the report of a musket—as the hard sublimate of speech I had curtailed through years, all the moments when I had silently inclined my head, these suppressed words of outrage now become indurated into some dire rhetoric, an oration so loud and so decisive, 'twould cause bodies to topple, and walls to fall, and I might surge forwards with the others—for so I saw us now, Negroes of the King's Army, unleashed at last, our fury speaking, and never more to scrape before the cruelties of gentlemen. This, from one who was ever pacific in nature.

So doth a man change from one moment to the next. So did I change, and become by degrees, without knowing, a soldier.

Beneath maples turned scarlet, scarlet soldiers sawed, as fire turns upon itself, devouring.

We presented *The Blockade of Boston*, Major-General Burgoyne's farce upon rebel hypocrisy, as one of the most celebrated events of our hivernal concert series. It was to be the last concert I played.

The preparations that evening were hectic, for it was to be acted by the officers themselves for the entertainment of not simply their peers and commanders, but also their troops, who were become restless with their long confinement. The officers, little acclimated to the exertions of drama — and the great rule, I have found, with stagecraft is that *drama begets drama* — filled the retiring-chambers of Faneuil Hall with their shouts and remonstrances as they were painted and clothed. There a man who had but a few months before stood proud upon the field, conducting men down some declivity with bayonets fixed, now, flustered with comedy, repeated lines while his valet drew lids upon his eyes. There drummers who sounded the advance and retreat across the battlefields thumped upon the skins of their raucous instruments, judging the quality of the attack. Here a man dressed as General Washington in hay-filled wig brandished a rusty sword.

In the midst of the preparations, Mr. Turner approached me. "Augustus," said he, "a moment."

I stepped aside to allow passage for a bustle of men who dragged a wooden howitzer.

Said Mr. Turner, "I have, at long last, recognized you. Some years ago you played a devilish ugly Tartini article for a subscription concert."

I assented; and he, in his curious way, was not unforward in his praise, saying, "Excellent. I recall it as a beautiful head-ache. *Con spirito.* Perhaps *con spirito maligno.* There was about it a whiff of sulphur; maybe *sal ammoniac.*"

I averred that I was honored by his recollection, no less than by his attendance upon the first performance.

"Perhaps you should play a more prominent part in the orchestra."

"You honor me with your notice, sir."

"Famous," said he. "Cracking. For our next concert, I shall shift you to play with the first violins."

"May I express my gratitude to you for the opportunity, no less sweet for being unsought, and the hope that I shall prove in every respect—"

"'Tfaith, you'd dull a man to death. Go move chairs."

We organized the chairs before the dais and lit the candles upon the stands so that the hall sparkled with illumination. My spirits were in a tumult: On the one hand, my heart trembled with anticipation of future performance; and I found myself surprised with hope that the siege should never end—for did it end, there ended also my freedom in this band, this glorious exercise of all I found most pleasant and agreeable; and I absurdly wished we could remain here, ever stranded, nestled in this tenuous moment; and yet, at the selfsame instant, I thought on those who encircled us, threatening, and wished my joy at the liberties I now took could blast them where they stood, that the brilliance of defiance might destroy forever those who prated of freedom and denied it so coarsely; and having thought thus, I found my hands wishing for a more devastating instrument than a violin; and scarcely was sensible of which emotion extended dominion over my disorganized nerves.

I tuned, frowning, and concentrated upon the music at hand.

The seats were filling with officers in full uniform and their ladies; in remoter areas, the rank and file were admitted to celebrate their favorite Regimental commanders in this act of buffoonage. In the farthest balcony, unaccompanied women in masks raised their fans to obscure their pox-marks, observed by men guessing at identity.

We sat through a farce entitled *The Busy-Body*, with jests regarding stays and lecherous inspections of bosoms.

When its *badinage* was completed, we picked up our instruments and began to play the overture for *The Blockade of Boston*.

For the benefit of the untried officers who acted in the piece, we had sat many times through some portions: General Washington seducing a widow, so he might melt down her family pewter for bullets; comic numbers for rustic paupers singing of their sheep;

a chorus of effeminate Harvardians, full of the pious cant of Puritan theology, which sour ephebes spurred on rough apprentices to fight for them and then wept and hid when battle began, terrified they should lose their lives or, far worse, their fortunes; we had seen also a bumptious dialogue between two ragged colonial majors, one a shoemaker by trade, the other a dentist's apprentice, each protesting their fellow-feeling while picking the other's pocket. Finally, I had witnessed with some interest a ballad we played mocking the rebels' Congress for crying, in the midst of wealth and luxury, that England had enslaved them, while all the time holding slaves themselves and trading Negroes at cards.

We finished the overture's concluding *fugato*. The action opened in Watertown, which was painted upon old linens; General Washington stomped out from the wings, his jacket ill-fitting and crude. He opened his mouth to speak the prologue.

Abruptly, one of the King's soldiers, dressed in the costume of a serjeant of the militia, rushed out the wings and sprinted to the center of the stage, shoving the Commander-in-Chief of the rebel faction to the side with little ceremony — and declared in Hibernian accents, "Turn out! Turn out! They are at it, hammer and tongs! The rebels!"

He paused, the audience gaped; he cried, by way of amplification, "Tooth and nail!"

The theater was for a moment silent.

Washington, knocked asunder, reeled and brayed, "I say," seizing the King's soldier by the arm and struggling with him.

The two wrestled there for a moment, which sight was enough to actuate laughter and applause in all who watched — as the two grunted there — until the King's soldier, bursting free of

Washington's elbows, cried, "What the deuce are you all about? If you won't believe me, by Jesus, you need only go to the door, and there you will see!"

Despite the action of the drama was somewhat confused, the audience still liked it well enough, it clearly conducing to the debasement of the rebel General, so they laughed again; but the story became even more unaccountable as the soldier addressed the audience again, pleading, "Sirs! M'lords! At Charlestown! The rebels are attacking the mill-dam at Charlestown!"

This time, there was no laughter; merely an astonished silence. An anxiety at what was real and what was display beset us. Some few men started to rise from their seats.

Major-General Burgoyne, dressed as a cow-herd, rushed onto the stage. "It is not in the script!" he cried. "The man speaks truth!"

For one moment longer, stupor held court; his scepter was absolute and we all were subjected unto him.

And then chaos usurped with his animal junto.

Officers rose and there was a general clamor; a woman wailed; from the wings, through luffing *coulisses,* men ran panting, wiping paint from their faces upon their oznabrig sleeves. There was a struggle on the stairs. The doors bristled with men in panic. Officers hauled themselves off the stage, shoving and pushing amidst the orchestra as we hastily turned aside that they might pass — one slid beneath the harpsichord for avenue — while in the audience, men groped to climb over seats, heaving themselves up, boots on velvet cushions; ladies rising and sitting; one fainting; cries for help; no language left but jabbering.

I held up my violin so it might not be smashed by colonels who clambered over my lap.

Regimental commanders shouted for order, but there was no maintaining it. Chairs were kicked over. Women suffered the assaults of their neighbors climbing towards freedom.

Gradually, the theater emptied, Mr. Turner shouting to us that we, at least, must remain stationary and minimize, rather than enhance, the violence of the rout.

Once the way was clear, we dispersed toward the doors.

In the market square, we found ragged companies forming, several led by men habited as milkmaids.

As I wandered home — little fearing, amidst the confusion, any harassment — I passed individual soldiers sprinting down alleys, seeking their station.

In the streets, companies marched.

Through the ways of the city, I heard the call of the drums, beating the soldiers into formation.

At Mrs. Platt's house, we ascended to the roof, where she had watched the burning of Charlestown some months before. Sally and I prepared tea and brought it up for the widow, Dr. Trefusis, and her old servant, Jacob, who was wrapped in blankets.

Not much could be seen on the other side of the channel; bursts of flame that illuminated only smoke. As we observed, Dr. Trefusis delivered a proud oration on how none could truly see, but all the world was smoke, flame, and night; and we stumblers in that obscurity, glimpsing figures that struggled and fell; which discourse I could not attend to, for my thoughts were deep engaged upon another matter.

"What," said Sally to Dr. Trefusis, "will you be diving off the roof to your death, now you've said your pretty speeches?"

Swifts roused by the volleys rose and called in darkness.

There are vistas which not only gratify with a demonstration of geography, but which act as the cartographers of our history, mapping time itself; so, then, this prospect: which took in, at a swivel of the head, the spires of Boston, its brick houses and slate roofs, its hills, on which campfires burned and murky Redcoats paraded; and indeed, one could make out, featureless from this vantage in this dark, the Novanglian College of Lucidity's townhouse, where I had spent my youth; and there, across the Bay, were ships of the line awaiting combat, quiescent and pregnant with menace; their tenders cutting across the waves; and to the northwest, across the Charles, the heights of Breed's and Bunker Hills, which I, with my own hands, had helped fortify for the rebels, at the side of Mr. G——g, but which works now were in the hands of the King's Army, and hotly disputed. Far in the blue distance, I believed I could see the hills of Stow and Concord and Canaan, where Mr. Sharpe and Mr. Gitney still dwellt, for all I knew, in their experimental chambers, conducting trials in the dead of night. Behind us, the moon shone down upon the mudflats of Roxbury, where Dr. Trefusis and I had struggled for our lives against the rising tide. Bound here together beneath the wind and touched by the tide were rebel and regular, Tory and Whig, all scrutinizing each other across the blue spaces between them, awaiting the moment either might rally and seize the landscape for their own.

Across the Charles, the calamity was bright and confusing.

They had, in impudence, chosen this night, the night of our festive lampoon, for their attack, knowing our officers engaged in the drama; there could be little question of that.

And 'twas as if one said to me, *Play as you will. Elsewhere, the battle commences. Play your sweet tunes, boy, and stay away from the business of men. Forget justice, for you have what you desired.*

I peered across the Charles. My palms wanted detonation. I held out my hands toward the minute battle, and yearned to feel the full shock of the blast, to tear away at the enemy's vile obstinacy, which kept us corralled; to feel the full eruption of justice visited upon them.

There could be no safety, no repose but illusory while such deeds went on in darkness.

I smellt the smoke blown through the black air.

We later heard that Major Knowlton of the rebels had led two hundred men to Charlestown to assault it; they making their way across the mill-dam. They burned houses that night, killed one man, and took five prisoners.

I know only that I looked across the houses, inlets, and isles of my youth, and was sensible that I had to leave them behind. There was staged a great transformation in the world, and when 'twas done, nothing would be as it had been; and nor could I be. We must lay aside one thing to grasp another.

I stood upon the flashing of the roof, and watched the houses burn.

A week later, we gathered to rehearse Mr. Arne's music for *Zara,* which play would be staged by Major-General Burgoyne. Indeed, there was fine melody; indeed, there was counterpoint well worked; the dances were the very type of grace and elegance; but I little relished them.

So soon as we were dismissed, I sought out the bassoonist who had spake to Sip and me of Dunmore. "Sir," said I, "sir, a small matter . . ."

We held our conference in the marketplace, near a gang of children playing at some game, clouting their friends with rope.

"Sir," I entreated, "I wish to know what happens to the south."

"The south," said the bassoonist.

"The matter we spake on in the manufactory."

He nodded. "I have the best of news," said he. "You ain't heard?"

"I have not."

"You will like this some," said he.

"Indeed," I said, my heart fair jumping into my mouth.

He smiled. "Heard it day before yesterday."

I asked him to tell me; and tell me he did.

[VI.]

THE KINGDOM ON THE WAVES

drawn primarily from the Nautical Diary
of Private *Octavian Nothing*, copied, enlarged,
and embellished by his own Hand

When thou passest through the waters, I will be with thee; and through
the rivers, they shall not overflow thee. . . . For I am the Lord thy God,
the Holy One of Israel, thy Saviour: I gave Egypt for thy ransom,
Ethiopia and Seba for thee.

—Isaiah 43: 2–3

Time is like a river made up of the events which happen, and a violent
stream; for as soon as a thing has been seen, it is carried away, and
another comes in its place, and this will be carried away too.

—Marcus Aurelius, *Meditations*

By His EXCELLENCY *the* Right Honorable JOHN Earl *of* DUNMORE, HIS MAJESTY'S LIEUTENANT *and* GOVERNOR GENERAL *of the Colony and Dominion of* VIRGINIA, *and* VICE ADMIRAL *of the same,*

A PROCLAMATION.

I have ever entertained Hopes that an Accommodation might have taken Place between GREAT-BRITAIN and this Colony, without being compelled by my Duty to this most disagreeable but now absolutely necessary Step, rendered so by a Body of armed Men unlawfully assembled, firing on His MAJESTY'S Tenders, and the formation of an Army, and that Army now on the March to attack His MAJESTY'S Troops and destroy the well disposed Subjects of this Colony. To defeat such treasonable Purposes, and that all such Traitors and their Abettors, may be brought to Justice, and that the Peace, and good Order of this Colony may be again restored, which the ordinary Course of the Civil Law is unable to effect; I have thought fit to issue this my Proclamation, hereby declaring, that until the aforesaid good Purposes can be obtained, I do in Virtue of the Power and Authority to ME given by His MAJESTY, determine to execute Martial Law, and cause the same to be executed throughout this Colony: and to the End that Peace and good Order may the sooner be restored, I do require every Person capable of bearing Arms, to resort to His MAJESTY'S S T A N D A R D, or be looked upon as Traitors to His MAJESTY'S Crown and Government, and thereby become liable to the Penalty the Law inflicts upon such Offences; such as forfeiture of Life, confiscation of Lands, &c. &c. And I do hereby further declare all indentured Servants, Negroes, or others, (appertaining to Rebels,) free that are able and willing to bear Arms, they joining His MAJESTY'S Troops as soon as may be, for the more speedily reducing this Colony to a proper Sense of its Duty to His MAJESTY'S Crown and Dignity.

GIVEN under my Hand on board the Ship WILLIAM, off NORFOLK, the 7th Day of NOVEMBER, in the SIXTEENTH Year of His MAJESTY'S Reign.

DUNMORE.

(GOD save the KING.)

[An open letter from Patrick Henry, Virginian Patriot. He had recently led a force against Governor Dunmore.]

SIR,

As the Committee of Safety is not sitting, I take the Liberty to enclose you a Copy of the Proclamation issued by Lord Dunmore; the Design and Tendency of which, you will observe, is fatal to the publick Safety. An early and unremitting Attention to the Government of the S L A V E S may, I hope, counteract this dangerous Attempt. Constant, and well directed Patrols, seem indespensibly necessary. I doubt not of every possible Exertion, in your Power, for the publick Good; and have the Honour to be, Sir,

Your most obedient and very humble Servant,
P. Henry.

HEAD QUARTERS, WILLIAMSBURG,
November 20, 1775.

By the REPRESENTATIVES *of the* PEOPLE *of the Colony and Dominion of* VIRGINIA, *assembled in* GENERAL CONVENTION.

A DECLARATION.

WHEREAS Lord Dunmore, by his Proclamation, dated on board the ship *William*, off Norfolk, the 7th day of November 1775, hath offered freedom to such able-bodied Slaves as are willing to join him, and take up arms against the good people of this Colony, giving thereby encouragement to a general insurrection, which may induce a necessity of inflicting the severest punishments upon those unhappy people, already deluded by his base and insidious arts; and whereas, by an act of the General Assembly now in force in this Colony, it is enacted, that all negro or other slaves, conspiring to rebel or make insurrection, shall suffer death, and be excluded all benefit of clergy: We think it proper to declare that all slaves who have been, or shall be, seduced by His Lordship's Proclamation, or other arts, to desert their master's service, and take up arms against the inhabitants of this Colony, shall be liable to such punishment as shall hereafter be directed by the General Convention. And to the end that all such who have taken this unlawful and wicked step may return in safety to their duty, and escape the punishment due to their crimes, we hereby promise pardon to them, they surrendering themselves to Colonel William Woodford, or any other commander of our Troops, and not appearing in arms after the publication hereof. And we do further earnestly recommend it to all humane and benevolent persons in this Colony to explain and make known this our offer of mercy to those unfortunate people.

EDMUND PENDLETON, President.

[A letter from Dr. John Trefusis to Dr. Matthias Fruhling of Philadelphia]

The *Marvel* Frigate
November 18th, 1775

SIR —

" 'Nunc, o lecta manus, validis incumbite remis;
tollite, ferte rates, inimicam findite rostris
hanc terram, sulcumque sibi premat ipsa carina.
Frangere nec tali puppim statione recuso
arrepta tellure semel!'"[1]

"Friskish dotard," thou criest — "why dost plunge into thy letter so?" Indeed, sir, say I, for I am awash on the seas of chance and giddy with their heaving — and thus I spew. A packet on its route north passes this skirling barque, and I shall hand this billet off to one I pray shall deliver it unto thee, most generous friend, so thou mightst convey to thy brethren at the American Philosophical Society the startling word of what *new experiments* here transpire.

---

1 "Now, my chosen men, draw hard upon your oars; lift the prow, drive our ship-ashore on the beaches of the enemy, cleave a furrow in the foe's land. So long as we find a safe foothold there, who cares if our ship founders on the shore?" — Virgil, *Æneid,* Book X [Editor's note]

I head now for the Virginia Colony in the company of my *quondam* charge, the Negro boy Octavian—in which country, he avoweth, he shall rise in arms against the vile practice of slavery. "Sir—," thou protesteth, "seaborne? How now?" To which my answer is, *Oh pish, sir, 'tis a tale of poison, escape, and desperate flight; surely of no interest to thee.*

There is aboard this ship a spirit of expectation which delights the heart as it vivifies the senses. My boy Octavian, having spent some days abed, never having traveled upon the water before, so that his vitals were involved in uproar, now prowls about the decks impatient of our destination. Ah, ye gods! It makes me long for youth and fire. I come to the end of things, dear friend, and he waxes mickle; my tides have gone slack and flaccid, while his swell newly to proxigean spring and rush through the gut.

He doth not yet know that he must someday die; which oft is the key to immortality.

By such potent ignorance, all may be changed.

Thou mayst report to the Philosophical Society that the child's education continues, though he is delivered out of the shackles of Gitney and Sharpe. The experiment now rests in Octavian's hands. I instruct him in epistemics, and he learns his own lessons in government. He has a little book, in which he intends to keep a maritime diary, which I trust shall be a record of great moment, when viewed with the hindsight of years. He that would triumph over the petty trickery of fate must indite history at its source.

In one respect, I regret, his education has ceased: Thou mayst recall he was a prodigious fiddler; and of late, circumstance hath allowed him to borrow a violin of a gentleman of Boston, and fate bade him play it. But with our departure for the south, which I have arranged comformably with the boy's ardent wishes, that instrument was left with its owner; and I can observe the boy's yearning for the bow and catgut, those his solace and his song, his very boon companions.

Our voyage south, though fraught with fear of foul weather and pert rebel brigandage, hath passed without incident; the shore for the last several days being but a collection of miserable hovels, forests hacked to their roots, a smoldering field in New Jersey, and meager cattle. We are anchored tonight off the coast of Delaware, where there stands, on the bank, a great ironworks — a bloomery and slitting mill — all cold and neglected. This evening, we meeting with the packet bound for New-York from Virginia, we halted for exchange — and have received most startling intelligence — which I hasten to scrawl to you, though I keenly want Mercury's marvelous avian sandals to deliver it with greater expedition than lazy water.

We have for some time heard tales of Lord Dunmore; that he hath fled his palace; that he sitteth enthroned upon a ship-of-war, the ground itself having grown too hot for him to walk upon. We have heard that he threatened a general manumission of the slaves and to burn Williamsburg in one great conflagration; and that many

Negroes were fled to him, and that he sent out raids through all the rivers and their convolutions to seize upon chicken, duck, and beef for his Marines, and to punish those would not swear loyalty to the King.

But now such things are heard — of which thou shalt, i'faith, get fuller news on this same packet: Dunmore hath fought his first great battle at a place near Norfolk. The rebel militia, hearing that Dunmore approached with a force, set an ambush to trap him; but seeing our grenadiers of the 14th marching relentlessly upon them, the cowards could not withstand the loft of bearskin and the rattle of shot — and either ran, or were taken. And this is the delight: Both the rebels' commanding colonels were put in irons; and *one* — I recall not his name — *was captured by two of his own former slaves,* who found him hid cowering in a swamp. *Dies mirabilis!*[2]

This victory hath heartened those upon this frigate greatly. Dunmore's situation, though uncomfortable, may prove now to yield to scenes of more perfect success; for though his colony is in disorganization and the rebellion there flagrant, still, his force hath shown itself formidable and only gains in adherents — for indeed, indeed, Dunmore hath carried out his rumored design, and offered freedom to all Negroes such as will desert their rebel masters and list in his cause. He hath formed a Regiment. Already, there are hundreds have flocked to his standard — and

2 "Miraculous day!" [Editor's note]

have taken up arms—and are gratified with the name of *Lord Dunmore's Royal Ethiopians*. The rebels may gnash their teeth as they will.

Would that thou wert a gambling man so we might take sides; for I know thou cleav'st to rebellion, and I cleave to entertainment; and my feet almost fall to dancing when I think of long odds and a woodland alive with black escapees. Detonations, sir, shall follow.

An ensign of the 14th came on board our frigate to deliver the particulars, of which we had formerly heard but rumor; and when he had done so, the spirits of all were in great ferment. Octavian could scarce remain within the compass of the gunwales. Others wished to push on to Norfolk, invigorated by the word of success. All talked of the rebel colonel trussed and bagged by his own two slaves, that had been whipped by him previous—and there was an elation in this tale of justice reflected in all eyes.

Amongst the glad faces and the looks of triumph, one aging Negro in the crew could be perceived crying; and, wondering at his tears, I inquired of him why he wept.

He raised his arms in a gesture of enthusiasm; and in a voice thick with his weeping, recited the Psalm:

"When the LORD turned again the captivity of Zion,
we were like them that dream.
Then was our mouth filled with laughter,
and our tongue with singing:
then said they among the heathen,

The LORD hath done great things for them.
For indeed hath HE done great things for us;
      whereof we are glad.
Turn again our captivity, O LORD,
      as the streams in the south!
They that sow in tears shall reap in joy."

It was most affecting.

Though my bones are eld and weary and my skin is *rough as is the houndfish's hide,* still doth my whole spirits tremble in agitated liquidity to see the issue of this coming campaign—in which so much shall be done to ensure, thou, my dear friend, dear because compassionate, that thy rebellion shall truly give birth to *liberty.*

Gamble how thou wishest, sir—

"Hos successus alit: possunt, quia posse videntur."[3]

                  So says
                              thy humble & affectionate,

                              Dr. John Trefusis

3 "They are strengthened by success; they can triumph because they think they can triumph." — Virgil, *Æneid,* Book V [Editor's note]

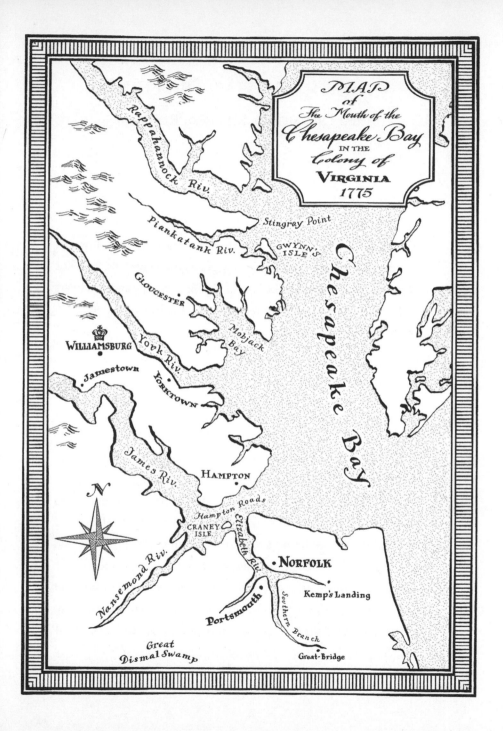

The ITINERARIUM
of Private OCTAVIAN NOTHING,
Lord DUNMORE's Ethiopian Regiment

Thus do I begin. Here commences my record—taken down in the hope that a record of such a struggle as here impends shall not be found uninteresting to the eye of future curiosity and the heart which thrills with compassion and is stirred by high deeds. So thus, on this day,

November 21ˢᵗ, 1775

We are arrived at Norfolk. The town is of a good size, and its waters swelled with the ships of Lord Dunmore's fleet.

We came to anchor at about three o'clock. There was a great bustle. Boats were prepared, that the passengers might disembark.

The moment being come that I should be rowed ashore to transact my enlistment, I bid a brief farewell to Dr. Trefusis, and hope that it shall be for but a short time, until we both have found our lodgings. As we embraced, he could not forbear to shed a tear. I fear I shed none, anticipation of coming adventures blotting out remembrance of those past; I fairly trembled with eagerness to reach the shore. I thrilled to that truth too sweet to be believed:

that as I entered the Army, I should be freed in the eyes of the law —
no stricture should bind me, no paper should hold me. Not simply escape,
but freedom itself. 'Twould be a half an hour; an hour — but this
same day.

The transit from ship to shore, meandering between hulls of schooner and brig, our oarlocks rattling monotonously, seemed to me interminable, so fired was I at the promise at last of landfall and recruitment; I strained forward, too, at the possibility that Bono should be presented to view at any moment; that by tonight, I might share a cup with him, who had been my only friend and brother throughout my youth.

I was conducted by a soldier to a warehouse requisitioned by the Ethiopian Regiment as a barracks, and there presented to a white serjeant by the name of Clippinger, that he might transact the enlistment. He asked me a great number of questions — *viz.* "Where d'you come from? Name of your master that was?" — to which he did not mark the answers, they being transcribed by his Corporal, a Scotsman named Craigie of a rough look and the letters *G.R.* branded upon the flesh of his forehead.

"Your name?" said the Serjeant.

"Octavian," said I.

"Your surname?"

I considered. I would no longer be called Gitney. "I have none," I said.

"And ye don't have no master."

"I have no master, sir," said I, "except the King."

To the tattooed Craigie he said, "Write 'Octavian Negro.'"

"While I would not trouble the Serjeant, I would beg —"

"What then?"

"If it please you, sir, put down nothing for the surname. I would rather be called nothing than be named only for my race."

Serjeant Clippinger gave an insalubrious smile. "Octavian Nothing?" said he.

I regarded my name. Knowing not who I was, it seemed a fair enough appellation.

"Octavian Nothing," I agreed.

And thus it was inscribed.

So terrified was I that some irregularity would interfere with enlistment — some unforeseen objection — I perhaps answered with too great an exactitude, too punctilious a range of detail — desperate for approbation. When he asked, "Whether ye fought previous," I thought in terror of my service with the rebels, and answered, "I have — through circumstance, not design — thrown in my lot with a regiment of — previously — but only as a slave — fought with — or built fortifications for —"

"Sweet Christ. No sermon, boy. A yea, a naw — no more, hear?"

I said, "Nay," and his questions continued. I stared bewildered at the young Serjeant's face — dazed not by his words, but by his features, his speaking mouth, his pimples; for in the last moments of my bondage, I was cast back into my years as a sort of half valet — unable to hold any thought but that I should hate to shave him, for that he would suffer cuts and scold. He asked his questions, and after each, I drew the razor down his pimpled cheeks in my helpless fancy, and saw him bleed.

And then I found that the time for questions was through; and he bade me place my hand upon my heart.

'Tis the moment, thought I—but scarce could understand it.

There was no ceremony to the oath he bade me swear. He, presuming I could not read, spake phrases regarding my loyalty to the Crown, and I repeated them without sense of their meaning—*be faithful and bear true allegiance … His Majesty, King George III … crown and dignity … abjure the works of Rebellion …*

And yet, those words were of infinite potency: for until then, I was a slave, though fugitive, bound by the laws of my country to Mr. Gitney and his house; but having spake the words of loyalty to my King, having been inducted into his service, my bondage, inherited from my mother, was, in accordance with the Governor's proclamation, at long last dissolved.

At the final word—which was *God*—I baulked, and could not speak—and choked the word—"Gah"—sensible that in the space of open vowel, with the tongue touched to palate on the *d,* the oath would be complete, the enlistment accomplished, and I could never again be legally taken—and twice I stuttered—entertaining a hectic fancy that I should never speak it out, and so must remain bonded—gagging—but there it was—*spoken*—and Serjeant Clippinger was already turned half away, having accepted my first assay as sufficient.

As were it some spell (for such it was, that burst through chains that stretched from America's shores to the palaces of London, the fastnesses of distant Oyo, fetters that bound together ships' ledgers and the firearms of kidnappers and the combs with which I plaited Mr. Sharpe's damp hair) I imagined the air should crack, the Atlantic sky yield forth its cataracts, and Hell itself howl misery.

Serjeant Clippinger hummed and hunted through papers. He held out a roster for me to sign, and indicated how to draw an X. I took his quill, and wrote my name.

Octavian Nothing, Negro.   Private, Major Byrd's Com.
Nov. 21st, 1775.

O Lord — who hath taken mercy upon the afflicted — praised be Thy name.

The room was but an accounting room, with desks and rectangles of sun; and yet it was in that room that the curse fell from me, the curse of sixteen years, borne with me from my mother's womb — and for the first time, I knew freedom.

❦ The Serjeant gave me then my uniform, which was but a shirt of coarse cloth, emblazoned upon the breast with the words, *Liberty to Slaves,* to be worn with my own breeches. The stitching of the motto was none of the finest, being accomplished by women attached to the Regiment who did not know letters; but still it was with awe that I received it, thanking him with bows and courtesies.

He received these marks of gratitude with distaste, cutting short my thanks to order me out of the room.

I have spent the afternoon in getting matters settled; being presented to the others of my mess, awaiting judgments upon my situation by sundry officers, and seeking out the Assistant to the Quartermaster to obtain my blanket, rucksack, and such other accoutrements as we are required to purchase on account.

In the warehouse, on the street before it, in the nearby square where the Regiment paraded — as I make my way through these places, I see everywhere Negroes in uniform — and on each breast, that triumphant and defiant motto, *Liberty to Slaves*.

I cannot suppress my rejoicing, and grin full on at these soldiers; who some, regard me in puzzlement; others, in scorn at my excitement; and yet several have returned my idiot jackanapes smile, as if to say, "*I know, my friend.... I know.*"

As a free man, I am dressed far more meanly than I was as a slave, when I wore silks and lawn; and yet, there could be no finer raiment than such a shirt as this, though the smock be coarse as hum-hum.

I supped with my mess. Despite their welcome, I could not bring myself to speak much at our meal, so sensible am I of my youth and inexperience, so anxious am I for their approbation.

Two others of my age, called Will and John, were today enlisted, having just arrived in the morning through the swamps. Two days ago they fled their master, having heard news of Lord Dunmore's proclamation, and have spent the last two nights in flight across plantations.

But four hours ago, they were fugitives, creeping in bushes, hearts apound, danger surrounding; and now, they sit giddy with escape, surrounded only by companions, drunken on the airiness of flight, recounting mishaps.

"We got apart," said John. "There was dogs, and we got apart."

"We has a sign," said Will.

"A sign — we has this sign — if we get apart."

"Wild turkey call. Our sign. Wild turkey."

"So John gets apart during the dogs."

"No, Will gets apart."

"I say: John gets apart, and he hide in the bushes."

"And Will crawls—"

"I hear the wild turkey."

"He crawls."

"I crawls to the turkey."

"He make the call back. He whispers me, 'John! John!'"

"And ain't no answer."

"He make the call again. Then, 'John!' He say, 'John!'"

"Ain't no answer, 'cause it was a wild turkey."

"In the bush."

"A actual wild turkey."

"And Will's there, whisper and whisper, turkey and turkey, and the turkey come out, and I'm laughing behind him."

"He laughs! On the ground! I ain't laughing, though."—But laugh they both did, now in safety. They waved their fingers before the embers of our fire.

Sensible that I should speak and join the frolic, I opined that I should like to hear their especial call, having never heard human imitate that animal's cry.

John nodded, put his hand to his mouth, and made a fierce noise, at which much of the mess was astonished.

"Sweet Lord," said Will. "Ain't no turkey."

"That's my turkey."

"Never no turkey. You got a harbor seal there."

"Harbor seal!" said John, and threw his arm around his companion in danger, and they laughed so hard that the tears ran down their faces.

And all the company laughed with them; for most were drunk; and we who were sober—we still wore shirts on which it said, *Liberty to Slaves*.

November 22nd, 1775

First day of service; my hands are weary with digging. We were awakened before dawn to begin a fortification of the town. This day spent in the construction of earthworks.

Our situation, I find, is thus: Williamsburg — its Palace and its House of Burgesses — lies utterly abandoned by all royal authority, and is now the haunt of rebels. As we have heard, His Lordship the Governor resides here in a ship off the shore of Norfolk, surrounded by his small fleet. He victuals himself and his little army by sending out small sail with landing parties to seize upon such provisions as are necessary — flesh and fowl — from rebel farms and plantations.

Though the rest of the countryside is, say some, a scene of riot, we are strongly placed here in Norfolk, with excellent approaches by sea and a control of all approaches by land. The Army hath raised stockades and breastworks to the south — to secure the road whereby goods are brought from the Carolinas — and to the east.

The rebels hath marched upon us here, spewing their calumnies and declaring their hatred for Lord Dunmore, our liberator, and for this Ethiopian Regiment; but they have been halted by our troops in the swamps below this place, where they remain, facing our stockades. They menace and wait to advance. Many of our number still speak with joy of our victory in the swamps securing the avenues to this town. Norfolk's situation may be as perilous as the investment of the Army in Boston; but there is more taste of triumph here in the air of the barracks than there was in the very feasts of the decorated officers on Marlborough Street.

My own lodgings here are humble: There are thirty-five of us laid in a warehouse by the wharves. There is but one fire-pit in the room, and the draughts are troublesome. My sleep was fleeting, and my bones, when I rose, sore.

I write this at the supper hour. It has been twenty minutes writing. I find myself concealing my quill from the gaze of curiosity.

I yield to discomfort; the arm aches. I set the quill down.

November 23rd, 1775

Morning — occupied in digging earthworks.

I have received a note from Dr. Trefusis, who is settled at a tavern in town. At the next available opportunity, he will seek me out — as I am not permitted to roam the streets.

This day, received my firelock. Our Regiment is armed from rebel stores seized in raids earlier this month. Mine is an old Charleville musket. Curious to consider that, were it not seized, this very musket had been used against us. The stock hath been polished by the enemy's hands.

Afternoon, drilled without powder. Corporal Craigie, the Scotsman with his forehead branded, called out the commands, saying we *maun needs listen well or we shall surrender in confusion*. I listen, but succumb to anxiety — lose all distinction between left hand and right — fumble the musket — find myself marching into my companions.

The gun makes not the soldier.

November 24th, 1775

This day, all hands to digging a fosse.

Afternoon, drilled: for two hours, the loading of the guns, and for another two, exercises in the fields, facings, wheelings, evolutions. I am the worst of soldiers.

No word come of Pro Bono. None have heard of him here.

The snoring in the barracks is considerable. I am in some difficulty to sleep. The air is frigid and floor unyielding.

November 25th, 1775

Snowed this day, so we could neither drill nor build our earth-works. We engaged in some few brief exercises, but were ragged in our showing. Several of the men have no shoes, protecting their feet with rags wound around them only, and their discomfort was extreme. When we returned to the barracks, they lit a great fire to thaw the ice around their feet and lay shivering, arranged radiant around the flames. There being no chimney in the warehouse, we were obliged to open a window at the upper story to release the smoke, which also swiftly draws out the warmth.

I fear sleep tonight will be difficult.

It is rumored that a great force of rebels approaches from the Carolinas. I am told by Will that I should not fear Carolinian numbers so much as Virginian sharpshooters, who, armed with rifles, can far outreach the musket in range and fatal accuracy. Their uniform is simply their hunting-shirts, on which, it is said, they have embroidered the words *Liberty or Death*.

The fear of these shirtmen expressed among our ranks is so great that they might themselves be messengers of Hades, for they appear in the tales of those who have fought them in earlier battles as faceless and invisible, a loud *crack* and a death, and they are gone.

We spent much of our day without activity. For a time, we were entertained by Will and John's ready store of wit and comic roguery as they engaged each other in kicking games. ("Stand still! I get two on your shin!"—"Not true! Don't count!")

The wind made its moan about the walls of our rude barracks, and we all fell silent, thinking perhaps on the rebels who await us. Without employment, we had little to do but listen to the boards rattle. At length, our dinner being completed, I took the opportunity to read in Virgil.

After a time, I glanced up from the trance in which the tale had engaged me to find the men of my mess staring mistrustfully at me and at my book.

"You read," said one fellow, and it was not a question; but an announcement of that fact, so that all might know.

Covered with blushes, I hid my volume, but they knew it was there, this artifact of the conqueror.

November 26th, 1775—Sunday

This day, continued work on earthworks and drilled on the square. I am apprehensive about the use of the firelock, and pray I acquit myself well in the day of trial.

In Boston, we should not undertake such labor on the Sabbath.

The inhabitants of Norfolk turned out to watch us drill, alarmed by our volleys. Upon their countenances, looks of apprehension. For some hours, they surveyed us. The men wear red rags sewn to their chests, which has been lately required of them as proof of their oaths to the Crown and to Lord Dunmore. I do not venture to say whether their hearts are as stalwart in our support as their chests suggest. I perceive that they little relish the marching of Negroes before them with firearms.

Boys call out names as we pass on the streets.

At the barracks last evening, a grand ball, which convocation was attended by soldiers of all companies and by many of the women attached to the Regiment. These Sabbath-day dances are the long custom among the plantations and farms of this Colony; but I have never seen the like. My delight may be imagined.

The music was loud and joyous in the extreme, sung, beaten upon drums, and played upon simple lutes and *chitarrones*; the dancing, though marked with great *bizarrerie* in its movements, was intoxicating in its strangeness and exhilarating in its exultation; and, despite what I had been told at the College of Lucidity of the dancing of slaves, it was executed with complete propriety: There was no intermingling of the sexes, but each maintained its separate steps and songs. There was great commerce and discussion between each dance, often beyond the scope of my understanding, the whole room a very Babel of rich tongues and alien conversation.

Though most speak English as their mother tongue, there are some, newer fetched from their country, who spake two languages or three before ever they heard our British speech. When I think upon their excellence of parts, their facility in the vaguaries of our Anglo-Saxon cant, I am ashamed at the pride with which my masters regarded my own slender accomplishments.

Some here have not spoken their own tongue for ten years, for twenty, separated in the auction-yard from their countrymen and sequestered, that they might not conspire; and now they are reunited with those who know not merely the same verbs, but the same cities, the same rivers, the same gods; and so everywhere one hears English overthrown with delight, and alien discourse entered into with ardor.

When in English, 'twas thus: "No, sir, this, this — Aye, you, this" — There was much negotiation, and a tune played or sung, taken up by others, learned by those newly hearing it. Observing these exchanges (and too timid to speak or sing), I at last understood the full breadth of their endeavor: These drummers, these dancers were ripped from nations more distant from one another than Lapland and Spain, speaking a wealth of tongues, praising different gods; singing different songs with instruments only alike as violin is to viol. And in the thatched quarters of the plantations had these people of disparate nations gathered once weekly to *sing their songs in a foreign land, though they are but sojourners here;* not the songs of one nation, but the music of many, sung in as many tongues. Each plantation hath thus strummed and beat out its own peculiar suites, its own lively airs, its customs negotiated through use. These plantation festivals are become an act of general composition, wherein dances forged from the rites of different cities, tunes taken from one kingdom and given new words in the language of another, codified if applauded through weeks of repetition. And here, in Lord Dunmore's Regiment, the singers meet and exchange and bicker over variations, all eager to have their song known.

Some sang burlesques upon their masters. Others honored Lord Dunmore, our liberator, most generous of Governors, bravest of commanders. One of the regimental drummers played most miraculously upon a drum of his own fashioning. Those near me informed me that he made the drum speak, and that it chanted the praise-songs of his people in ancient times and their exploits martial.

His praise-song being completed, the women sent forth a maiden to sing who must be a favorite among them; being graced not only with elegance of gesture, but symmetry of feature and comeliness of form; and she sang a lamentation in her tongue which could not have been more interesting and affecting.

I cannot write too much praise of this girl. Her every movement was fascination. Her hair was close-cropped; her dress was modest; her voice compelled attention.

I would gladly have heard more of her solemnity; but following her performance, the music ceased, the fire was banked up, and conversation became general.

There were many stories this night; several recounted in tongues I knew not to groups of four or five; a few sung; some ancient tales told. Many related the stories not simply of antique times, but of their flight from their owners, which seems a ritual of our Regiment, the telling of these tales, of which each of us has one to relate; and among the auditors, there was much laughter at the ingenuity of contrivance, the boldness of deceit, and the gullibility of white *hauteur*. To whit, Will and John told again of their turkey call. One man told of his flight that he had stolen not only some few silver buckles, but also a bridle from his master's stables; and so far from him proceeding in dead of night, in silence and stealth, he walked through the woods in open daylight shouting, "Bellerophon!" as loud as he might; and when white men approached him, he explained that his master's horse was fled, and he sent out to capture it. Another man was a day from home when he espied the slave patrol approaching upon the road; and he repaired into a yard and split wood until they passed. Others spake of boats stolen, of rivers navigated, of days spent humming on smacks.

Following these tales, a man rose with his wife held close to him, and both spake their tale; how the wife had lately been great with child; and how as she grew, she was beset by new hungers, there being no meat allowed the slaves in that place, but only corn. She worked in the master's kitchen, and could not forbear to snatch some few shreds of chicken from the preparations she was daily engaged in, to ward off the terrible famine that wracked her gravid frame. She was taken in this theft, and condemned to be beaten. The master seeing that she could not well support herself under such duress, he determined that she should lie upon the ground while receiving her punishment, with a small ditch dug for her stomach so the child should not be harmed for the crimes of the mother.

The husband told us, "He give me the shovel. He give me the shovel, and he say, you dig the place for the belly. And I weeping; I weeping, and no wise could dig. But Mr. Spritely, he say he whip her more if I don't dig; he say more strokes if I don't make the hole; and so I takes the shovel."

And so he dug, and his dear wife was laid upon her stomach and whipped; and as, three weeks later, he dug another trench, this one in which to lay the stillborn child, he knew they would run; that death itself was not terrible; and a month after that, they had lit out for Lord Dunmore's flotilla at Hampton.

This narrative was greeted with tears and sung expostulations, prayers and awful wailing; and the women began a song, which transfixed me not in small part because the damsel, with modest blushes, chanted with the chorus, and in the midst of it, sang a solo. I inquired of those around me what the maiden sang; and found finally one who spake the language; he informing me that 'twas a praise-song, as men would sing of their forebears; but that she sang not for deeds done, but for those as yet undone.

The maiden sang the praise of our Regiment, a prayer to her gods for our victory; she sang that we should be remembered by our descendants, and that, triumphant, we should be those who would lead the dead home from their long exile, and end at last their hungry wanderings.

Today, all hands to fortification.

A thing which troubles me: I am sensible of a silence that accompanies me in all conversation. It stops up my mouth and the mouths of others. My own voice galls even me; it oppresses me like a silver fork scraped across porcelain.

Not so when we are upon fatigue: When we dig, bind, do any of the work of entrenchment — these things I know from long practice — I am one of the number. There is no distinction of habit or effort.

But when we sup or dine, I know the looks my voice will invite, and I cannot bring myself to speak. I am ashamed at my words before they scape the teeth; I clutch my trencher on my knees; I discover myself practicing all the arts of concealment which I learned in my years of service, when I little wished notice from Mr. Sharpe. I say nothing which might offend; I respond if questioned, so as not to draw interest through unoccasioned silence; I do what is asked of me; and most of all, I observe.

Among the Collegians, silence was protection; among the rebels, 'twas grief. Among the members of the orchestra, 'twas policy; and among the work crews, 'twas prudence.

I do not know what it signifies here, where there is no purpose of concealment nor need of diplomacy; and I am tired of it.

I may write this, that *I know not;* but I do know on several heads why I am ashamed here; one being, that in this company where all have a story of suffering, all have a history of grief and a narrative of flight, I am suddenly the least of them.

A new youth, a boy younger than me by a year or two,

enlisted this day. He labors under an affliction in his speech, acquired through long habit of degradation or sudden excess of horror. When he talks, his throat or tongue will of a moment seize up, and he be unable to speak more. I fully compassionate in his distress, having but the other day, when enlisting, felt I should never speak a full word again. A gentle soul, already long and spidery of limb and uneven of tooth, this boy was introduced to me in the evening in some embarrassment. He said that it had been told him that I could *read*; which accomplishment I could not deny. He asked me then to read his badge; which I did, saying that it read as all of ours did, *Liberty to Slaves.*

He told me that Serjeant Clippinger had howled when he had seen it, jeering that the woman had sewn it wrong, and it was a perfect fit for a three-toothed black coxcomb like himself. He asked me again, earnestly, to con it out; and I admitted that the letters were not formed in complete perfection; that it resembled somewhat, *Liberty to Slane,* with a wriggling trail after the *e.* I inquired if that was Serjeant Clippinger's reading; and he replied glumly, *Liberty to Slant.*

Upon hearing this, Will and John broke into great laughter and patted him on the back, crowing out the motto, tilting comedically, embracing him until he too laughed. The men now call him *Slant,* which would be wounding, were it not exclaimed with such an achievement in the "Liberty" that the "Slant" might be righted with balance and equanimity.

And the men now call me *Buckra,* which is their word for a white man; for having seen me read, they say that I am a white man hidden in a black skin.

And I have just called them "they."

Dr. Trefusis's ingenuity is marvelous. We have been here but ten days, and he has got himself introduced into the finest houses in Norfolk; he has written to Lord Dunmore, describing his experiments and begging permission to visit with his ex-slave Octavian Nothing; and he received a written pass, that he might spend one hour with me this evening under the pretext that my lessons must continue, if his philosophic endeavors are not to founder through disuse. He was merry, and we sate in an office in the warehouse while he feigned instruction and I feigned learning.

Serjeant Clippinger could not conceal his distaste and jealous suspicion of this connection, and scrutizined Dr. Trefusis for all the marks of a spy. Throughout the time of our discourse, he paced past us, frowning.

Our hour was spent pleasantly. I wished to speak to him of my silence; of my name, *Buckra;* but he was so giddy, his hands strapped about his knees, rocking, that I could not.

Dr. Trefusis informed me that he is become marvelous familiar with various of the local gentry and the officers, and has been entertained in parlors of the most gracious rank, having merited introduction by the rumor that in his youth he was in attendance at Versailles and Sanssouci.

The principle pleasure of these audiences, says Dr. Trefusis, lies in referring to royalty without either revealing or denying the closeness of his connection, *viz.* "You know, sir, His Majesty, Frederick of Prussia, once said after supper . . ."; or "Philippe d'Orléans, of course, was no enemy to flatulence; I recall Louis

XIV used to jest about how his late brother held contests in after-dinner eructation *en famille*," which careless talk greatly discomfited his hosts, who wished to determine the rank of the man to whom they spake.

"Am I tramp or baron?" mused Dr. Trefusis. "My wig saith baron, but my odor saith tramp."

"'Sdeath," Serjeant Clippinger interrupted, "you're to be teaching the Negro somewhat, sir, yea? Or absent from military property, if y'please."

"I am indeed teaching him," Dr. Trefusis insisted. "About odor, which is what Locke would call a *secondary quality of bodies*. What is unexpected is that time has a smell, Octavian; how else might we explain that old men exude the scent of years?" He held his wrist to his nose. "'Tis startling when one acquires it oneself."

I inquired, "Is it not surprising, sir, that despite its long continuance and your constant intimacy with it, you can smell it still?"

"Passing over your delightfully clumsy reference to the extremity of my age, it is indeed surprising. The human primarily observes change; those things which remain unchanging become invisible to us. A smell to which we are long accustomed ceases to be a smell; objects hung upon the wall for years no longer garner interest."

I remarked that I had thought the same of a shackle (when I was sitting enchained) or a bit in the mouth.

Dr. Trefusis, noting that Serjeant Clippinger had passed on, asked intently, "What mean you?"

I said, "A shackle on the wrist the first day is an outrage; after weeks or months, it belongs to one, and one would feel nakedness without it."

For a long while, Dr. Trefusis regarded me warily. Said he, "Indeed. Indeed. One forgets that one is shackled. One forgets that one smells. This focus is necessary for our operation: Did we see every brick and tree anew each time we saw it, did we encounter every personage we met as an infant does, were we sensible of every outrage every moment, perception had disordered us to so great a degree we should not be able to carry on the business of life. So what the senses notice is primarily *that which doth change.*

"And yet," he mused, patting at his waistcoat, "the change from youth into age one perceiveth not. You awake one morning, and find you have smelled of old man for some time. You have been deceived by the passing sameness of days; they have accumulated upon you like powder. A vaguely"—he sniffed—"moth-scented powder."

"D'ye say," said Serjeant Clippinger, returned with sarcasm heavy in his voice, "that this lesson is to make a better soldier of him?"

"Indeed, Serjeant. It improves him."

"He don't need improvement," said Clippinger. "He's a private."

"I would think," said Trefusis, "that to make a man a good soldier, you first must make a man worth losing."

December 1ˢᵗ, 1775

All hands to fortifying the town. In the afternoon, drills.

Supped with Slant, the gentle, timid arrival of the other day, and another youth, Pomp. The boy Slant suffers some disorder that causes him to choke upon his words. In the course of common speech, 'tis but a hesitation. When he is excited, however, some fist doth clutch his jaw or some finger pinch his tongue; no sound comes forth from the working mouth, and shame fills his eyes, that he cannot speak. I fear to think out of what grim circumstance this arises.

We sat upon the dead grass and ate our rations as we watched Will and John, who are the favorites of our company, engage in their antics by the berm.

This amiable Pomp hath a fund of stories, delighting particularly in those most horrible to hear, and I, giddily diverted not only by his wonder-tales but also by this hour of companionship, begged him to favor us with descriptions of the world's chiefest monstrosities. He thought hard upon it, smiled widely, and informed us of his two most favored water-beasts: the Scottish water-bull which lurks in Highland tarns and waits to devour the child dangling his fingers in the peat; and the *ninkenanke,* the dragon of the Gambia, which devours goats and men, pulling them shrieking into the mangrove swamps. The latter beast hath, says he, a diamond in its head.

Slant, who is tall in stature but still a boy in years and spirit, was much affected by these tales, thrilled with fear and pleased with the discomfort; after our dinner, when we sate about the fire, he asked Pomp *whether he— ... believed such monstrosities.*

"I don't reckon so," Pomp answered. "Except saving when I'm out with my cattle in the swamp at night, and no stars. Then I believe everything."

Slowly, friend Slant nodded. He kept his eyes fixed upon the flames.

"I don't mind to tell you," said Pomp, "and this is truth: There's a lake near where I keep my cows, and each night, a column of light come straight down from the sky and search out the middle of that lake."

Greatly intrigued, I asked whether he had seen this illumination and sought its source, saying that this was a worthy object for the inquiries of philosophy.

He nodded solemnly. "One night," he said. "I went to see it."

Asked Slant, *did he know what it — what it was?*

Pomp said, "If I seen that there's a light sometimes come down from the stars and burn on a lake, you reckon I go paddle out and see where it come from? After the once, I never seen that damn lake again after dark." He laughed; then, seeing Slant's fear, he took pity and said, "I sleep better, nights, knowing that light's an hour walk away from my tent, sitting on the water. If there ain't no light, I wouldn't sleep so good. Then there ain't nothing but darkness. Then you don't know where the danger's really hiding."

This day, for the first time, I fired shot in our drilling. I am no exquisite marksman, and almost dropped the piece when it fired. It is incomprehensible that I shall use this weapon against men of flesh and blood. I fear I am the worst of soldiers. It takes near a full minute for me to load.

Tonight, the visit of some of the women to our fire, and some singing. The maiden was among them; she chanted at the request of the women; I blush to relate it, but I (pridefully) painted in my fancy a scene where I played the violin for her, and she was delighted.

December 6th, 1775

This day, all hands to raising a redoubt and securing emplacements for the guns. The cannons are aimed, for the moment, at cattle upon the glacis, and children batting at the sky with sticks.

Still do our numbers swell with those who flee to join us. This day a man named Peter, of some thirty years, was admitted to our Company. In the evening, when we were retired, Peter recounted his tale of escape to such as wished to listen.

He was all his life in the service of a Major Marshall, who is an arch-rebel among the provincial militia; and come the commencement of the rebellion, Peter said to his master, "Sir, if you want the freedom, why don't you give me a little sip of that cup, too, if it please, sir?" His master would have none of it; but scolded him for his importunities.

Peter, serving his master as gentleman's man, traveled with the rebel army as they marched to launch their assault upon Lord Dunmore and our gathering forces at Norfolk. They were, as is known to us, stopped in their progress at Great-Bridge, and here they now rest, entrenched, frowning at our stockade across a great marsh.

The rebels being so poor in numbers, Peter was given a musket and told he would sally forth as a soldier, when the time came to attack the stockade. "I tell him," said Peter, "'Sir, I ain't going to fight them Royal Ethiopians.' That's what I tell him, boys — I ain't going to fight you — and he said, 'You will do what I tells you to do,' and scritch and scratch and done."

But one night, when Peter was sent out to victual several snipers who occupied houses on an island in the marsh, he found himself in the midst of an action, the Royal Ethiopians attacking; and when the Virginian shirtmen retreated, Peter did not flee with his rebel masters. They little noted in the confusion when he remained upon the island, nor when he stole down into the marsh and followed the Royal Ethiopians, hands up and whispering for quarter.

He was taken into custody, questioned closely, and eventually was hied to Norfolk, where he has enjoyed an audience with Lord Dunmore himself. "Lord Dunmore," said he, "he asked me questions hisself. He wishes especially to know what I seen, and I don't mind to help a man such as Lord Dunmore is, the Governor and all. I tell him, 'I tell you how it lies, sir. Sir, right now, there ain't above three hundred rebels there, at the Great-Bridge. You best move quick, sir, Your Honor, you best.' I reckon that he will, based on my intelligence I brung him, because I say, 'Sir, you best move soon, because in a few days, they bring up them cannons from North Carolina, they get them here, and they'll shiver your little wood fort into splinters. Three hundred men right now. Just three hundred. But they get their thousand Carolinians and their cannons — you and the Ethiopian Regiment is through.'"

I surveyed the faces of the men as this tale was told; we none of us like his pride in predicting disaster, but we like less the sound of those cannons.

Thus the tale of Peter, our new recruit.

❦ There followed talk of circumstances near Great-Bridge. While we have been laboring here, raising fortifications around Norfolk, against the rebels break through our lines and assault us, there are daily small actions and sorties in the swamps to the south: houses burned, raids on entrenchments, mortar shelling, a few dead from snipers or volleys from our stockade.

Slant, Pomp, and I listened for some time to these accounts, and then, the talk turning to other subjects, we whispered among ourselves. The three of us do not speak loudly in our barracks, perhaps because we are sensible that these are men, and we are boys; these others are whole, when we know ourselves broken.

To calm Slant, who now looked about him with unease, I told them of a battle joined between the Romans and the Albans: It was seen that the slaughter from the meeting of their two armies would be senseless and complete; so the two generals came to agreement that, as there were triplets in each army, the two sets of triplets should fight to determine which army would be the victor.

"It would be a fine . . . way to decide," said Slant, "with less of killing."

Now Pomp had a look of dreams in his eyes, and bade us imagine instead how the battle would appear, were one a triplet: the long afternoon; the armor in the sun; seeing your own self cut down again and then again; and killing the same man, only to have him rise, just winded, and raise his sword to finish you.

I asked them what they wished out of our present conflict.

Slant answered that he wanted to have many children, and a farm, and a plump, good wife.

Pomp said: "I suppose I wish to be a hero."

✍ I have just set down this account of Peter's arrival and our discourse; and now it is late, and I am beside the fire, and I think with anxiousness on the stories of those skirmishes to the south of this town, which even now preserve us from the enemy.

We have not seen that violence here. We are not sensible of it. In this town, all is linearity and training. To fire muskets is not an act of war, but a routine with which we, ranked in concert, take up the hours between ten and noon. A fortification is a task, a line, a curve, not a bulwark. The arts of war are mere geometry.

The regularity of drills has soothed, rather than excited, my more ardent passions; and I try now in vain to paint what those orderly ranks shall look like, were there grapeshot tearing through us, raining metal droplets from the skies on our open mouths.

I recall the strife upon Hog and Noddle's Islands, when the grass burned and the beach puckered with the shot of Marines. I put my life at hazard there, which some might account valor; but I knew it for the rashness of despair, the precipitation of utter despondence. Now that I am actuated by hopes more active—by anger at injustice and demand for benevolence—I fear I shall not be so reckless of my life.

I have wondered lately about death. I attempt to recall that it is but an assumption into a better realm; and yet I cannot envision past the stifling eternal silence of it, as were one locked in ice, with the world entertaining its commerce above—and I lying cold, below, aching to move, with the chill invading the flesh.

I had best prepare myself for action; the word is, it shall come soon.

✤ "There was once, there was a man," said Pomp, delighted narrator of horrors, "there was a man so afraid for dying, he make a deal with Death himself. A true story."

"A true story," said Slant in teasing tones.

"True. I knowed this man."

"Then wh—, wh—, what was his name?"

"See, it don't matter. He make a deal with Death. James Wippleson. Of Nansemond County. He calls Death to him out in the forest and he says, 'I don't want ever die. What I got to do not to die?'

"And Death, he says, 'Aye, Mr. Wippleson, you don't want die? I make a fine deal, sir. You don't kill nothing—not one single thing—and so long as you don't make work for me, so long as you don't deal death, you don't die.'

"This James Wippleson, he thinks this a fine deal sure, so he shake Death's hand, all bony and crunchy. He shake it. And Death laughed, and he gone in a trice.

"This James Wippleson, he standing there at the edge of the forest. And the sun coming up. And James Wippleson, he standing there and he see all the living things — the birds and the trees and all the plants — and he's joyful he alive.

"So he starts off for home. And he ain't taken one step before he sees: grass under his foot, and the bugs in the grass. And the crickets and the spittle-bugs. And all those tiny little things. And he can't step on none of them. So he stops walking. And then he realize, he can't eat. Can't kill no plant or no animal.

"And he look around again, and his life is over every second. The fly land on his arm, the mosquito-bug. And he can't hit it. And no way he can walk out of that field. So he stand. And he stand.

"All he got — all James Wippleson got for his . . . See, his immortalness, it's a terrible thing. Because immortalness ain't nothing but an endless carefulness. A man can't live his life forever. James Wippleson, he still standing there, thin as a rake, seeing as he can't starve, still standing there, not moving. And people go by and watch him, but he don't say nothing to them or budge none. Because if he move like he alive — he dead."

Thus the sermon and the text as we await word.

December 8th, 1775

Drills and exercises.

The command comes down from Major Byrd that we are to rest after supper but with our bedrolls and rucksacks in preparation.

It appears we shall march tonight.

December 15th, 1775

For some days, I have not written here. Opportunity for transcription was wanting, though matter was abundant. And after the battle, I could not write of it; words seemed insufficient.

We were occupied in the usual manner on the day of the eighth. We being ready to retire following our labor, we received orders that all companies should instead be prepared for deployment, but no word of our purpose. Accordingly, we returned to our barracks and ate our supper, prepared our weapons, and then waited uneasy for further command. Many of us fell to sleeping.

The guns had just gone off on the ships to mark the evening when Corporal Craigie appeared and ordered us form into rank.

Slant rose next to me. Pomp clasped him upon the arm, as he had seen men do, and, like a man, said, "Don't you fear."

Slant gave a look expressive of rebuke. "Just because I — stutter," said he, "don't mean I'm afraid." He grimly turned and rolled his blanket.

I myself felt no fear as we passed out the doors; but this was not so much the effect of temerity as of the strangeness of the hour and the darkness, and the mystery of the errand.

We assembled upon the square; we marched out through the streets of Norfolk, encountering a great parade of soldiers with whom we joined number. When we were free of the houses, we could espy the length of our column, which was great, the march being led by the regulars of the 14th Regiment and a small detachment of the Queen's Own Loyal Virginian Regiment. We were cautioned to make no sound, though the scudding of our feet on the road made a continual grinding, histle, and scrape.

I did not know whither we headed, but I fain would *be there, be there*—wheresoever *there* was—desired to be already engaged in confrontation, the terror full and present before me rather than measured out in paces of a foot and an inch.

We walked for hours through the country; our Regiment stopping only once, that those of us with shoes might lend them to such of those as marched without, and thus give them some respite.

Pomp was one of the unshod, and gentle-hearted Slant and I vied to proffer relief. He took my shoes, and watched me wind my feet in cloth to protect them from the extreme cold. He expressed his thanks; raised himself on his toes to even them out in too cramped a space, dropped back upon his feet, and said, "Now the big contest." He squinted along the line. "We look like them armies of ghosts that walk through the skies. You know, damned. They seen them there in England, marching. True. True story." Then he said to me, "You ain't told us what you want do, when we won. When we has our triumph."

"I would like," said I, tying a knot at my ankle, "to play violin in an orchestra. Symphonies of Arne and Sammartini."

Pomp regarded me with some amaze; Slant said, "Friend, you— . . . when you are there playing the music with the candles and the . . . fine ladies, you think back on this moment, tying you rags to you feet." He smiled and offered me a hand to pull me up.

We set off again, our number sunk in complete silence. We passed farms and villages, lone dogs crying out at our vast column. Their voices were sharp and small, and their warnings were unheeded.

As said Pomp, we looked like an army of phantoms, marching upon those roads. Our faces were sullen. In the absence of warning or explanation, we watched carefully, lest the enemy burst out upon us. There was no assault, however, and nought disturbed the countryside as we marched south toward the front.

I must own that the two hours I walked without shoes were in the highest degree uncomfortable, not only for the roughness of the cold earth against my heels — which were not hardened as some others' had been by years of such abrasion — but also for the extreme cold, which first chilled, and then dulled, the toes to insensitivity.

We passed through homestead and swamp, traversing a distance of perhaps ten miles in all. After a time, the darkness was so great that we could see little.

Some hours having passed, we were cautioned again to remain silent; and we found ourselves filing into a stockade in a broad marsh. Within, the stockade was cramped, some five hundred men gathered in a small and incommodious yard between tents.

We did not know where we were come, or what this march portended; though now that we were within the stockade walls, there was a continual whispering and muttering of intelligence; 'twas said that we were at Great-Bridge, and that the enemy was across a river from us, and that we should be called upon to defend the approaches to Norfolk. Peter, he who had lately escaped from the rebels, vaunted to all who would listen that it was his intelligence had convinced His Lordship to launch this expedition; for which no one knew whether to thank him or cuff him, and so we turned away.

It being perhaps three or four in the morning, our officers informed us that we could sleep for a time, each regiment directed to gather around their own campfires — all of which blazes were meager. There were some two hundred Negroes of the Ethiopian Regiment present, clustered around three flames that scarce would have warmed ten.

I was half way between waking and slumber in the dark corner of the stockade, shivering beneath my blanket — my shoes once again my own — my spirits ebbing with fatigue. My gaze was fixed without object upon the encampment, the dim figures who, an arm or a cheek caught in the distinguishing gesture of flame, huddled or moved about the mob of soldiery. Before me, half-seen, men lay on scant blankets, or smoked pipes and chafed their arms; near me, six soldiers on their knees offered prayers together; Coromantee fellows muttered poems or praise-songs to each other to prepare for battle; white grenadiers drank toddies and cracked nuts with their teeth. An older man of some fifty or sixty years walked among the others of our Regiment, offering a compound in a bowl which he spread on muskets as a blessing. Many shunned him; a few nodded, and handed him their weapons; he rubbed the unguent on the stock and muzzle, all the while whispering to the firearm coaxingly in some unknown tongue.

He came to a figure twenty feet away from me and offered his compound; and a voice replied, "What's this, some fashion of luck grease? A man don't need luck grease when he's every inch of him superlative."

This voice thrilled every nerve of my being — caught at my heart — for I knew its accents as well as my own.

I rose, disordered with delight, trepidation, confusion — I know not what — and said — louder than I liked, "Bono? Pro Bono?"

For my voice, I received hard stares from some around me, but jubilation at reunion confounded any sensibility of censure; and I rushed to his side as he twisted his head to face me, swore, and, in a voice of doubt, called my name: "Octavian?"

He half rose; I half sat; and hung thus between earth and air we grabbed at each other's fingers — and he cackled a laugh, and clasped me to him. "Your Supreme Regal Highness Octavian Gitney," he said, wonderingly. "This is a joy," he said. "This is a genuine joy, to see your little cry-teary sulky-boy face." Stepping back from our embrace, he swore, "Sweet Moses! You got a muscle in your arm. I felt it — a full muscle. Don't you fret yourself, Prince O. It's probably you been reading complete collected works instead of little poems."

"I am no longer Octavian Gitney," I said. "I am now called Octavian Nothing."

"Well, I ain't Pro Bono still. William Williams, Private. Like I told you, next time you saw me, I have a new name. So, sir."

We extended our hands and shook.

"William Williams," I repeated in wonder.

He explained, "They seem to favor the English names, the white folk. It's my interest to please their affable selves at every o'clock of the day. So I reckoned the pale, forgettable names was the best. Two, where one wouldn't do. I tried John Johns and Richard Richards. Richard Richards set a barn afire and he slain a sheep, so now I'm William Williams." He frowned. "I warrant I missed something fine with Henry Henry. But there is time, sir, there is plentiful time in this war for Henry Henry and, if I commence English, for Aubrey Aubrey, too."

He bade me sit, which I did, and we again expressed our

mutual pleasure at our reunion, following which he asked after my fortunes, inquiring how long I had been at Norfolk. I answered him, and asked of him the same, and he replied to my counter-interrogative that he had been at Norfolk since Lord Dunmore had arrived there from Hampton; that he had been in His Lordship's service since the summer, when he had found his labors elsewhere inconvenient; but any further disclosures on this lively subject were interrupted by another fervent question — for said he, "Your mother with you? She come down from Boston?"

I baulked. I had not considered the question. Of course he did not know; 'twas as if I conceived that some shudder would have reached him, who was so close a companion to us; as it is said that when Lisbon shook in the great quake, the spires of Boston quivered.

But unprepared, as I say, I baulked.

He studied me. "Prince O.?" he said.

Judge of my emotions upon being asked to recount her tale.

And I am ashamed to say: After long delay, I answered, "She is in excellent health. She — she sends her compliments and asks me to convey her deep affection and regard."

At this, he smiled. "Princess Cass," he said, in a tone of reverie. "When you seen her last?"

"Three months hence," said I; then, "Four months. April."

Bono, twitching my shirt, corrected, "That's eight months."

"When I last saw her, she sate in the garden —"

"And you left her behind? When you run?"

This was sudden; I could not speak. My mouth was, I know, open.

Around us, men slept upon the ground, or with subtle convulsion, approached the small fires. The watch walked the walls above us, their muskets at ready.

"She is a beauty," said Bono. He sat back and pulled the edges of his blanket around his knees. "Which garden?" he said.

I begged his pardon.

"Which garden?" he repeated. "Was you back at the College?"

My wits were so disordered that I answered yes.

"After the rebels surrounded the city?"

Once again, I answered yes, miserably.

He said, "Reckon it was too early for the delphiniums." Uncertain, I nodded; he continued, "Only damned parcel of labor your mother's ever tried her hand at. That garden. She and Mr. Gitney, ordering me up and down the borders. The names all jumble up in my head. Your lupine and your sweet-sultan and such."

Again, I nodded. Soldiers were rushing about near a white marquee, carrying casks.

Bono said, "She is a treat in that garden. That's a very fine place to see her. She fix the borders different this year? She and Mr. Gitney had a plan last summer."

"I regret I am not aware," said I.

"They was going to have a switch in the midsummer. Take out the foxgloves when they die, put in the chrysanthemums, take out the daisies and the pansies and such, put in the — I can't recall — the phlox or such." He considered. "Lupine and foxglove. Them, they always muddled me. Both tall." He asked, "You don't know how the garden was?"

"I left, regrettably, before it was in flower," I said. "In April."

Bono nodded. "When a man puts in work, he wants to know it will bloom."

I wished we would speak of something else. Three men dragged an ammunition cart through the mob of bodies, hissing to waken the sleeping.

Bono wrapped his hands in his sleeves. He said, "The enemy, he's sitting, guess a half mile from where we is. We been here since the middle of November. We've had some skirmish. They send some fool across to us, we fire our guns a couple of hours; we send someone back, their snipers fire, we retreat, but no one can move a damn inch. Other day, me and a few others, we go and burned some houses."

"Why are we brought here tonight?" I asked.

Bono shrugged. "Sally forth," he said.

He pointed to places that lay unseen through the stockade walls and told me about each: the mud around the fortress, which made it impossible to build rampart or redoubt; the village across the bridge to the south, now fortified by the rebels; the church where their insolent boys shimmied up the steeple to peer at our walls; the earthworks, lightly guarded, where the rebel marksmen lurked.

"I have heard," I said, "that there are a mere three hundred entrenched in the village."

"Don't rightly know," said Bono. "I reckon more than three hundred."

For longer we sat, content to be in company once more. At length, Bono opined, "I don't believe those impatiens will ever grow near the pine tree. What do you reckon?"

"I believe I was informed that those near the pine tree are nasturtiums."

"Whatever they is, I warrant they won't grow there. Too much shade, and those needles choke them off."

I was full of misery at my lie, but I found I could not disabuse him of it — I could conjure no words sufficient. And this was, perhaps, my secret desire: Though my mother would be dead for Pro Bono Gitney, for Private William Williams she was still in the garden; when we returned, she would be perched there in straw hat and bright India chintz, exchanging daisies for phlox; and she would stand and hold out her arms to us — "Octavian! William!"; and we should run to her and tell her our triumphs, our travails; and sit throughout the long afternoon.

In the darkness just before dawn, they called us to rise. When we stood, I saw for the first time that I was grown taller than Bono.

✹ Before dawn were we summoned; we went to our companies and assembled. Pro Bono and I, being of different companies, were of necessity separated, and we bade each other a temporary farewell, and he fell away from me as images succeed one another in a dream; officers hissed orders in the gloom.

We were arranged into ranks six soldiers wide; then told to stand without motion until ordered to march, a column of some five hundred men coiled in the belly of the fort, crammed phalanx to phalanx. For twenty minutes, we remained in our places, the officers walking among us. I could not forbear to notice that none offered my company any plan.

On one side of me stood Slant; on the other, Pomp. Pomp put his lips against the barrel of his musket.

Wishing to speak for proof of companionship, and knowing his delight in tales of superstition, I asked him, "Is your rifle anointed with luck grease?"

"Ain't no luck grease going to help," he said. "It's steel and lead, now." And then, in the voice of a child, he recited softly, "Steel and lead."

We stood shoulder to shoulder for some time; until, my eye being drawn by a motion in the far part of the stockade, I saw that there was activity at the gates. The great doors were opened.

A company of soldiers issued out. The doors closed again.

"We have begun," I said to Slant beside me.

He wished me luck, calling me *Buckra,* and I wished him luck, calling him *Slant;* and then we fell silent, and awaited our turn, biding our time in that endless queue that convolved there in the night stockade.

We heard the great guns begin to fire; we heard volleys, and yet knew nothing of what this signified.

Then after some minutes, we heard the small arms cease, the cannons continue. Between the blasts of the great guns, there was an unsettling silence to the battle.

We betrayed signs of restiveness. We could not place our feet comfortably on the ground; for we were impatient that they should carry us toward either death or valor; toward, at all expenses, events that could be known.

Another division issued forth, and we all progressed forward by some forty feet in our queue. Now we heard no firing from without.

Abruptly, several rows behind me, there was expostulation — and when I turned, I saw that Peter, the sometime servant of the rebel commander, fought his way out of the column, complaining, "*I ain't going out there. Don't send me. You can't send me out there!*"

Serjeant Clippinger strode down our line, demanding we face forward, *black devils* — and yet, facing forward, we heard the *contretemps* continue behind us: Peter's voice, Clippinger's oaths.

Again we shuffled forward toward the doors. Now Corporal Craigie walked past our ranks, calling out to us, "Brave billies. Brave, brave. Strike against your masters."

Again, the line moved forward, and now the gates had almost swallowed me; I was almost out upon the plain. Sashed officers stood near the gates, watching the progress of the procession, leaning upon their spontoons. I heard one say, "By God, this is idiocy."

And another, "It puts me in mind of the church vestibule. The choristers and deacons processing." He softly intoned "Our God, Our Help in Ages Past."

We halted for a moment. I looked at Slant, whose eyes rolled toward mine; and we both saw the skull of the other.

Then we moved on; and out into the dawn.

And so we found ourselves at sunrise upon a wide, marshy plain, all shapes gray and indistinct, with the sky a seam of red. The landscape was thus: A bridge stood before us, on the other side of which lay a small island with several houses standing, and several more burnt to heaps; and beyond that, a morass, forded by a causeway; and beyond that, just visible in the purple gloaming, the entrenchments of the enemy.

We were afforded that brief glimpse of the terrain — the soldiers of the 14th already marching across the bridge toward the enemy encampment in their rows, six by six; and we in rows to follow them.

to North and South Carolina

to Portsmouth

Church

Woods

Woods

Village of
Great-Bridge
Occupied by
Rebels

Causeway

Rebels

Rebels

Marsh

Island

River

Fort Murray

Marsh

N

To Norfolk

A maneuver so simple — a frontal assault. A bridge, no other path to follow; and the grenadiers led us into battle.

Surely, thought I, *we are not marching straight into the enemy fire. Surely we are not marching upon the bridge, upon the narrow causeway. Surely we are not presenting ourselves to them in the middle of an open marsh without any protection nor cover nor guile.*

Once again, we paused; and one of the great cannons blasted — all of us flinching at the roar — and shot hurled over our heads and rained upon the enemy. There was little sign of activity in the village behind the rebel lines, for it was hardly in their interest to appear above their trenches and petty escarpments while the guns were trained upon them. They might wait in perfect safety for our approach.

We began again to march.

My rank gained the bridge, loud upon the wood, and the river ran black beneath us. I was hemmed in by three men on one side and two on the other; I could not see before me nor behind, save heads behind me, heads before; I could hear only our feet beating on the planks, could smell the cold, the sweat, and the marsh; nothing more was there to guide me; and we marched on toward the enemy redoubts.

Now could I see black smoke above the ranks before me, rushing through the brown and red air; our advance guard had torched the last houses on the islet.

I could not see what transpired in our first ranks, the men of the 14th; I heard shouting, but was hemmed in by replication: rows of muskets, coarse shirts; bare feet gray upon the yellow wood of the bridge; nothing but lineation, grimaces within ranked order. Slant's eyes were not open; for several steps he walked with them closed — praying, I suppose, or blotting out that dawn, that pitiless approach.

Authors, in their prefaces, their blushing bows and courtesies to noble patrons, their deep congees, lace-wristed, will oft protest that their pen is not equal to their subject; and yet, now I tell you — this is true: I can in no wise convey the sensations of battle. There is no language which can tell of its intensities — the way the body seems covered with eyes — and yet blind — the way all skin clamors of danger and berates you to move — no man may write of what it is like to be *sheathed in danger* — all limbs alive with it — all senses reeling —

Good God, have mercy upon us.

I found abruptly that we were upon the little island, buffeted with warmth. Houses were toiling in flame. We halted our march again, and we waited.

The smoke upon the islet parted, and for a moment, from that vantage, we could see our column begin its progress across the causeway.

At our head marched our fine grenadiers in their brave red coats, their bearskin shakoes. They marched in time inexorably toward the enemy. There was a brief volley; a few rebels who could not hold their fire, terrified at the approach of their King's army, let loose a round without harm to any.

The drillmaster's wisdom quoth that the mark of the true soldier is not the ability to fire, but the courage to hold one's fire; that the expertise is not in the hot moment of engagement, but in its delay. A soldier must know the range of his firearm, lest he blast away once with impotence, only to give the enemy thirty seconds or a minute's grace to approach and fire with leisure and accuracy as one fumbles, exposed, tearing the cartridge and priming the pan. The Virginian rebels knew this: Their rifles' range and accuracy extended far beyond the feeble throw of our muskets. It must be ascertained that they had been given orders not to fire until our column was within fair range of their weapons.

The grenadiers had affixed their bayonets; they marched our ranks straight toward the earthen wall of the enemy, exposed to fire from all sides, with their Captain leading them in haughty stride.

I know not who devised this strategy. I cannot think on it with equanimity.

Abruptly, we were almost blinded there upon the isle; the smoke of burning houses inhaled us, and we were within it.

We saw quick glimpses of the enemy lines: heads and rifles now raised, watching the futile approach, waiting for a moment to fire. They were many. I suspected that they numbered far more than three hundred. The smoke again hid them.

We waited, rubbing at our eyes, coughing. We knew what was to happen.

Another glimpse: the enemy crouched along their walls, all guns trained upon the head of the column.

There was nought we could do but wait.

The grenadiers, six by six, marched straight toward our adversary.

When our ranks were within fifty yards of the breastwork, the massacre began. The Virginian sharpshooters opened fire, aiming particularly for the Captain and those who marched in front.

A glimpse: the Captain down, struck in the knee; several more were dead beside him. He rose, tottering, and he shouted that all was well; he charged forward, limping, his men behind him.

Again, we could not see.

It is said that he even touched the earthwork wall before he died; before another volley; before there was not enough flesh left upon the bone to support him, not enough meat for motivation; and the apparatus collapsed. The rebels turned their rifles to new targets and tore down rank after rank of proud grenadier.

The latter replied; they buckled, but fired; they advanced still in that hail of lead. They were ranked by sixes, though, and so were constrained in their firing, only a few able to present at once; and the causeway afforded no cover. The fire upon them was hot and brisk and, as I have said, it was a massacre.

Again, a glimpse: The 14th Regiment still marched forward over the bodies of the fallen. They still, despite all, marched upon the enemy.

I have never seen such bravery before; and I hope never to see it again.

Aghast, we watched: Grenadiers flew backward; grenadiers screamed; we saw hats topple; a body, relieved of impulse, rolled down the side of the causeway into the swamp.

Then we were lodged within gray, the smoke thick around us, and we coughed and slapped at our eyes, scarcely able to perceive our own limbs; with the heat of the flames all about us. We heard the rebel volley and the grenadiers' response; another rebel volley, and another; and then, through the smoke, the 14th Regiment's drums beating retreat — and then our drummers — and we fled with little form or regulation.

Now came the panic visited upon me and upon my brethren in arms; now came the horror at nothing known, dim things heard — shouting and running — and my only safety lay in the solid men arrayed around me—in the cruel hope that another chest, another shoulder would snare a bullet before it struck me.

We emerged from the smoke and found the bridge before us; but we saw also that the rebels had now organized their lines to the west, curving around us. They had flanked us with ease—they fired upon us from the side—and we, enfiladed, fled—hearing cries as men fell behind us.

Now it was a rout. Bullets were flung among us—I saw men collapse before me—or grab a limb and topple—rise up—and stagger. I passed dead upon the bridge—men prone with their arms hung over the river—*Liberty to Slaves* on shirts of corpses—and a man fallen in the river who bobbed there, drowning, holding up a red hand. It was, I saw, not his own.

He struggled to save another.

I watched him struggle; and know now that I watched him without motion, having stopped my progress, staring stupefied at the destruction. I was become Observant, as I had been in my child years; unable to do aught but stare—and men ran past me—and there was firing all around me—and I could not protect even my own frail form.

What I recall was pity, a sorrow so great that I could not move to save myself.

I am ashamed that I stood thus, able to save neither myself nor any other, serving to do nothing but block retreat.

I do not know how long I stood upon the bridge with fire behind me and gunshot around me and soldiers galloping away from the enemy, clutching their muskets to their chests.

Will was beside me—tears on his face—and he sobbed that

John was hit, that friend John was down. He was gesturing in frantic wise back toward the island — and pleading with me that it was John's arm, just his one arm, and they can cut off a arm, they can save a man, pleading that I go fetch him so they could cut off his arm.

I did not know what to reply. The Ethiopian Regiment was now past us, and we were engulfed by the regulars.

As we stood astounded, jostled, swore at, one of the 14th shouted, "*Move, Negroes! You're not serving at table now!*" and he shoved me and compelled me forward, me stumbling upon the planks, until my legs regained their activity, and I too fled, and Will fled with me, weeping, and left his friend upon the island to be picked up by the scavengers of the enemy.

Will wished to go back — he struggled — but I had his wrist, and shouted that he could not; that he must come with me; that to go back was death; that if 'twas but his arm, John would be waiting for us within the stockade.

"He fall!" said Will. "Fall when he was hit." He looked back toward the isle, which was nothing but smoke. He no longer fought to return there.

I guided him forward, and we ran the final feet behind our lines.

We were back within the stockade, confusion all around us, men screaming at each other and officers bellowing for order, the drummers playing tattoos to draw us to attention.

I dragged Will to the corner where our Regiment had resided an hour before. He cried again that we must issue forth and seek out John, friend John; and I did not know what to say to him, for I fully believed that return to the isle had been impossible.

And as I spoke comfortably to Will on one side, I sought through the confusion for Bono; and I saw rage and fear in all quarters.

I spied Peter struggling in the arms of several of our Ethiopian Regiment while white officers shouted questions at him. He had, it appeared, continued to refuse to issue forth, crying that marching on the rebel there was death, sir, utter death; though he himself had recommended the seasonability of attack.

An officer bawled at him, *"Can you count? Can you, man? Can you count? Can you count to five hundred? Can you count to a thousand?"* as Peter cried, "Please, sir, they must have come up new, those men, sir, please. Please, Corporal, you know I ain't—"

Corporal Craigie hit Peter across the jaw, once each side, until the man's mouth bled. His head hung; he was thrown down upon his knees. They took out rope to bind him.

Amidst these alarums, Will pleaded still with men around us to take him back out to the island; that John could be saved; that they had come so far together, he could not leave him.

I could not abide it.

It was almost full day. I looked at the confusion around me, the ruination. I did not know whether our losses were great, or whether they simply seemed so. I knew only this: *We had lost. We had lost. We had lost.*

✤ The battle being over, full day was come. We sat in the stockade, blind to our surroundings. There was but one event in the sky, about noontime: a flight of geese.

We most of us slept an almost ensorcelled sleep, astounded by our fatigue. I awoke to find Pomp sitting near me, chewing seeds and spitting the husks into his hand. My weariness was so complete that I fell back into slumber, little heeding the objects around me.

I was gratified by a sight of Bono among his Company. He hailed me, and I went to his side; we clasped each other's hands.

The word, his companions told me, was that we were to abandon the fort, the commanding officers nourishing no hope that the position could be held, did the rebels attack, their numbers being so superior to what we had been informed, and soon to be augmented, 'twas said, with Carolina militia. It was the surmise of many, Bono loud among them, that we were to fall back to Norfolk, to repair to the new entrenchments dug around that town and man them for all they were worth. I averred that the fortifications there were not in a complete state of readiness, but we could imagine no other strategy. With some pride in my familiarity with the situation to the north, I sketched the disposition of Norfolk's new entrenchments in the mud, and Bono and others hunkered around us spake manfully of approaches and defense; and I was proud to be of their number.

In the afternoon, all hands were engaged in preparations to abandon the stockade. The tents and marquees within the yard were struck and bundled into carts. The dead were buried without the walls. The sentries still patrolled above us, surveying the marsh and the burning hamlet, and when they were relieved of duty, they spread word that our wounded brethren had been carried over the enemy's berm with an astonishing gentleness and civility.

By night — when it was too dark for the piercing gaze of the adversary — we formed and took up our line of march. We left the place secretly — it was utterly abandoned — some four or five hundred of us issuing forth in a dismal parade to the north. In our wake, the cannons were spiked, and the muddy ground churned with bootprints and littered with the trash of war, comprising snapped buckles, bloody shirts, neglected spades, here a bayonet bent or a stub of candle, a burst barrel, or planks.

We left in silence, as near as we could, to ensure that the rebels would not know of their victory until we had gained Norfolk again.

Through the night we marched with the wounded on carts beside us, crying.

The next day's dawn found us entering into Norfolk. It was the Sabbath, and the church bells rang.

Women on their way to service stopped and watched us in a line; they wore red cloaks, and their necks and faces muffled, so that all that shewed beneath the head-cloths were the eyes, which followed our ragged train.

The faceless congregants watched without speaking. We meandered past them, but a few of the regulars raising their hats.

Farm girls and fathers on horses watched us pass in wonderment; until, a cart come up wherein complained some of the wounded loudly—"Water, ladies, we beg of ye, water!"—several of the girls, moved to pity, darted back to a well and scurried down the line with a bucket, quenching this thirst and receiving the blessing of the fallen. I know not whether these angels of mercy were Loyalist or rebel; I know that they were moved to the quick, however, by the sight of the dying, and took a small pity, for which I felt gratitude myself, the act restoring memory of compassion.

We passed through the outskirts of Norfolk, and the people of that town surveyed our bedraggled carnage with a gray, defeated mien. With Great-Bridge fallen, nothing stood between their town and the rapacity of the enemy. The citizens watched keenly where we wended; for we did not return to our warehouse barracks; but we were mustered upon the docks, where boats and transports were in a readiness.

We fully anticipated that at any moment we should be detached and sent to the earthworks to begin the long wait for the rebels; we were in constant expectation of orders to take to the dirt ramparts and stand to arms, there to defend the safety of the loyal denizens of Norfolk, the honor of our King, and the dignity of our new-granted freedoms.

It was therefore with confusion that we observed companies boarding transports. They were rowed out to ships. It took us some minutes to realize that we would not be guarding our redoubts. We were retreating not simply from Great-Bridge, but from Norfolk itself.

We were astounded. That we should be asked to abandon not merely our southern approaches, but the town, having spent the better part of two weeks fortifying it; having cracked our hands and wearied our bones digging, hauling, raising embankments, affixing stakes, and settling gabions—this directive was greeted with outrage. We were not unforward nor imprecise in our criticism of our officers, muttering that cowering timidity was but poor cover for past incompetence.

Pomp spake angrily of the circumstances; and Slant, once he saw that others would speak with the voice of censure, joined his voice to Pomp's. Will spake to none; but stared, hollow-eyed, at the ground.

We were, over the course of some two hours, herded onto boats and rowed out to ships that sat at anchor in the river. My company was posted aboard the *Crepuscule* sloop-of-war.

The populace of the town little relished this evacuation. They attended in great crowds and watched, and we were sensible of their distress; for they had all sworn loyalty to Dunmore and to the King, and now they found themselves abandoned.

One man I saw tore off the red kerchief sewn to his breast, emblem of Loyalty, and cast it on the ground, turning from us in disgust. Women wept; children stared in wonder. It was no secret that the rebels despised the town of Norfolk for its pandering to Dunmore and his troops. There was every expectation that they would, at best, hang those who had colluded and performed their duty to the Crown; and that at worst, they would ignite the whole of the port and burn it to the ground.

Thus it was that later that afternoon, we saw the Loyalists begin their own evacuation of the city in preparation for its occupation by the rogue militia. The grander Tories came to the quays with great trunks and with cages for their birds; many had ships from which their fortunes were derived, which schooners or brigantines now would try their fortunes in even hotter waters.

Once aboard the *Crepuscule,* we were sent below to the ship's one lower deck, a dark and windowless place. We crouched there, awaiting orders, expecting still to man fortifications, but no order came. After a time, Corporal Craigie informed us we would be spending the night upon the ship, and that we might settle upon the few straw mattresses provided to us, and draw lots as to who should enjoy the hammocks.

Nor did we return to shore the next day, but took our exercise upon the deck of the ship, beneath the watchful eye of the sailors.

Around our sloop-of-war lay a great confusion of ships, a floating town. There had been great numbers of them previous to our retreat, but now, with the threat of rebel incursion even greater, others had made for the port, that they might be protected by the guns of Lord Dunmore's Navy. Countless crowds of them were at anchor, from the smallest fishing pinks and hoys to the great three-masters sitting at rest.

The wealthiest among the Loyalists had fled already to their ships. Now upon the docks gathered the Loyalists of the middling sort — leather-aprons; shopkeepers who knew that no quarter would be offered them did they stay, no mercy from the rebel Sons of Liberty, once their sympathies were known; smiths, chandlers, and butchers — all begging passage, any passage, for them and their family. They brought chests with what they could save of the instruments of their trade. Their wives sighed; and sometimes great arguments broke out upon the docks between men vying for passage, or between man and wife, the air full of remonstrances regarding which especial chair might be saved, or whether the gilt mirror would survive embarkation. A child cried for cats left behind in the barn.

They were taken off onto small snows and brigs, if that they could afford; and others, finding no route of escape upon the water, fled the town by land, praying for mercy.

Then, the day following that, came the most desperate to the docks — many who had fled to Norfolk from the raving countryside, leaving behind all they had, and now had to flee again without benefit of coin or goods to barter. They pled with the few who still loaded sideboards and escritoires into tenders.

We stood listless upon the deck of our sloop-of-war, with no employment but to observe the rout.

I could not countenance that we would abandon the town. 'Twas strongly fortified — stocked with Loyalists — our Governor's last refuge upon the land. We wished to defend; we demanded confrontation; we felt all the transports of issueless rage, thinking of the rebels and their cries of self-congratulation.

Even now, I cannot abide this retreat. My hands are empty, and I sit enwombed in a ship.

Yesterday, the fourteenth of December, the rebels passed through our unmanned fortifications and entered the town of Norfolk unopposed. We still floated in the harbor.

They occupied the town; and we, yards from the shore, heard tales of skirmish and indignity. As the enemy marched through the occupied streets, a few desperate Loyalists fired upon them from gables, then slid down roofs on their bellies, and fled.

Last night, when the rebels reached the quays in their march of invasion, we heard musket- or rifle-shots fired at our fleet, and hoped to acquit ourselves in a contest with these bold scoundrels. We seized upon our weapons and awaited commands.

'Twas no attack, however. Merely a frolic by a few rebel sots. A cocksure, drunken game. We received no orders for reprisal.

Today, the docks were empty of commerce, the wide squares untenanted. We saw snipers take posts in warehouses with feline swagger. Once, a line of picket-guards came down to the dock, made a mock obeisance, and shouted, "All hail Lord Dunmore, King of the Negroes!" then fell about, laughing.

It was not an unfair epithet, though meant unkindly. With the flight of the Loyalists onto ships, royal power in this execrable Colony is restricted into still more minute compass. Williamsburg fell months ago, and with it the Palace and the House of Burgesses; then Norfolk County; then the approaches to Norfolk; and now Norfolk itself is not ours. Only the waters are ours; and how may one build on something so mutable?

Governmental authority no longer hath any purchase on land; chaos and the mob of slave-drivers rule all; and we are left, a tiny kingdom on the waves.

December 16th, 1775

Very cold this day. My company still confined to the *Crepuscule* sloop-of-war.

At noon, we were ordered to march out upon the quarterdeck to witness the execution of a traitor.

Our number being arrayed above-decks, and observing other companies of our Regiment similarly awaiting this deplorable demonstration, we were bade to remain silent for a space of minutes, until Peter was brought forth bound and blindfolded.

We could not hear what Captain Mackay read of him; the damp wind interfered with the oration. We could hear Peter beg as they fitted the rope to him, and I shall not soon forget the first cry as he was hauled up on the foresail yard. We were instructed to watch him while he kicked.

It was cold on the deck where we stood. Some minutes later, his corpse was lowered, trussed, and thrown into the river. This being done, we were permitted to once more go below.

Rumor reports that he was offered freedom by his master, Major Marshall, to lie regarding the weakness of the rebel force and to misrepresent their preparations to Lord Dunmore; though others speculate that he simply could not count. We know not what wrong he might have admitted to the Court-Martial that must have tried him. We know merely what disasters his mendacity occasioned. I believe he sold us.

As his body was lowered, the rebels on the quays who smoked and watched applauded.

☙ There is little to occupy us upon the *Crepuscule,* now that we have witnessed the death. It appears we may be confined to this ship for some time; and more particularly, to its lower deck. These quarters are not commodious: I count forty-two of us in this strait-ened space, three of which number are women; and we are kept fore by the ship's numerous crew, who crowd aft and jealously guard their hammocks.

Since our evacuation of the town onto the ships and trans-ports of this fleet, there has been little employment for us; and having nought to engage us, we spend much time sleeping. No one, it seems, relishes wakefulness.

When we are permitted to walk the decks of our ship, either for exercise or in the commission of our watch duties, even these tedious rounds are a welcome shift from the lower deck, which is dark and noisome. We stand gratefully beneath the rigging and line the rails.

On the decks of other ships, black men wander as we do, without aim; and they seem not another company, but our own; as were there but one ship, one fraternity of specters which is reflected in the frigid, misty air.

We see also white Loyalists of Norfolk upon their pleasure-boats now laden with clocks, bedsteads, and inlaid secretaries. They are as doleful as are our sable number, or perhaps more so, for they have lost their homes just a few days previously, whereas we became accustomed to losing ours years before.

Slant and Pomp are often my companions; each of us finds the company of the others not uncongenial. We have, indeed, little held in common to speak of, but Slant was reared and raised by the River James, and tells us of its ways; Pomp and he trade tales of livestock; and, I disclosing my past service, they have asked me to tell them of the rebel camp outside Boston, and my actions there. We stare at the ceiling, and Pomp sings songs beneath his breath he learned while herding.

The rebels become bolder, and now patrol the docks of Norfolk by day without apology or shame. They will not suffer any food nor other articles to be purchased from the wharves, and our fleet does not abandon the port entire; and so we float here, and they parade there; and both sides regard the other, well in range of volley or lob.

Our meals are but choruses of complaint. Directly we boarded the ships, the quartermaster dictated we should be switched to salt rations. We eat our few ounces of poor, scalding pork with little gust.

At night, we are slung together for warmth. We all lie in the belly of the *Crepuscule* and gaze into the darkness, awaiting sleep impatiently. Among us scratches and lumbers Vishnoo, the shipboard tortoise kept so that he might dispose of the roaches that hang on the beams and scuttle into the straw of our mattresses. Though his kind be proverbial for sloth and torpescence, 'tis he who remains awake the last of us; and I imagine his black eyes still glittering alone in the dark, his ancient visage surveying these curled mammals with their tricky hands and shocks of pelt; wondering that such soft things, once they fall, will ever rise again.

December 17th, 1775

Today, another feast of distasteful intelligence. We are stricken with it.

We received notice of the lists of prisoners seized by the enemy at the Great-Bridge; that John, of our number, has been taken alive; and that he and thirty others are to be exported and sold at the foreign ports in the West Indies, the Sugar Isles.

They are sold for profit; the rebels inform us that the sale shall reimburse owners and fund commissions and weaponry for the rebel army, that the criminals might more efficiently defeat us.

We may be sure, however, that this exportation is transacted not simply for the emoluments of sale, but for the instruction of awful example. They wish to show us where we all shall be con-ducted: those island colonies we weep to hear named, where precise calculations of plantation œconomy suggest it is far less expense to work slaves to death and buy new, imported from Africa's shores, than to care for those already there.

At the same time, we receive word that as the rebels swept through Great-Bridge, Gosport, Kemp's Landing, and last, Norfolk, they have taken prisoner all who still wear the red kerchief of Loyalty upon their breast, or any reputed to be favorable to the King's cause — such individuals as, having pledged their fealty to Lord Dunmore, now find themselves, poor wretches, deserted by our retreat.

We hear also of the punishment accorded them: The enemy has chained each white Loyalist to a black man taken in flight to Lord Dunmore and our Regiment. They are marched, thus paired, black and white rattling together, to Williamsburg for judgment.

In the estimation of our enemy, there is no greater indignity, no sharper shame, for a white gentleman than to be thus twinned. We hear that some spake against it and said it was too great an outrage, but the rebels have replied in their broadsheets and papers that it is punishment condign that the damned Tory dogs shall be shackled to the black cattle they consorted with.

They marched one coffle of these paired prisoners across the docks of Norfolk, that the Loyalists on board their ships could see what fate awaited them. There was no jeering then by the rebels, no laughter, but only eyes that surveyed us and warned.

At noon, some hours following the announcement of John's sad fate, Will fell to beating a fellow soldier over whom should receive an extra ladle of bone and broth.

Only a few blows fell before we took his arms and dragged him back. His rage cooled quickly, and the transports of ire gave way to the listlessness of despair. He pushed us away, but did not heave himself up and quit the place, there being no space for him thither to flee, that he might seek the solitude of his thoughts; for we all were crammed in that small quarter.

He has laid himself transversely upon the deck where we sit, and stares inert. So we crouch in silence, and we each of us entertain the same vision: the fields bleached with sun and hacked cane; the scalding steam of the boiling-houses drifting through the brake; the eternal rows of men scything in gangs; and pushed out among them, the boy, hand useless, armed only with his turkey call.

Dear God; dear God; what Thy creations do.

This evening, a surprising turn: An ensign sought me out, groping along through the gloom of the ship, pressing between the tight crush of soldiers, and informed me that I was to go above, from thence to be conveyed to the fleet's flagship, the *Dunmore*.

This perplexing intelligence was greeted by Pomp and Slant with looks expressive of wonder; and no less did I view it with astonishment, having no call to appear upon that meritorious ship, and no quality nor rank to distinguish me. I left my brethren rapt in conversation regarding what this mark of special notice might signify.

When I emerged above-decks, I discovered the cause of this unusual request: Dr. Trefusis awaited me in a boat which should deliver us to the *Dunmore*, where, he called up to me jollily, I should have the honor of acquitting myself upon the violin before His Lordship. "Come, come, i'faith!" cried he.

I was, at first, too startled to know of my sensations, staring down upon him, almost uncomprehending. He entreated I should climb down to his shallop and gawp later. I protested I had no violin; but, said he, 'twas no matter; one should be provided. With this faint assurance, I descended to the boat and we set off between the great prows of the fleet.

Dr. Trefusis informs me he hath found refuge aboard a Tory's ship, and making inquiries, determined the location of my company. As he is considered by these people a philosopher of note and a friend of kings, 'twas no arduous task to gain an audience with His Lordship the Governor; and having done so, he offered my services as violinist for this evening, in hopes that I should thus distinguish myself.

He was greatly solicitous of my welfare following the battle, and asked me many sharp questions regarding it; which queries it was not in my power at first to answer. I longed to recount to Dr. Trefusis what had transpired—but could not. Our hearts are too heavy with our defeat; we scarce can speak of it to each other upon the ship; and so, being unable to speak of that awful scene of massacre and flame, I informed him only of the pleasant news, that our dearest hope was realized, and Bono found, though now named William Williams. Dr. Trefusis rejoiced in the intelligence, and has determined to find our dear friend, that he might speak with him again.

"I still shall hear of this battle," said he, pointing a finger at me, "but for the nonce, tune yourself." With this, he lifted a violin in its case and passed it to me, he regretting deeply that "you shall find, I fear, 'tis no Cremona fiddle"; but 'twas the only instrument that might be flushed out in such short order from amongst the effects of Norfolk's Loyalists.

Tune I did; and found that, indeed, the instrument was none of the most euphonious. I played my fifths and my scales, which, lapping gently upon the bulwarks of the ships we passed, drew sailors to the rails as we rowed on.

The *Dunmore* is a grand ship, not the largest, but renovated for display of its wealth and puissance; and it looked prodigiously fine in the evening, the gilding still catching the last light, the decks lined with Ethiopians of His Lordship's Company in livery, standing by cressets, facing out implacably at the shore—more impassive in their features than the tritons and dolphins which disported themselves in silver foam upon stern and stem.

We boarded, and found there a whole company of guests awaiting Lord Dunmore's favor. Dr. Trefusis commended me to one of my fellow-soldiers of the Royal Ethiopians, which fellow informed me that I should perform in a small closet adjoining His Lordship's chamber, there being insufficient space for a musician within the room itself when others dined.

Accordingly, I waited among members of His Lordship's Company, all severe of mien and proud of bearing, while preparations were made for the supper; Dr. Trefusis, as we waited, turning upon me gazes proud, or comforting, or comical by turns.

At last, I was conveyed into the closet where I should play, the door being left open but a small space so that the guests could hear the music. I struck up a pretty minuet and watched through my sliver of the doorway as they all entered, my preceptor among them, and sat around the table. His Lordship himself I did not see, he being concealed behind the door; but I could hear his casual and commanding accents. Though the gentleman is a Scot, there was none of the Caledonian in his speech, but instead the easy air of Whitehall, Saint James's Palace, and Vauxhall.

They supped; I played; they spake; I barely hearkened to what they said, so involved were my wits in recalling sonatas enough and dances, so that there should not be a silence from the closet in the midst of their revelry. Over-awed as I was to be in the presence — or almost so — of those officers and advisors upon whom the fate of this Colony doth depend, my apprehensions of failure were great; thus anxious, I could not gain any sense of what their discussion compassed, no understanding of their words — and their communications seemed so intricate, they spake as if they were not men, but rather gods, gathered over some ambrosial collation, discoursing thus:

"Gentlemen, if the parties were to proceed upon the second action with the expedition with which they have undertaken the first, notwithstanding the difficulties therein, should we not find that object achieved which cannot but redound to the greater glory of such actants as might disculpate us in even the ungrateful eye of the enemy, rather than submitting us to the excoriations of the same?"

Opined another: *"The first bespeaks readiness, gentlemen; the second, foolhardiness. While the former exhibits all the virtues of valor, the latter suggests a profligacy of force; and it should be a terrible issue should waste follow sacrifice."*

"Sirs, while I would liefer commend the nobility of restraint, here must I endorse rather the vigor of lively opposition, lest, peradventure, we nd that inaction is in itself the occasion of profligacy."

I could understand not a word of it.

'Twas like a dialogue spake in a tongue of pure light and clear air. I remarked favorably its buoyancy, which stirred the heart at the thought that such excellently spoken men determined our fate. I rejoice still in the comfort of its incomprehensibility.

Lord Dunmore did not speak at first, simply listening to his guests before unfolding his own schemes and views. When he did speak, it was in the voice of judgment, saying merely, "Quite," or "Indeed," or "Aye," or "There's reasonableness, gentlemen."

Dr. Trefusis, I could tell, quickened them all with his ardor in promoting the excellence of the Royal Ethiopians, our willingness to fight, our profound interest in our success in this contest.

Then they closed the closet door to exact more privacy, now that the servants were retired; and I became so involved with the labyrinthine concerns of Tartini that I no longer could listen even to the faint words spoken. The next hour passed in delight at music, familiar conversation again with the dearest and most speaking of instruments; playing melodies that brought before me, in all the tincture of poignancy, our spirits before the battle; the approach toward the enemy across the causeway; the rout; the volleys; aghast, my inaction upon the bridge; the bodies in the mire; the march back across the miles to Norfolk; the stench of our hold in the *Crepuscule;* the loss of John, frolicsome John, transported to the Sugar Isles, than which no fate could be less sweet, more bitter, more disgustful.

"Strike me blind!" exclaimed His Lordship. "Who is the article playing for us upon the fiddle?"

"Ah! That, Your Lordship—that is a soldier in your Ethiopian Regiment," said Dr. Trefusis loudly, rising from his chair. "Private Octavian Nothing. I spake of him yesterday. I am eager to present him to Your Lordship, if Your Lordship would be so indulgent."

"He is a prodigious sad fellow."

"I believe he laments our late loss."

"Very correct, too. Excellent, excellent."

The door was thrown open. In the presence of such nobility, I lowered the fiddle and bow, and fixed my eyes upon the ground. I heard Lord Dunmore rise; saw the approach of his shoes.

"Your name, soldier?" said he; and I told him, my gaze upon his buckles. I bowed and thanked him for the favor of his notice.

He declared genially, "You're a fine fellow, ain't you?"

Dr. Trefusis expatiated at somewhat galling length upon my achievements; which accolades Lord Dunmore received with kind pleasure, saying, "Faith, excellent! Excellent! You are brave boys, all of you."

Said he to me — and this I shall recall until my final hour — said he to me: "We shall make you proud to serve us, soldier."

I thanked him reverently — but he continued, "We are already proud that, at all adventure, you chose to enlist at our sides."

"Amen," exclaimed Dr. Trefusis, his voice flowing over with joy.

I again thanked His Lordship's buckles for the honor of their notice and more, remarked that it was very like his beneficence to think upon the sacrifices made, the hazards run, by my brethren to escape to this our Regiment; and vowed that we should acquit ourselves so valiantly that he should never have cause to regret issuing his Proclamation drawing us forth from shackle and shanty.

At this, the company all clapped, and His Lordship returned to his seat; my heart swelling with adoration; swelling, at the same time, at the transports of sadness at what had already been lost; and at the promise of hope for new battlefields and victories as yet unwon.

Later, we were rowed back through the night, which was become greatly frigid. Dr. Trefusis reported, delighted, that he had convinced His Lordship to grant a letter allowing my lessons to continue. I, however, wished to hear more of what Lord Dunmore had said of the present tumults. Dr. Trefusis put his finger to his lips, and would not speak before the sailors who rowed us.

When we gained the *Crepuscule,* he climbed out as well, and said he would come below with me for a short space, that we might discourse more fully on what he had gleaned at His Lordship's table. Trefusis displaying Lord Dunmore's letter, he was admitted, and we passed into the lower deck, where my companions awaited me, rowdy until we appeared; silenced in a moment by the sight of a white man among them.

Pomp, at last, asked me what I had seen upon the *Dunmore* frigate, and I recounted the facts of the case; that I had played for His Lordship's table, but that, being in a separate chamber and anxious of address, I had neither seen his face nor heard his schemes. I told them of his word to us — that he *should make us proud to serve,* which announcement made all more easy in their minds. This being said, I asked Dr. Trefusis what he had observed during the dinner.

He reported that Lord Dunmore expresses none but the most sanguine expectations of our future success, though he admits that the setbacks of the late battle were great. The rebels' criminal ardor shall cool, says he, when they see how great the number is of those loyal to the Crown; and His Lordship has dispatched an agent to the northwest to rouse up the Indians in the King's cause, having treated with the Shawnee last year. Dunmore expects that at any time, he shall receive additional troops from Florida or from Boston, and the summoned Indian and Canadian forces shall march down from their territories and sunder the Colonies in half, depriving the infernal rebel associations of their communication.

So spake His Lordship—grandly—but, said Trefusis, "I have other views of the man." With a smile of satisfaction at his own sagacity, he continued: "Here is what one must know about Lord Dunmore. Whenever the man unrolls these hopes and schemes, he clutches and chafes his own wrist without cease. D'you see? His opinion must be entirely discounted. One cannot repose the slightest trust in a man who holds his own wrist, boys. It suggests that he wishes someone else would hold it for him. It suggests he feels there is not enough in the world to steady him, and must needs hold on to himself alone for balance. Ye gods, I would liefer listen to a thumb-sucker."

The assembled, who knew not Dr. Trefusis's prankish humor, little knew what to make of this curious discourse. I saw their eyes bespeaking confusion at this raillery, sorrow to hear our liberator mocked thus, and anxiety at what His Lordship's uncertainty might mean.

My tutor explained that, seeing the fretting at the wrist, he had begun a more delicate questioning, listening not simply to His Lordship's bright hopes, complaints of past misfortunes, and brash gasconades, but to His Lordship's doubts; and these are the fruits of that auditory: His Lordship has received no word from the Ministry in England for some six months, and clearly feels terror that he is alone, floating with his tiny fleet in a sea of rebellion. There is no sign from the King, no help to be had from the Secretary of State, no indication that anyone in Whitehall knows that government in the Colony of Virginia is fled the capital, that the House of Burgesses is shut up and the courts at an end. His Lordship awaits reinforcements; but he does not know if they shall come, nor whether anyone even knows that he requires them.

The faces of the men in my mess—of Slant, Will, and the others—grew alarmed or slackened at this insight into our commander.

Thus Dr. Trefusis's visit. We discussed our plan of study: I continue with the Locke seized from Mr. Jonathan Gitney's library; for Latin and for pleasure, the *Æneid* again; for Greek, Apollonius of Rhodes's tale of the *Argo*'s voyage to find the Golden Fleece. Dr. Trefusis says it behooves me to remind myself of the heroics of men who seek the impossible in ships.

☙ I had set down the quill—though I have no occupation but to write—and I take it up again. I must add to my account that my nerves were agitated within me at Dr. Trefusis's discourse, and (it shames me to say) I felt myself not entirely well dispositioned towards him, who is the kindest and most generous of men. When we went above-decks for me to conduct Dr. Trefusis back to his shallop, he paused and said that I seemed out of my humor; to which I replied that the battle weighed heavily upon me. He entreated me again to tell him of the events, now no mirth in his demeanor.

It was then that I told him of the battle—so much as I could—and of my fit upon the bridge that left me without motion; I confessed my cowardice in freezing thus, unable to stir my limbs. He hastened to mollify me.

"'Twas not cowardice," said he, "but overwhelming compassion."

"It served no purpose," said I. "No one was saved."

He smiled kindly. He said, "Socrates served as a soldier in the Athenian host. At Potidæa, he became so engaged in a question of ethics that he remained standing in his armor, unmoving, insensate, for a full day and night altogether."

"I do not care, sir," I said. I told him: "I do not care a whit."

The old man's face fell; he was in some confusion, before he regained his pride, and with a hint of a gentleman's *hauteur* said, "Octavian, I was merely attempting to soothe —"

"Did you need speak of Dunmore's doubts? Did you need tell us he was foolish and uncertain?"

"I was attempting, Octavian, to reveal the truth of —"

"You spake thus, sir, to vent wit, so that you might regale us with the acuity of your observation. The comedy of the wrist."

If he had been previously startled, he was now stunned, even frightened in his demeanor. And still, ruthless fool, I continued: "Sir, you may jest at the foibles of His Lordship — because you are —" (I could not say it) "—because you are as you are, sir — but for us, this expedition — sir, this expedition — it is our sole hope. If it fail, we die. We are transported to the Sugar Isles. We are hanged. I beg you: do not jest with our fates."

At this, his heart melted, and he wept a tear and embraced me, begging my pardon and calling me the most excellent of beings, the most tender of grandchildren. He said he was abject, and told me his stomach was taken sick with the very thought of his vanity, and praised and thanked me profusely for my candor. I could not retain any anger against this gentle soul, my longtime benefactor, at this display, and I begged his pardon for my harshness; and thus, reconciled, we parted, both more secure in the other's affection.

✣ It is near midnight. I think on those who are chained. John clipped to a Loyalist and forced to march.

The ancient tyrant Mezentius of Etruria, punishing his enemies, bound each living prisoner to a corpse and left them thus, shackled face to face, until the corruption of the dead involved the living. Saint Augustine hath writ that this is the very type and emblem of us mortal beings: the shining soul that must drag around the corpse of the body and its vile decadencies.

I am sure that many of the gentlemen Loyalists imagined themselves in this way as they toiled upon the road to Williamsburg, paired disgracefully with Negroes: the civilized mind chained to the brute brawn of the flesh; the quick, living spirit tripping at the drag of those already headed for a distant Hell.

But is it not also thus: the living man, black and desperate to run, cursed by his connection to the white, devouring ghost?

Again, I take up the pen, with nought else to occupy my hands. Word from a midshipman: 'Tis said that yesterday, there was a skirmish on the river when two warships attempted to seize upon fresh water at a distillery; they left unprotected a snow, which could not follow on so fast, and it was taken by the enemy.

This morning, Serjeant Clippinger grew drunk upon rum and became loud, complaining of his command over Negroes, and that he was cursed to be thrown onto a hulk where every private stank like a pit and not a man could speak decent English, but he was like to hear a babble of Guinea tongues and the fiddle-faddle of murderous Coromantees; and that even his own Corporal (by which he meant Corporal Craigie) spake a blithering stew of English and Scots, and that never should he receive preferment, trapped in this damned Regiment rather than in one of those founded and numbered by our sovereign; and that he should have stayed a poor Spitalfields prentice toiling at the loom; and there ain't no hope; no hope at all, boys, so we might as well drown and go to the Devil; and more to this effect. The Company's captain, hearing of his stupor, sent for him to be removed and slapped; but by that time, he had around his form recumbent a ring of men — Will, Slant, and me among them — and we had all heard his vile opinions. We know now the quality of our command.

This, then, from our own ranks.

And from the enemy: When we were above-decks taking our recreation in the afternoon, one of the rebels called from the shore, "Boy! You, boy! Do you have a fine Negro soldier name of Major-General Quash on board? Major-General Quash Andrews? You acquainted with the Major-General? Could you tell him I need my laundry done snip-snap? He left it soaking."

A great laugh went up among the rebels.

"Tell him come home, and I need the shit be cleaned out my breeches."

We stood silently and did not meet the eyes of the enemy; nor each other's eyes.

We await some confrontation.

❦ 'Twas after dinner that Pomp came to tell me my presence was required upon the upper deck. Upon ascending, I was confronted by the most welcome of spectacles: Dr. Trefusis and Bono both having just come aboard, conferring with Serjeant Clippinger. As I approached, I saw that my dear *philosophe* spake in terms of remonstration to the Serjeant, which officer protested their presence on the ship. Trefusis, however, had procured a letter from Lord Dunmore which approved my lessons in philosophy and language should continue; and a letter of commission that transferred Bono to my company. The latter is a great cause for rejoicing, though perhaps of little surprise: The white officers generally account our sable troops as number without face or footprint, and approach questions of our regulation with indifference and irritable neglect.

So soon as Serjeant Clippinger was dispatched, and retreated with a scowl little calculated to welcome, Dr. Trefusis and Bono made merry in quiet tones at our reunion. Dr. Trefusis had sought out Bono in the morning and sent him a letter to inquire whether a transfer should be an agreeable and desirable circumstance for my friend; and had encountered nought but approbation for the scheme.

I was rejoiced at this prospect, for, in truth, I have now together in one place all of those who remain most dear to me; though this I cannot say out loud, for fear Bono should note the absence of one inestimable being from that roster of tenderness.

We betook ourselves below and sate ourselves with great satisfaction. The pleasantries being accomplished, Bono asked of news. Dr. Trefusis replied that there was no news but starvation — so many of the Loyalist citizens upon their ships having prepared inadequately for a stay offshore. Bono then inquired how Dr. Trefusis himself was accommodated; to which the philosopher replied that though he was ill fed, he wished we could reside with him in his space upon the *Betsey* brig, which delightful little chamber had been vacated for him so soon he made mention of his hearty jests with Frederick the Great. Following this, Dr. Trefusis pressed Bono to hear of his adventures, and of what had transpired since last we had seen him — the doctor having last seen him bundled off to Salem for shipment a full year before.

"I should be pleased to tell you the story of my travels," said Bono smartly, "really I should, and a cracking fine tale it is too, sir, but I beg your pardon, you has work to do. Teaching Prince O. And reading and such."

Dr. Trefusis importuned him to recount his adventures — to which my own wishes ardently assented — but Bono offered only theatrical refusal, saying he knew Trefusis had a letter from Dunmore that said we should be philosophizing, and we didn't want to disappoint our Serjeant there.

Nodding, Dr. Trefusis asked me to fetch my Locke; which I did, receiving a baleful interrogatory look from Clippinger. When I returned, Dr. Trefusis was sat with his arms around his thin legs, as I remembered him so oft sitting in the school room in the College of Lucidity, laughing at some witty chaff of Bono's.

Trefusis took the book and searched it, explaining that today's lesson was on travel, location, place, and the relative nature of motion; which, said he, would be illuminated by an excellent example of alteration in location by Private William Williams.

"Read it now," said Dr. Trefusis. "Later this evening, transcribe it for better understanding."

I stared down at the page; and well can it be imagined how little I perceived of the meaning of Mr. Locke's disquisition on space and place; though I shall transcribe and seek to understand. What I recall of our evening is not the words of that most eminent of rationalists, but the sensibility that those dearest to me, the supports of my childhood and instructors of my youth, were gathered again in company with me, and that there was great comfort annexed to sitting there idle — together — crouched upon the stooped lower deck of the *Crepuscule,* hearkening to Bono's tale while others played cards or muttered or slept, and Vishnoo clambered along the planking, seeking his insect meal.

And Bono, beginning, spake thus: "I was sold to one Colonel Clepp Asquith of Burn Acres. I served him as a valet. You know Colonel Asquith?" he asked Dr. Trefusis.

"I was never gratified with a personal introduction," said Dr.

Trefusis. "I saw many letters by his hand regarding the finances of the College."

Bono nodded with impatience. "He's a—what can a person say? Mr. Asquith is one of them men who's like a tipped-over scuttle, see? He has one of the pointy, low guts that a gentleman can have. And a face like that too, a pointy, low round face. That didn't make it no easier when you saw how many of the little Negro babes on the plantation had his pointy, low little nose and little mouth. Or maybe that was just in my fancy. I started to see his pointy, low self everywhere I looked.

"First I got there and he had me as just another house servant, but then one day he saw me look over his shoulder at a newspaper that had some word of a Negro uprising and he was sensible that I seen the matter and understood it; so he had me whipped for knowing the science of reading—ten lashes—and then elevated me to his valet."

(And I read, without much marking:)

> I shall begin with the simple idea of SPACE. I have showed above that we get the idea of space both by our sight and touch; which, I think, is so evident, that it would be as needless to go to prove that men perceive, by their sight, a distance between bodies of different colours, or between the parts of the same body, as that they see colours themselves: nor is it less obvious, that they can do so in the dark by feeling and touch.

"So if you never met him, how much you know about Clepp Asquith?" Bono asked Dr. Trefusis.

"The impressions he made upon me suggested he was not of the sagest, nor of the most excellent of men."

"Sir, he may have paid for some of the College, but he hated it, too. Surely, he employed me to write him notes and to read some small correspondence, but it raised up his ire devilish—*devilish*—that the College had taught me to read; just as it raised up his ire that the College done experiments on time and the soul and such instead of on crops and metal and baking and such. That and everything else got him storming, on a general head—that there ain't enough respecting of degree in the North, and that up yonder, barbers and bootmen—he always said that, 'barbers and bootmen'—that up yonder, barbers and bootmen sat next to the first men of the Colonies and talked to them like brethren. Sweet Jesus, he would yell and curse about the Northerners and their fool leveling Puritan ways and they were a lot of sickly old schoolmarms, didn't understand a single thing regarding the nicer points of business.

"And after a while, I started to remark that whenever there was some talk of the North—one of the mobs done something he didn't like, or a reverend arguing for schools, or some Negro gents presenting a petition in Boston for their freedom, or (murder!) that book of poems by the Negress—he'd start all fulminating: *Oh, the meddling scoundrels in New England! Their leveling! Their freaks!*

"And then, he search out some reason for to whip me.

"Every time. I looked over the top of his head to the hall clock, and the longest it took was one hour and thirty-three minutes. Some fool reason. They wasn't the right shoes or the candle is burnt down too low, boy, or just for having a look. He said I had a certain look. And he order me outside and whip me hisself and all the while asking me if I was clever, if my dear sweet College ever taught me to read stripes. And I kept quiet and bided my time.

"He had a daughter, I mean a white daughter, name of Fanny. She was—sweet mercy in a firkin—she was a gruesome little baggage. You know, sir, I love the dear darling squat children, especially when they're spruce things that either answer smart or that stare in a long-lashedy kind of way, like our minikin Prince O. here used to be before he a-muscled himself up—but this damn thing was some imp out of Hell. Maybe ten or eleven. I knew her and the truth of her from one of the first days I was there, when I seen her playing with some little girls—six or seven years, these girls—they was the daughters of a neighbor planter. She brought out her dolls for their games, and one of the dolls was a black doll made from rags that was given her when she was a little girl by her maid, who'd suckled her, her mother being too tender to do so herself. Fanny and these neighbor girls, see, were at play, and one of the small girls took a white doll in a dress and began having fits yelling at the black doll, making all this chastisement in some high, squeaky voice. 'You breaked another plate, Masie, and you ain't fit to serve in a respectable house' and such-like. Like she must hear her mommy or her dada say.

"And Fanny—who could tell her halt, that ain't what a lady does—instead Fanny breaks off a stem of grass, and gives it her, and puts it in the doll's hand, and together, they make the little white doll whip the black one.

"And Fanny puts on some African accent, and starts begging mercy—'Oh, de missus whip me some! Oh, missus!' and such-like. And these tiny girls, they start to laugh and whip the doll harder to urge the whole jest longer.

"It made my heart sick, and I could not barely stand in that yard without fleeing. That's when I knew sweet Fanny was a species of demon.

"Now, I don't know rightly what made Fanny fascinated with my person, and longing always to hurt me special, what called her eye to me, but I warrant it was due to me being a wondrous handsome brute. That's a burden that a man has to carry upright, sir, and I may suffer—I may suffer awful, boys—but weep me no tears."

"You have," said Trefusis, "made your peace with your Maker."

"And gentlemen, I myself cry no tears for me. No, sir, I don't. Because it crunches up the features. Detracts from the regularity."

"I can see that if we allow the slightest divagation on the subject of your charms, we shall never have time to hear the tale of your escape."

"Sir, the shape of my jaw alone could furnish enough talk for a whole of your symposiums."

"Symposia. Doubtless."

"Look ye, Prince O. actually almost smiles."

(Bashfully, I returned my gaze to Locke.)

SPACE AND EXTENSION.
Space, considered barely in length between any two beings, without considering anything else between them, is called DISTANCE.

Bono continued his tale: "So, as I say, Fanny, she conceived a great hate for me specific. I don't rightly know why; but that girl enjoyed tormenting me, and so, oft when her father was in a ranting state because of the fools of New England, his reasons for whipping, they come from Fanny.

"I can recall . . . Here, sir, one example: One day, it was beastly hot, a devilish hot rainy day, and Miss Fanny didn't want to go above-stairs to her chamber to change her dress, because her paint might melt. So her father says to me to go up and fetch down the gown the maid left out on the bed. Now, her maid is there, sirs; she is present in the chamber. Miss Fanny's maid is the correct one to fetch her dress. But I bow and say, 'An't please your honor,' and I step up the stairs and fetch the dress down and ask where they wish me to lay it, that she might change into it and such.

"Fanny says, she says, 'That ain't the gown I am to wear for supper; I wish for the gray. That ain't the one I asked for.'

"I apologize, and say this is the one I found on her bed.

"She says, 'You got the wrong one.'

"I says to Colonel Asquith, 'My apologies, sir. An't please your honor, this was the dress was laid out.'

"'That was laid out earlier,'" says Colonel Ass. 'Before the rain started. Now she wishes for the gray. She wears always the gray, boy, when it rains. Always.'

"At this I cannot forbear, and I say, 'When it *rains,* sir?'

"And he says, 'Don't be an impertinent fool, boy.'

"And I can't forbear—because I am an impertinent fool—saying, 'I was to guess her mind from the *weather,* sir?'

"And he calls that insufferable vanity, and swears that I am a black scoundrel, and I say, 'Sir, begging your honor's pardon, sir, I beg your honor's most gracious pardon, but I have a nation of trouble knowing people's thoughts by looking at the clouds, me being a gentleman's valet and not a old Roman prophet.'"

Bono ceased his speaking.

"Lord Jesus," he swore; and for a moment there was silence. I looked up, and found he was almost in tears. "Lord Jesus," he repeated. "I still have them scars."

We sat soberly; we none of us could speak.

After a time, Bono resumed his tale. "Now, people was always at the house, talking sedition, just as up at the College. Colonel Ass and his friends might proclaim that the Boston mob is a danger, but they applauded all that talk of liberty. I presume, sir, from what I could tell, that they was wound up in that same scheme to purchase Indian land—"

"Indeed," said Dr. Trefusis. "Mr. Asquith was one of the foremost investors in that scheme."

"That same scheme. So they was always making plaints about Parliament and the King's Ministers being no respecters of property and how government was builded to protect the natural right to own what you own and how there was rumors—mark you—rumors that Lord Dunmore even spake of freeing the slaves if the spirit of rebellion came to Virginia.

"It was that last that I heard. I knew my master and his crew was preparing for a stand—they had recipes from you at the College for gunpowder, and they was making experiments in getting nitre from the floors of their tobacco houses. They was setting up a factory to make the powder. They was ready to fight; and I said, 'If they're ready to fight Lord Dunmore, time may come when I am ready to join him.'

"And not too long after, that time, it come."

FIGURE.
This the touch discovers in sensible bodies, whose extremities come within our reach; and the eye takes both from bodies and colours, whose boundaries are within its view.

Thus did I read in counterfeit of study; but I could not comprehend its meaning, so bent were my ears to Bono's tale:

"So it happens that Mrs. Asquith is having a grand ball. Her particular acquaintance is come for overnight, and then the next night, there is a full ball with all the neighboring houses. There was among that crowd several especial friends of the little Asquith imp, and Miss Fanny was ever so delighted they was visiting. The first night, Miss Fanny and her friends are in the parlor, and Colonel and Mrs. Ass and their guests are out visiting at another house for the evening. Before the Asquith Seniors take leave, they says to me, the Ass Seniors, 'Bono, you make sure the girls got everything they wish,' and though that ain't my watch, I bow and says, 'As it pleases your honor.'

"I spend some time, a part of an hour, polishing my master's shoes, and then I hear screams and laughs from the parlor and I bethinks me it is time to see whether the ladies require any little thing. I introduce myself into the parlor and they's all giddy, and I inquire if there is any way in which I may be of service; that the kitchen is at their command and such.

"One of them says that I has polished manners, and I bow, but Miss Fanny is bellowing over it all like Captain Stormalong that she wishes me to fetch them her mother's diamonds — Peruzzi diamonds some of them — corsages and aigrettes and such — so the girls can dress like ladies and romp.

"Now, this is a surprise. I express my regrets that I cannot oblige her, but I aver that should she wish anything within the compass of my et cetera, surely I shall speed to et cetera.

"She says, 'You will get us diamonds or be whipped as you were for the gown.'

"Once again—and now my ire was rising, but I was most cool—I say that I regret I can't oblige an indulgence that her father should find wanton and improper in a young lady and et cetera, and she says softly, 'You will oblige us.'

"At this, there wasn't no course but insolence, so I says, 'Miss Fanny, I tell your father that you and your friends played flying duchess skip-jump with the diamonds on, and you gets a greater whipping than ever I will.'

"There was silence then—this terrible silence—and she stood up and smiled at me. She said—very soft now—she said, 'You are my djinni. You are my magic spirit. You will get me whatever I wish.'

"I did not reply.

"So she said, 'Otherwise, I shall tell *mon père* that you touched me.'

"She delivered that word, then she stared with all this hate; and I stared right back; and our eyes . . ." He couldn't finish the sentence, but said, "And my heart retreated, and I went and fetched them down some gauds; bethinking the whole while that I should be whipped for touching the jewelry, but that if I didn't give her the diamonds, and she delivered her message of me touching, the Asquith Seniors would be tripping over theyselves as to whether I should be burnt first or hanged.

"I delivered the jewelry boxes, and she smiles again and says, 'Now you may give me a kiss.'

"It was death. It was death, sir. I could not do a thing in one way or in another. It was death. I ain't got no thing to say to her, no witty thing, and no . . . No thing. I ain't got no thing. So I bow and I left the room. I heard them cackling behind me.

"And I knew then that I must flee. I must needs flee or I was soon dead."

(And I read, without apprehending:)

> In our idea of *place*, we consider the relation of distance betwixt anything, and any two or more points, which are considered as keeping the same distance one with another, and so considered as at rest. For when we find anything at the same distance now which it was yesterday, from any two or more points, which have not since changed their distance one with another, we say it hath kept the same place.

"I knew I had to run, and I knew it was Lord Dunmore or nothing. I reckoned that I could make my way during the ball, there being confusion and many servants, all comings and goings. And I should have just fled—but I couldn't forbear revenge. I could not forbear revenge."

"Revenge," said Dr. Trefusis, smiling widely and stretching his hands around his knees, as he could not be more delighted by this welcome turn in the narrative.

"Now. All night, I lay and I bethought myself—*how to leave so I won't be forgot?* And behold."

"*Ecce,*" said Dr. Trefusis.

"Look ye. Now, when I was at the College, one of the experiments I assisted at—it was an experiment with paint. Metallic paint. Lead and bismuth. You recall, sir? We all wore cloths over our mouths?"

"I recall it. Paint for the ladies."

"For the ladies, as you say. For their cheeks. An excellent complexion in a gallipot. And I remembered Mr. Gitney telling me that what you was all laboring at was an old problem: that the bismuth, or mayhap the lead, acted with any sulphureous exhalations in the air —"

"Ye gods, you are so far at present from being comprehensible —"

"Hark and shhh. That sulphur in the air acted on the paint and turned it black."

"Indeed. 'Tis a thorny problem."

"So in the morning, I went down to Mr. Asquith's gunpowder house, where there was two men concocting the powder, and I delivered a message that Mr. Ass was desirous of a sample of liver of sulphur. I recalled particularly, that's what we used in the experiment at the College. Liver of sulphur."

"Indeed."

"I told them Mr. Ass was observing his own experiments up at the house with his guests, some crook-bonneted scheme sent down by those Collegians up north. They laughed and they gave me the liver of sulphur in a sack, and when I asked, some vitriol oil, too."

"You carried oil of vitriol knocking about in a sack? It is infinitely dangerous, my boy."

"Dangerous? Oh, I quaffed swigs, sir. Washed my teeth with it. Sang, 'Hey, nonny, no.'"

"I'm sure. Continue."

"So I take the liver of sulphur up to my quarters, up where they stash us in the top of the house, and I begin crushing it with a stone. You have never seen any single thing crushed so fine as I crushed that powder. I reckon I spent an hour in the crushing. That was my preparation.

"Then come the ball, all the ladies are giving their courtesies, and the young gents, looking so fine, and Miss Fanny, she's demure. No little lady who threatened destruction to a man the night before.

"So there are the excellent gentry, all smiles and blushes, stepping their measures. First they have the minuets, then the reels, then the country-dances. And I take one last look at the young miss whispering to her friends and clapping, and her father in his fopperies, and I turn from the hall and go up the creak-crack old stairs to my quarters and move the bowl of powder to a closet near the dance-hall, where I know there will be a good draft going past. I hide the bowl in there and I pour in the oil of vitriol. The whole pot, it starts to smoke and it smells so awful and sulphurish I can't barely breathe. The smoke is all spreading. When I seen that, I know I don't have long, so I close the door to the closet and I bolt through the servants' door and I run on out of the house, quick as I can.

"I'm at the woods when I hear the shrieks. Because there was a devil of a stink, first, and I fancy that the young gents held their noses. And then there was louder screams, shouts. Because all the fine ladies, all the girls sweet-eyeing their beaux, have just turned black. All their face-paint. First dingy, I reckon, then smutty, then to rotting, then to coal, then to midnight. All of them."

We, his auditors, were enthralled—swept away in awe. "Bono," said Dr. Trefusis, "will you be my bride?"

"So I run through the little wood—"

At this interesting juncture, Serjeant Clippinger appeared. "This don't sound like any lesson, sir," he said to Dr. Trefusis. "On philosophy."

"Serjeant, we yet discuss mutability. Private Williams is providing us with an excellent example. He demonstrates how change occurs, and how the senses remark upon change."

Said the Serjeant with sarcasm, "As when you don't smell and then you do smell."

"You recall our conversation of the other day. Indeed. Though that, methinks, was not precisely my example at the time. Rather, when one smells constantly—of old age, say—one should no longer be able to mark the smell until it alter; or when there are objects hung long on a wall, the eye ceases to see them, until something is shifted. Or if one regards an officious myrmidon too lumpen to move for long periods of time, one ceases even to note him until he actually motivates himself and speaks."

"A myrmidon."

"Indeed."

"What is a myrmidon?"

"An ant."

"A speaking ant. I'll warrant y'art being cute."

"I'll warrant I have a warrant, ha ha."

"He has the letter, Serjeant," said Bono.

"The letter!" exclaimed Dr. Trefusis, producing it from his coat. "I do indeed have the letter. From John, Earl of Dunmore, Baron Murray of Blair, of Moulin and Tillimet, Lieutenant and Governor-General of His Majesty's Colony and Dominion of Virgina, and Vice-Admiral of the Same, '*Sir: It is my wish that Dr. John Trefusis shall be granted*—'"

"Indeed, sir. I read the letter. I will hope that there is no treasonable intelligence exchanged here, as I don't hear no philosophy."

"I avow, Serjeant, we shall commit ourselves wholly to philosophy without a grain of intelligence intermixed."

"You ain't witty," said the Serjeant, turning away. "Y'art just an old man who can only find Negroes to laugh with him."

He left, pacing the deck, and Bono inquired, "What is a myrmidon?" to which Trefusis rapidly replied, "Good God, sir! Continue!"

"I run through the woods, at once applauding myself for my wit—"

"Well deserved, sir. Well deserved."

"And at the self instant, I am grinding my teeth because I am a vain, proud, revenging idiot and shall be run down because of it. Certain, they knows I'm gone within fifteen minutes, I reckon. Soon I can't hear the protests at the hall no more, but I can hear the dogs. They've let the dogs out.

"I can hear them approaching. I tears through the woods— knees up—and over some fields. I know the general way. But there are horses on the roads and I'll warrant alarums.

"It's not another twenty minutes before the dogs are on me.

"I can hear them a-crashing through the leaves. And thrashing. And I see torches through the trees, and I hurry quick and hide me in the bushes. But no avail. They going to find me.

"Then—it's now I smell a thing. Not just the sulphur on me. Sirs, with my sulphur, I am attracting the curiousness of a skunk. Walking through the bushes to me as bold as Sunday.

"Every inch of me wants to run. Its stink is prodigious—my eyes is near watering—and the hounds is coming—by God— what does a body do?"

"Indeed."

Bono rose. "Sir, I reckon our time is over for today. My deepest apologies, an't please Your Honor."

"Sit! Plautan varlet! Speak!"

"Oh, me, sir?"

"Sit!"

"Do you order me, sir?"

"Speak!"

"By your grace, sir." He sat. "So the dogs is coming close and the skunk is already there and I'm shivering with fear and my eyes is burning and the skunk, he sees me, he sees my bulk, and *spang*—afeared. He lifts up his tail and sprays me and run off."

Dr. Trefusis made a noise of great disgust.

"I—it's what I can do, just not to vomit. My eyes are burning. I tell this all as a jest, but it was—I was wracked, sir. I was in the bushes, wracked. And death to retch. Death to make any solitary sound. All curled up, and can't move. And the vomit in my mouth. Can't move, but—oh, Lord, sir. It was horrible.

"The dogs, they sniffing closer, and the men calling out, 'Something here! Something here!' And I'm in the bushes praying to keep still. It's too dark to see. I can't see a thing. The whole pack was coming straight for me. That I could hear, and I put my head under my arms and prepares for the biting.

"But then, the dogs—the dogs smelled the spray. They smelled it and started whimpering back. The men behind them, they shouting, 'It's a damn skunk! Call 'em back! It's a skunk!'

"I wait and I wait, and every few minutes, the burning again, and all down my throat, and—sweet Jesus, there's no smell like as . . . I can't even say how deep that skunk smell is. You can keep falling through parts of that smell and there are other parts, whole other rooms and wings you ain't known about. That is one devil-ish power of a smell."

He smiled with some satisfaction in the rapt attitudes of his hearers; for both of us could not have been more attentive, though I, for empty shew, flipped the pages of my Locke.

"That smell, gentlemen, is what brought me here today. That smell is my salvation. The next week, I walk along the riverbank, walking all night. And where I hide, nobody wants approach me. No farmers, no magistrates, no slave patrollers. One breeze and they keep their distance. No way they's coming into the bushes after that.

"After a day, I got famished, and so I killed a sheep and took him to a barn I reck'd would be safe and lit a little fire to cook part of it. Some slaves saw the light and come in and I say I'm Richard Richards and this here was my sheep and did they wish a leg? For a while, they eats and I eat and we are all genial; them asking me questions and me telling them stories as to how I'm a honest Dutchman new come from the Antilles. Then I see that they is waiting for us to finish before attacking me and turning me over to their master, so they is fussing with rope and one has a machete. It was then or never, so I burst for the door and there was a scuffle and I take a firebrand and swing it around and push them down, and I throw the burning stick into the hay and run, and I believe that barn burned behind me. They was running down the slope after me, and there's the river in front of me."

"By God," said Dr. Trefusis.

"Prince O., you recall when we was up at Lake Champlain?"

I answered, "It was a most gratifying time."

"That it was, sure. And I watched you close while Lord

[229]

Cheldthorpe taught you to swim. You out there a-wiggling your little twig arms."

"You said there were channels to cross."

"So there were, Prince O. I knew then that when some tries to flee through the woods or such, they come to a river, and it's a wall; but for me, I wanted it to be a road. I wanted it to be the very gate wide open. And that's what it was, now. Rivers don't stop me. I swum in Boston Harbor. I swum out in Canaan. And now I swum in Virginia."

I saw the Serjeant's eye upon me from across the room, and dropped my own gaze to the page, where I helpless took in several incomprehensible paragraphs regarding place, chess pieces, ships, and substance. While my eyes were thus burdened with the page, however, my ears were free, and followed Bono's tale.

"I swim, I walk, I swim.

"Long last, I get near Williamsburg. Hide in the bushes. Every day I been bathing in the river. It's not so much my skin that smells still, more my clothes. They have a reek. That last day, I washed there again in the James and saw the laundresses mashing the clothes and talked real sweet to them and offered to do some wringing. They says thank you kindly, and ain't I a good fellow; and so soon as I got my hands on some breeches and a shirt, I sink them under the water and put a stone on them with my feet and then keep wringing, and then the women smells my own clothes and it's, 'You ain't no man to be doing laundry!' and 'What you play at?' and them cursing me. I laughed and they takes the rest of their clothes and frumps off down the riverbank. I wait a few minutes and get the breeches and shirt out from under my feet and go to dry them.

"That evening, I present myself at the Palace. I guess I speak to a factotum. It seems His Lordship is not at home; he's fled on board a ship, but if I wish, the factotum says, I can sleep in the stables with another little crowd of Negroes awaiting His Lordship's pleasure. Eleven or so of us who'd fled, hearing rumors.

"Since then, I served Lord Dunmore. I served on the first ship, the *Fowey* man-of-war; and then back to the Palace, where I stood as a picket guard when the population was got all restive. Then when he fled again, there was more of us—and we went with him, and you know then. We drifted up and down the river. We was sent out on nights to catch some poultry from farms. We steal cows so the Marines can eat. Other times, we pay for forage, if it's Loyalist. We hope.

"For months, I been on the river, up and down. I was with His Lordship for our first skirmishes, when the rebels all run away. I can't tell you, Prince O.—I can't tell you the fine sensation of victory. When you run on their heels—and they fleeing, like we always fleeing—they running before you—scared—and you chasing—when those boys caught their own master in that swamp—sweet dicker of mercies—I ain't a praying man, but that night, I fell on my knees. I fell on my knees under the stars and thanked the Lord who delivered me out of all distresses.

"That was Kemp's Landing. Then I was posted on garrison near Great-Bridge. We heard the Proclamation read. And Prince O.— Prince, we seen some terrible things—we seen that battle—we seen things that chill the blood—but there's one thing, still: We is free. That's the great change. In all legality, we is free now."

I believe the eyes of both auditors now were full, though Bono would not admit of tears himself; and that excellent and ingenious man, so like a brother to me, voice tremblant with his passions, said, "This is the war where we change. This is the trickster war. It's where we disappear, just like they desire us disappear. I spoke it you before: They wish us blank," he said, gesturing without thinking at Dr. Trefusis, who was the nearest exemplar of the white race. "They want us with no history and no memory. They want us empty as paper so they can write on us, so we ain't nothing but a price and an owner's name and a list of tasks. And that's what we'll give them. We'll give them your Nothing. We'll give them my William Williams and Henry Henry. We'll slip through and we'll change to who we must needs be and I will be all sly and have my delightful picaresque japes. But at the end of it, when it's over, I shall be one thing. I shall be one man, fixed, and not have to take no other name. I shall be one person steadily for some years."

He took my shoulder. He shook me. "This is why we got to win," he said. "We only lost one battle. We got to win, Prince O. If we ever wish to be one person, we got to win."

For Dr. Trefusis:
SYNOPSIS OF LOCKE UPON MOTION AND PLACE

Locke giveth this example of motion and place: That if we leave a chess piece on a board, and move the board, we still say the chess piece hath *stayed in the same place;* for we judge its movement according to its place on the board, not relative to the room or the table.

Further, he saith that the chess board, neglected upon a desk in the cabin of a ship through the night, *stayeth in the same place,* to our mind, though the ship hath moved across the waters — for motion and place are relative.

So be it; but, sir, I wish, whether motion is relative or no, we would move. We have all traveled far to get to this place, though this place alter as our camp alters from shore to ship and our ship shifts on its anchor cable.

We are prepared to prove ourselves again and redeem our loss.

☙ As I conducted Dr. Trefusis back to his shallop, he said to me, "I divine that Bono seems under the misapprehension that . . ." Dr. Trefusis could not continue, soured his visage, then made another attempt, this time more gentle in his tone. "Upon our meeting, Bono expressed his happy anticipation of seeing and speaking with your mother again," said he.

I did not respond.

"How long?" asked Dr. Trefusis. "When wilt thou tell him?"

I could not speak. We had reached the quarterdeck.

"The portions of our history you have related to him are incomprehensible," said Dr. Trefusis. "You have told him that we decamped and returned to Boston just as the siege began and we should have fled. He does not understand why, you assisting with

His Majesty's Army in Boston, you did not seek out your mother, if she was there as well. He believes that you left her behind."

I said simply: "I did."

He frowned. "Oh, my boy," said he, in a lamenting tone. "Oh, my dear boy. Do not take that weight upon your shoulders, or you shall never rise from your knees."

✣ It appears Bono is known among our Company, and is a favorite already of many. No sooner had he and I settled beside one another, than Bono was asked with surprise, "You friend of Buckra, before you come to Lord Dunmore?"

Bono saw that by "Buckra," I was meant; and replied, "Oh, I known Buckra since we all had to wipe his behind and weigh the leavings."

This was not, perhaps, the introduction I would have wished, contributing little to my own stature or ease; and I find myself fervently wishing that he could have refrained from referring to that gloomy period of my infancy and its galling rituals. Still, however, Bono is too dear to me, and I admire too greatly his facility with others and fear too much his wrath if corrected to protest; and so I swallowed shame and smiled when the rest laughed.

December 20th, 1775

Quiet aboard the ship.

We had a one-day flux, which we feared was a bloody flux. 'Twas, I think, the pork, which Slant said was slimy before cooked. We all were violent in our disturbances; but once ejected, the meat's evil influences seem to have passed.

We hear that the citizens upon their schooners, brigs, and snows suffer greatly from hunger, for the rebels will not allow them to land and purchase provisions. I did not go above-decks today, being too ill; but those who did, say there are many sallow faces to be seen upon the fo'c'sles of other ships.

December 21ˢᵗ, 1775

Today arrived the *Liverpool* man-of-war, a frigate of twenty-eight guns, which eases our mind somewhat. We heard a great cheer go up from the rest of the fleet upon its appearance, as were we delivered.

We know not what command awaits or what the vessel's arrival portends; but we tallied this day, and we have now five sizeable fighting ships—the *Liverpool,* the *Otter,* the *Kingfisher,* the *William,* and the *Dunmore*—as well as assorted schooners and sloops-of-war. I was on the larboard dogwatch this day, and so could observe the positioning of those ships, it appearing that we are preparing for some great action against the town of Norfolk.

The ships are arrayed thus: The *Dunmore* sits at the northern end of the town, the *Kingfisher* at the southern, and the *Otter* and *Liverpool* between them. They ride with springs on their cables, tampions out, as if prepared to open fire and level the town with broadsides.

They shall not mock us for many days longer.

I believe the presence of Pro Bono—or as I should perhaps call him, Private Williams—shall change much for me upon the *Crepuscule*. He is known to many of the men of my Company, having been present before the Regiment was formed, in those months when the Governor's black forces were smaller, before that body were divided into distinct corps. Both his affability and his harshness compelled others as they did me; and he hath been admitted into a great variety of circles of friendship and amity that remain generally closed. His art in greeting, in laughing, in commiseration, in knowing when to speak and when to keep silent, is prodigious, and causes men to admire his practicality and sturdiness, and women to enjoy his ease, wit, and scurrility. He was, in short, a favorite among our number instanter, and continues so.

Over the month since my arrival in this distressed Colony, I have, as might well be supposed, been sensible of a whole realm of social niceties, rivalries, and alliances in our Company about which I understand little. These, Bono illuminates for me in asides, and for the first time, I fully comprehended the magnitude of human story in our endeavor and the intricacies stashed like clockwork behind the regularity of our uniforms.

Yesterday, I witnessed an argument between two of the men of our Company. At dinner, an old man burst out yelling in his tongue; the object of these expostulations being one of Bono's friends, Charles. Charles would not face the old man, but turned his back to him. He would not meet the elder's eyes, but, even in these cramped quarters, swiveled and contemplated the walls furiously. The old man snatched at his shoulder, importuning him still

[239]

in a language unknown to me. Charles remained in his situation, unmoving.

I asked Bono if he knew the reason of this altercation; and he answered, "The reason for this altercation? The reason for this altercation is once you lose your teeth from old age, you wish especially to bite people." When I inquired further, he explained, "They're both of the Ibo nation, Charles and the old article, Better Joe. Charles, he been here in the Colonies since he was eight or nine years. But Better Joe was already old when he was took. He was some species of wizard in Africa. He was the captain of some spirit club up in the Ibo highlands.

"So they join this Regiment and meet each other, and Better Joe sees from Charles's scars he's an Ibo, and he thinks, 'Now, here's somebody going to pay me some mind.' For three months, he been saying he wants to be Charles's teacher, show him mysteries. But Charles don't even want to think about any of that. He already saw his gods beat once when he was a child. They didn't do a single thing to help him when he was took and then they forgot him entirely when he and his family was on the ship. So he don't want to see some creaky baggage who gets whipped and spit on — some addled, sad old dotard who can't shave without he cuts himself — saying he's the voice of the sky or the dead or all powerful or such. The old man just reminds him of defeat."

These things, Bono explained to me.

And he continued the chain of stories, explaining that Charles could not abide the looks or Efik speech of yet another man, Jocko; for Jocko, sharp and sleek, had been employed in one of the great Canoe Houses of Old Calabar, which had sold Charles, and Better Joe, and countless thousand others, to the white men whose ships lay out in the bay. Charles recalled too clearly the cruelty of his Efik captors, taunting him and his father, telling them that the white men had sharp teeth and purchased slaves to eat them soulless. When, rowed out to the slave-ship, they first saw the white men peering over the gunwales, Charles's father had despaired, cried a prayer, lifted up his hands, and made a valiant attempt to strangle his son with their chains, that he might end the boy's agony before the slaughter to come; that his son's spirit might remain, at least, in Africa and find its way back up into the hills.

"His father had his arms and the chains round his neck," said Bono. "They pulled the father off."

I could not speak for horror.

"The father died a few weeks later at sea. So now Charles can't abide an Efik."

"He told you this?" I asked with some incredulity.

"This is a time for speaking," said Bono. "All of us, we come here, and we been nobody for a long time; and so we want to tell a tale."

"Did you tell them yours?"

He shrugged. "I told them enough," he said.

Many of our number have never known the Africk shores, but tell the tales of parents removed decades before, who were attached for debt, or taken in adultery, or captured on slave-runs made in the name of warfare, some petty difference elevated to conceal the greed for human chattels — for when a nation needs despoil another to produce captives, they find a reason.

They speak what they have heard of the warrior-women of Dahomey, or the child-soldiers of Morocco; of the great

Mohammedan universities of the north; of the wise men of Islam, the marabouts and *mallam*s, fabled throughout the continent for the sorcery of script, who write charms to be rolled in amulets, and who sew on the tunics of warriors sorcerous sigils of protection to keep them safe. They speak of the *travado* clouds which darken the Gold Coast; of the fierce harmattan winds, which boreal blasts itch and turn black men white; they tell of the mangrove marshes of the Windward Coast, where stand ancient stone circles, and where the canoe-men hunt their human chattels. They tell of the great herds of the Fulani, who peddle their hides even upon the Slave Coast, whence my mother was dispatched. They speak of small things: the intoxication of kola nut, or how no food hath tasted right for these twenty years without palm oil.

These tales of Africa I remember best, because of their strangeness; but most of our Regiment have never seen the country, and remember it only as a place of legend. Thus, there are many stories of the Colonies, too. One man learned the art of furniture-making from his master, and thereafter assisted in his master's shop, which was a great pleasure to him. He speaks of the glories of joinery and its satisfactions. He talks of how Christ was a carpenter, and how he is blessed to follow in the same profession.

Another man was apprenticed to a farrier, that he might save his master the expense of having his horses shod; but his apprenticeship ended when two white farriers, angry at the loss of custom occasioned by the training of slaves in this art, threatened to kill him, did he continue to learn the trade; and his master deemed it prudent to withdraw him, and place him instead in the field.

There are tales of escape, many as wily as Bono's own. Three men who set off together for Dunmore's force, fearing detection, bound one of their number and led him on a rope; those passing by upon the road presuming that the slave thus bound had escaped and been recaptured by the other two. White men jeered as they rode by. When the bound man was fatigued, the three shifted the rope to another of their number, and so made their way over days to Hampton and Lord Dunmore.

So, tale after tale. Indeed, they are tales of hardship, but notable even more for their bravery. For every man, every woman, every child upon these ships, there is by necessity a romance of adventure and flight; this ship a book of stories; every one has his heroism, her ingenuity; all their close escapes and desperate relief.

So doth Christ in His mercy often supply courage and industry equal to adversity, that His creations might meet their travails.

I set these stories down so that the deeds of our Company may be remembered; and more, so that as we sit here, raging at our leisure, despising our impotence, awaiting the order to attack those who mock us from the shore, we may recall what we have already undergone — and we may remember our enemy in preparation for marching out against him. And I record them because when we or our forebears passed over the water on ships, we lost our names and our stories; and now, in these ships, moving upon these waters, we shall regain them.

Pomp was employed by his master as a cowherd in the Great Dismal Swamp, and oft saw refugees flee past him, but had no stomach for flight. He tells us of the legends of that place: In the curdled depths of the Great Alligator Swamp, says he, the beast for which it is named is so vast it can devour a cow in one snap of its jaws. Or this: One day, as Pomp tended his cattle, a man appeared to him and told him of a fabulous town of runaways in the Swamp, complete with their own houses and streets, and roosts in the trees, and a governor in a strong hat.

Pomp is a fellow given to dreams, and did not much mind his tedious days nor his isolate, swampy environs. He took pride in knowing the ways and mires, and was, after his fashion, content to be employed away from the eye of censure and the lash. He should not have flown, but for this circumstance: His master's cattle were marked upon their ear, one cut to signify his ownership. Another man's slaves, seeing this mark, recommended that their own master take up a sign of two cuts upon the ear of his cattle; and then, at night, coming across Pomp's cows and bulls, would give them an extra cut upon the ear and claim the cow as their own. By the time Pomp had detected this piece of deception, five or six cows were missing, and his master so wroth that Pomp scarce knew what to do. Though perhaps if Pomp had remained and had simply informed his master of the source of this base trickery, his master had pursued an action against the neighboring farmer without prejudice to Pomp; still, Pomp, being too full of imaginations of disaster, decided upon flight, and traversed the route north from the Great Dismal Swamp to Norfolk with two kine driven before him, his excuse when questioned being that he drove the cattle to market upon command.

"I was very welcome at Norfolk," he said, "but I reckon, mostly for my beef."

THE TALE OF ISAAC THE JOINER

Isaac, the pious carpenter, was enjoined from his youth to accept the teachings of Christ, which doctrine he received with joyful heart. He being possessed of a memory excellent in its acuity, most especially for those things which stirred up the embers in his breast and reflected the scintillant glory of the King of Kings, he quickly conned long passages of Scripture, though not a word could he read.

At length, he found himself preaching at the Sunday night dances held near his master's house, and his sermons were not unwelcome. He spake of the end of bondage, and the Lord's donation of a soul to each human body, which soul could never be degraded nor yielded up; which spirits, when gathered in Heaven, would be of no low or high degree, and would wear no garments nor finery nor frip, but all should stand equal and justified before the Throne. Beautiful clothing, said he, and the jewels of the wealthy are of *tough, heavy fabric* when weighed upon the airy bodies of spirits; and shall either *drag the wealthy down*, or *fall away like so much chaff* through their excellent and imperishable spirits in that giddy moment of the end. He bade his brethren: *"Wait and be ready, for the Lord shall come."*

For this doctrine, as may be presumed, he was debarred from all preaching. His master indeed forbade him from leaving his quarters on Sunday nights, for fear that in preaching of equality before the Lord on High, Isaac might incite riot on Earth.

This was a tribulation; Isaac wanted sorely the camaraderie of his heretic congregation, their sweet witness; he missed the singing and tears, the prayers of love and fellow-feeling, the entreaties of sorrow assuaged.

Every Sunday, he knelt through the evening and prayed to the Lord, that he might be delivered and be freed to partake of God's Word.

And behold: At ten o'clock one Sunday night, his master came to him, and demanded he take up a scythe and go down to the chicken-house, for a body of Lord Dunmore's Negroes was landed and seized upon the fowls for provender.

So Isaac went down the hill toward the river with his scythe in his hand. He saw the ship waiting for him upon the waters, the boat upon the shore. And he saw the adversary stealing the fruits of his master's fields and paddocks, carrying off chickens and leading goats by ropes. They spied him and paused in their depredations.

He raised his hand in greeting.

"At long last," said he, "you are come."

And he went down to welcome them.

Slant's tale was most affecting. He told it me himself. Slant's childhood and youth were spent upon a tobacco plantation presided over by a benevolent widow by the name of Croak and her son, who was of Slant's age. The son deplored slavery and oft would grow into a fury at the sight of mistreatment of his mother's slaves. He saw to it that Slant and his fellows were not used unkindly; their diet of Indian corn, for example, to be supplemented with helpings of meat, and new huts built for such hands as did not live in the servants' quarters in the house.

When Mrs. Croak died, her son, not yet having achieved his majority, was helpless to interfere with the wishes of his trustees, whose discipline upon the plantation was much harsher than had ever been offered by the widow, their desire to profit from the farm being greater than their attachment to its persons. They discounted the boy's protests for their impracticality and sought to rationalize expenditure.

This was a severe period on that plantation, and saw many unhappy restrictions upon the small luxuries and freedoms the servants had been accorded. There was much toil, and still complaints from the trustees' overseers that the slaves were unaccountably lazy and devious. 'Twas in these years that the harshness and rigor of the discipline so made its mark upon Slant that he cannot speak without wrestling his words, and will not name what dire thing was done to him.

When Master Croak, the son, reached suitable age, he dismissed his trustees with curt thanks. He called his slaves all together in the yard. He spake kindly to them, and said, "You have undergone great hardship; and now shall be your reward. You know well, i'faith, I cannot abide the barbarism of your state. You have suffered indignities and evils that none should suffer. I cannot free you outright, for it would ruin me; but I can provide you with a small weekly sum for your labor, to be placed against your price, so you might, in three or four years, purchase yourselves of me and enjoy complete manumission. Once freed, you are at liberty, of course, to go where you will; but as you are like a family to me, I hope you shall choose to remain here, in this happy place, upon a footing as paid laborers. We shall be as a beacon to show those around us how great the bounty and fruits of amity may grow."

The slaves, when they heard this, clustered close about him and embraced him; and he embraced them, and none could forbear weeping. That night, he laid out a feast for them, and they danced and sang until dawn.

The gentry of the neighborhood, hearing of his pronouncement, appeared in the following days to protest, saying that he would incite a rebellion in the neighborhood if others heard of his system. To the supplications of reason they eventually added the insult of imprecation, calling him a young cur and a scoundrel and, moreover, a fool. He ejected them with celerity, and his servants watched with some satisfaction as these lords of the leaf stalked back out to their chaises, disappointed in their designs.

Following this victory, young Croak undertook various improvements in the servants' quarters, that each chamber might be warm in winter, cool in summer, and free of dirt and disease; and he altered substantially the diet afforded his field hands, proclaiming that work undertaken in health and in a spirit of felicity should always excel beyond the drudgery of the miserable.

Such was Master Croak's scheme.

It is to be deplored that the experiment failed utterly. The trade in tobacco was suffering materially due to the unrest with the mother country and the late crisis in credit. This depression of the market was compounded, on the Croak estate, by the antagonism of every neighbor, who made of every favor a dispute; and, in the end, of course, despite Master Croak's expostulations that there was in liberty a wondrous œconomy, there is a more wondrous financial potency to abject exploitation. Within two years the farm was bankrupt and the honest Croak was bankrupt, and had hanged himself in his bedchamber, leaving instructions in his will that all his slaves should be manumitted forthwith. It might well be predicted that the wider Croak family intervened before this instrument could be executed, and argued that the youth was clearly not of sound mind and so was unable to dispose of his property fitly. This necessitated a hearing to settle the contestation of the will.

A night some weeks ago, one of the overseers crept to the slave quarters, and alerted the hands that on the morrow, young Master Croak's uncle and aunt would descend upon the estate and secure the Negroes who remained until such time as their case was heard; and, the courts being suspended and the government in confusion, it might be some years before the suit was settled, and by that time, Slant and his kin would be accustomed to the yoke of tyranny; and, said the overseer, "Master Croak would not wish this. He wished you free. You all must fly tonight."

Most of them lit out for the western hills or for Florida; Slant stole a small boat and set out to join Dunmore. He was washed down the James and then rowed up the Elizabeth, and reached us when I have recorded, since when, he is delighted to have taken a new name, Slant, and will no longer answer to the old, which we do not know; though he has taken his master's last name, in memory of that tragic youth's attempts at generosity.

Thus the tale of Slant Croak.

THE TALE OF PRIVATE JOCKO

Jocko grew up among the great Canoe Houses of Old Calabar, and was accustomed to the sight of white men who visit that port for their dismal trade. One day as he walked along the street, he observed a small hut that had not been there two days previous, around which was a cluster of youths, all clamoring for admittance. The door of this hut would open, and one man would go in, and another come out. When they went into the hut, their hands were empty; when they set out from the hut, each of the men carried a sack with some small object in it.

Emboldened by curiosity at this mysterious transaction, Jocko approached and inquired about this practice; and he was told, to his great surprise, that

—Pro Bono—who some minutes ago seized this book out of my hands.

I protested—rose—he held it away, saying, "I have need of paper. Stay! I have need of paper!"

And perhaps our hunger and our anger at our constraint conquered both of us—for he persisted in holding it from me, laughing and saying, "What is this?"—whereas I was reduced to grabbing for it, crying, "Return it to me! Return it to me now!"

He said, "We must needs make a little sketch of the river and Norfolk and its approaches," and I watched the book swoop around my hands and I heard my own voice, the treble of a boy in skirts, wailing, *"It is mine! Bono—Private Williams! It is mine! Give it back to me!"*

"The boys and me are discussing strategy."

"Give it back to me!"

Bono thrust a palm against my chest to hold me at a distance, leaned the book on an upraised knee, and with the other hand, perused the pages. "What have you here?" he said. "You writing down things about us all?" and he called out the names as he found them: Jocko, Slant, Pomp, Isaac, Charles. I may be grateful that Charles and Isaac, who were by his side, turned their heads away, ashamed at our squabble. "What have you here?" Bono repeated.

"I'm setting down the stories of the Regiment in my Itinerarium," I said. "That they may not be forgotten. Our heroism. Give it back."

"Sweet mercy," said Bono. "Your Itinerarium." He shook his head. "You barely got your own story to write." His aspect was lowering, and he said to me, "Prince O., you consider these people, and then you consider your own self. You lived in a special bed, you ate beef every supper, you was taught to play the fiddle, and your biggest hardship was learning the present plural singular indicative in Latin. Do you . . . — Do you truly . . . ?" He frowned wildly and did not complete his sentence; my face burned in shame.

He tore out a blank page so that he might sketch Norfolk and its defenses for his friends.

He gave the book back to me, and I sit with it now.

Bono and his companions sit only four feet away, smoking pipes and murmuring.

I will not write more this evening.

December 23rd, 1775

In the last days, entreaties have been made by members of my Company that we might hold our accustomed dances, palavers, and protocols; which requests our commanders denied summarily, the hazard being too great at this time. Though the dancing was impracticable, there was nonetheless a great convocation of both sexes upon our ship and several others, a boatload of women and children from the *Dunluce* being added to the soldiers and the small number of wives and children aboard the *Crepuscule*.

I was delighted to observe that the comely young lady of such exquisite voice I had seen previously was returned, this maiden attended like one of the Parnassian sisters by a company of other songstresses.

It was, however, with some surprise that I encountered Dr. Trefusis among those boarding from the *Dunluce*, that ship being largely given over to the housing of women connected with the regiments. I begged him to explain to what we owed the honor, and he responded merrily that we owed the tearing great pleasure of his presence to the fact that he had been detected in fraud and ejected from his former berth. I inquired as to what fraud precisely, and he responded thus: When he resided in Norfolk, he circulated among families of the most exalted condition on the strength only of his wit and a forged letter of credit from a bank in London; debts mounting, inquiries had been made, and Dr. Trefusis's purse embarrassed. "I have always said, my boy, that a lace jabot is as good as a thousand pounds in trust at the bank. But yesterday I discovered that the precise figure is fifty-three pounds, eight shillings. I found it expedient to remove myself to the *Dunluce* transport and to take refuge with the washerwomen and trulls. My new companions are infinitely preferable to the old. Last night, a woman gave me a crab claw without asking a farthing for it, and I knew, in truth, I was finally moving in circles of the very first *ton*."

The festivities this night were louder than in evenings before, due presumably to the confinement of the sound in the hold of the ship; but it seemed as if the very act of suppressing the dancing spurred on the singing and the drumming upon the hull, upon hogsheads, the clapping of hands.

I have now been privy to several of these exuberant protocols; and of their music I have observed a great deal, and hope someday to learn the secrets of these consorts and write an account of the inexplicable tunings, the intricate complexities of rhythm, the simple *fugato* songs, as headlong catches, the rapt *recitativo secco* of their narration. This shall be a work for times of peace, when I have had more opportunity to study and learn.

My most ardent wishes were gratified with a performance by the maiden singer I had seen previous, though she sang in chorus with two others, delivering a ballad on the progress of the worm in corn. Even such mean matter, rendered by this maiden, ravished the senses.

Dr. Trefusis squatted by my side; and I presented both Slant and Pomp to him particularly, hoping that his frolicsome air would alleviate their habitual mistrust of white men, and they find as much pleasure in his conversation as I found in theirs. Their silence, however, betrayed their discomfort. When they perceived that Bono crawled and stooped beneath the beams, advancing crabwise through the seated crush to join us, 'twas too much;

Bono was an object of even greater fear to them than a white gentleman. Though he does not mock Slant's difficulties with speech, and uses him always with perfect politeness, it is clear that he withholds some hidden commentary; and none of us wish to be by when he, angry at our confinement or some recent rebel out-rage, sees fit to loose his bile.

He coming, they fled.

Dr. Trefusis did not note their absence, but as Bono sate him-self down beside us, greeted him.

"Your humble servant, sir," said Dr. Trefusis. "Excellent *ridotto*."

Bono said, "Ain't the same without the dancing."

"*Tant pis,* the ceiling is a little low. One brisk hornpipe and we'd all be bashed stupid."

Bono took ahold of his own head, and said, "Aye, I'll tell you, sir: too low, too narrow, too short. One more day and — I swear I can't abide this hunching. And the stink. Sweet mercy. What intelligence you got from Lord Dunmore?"

"I hear nothing from Lord Dunmore," said Dr. Trefusis. "I am become *persona non grata* in that quarter. I am no wise welcome in the stateroom imperial."

"You heard when we're going to attack the rebels, instead of waiting on deck, admiring their fine parades?"

"One must assume that we are waiting for word from Lord Dunmore's agent with the Iroquois Confederation. He is supposed to sweep down with them from the northwest and provide us with most welcome assistance."

"Well, when's he due? His Lordship's agent?"

"Connolly."

"When's he due?"

"You ask a fool and an outcast."

"Damn," said Bono, rubbing his hands once more upon the sides of his skull. "My gampapa warned me, never accept no invitation to get into the hold of a white man's ship. Said he had a devilish irksome experience once. Visit lasted some few months."

"I am sorry," said Dr. Trefusis, "that I can provide you with no more information." The song was ended; Dr. Trefusis turned to me. "Private Nothing is quiet this evening."

I did not disagree.

He smiled in a curious fashion — occasioned by I knew not what — and said to me, "I must present you to someone." He rose, ducking to avoid the beams. "Follow."

I attended him as we stepped among the crowd. Men sat skewed against their wives; children passed Vishnoo the tortoise between them, hands reaching, as he ducked and scrabbled to resist the hardships of their affection. It may well be imagined what emotions passed through my breast when I saw Dr. Trefusis's goal: the comely girl who sang such exquisite arias.

I was startled, convinced my tutor possessed the power to scry the thoughts of mind and heart. Dr. Trefusis leaned back to me and confided, "Your eyes, sweet child, hang out for all to see like the globes on a pawn shop."

Reaching her side, Dr. Trefusis engaged in a low bow, saying, "Mademoiselle, may I present to you Private Octavian Nothing of Boston." And to me he said, "Miss Nsia Randolph of Chesterfield County, Virginia. Lately cast off the name of Sarah."

I had wits sufficient about me to bow; and then stood and regarded the girl, who regarded me.

I knew not what to say.

"Real pleased, sir," she said demurely.

Dr. Trefusis smiled upon both of us.

"You . . . sing," said I, "with great skill and beauty."

Miss Nsia lowered her head.

So we stood.

I am not unschooled in the arts of gallantry, but my lessons were administered through observation rather than practice; and I found myself unpossessed of even the slightest article of sense. I cast about for topics, and found none sufficient; ransacked my wits, but seized on no jot worth speaking; and feared that at any moment, she should turn back to the entertainment and so show her disregard for my person.

She did not turn away, however; and I could not.

After a silence had elapsed, Dr. Trefusis reported, "Private Nothing plays upon the violin." Dr. Trefusis personated a violinist, sawing upon the air. He looked upon me with eyes of encouragement.

She nodded and said, "You play fiddle?"

"Yes," I said.

To this, Dr. Trefusis added, "He speaks Latin and Greek as he were a gentleman of antiquity." This made, as might be expected, little impression.

"You is a soldier, sir?" she asked.

"Indeed," said I.

She hummed a note and nodded; and I, over-awed at her dignity, could not speak another word.

At this uncomfortable juncture, I perceived with no little confusion that Bono watched us, grinning a wide, jackanapes smile;

which cajolery threw me into more distress. I hardly knew whether I breathed.

"Splendid," said Dr. Trefusis. "I shall leave you two to twitter as you will."

At this, a panic struck me, and, he bowing to remove himself, I bowed too, and said it had been a pleasure to meet her, retreating after Dr. Trefusis, stumbling over the legs of the crowd.

He at length recognized that I followed him still, and turned. I was struck by his face, which was not so much surprised as disappointed to see me. Still, he nodded and walked on, back to our perch beside Bono.

Bono had seen the entirety of the transaction.

"She," he said, as I settled beside him, "is a very fair nymph indeed."

I did not appreciate his air of connoisseurship. "Her voice is of exquisite quality," I said. "Not simply the *coloratura,* though there is a lightness to it, but some of the duskier corners of it, a softness not so much—"

"I heard," said Bono, "when it gets real low, you can hear all of the intimacies of the mouth."

To this impertinence, I did not wish to reply.

"Her tongue," he said. "You can feel the back of her tongue all rise up—hm?—and all those secret spaces in the cheeks. Which makes a man think about the whole mouth and lips."

At this grossly familiar observation, I was, I must own, not devoid of considerable anger toward my friend, agitated by a frustration at his coarseness, his knowing indelicacy; that I could treasure the sound of her and the sight, and wish to approach her so worshipfully; and he instead reduce the balladry of her ancient kingdom to the indecencies of desire—this galled—and I wished to speak against him, but could not, for fear of him.

He asked me, "What you say to her?"

I could not reply.

He nodded. "I see. Ball lodged in the breech, sir?" he asked. And having thus spake, he could not forbear, but fell to laughing, laughing at me, laughing at his own idiotic jest—repeating it ("Ball lodged in the breech!")—laughing at my disapproval, at my timidity; at the depth of my discomfort.

I burned with shame.

I was not sorry when I was called above for midwatch.

The women soon filed out and were rowed back to the *Dunluce,* Dr. Trefusis and the girl among them.

Pacing the length of the quarterdeck, I thought upon things I could have asked Mademoiselle Nsia: the provenance of the songs and their meanings, who had taught them her. I clasped my hands and blew upon them and watched the shore for activity.

It was a dark night and cold. On other ships, lanterns burned; on one of them, anchored far down the river, the singing of another company continued for some time. Rough voices, thin as an insect's whine, were cast across the black river, the dark town, the shapes of ships on the water. There seemed a great distance to it, as could never be gained by skiff or tender; and yet it filled all of that silent landscape, and so was not lost to the night.

December 24th, 1775

All hands to cleaning our firearms today, in readiness against an inspection by the Captain.

The word came also that Command hath sent to the shore to demand provisions, so many going hungry in the fleet; and that the rebels hath refused to supply us at any price; and hath furthermore requested, "that if His Lordship must indulge in midnight orgies with his Negroes, that he at least forbid the wretches to sing, as it disturbs the town and frights the cattle."

For this great feast, so nettlesome to the Puritans of my own town, so celebrated by the pious of this, we ate starvation rations. The quality of the pork was not excellent, but we ate with great stomach for any morsel.

Pomp hath informed us that at midnight on Christmas Eve, the animals are reputed to speak, as they did around the manger.

"Tonight I going lay awake," he said. "And listen."

"I wonder," said I, "what Vishnoo would say, could he speak."

Pomp said, "I reckon it'd be 'I wish them roaches would stop their whining. My old guts sound like a Baptist prayer-meeting.'"

Slant did not at first understand the jest; Pomp explained, "The roaches, they talk too, then. In Vishnoo's stomach."

Slant's expression was intermixed with discomfort; he protested, "Vishnoo, he don't eat a thing that talks to him. No one eats a thing that . . . begs."

Pomp, sensible of our friend's more delicate sentiments, rushed to soothe: "No, not on Christmas Eve, Slant. No wise."

"Peace on earth, goodwill among men," said I.

Said Pomp, "Christmas Eve, those roaches all hold their little stick-hands in around with Vishnoo, and he ask after their auntie and they ask after his brother, and then it's toddies and then everybody together sing 'Wassail.'"

OH LORD, Thou who wert born amidst the wretched of this earth, Thou who didst not disdain the lowly shed, and who madest those of common degree Thy dearest servants, have mercy upon us in our troubles. Grant us Thy blessings in our endeavors of the coming year. If from Thy Throne in Heaven Thou canst peer down into this sublunary world, pity our distresses; and we shall serve Thee with gladness and singleness of heart; we shall rejoice all the days of our lives. Thou wert first a human child on this day; I beg Thee, now look upon us with childish compassion.

Prosper Thou the work of our hands, we beg Thee: Prosper Thou it.

AMEN.

[Letter from General George Washington to Richard Henry Lee of Virginia]

Cambridge
December 26, 1775

Dear Sir:

Your favour of the 6th instant did not reach this place till Saturday afternoon. The money which accompanied it came seasonably, but not, as it was so long delayed, *quantum sufficit,* our demands at this time being peculiarly great for pay and advance to the troops; pay for their arms and blanketing, independent of the demands of the Commissary and Quartermaster-General.

Lord Dunmore's letters to General Howe, which very fortunately fell into my hands, and were enclosed by me to Congress, will let you pretty fully into his diabolical schemes. If, my dear sir, that man is not crushed before Spring, he will become the most formidable enemy America has. His strength will increase as a snow-ball, by rolling, and faster, if some expedient cannot be hit upon to convince the slaves and servants of the impotency of his designs. You will see by his letters what pains he is taking to invite a reinforcement, at all events, there, and to transplant the war to the Southern Colonies. I do not think that forcing his Lordship on ship-board is sufficient.

Nothing less than depriving him of life or liberty will secure peace to Virginia, as motives of resentment actuate his conduct to a degree equal to the total destruction of the Colony. . . .

My best respects to the good family you are in, and to your brothers of the delegation; and be assured that I am, dear sir, your most obedient and affectionate servant,

George Washington

Starvation rations. There is word that a great fever is broken out on other ships.

Last night, shots and bombardment. A sailor informed us that the enemy fired upon the *Otter* sloop-of-war and that fire was returned from the six- and nine-pounders.

This day, the rebels again changed guard full in sight of our fleet, as if to mock us for our inactivity; they paraded with their hats hung on their bayonets. There is word that our Command hath sent an ensign ashore under flag of truce and issued an ultimatum: that the enemy must cease mustering their illicit guard within sight of the King's forces or suffer destruction.

We have heard of no answer.

I look upon the shore, which is but some four hundred yards distant, and it seems an infinite distance, as if we shall never cross that little space of water; as if we shall never change our state, but shall remain here in this clamorous, reeking hold for eternity, reduced to maddening idleness when all the country is roused for us or against us, waiting for alteration.

Greek Zeno and Parmenides, saith Dr. Trefusis, claimed that there was no change nor motion; fire an arrow at a target, reasoned Zeno, and it can never get there, for it must travel half the way, and then half that distance, then half that distance, and again, and again; so that there shall always be an increment of space between the arrow-tip and target. So do I feel here upon this ship; that even did we open fire with our artillery upon the shore, that the grapeshot should move with infinite halving through the air, endless division, never arriving, always suspended.

At the close of our lesson on Locke, Dr. Trefusis, who must needs catch the ferry back with the washerwomen to the *Dunluce,* observed with some concern, "You do not speak when Pro Bono is by."

I replied that Pro Bono was my elder, and I felt it unseemly to speak when my betters were conversing.

"That is no matter," said Dr. Trefusis. "In Boston at the Widow Platt's, you and I gabbled away the hours. Now you seem silent again, like that frightened youth I was acquainted with at the College, before he escaped and commenced a life of hazard. Where is your spirit of some months ago?"

I replied, "Perhaps I have not changed as you thought I had. Perhaps nothing changes, and there is no such thing as change nor motion."

"When Diogenes the Cynic heard, in a debate, that there was no such thing as change nor motion, he refuted the charge by walking about the stage during his opponent's speech, waggling his legs."

"I was mistaken in the notion that I was become a man; I am still a child."

"Octavian, we none of us reach manhood," said Trefusis. "That is the great secret of men. We aim for manhood always and always fall short. But my boy, I have seen you reach at least half way."

December 31ˢᵗ, 1775

A bitter frost. We have head-ache from double rations of rum and half-rations of beef. We hear a few scattered shots upon the water but none know what it signifies.

'Tis said that, should the rebels be bold enough to muster just once more upon the wharves, we shall launch an attack upon Norfolk and level it; the slave-driving rascals have received fair warning. Our commanders have days ago informed them of this determination.

Everyone knows this is the eve of assault: Those on watch say that they have seen great caravans of refugees fleeing from the invested town with carts piled high and wagons full of effects. The streets, say they, are full of bustle and flight. The shops close and there is an end to all commerce. Both sides, it seems, now ready themselves for the ultimatum to be touched off by new shew of rebel impertinence, and for the desolation to commence.

As I write this, the four Coromantees in our Company are gathered in a circle, chanting their prayers or praise-songs, telling tales of valor from their kingdoms, which ritual is conducted to prepare them for battle.

On the morrow, we all know, rebel and soldier alike, that the rebel shall muster with impudence; and we shall invade; and the battle shall be joined.

We are ready to play our parts.

January 4th, 1776

At three o'clock on the afternoon of January 1st, the new year 1776 hardly commenced, the rebels infesting Norfolk saw fit to muster their sham army upon the docks of that beleaguered town in the plain sight of the floating army of their rightful Sovereign; and shortly before four of the clock, as solemnly promised, our ships opened their full battery upon the shore, cannons blasting, and the battle for Norfolk commenced.

Below-decks, we formed as best we could in straitened space and umbrageous darkness. Though the *Crepuscule* was armed with but sixteen guns, the noise of their detonation was great, and as we labored to stand in the darkness, cannon blasts quaked the whole ship from strake to stringer.

We having no chaplain to confer benedictions, Private Isaac, the pious carpenter, performed that service; he reciting, in voice hoarse with emotion:

"'O give thanks unto the Lord of lords:
    for his mercy endureth forever.
To him that smote Egypt in their firstborn:
    for his mercy endureth forever.
And brought out Israel from among them;
    for his mercy endureth forever.
To him which divided the Red Sea into parts and made
    Israel to pass through the midst of it:
    for his mercy endureth forever.
But overthrew Pharoah and his host in the Red Sea:
    for his mercy endureth forever.'"

The smell of the powder and smoke bit in the air; the battle lay across my tongue already; I could taste its iron, and I wished to chew.

> "'To him which smote great kings:
>   for his mercy endureth forever.
> And slew famous kings:
>   for his mercy endureth forever.
> Sihon king of the Amorites:
>   for his mercy endureth forever.
> And Og the king of Bashan:
>   for his mercy endureth forever. . . .'"

From all about, the roar of cannons and shouts of orders reached our ears; the water itself which nestled the hull spake of the battle.

Within me, anger: thinking on the mockery of the black-guards on the docks, the fleering of the mob, the calumnies of burgesses; thinking on the self-love of grinning old white men with their watches on quaint fobs, and the tortures of the innocent, the gleeful pursuit of profit without concern, without benevolence, the pious preaching of lies — thinking of these, I could not abide any longer our cramped hold — and wished us loosed upon our enemy, a chance to strike a blow.

We issued forth upon the quarterdeck, and were treated to our first sight of the bombardment. The ships of the line blasted without cease and without opposition at the quays; the noise and commotion cannot be described; the air was thick and convulsive with explosion. The *Dunmore,* rigged and coursed with smoke like some spirit vessel, cast volleys of flame through its entanglements of cloud, and all its gray was incarnadined with fire.

On the shore, shot punched holes in walls; docks staggered; and as we boarded our launches, we perceived figures retreating among the chaos and confusion of the piers.

Our orders were thus: Under cover of a hot fire from the ships, we were to land, that we might burn and reduce to ashes the warehouses and stores closest to the water all along the wharves of the town, depriving the shirtmen of their wonted lairs, their posts for the commission of continued defiance. We were to do no more than destroy these haunts for snipers; this done, our work was complete; the docks should be secure; we were to return and await further orders. The rebels would be scourged from their roosts and out of range of the ships. We might then retake the town at our leisure. Norfolk should be ours again.

"An we meet with resistance in the brenning," said Craigie, "give ye na quarter—open fire. Y'art valiant men, and cam thus far; the likes of ye are not quick to submit now to the spite of the enemy and their snash. Make His Lordship proud of the Regiment that bear his name. Brave billies—brave!"

"Here's your moment, boys," called Serjeant Clippinger, unwilling for his exhortation to be surpassed by his own corporal's. "Aye, brave! Let's serve them dogs a dinner they deserve!"

We clambered down to the transports, and with mouths set and oars in our hands, we faced the docks and the enemy.

We drew upon the oars. The warm mist of assault crept across the waters and involved us, piling down from ship decks and gun ports, mountainous, sharp with fume. We swayed on the launches and rowed unsmiling toward shore as shell and carcass shot flew far over our heads.

Through the smoke we saw other launches put in from other brigs and sloops slipping toward the embattled docks. Soldiers sat with arms at ready.

The air beat with detonations like a heart.

"To him who remembered us in our low estate:
  for his mercy endureth forever.
And hath redeemed us from our enemies:
  for his mercy endureth forever.
O give thanks unto the Lord our God:
  for his mercy endureth forever."

On the *Dunmore,* I supposed, stood His Lordship, surveying the battle; he who had said *he would make us proud to serve him;* and indeed, I wished to prove His Lordship had made no error in freeing us; I desired us to demonstrate to all the world — the callous and the snide — that there was greater profit in sending us forth than in shackling us below. My choler was so risen, I longed for nothing more than confrontation; my fingers demanded engagement.

Our fleet of small craft being almost come to the docks, the fire from the ships ceased. A strange stillness prevailed over the scene as the stentorian thunder of bombardment yielded to the minuscule cries and commands of distant voices. We could hear sharp as raps the lapping of waves against our gunwales. There were blasts from an invisible horn and the rattle of drums.

Marines sat in the bow of our launch to provide covering fire while we disembarked; which precaution seemed of little utility, for the docks were now empty of all enemies. Come to the city pier, we stepped forth upon enemy soil and charged our muskets.

In the square there by the docks, we formed, an operation carried out not without some error, we being little acclimated to the choreography of street-fighting. Having so arrayed ourselves, we made our way along the pier, where others of our Regiment and the 14th were clambering up from the river.

We proceeded along the street, marching warily to avoid the assaults of guile unmoved by the fear of bombardment; the shops and warehouses to either side of us were evidently deserted. A dog ran before us.

Arriving at a bend in the embankment, we entered into the first warehouse there, a storehouse for some chandlery, and began setting it to flames, touching our brands to cordage and hogsheads. The rope received the flame greedily; the transports of greed were succeeded by the profligacy of utmost generosity; and soon the whole store partook.

In the next shop, empty of goods, there were signs of recent habitation by the shirtmen: blankets and mattresses laid upon the floor, clothing deposited in a corner, and recent ashes on the grate. Bono, Will, and I stood with our muskets at ready while the others lit the place afire with their burning torches.

Stepping back into the street, we could survey our handiwork in the first warehouse, which now blazed well from its windows, pouring black smoke toward the sky, the heat considerable even at a distance of some forty feet.

[273]

We passed over some smaller buildings, they lying in the lee of the burning buildings, and thus fated soon enough to catch fire; having passed them by, we entered a third warehouse, the roof of which was considerably compromised by the late passage of cannonballs — the peak blown off and the rafters visible. From without, through windows and a door ajar, we could see that the chambers of the place were in great disorder, some of the loft having collapsed to the floor.

We entered — heard a crack — and found ourselves fired upon.

That noise — and the true peril of our situation — it darted through my arms — I presented my gun — saw a muzzle, and fired.

I trembled; ducked.

He was dead, the shirtman; a man of about thirty, now bleeding from the cheek.

Three had fired; I was one among three.

It was then, observing the bloody face, that I took the measure of what had transpired: that we had encountered a bearded white man lying awkwardly upon a broken staircase, his leg crushed in the bombardment when the building was struck — a final stand, then, for one unable to flee; that he had fired his one shot, which went awry; that he had then known he should not have time to reload — cried out some name — which I could not recall — wife, perhaps, or child; that he had closed his eyes and averted his head as we fired back upon him, three muskets; one of which had sped.

I was not sensible then of the rebukes of remorse; nor am I now. I thought only of the muzzle trained upon me, and my response, which was requisite.

But I felt a soft hand upon my shoulder as I stood guard while the room was searched. "Your first kill," said Bono to me gently, with an air of kindness and a cadence of mollification. "One generous habit of a volley: You never know if it was your bullet or some other body's did the deed."

I regarded him with impassivity, I believe; for he wished me to be sorrowful, to wince at some degradation; but I was aware of no sentiment of horror. I felt, I suppose, a rage tall and consuming as the fires we set.

He continued, without need, "Don't regret it, Prince O. It was him or us."

"My only regret," I replied, "is that he left behind a musket rather than a rifle, which would have been a greater prize." I took a pleasure in Bono's startlement, his wariness.

We did not tarry, but Charles, who is ever practical in his considerations, swept in to secure the man's musket and powder horn. As he pulled the gun from the man's hands, Better Joe berated him in their own tongue, over some protocol or gesture necessary for quieting a murdered enemy.

Charles gave him a look of disdain and turned back to robbing the dead. Then Charles and Pomp lit the staircase on fire, and we left the man to burn upon this bier.

Thus my first kill.

We emerged from the warehouse to find our previous two conflagrations active.

Now in the outer air, a thought passed fleeting through my skull: *that I was so tender-hearted I could not bear to see Slant Croak upset at Christmas tales — but that I had now perhaps killed a man —* and yet there was no disagreement of temperaments. I did not feel disordered nor divided in the least.

Farther along the street, a detachment fired upon a house. The air was thick with smoke.

We proceeded back toward the dock. Two cats ran along the street, fleeing from the general destruction. Along the avenue, our drummer beat out commands, but we could not hear them sufficiently amidst the chaos. We heard the screams of a horse.

It was first down a side-alley that we saw more flame.

This spectacle arrested us with its strangeness; for the landing parties had been ordered to fire merely the docks and buildings by the water, not the town itself.

But we had no opportunity to deliberate upon it. We continued in our commanded destruction: We halted again to set fire to a shop, this time touching our brands to the exterior.

A detachment ran past us, shouting without reason.

Our work complete, the row of buildings all along the riverfront given over to flame, we returned to our landing and stood in formation, awaiting the order to embark. We could see that other portions of the town were indeed afire, some well inland. Corporal Craigie ordered us back into the launch.

When our other detachment appeared, they took their places; we pushed off from the shore and rowed toward the *Crepuscule*.

Now removed from the theater of action, we could survey the whole prospect of our assault; and it was then that we fully recognized the oddity of those flames commenced in the heart of the town.

I feared at first that the wind had shifted, and that our conflagration had, despite our precautions, spread inward; but it was the matter of a glance to see that these flames which now arose well away from the river bore no connection to those of our setting.

"Someone fired the houses," I said. "The roofs are burning."

"Some fool," said Bono, "don't understand orders. We want to take the town, not burn it down."

So we thought. But no sooner had we gained the *Crepuscule* than we heard word from one of the topmen of the true case — unutterable — astounding to believe.

"I seen it," said the sailor. "From the royal yardarm. It's the rebel." The man squinted at shore. "The rebel's firing the town."

It was beyond comprehension; but this was indeed the truth: The rebels themselves were taking up our work and destroying Norfolk.

We stood bewildered on deck after deck of that irregular fleet — brigs and schooners, sloops and barges, frigates, grand yachts and lowly ketches — soldiers and sailors, families fled from the town, husbands with their arms around their wives watching their homes burn — we all observed the spread of flame.

"Fools," said Bono in wonder. "There are some utter fools. I say, let them burn up the town. Let them burn it all up into atoms. When word of this is spread wide — they sack a whole city for no reason on God's earth — then some eyes, they are going to open. People got to realize that His Lordship has a few good words to say about lawlessness and treason and how we has to restore order. And maybe people, they will finally see what species of criminal is parading through the streets, calling theyselves friends of liberty."

We were ordered below. For an hour, we remained there. At that time, we received word that we were to return to land that we might bring off such stores and victuals as remained, and attempt to halt the destruction by the rebels; which we knew was, at that advanced hour, mere futility.

Being called to stand to arms again, we rose, stooping, and took up our muskets. Danger passed, we had accustomed ourselves to retirement for the night at least; and now that hazard was renewed, our spirits struggled with sensations of dread and doubt at what we should find in that uncertain scene of destruction.

Still, we embarked again and rowed toward the flame.

☙ Thus we landed, and entered the inferno.

The structures along the river were now nought but torrents of fire, liquid and rushing; whatever features as remained — lintels, doorframes, and roof-trees — were sketched with dark charcoal smudges in the midst of red activity. The city pier and square, however, afforded a place still for landing parties, and 'twas there we disembarked, formed, and began our mystified sortie. We progressed up past the Market House.

The streets were empty but of broken glass; the sky was black.

By the mast pond, where the great spars of ships lay refracted, we saw a little girl with a bucket, a vain and minute assay at extinguishing the flames. She looked upon our detachment with sullen terror as we marched by.

We crossed the Catherine Street Bridge to the more populous part of town, which now appeared without inhabitant. Watching for resistance, alert with alarums, we progressed past silent residences.

In some streets where no fire had yet reached, doors were ajar and windows smashed, prey to the depredations of rebel greed and the exercise of wrath.

In other avenues, there was no sign of the sack; gardens were unmolested; it had been any Monday morning, were the air not alive with insect ash, and were there a sun in the sky; were the sky above us not black; were there not a look of Judgment and the End.

❦ We heard shots and made our way swiftly to the site of battle, finding a detachment of Marines engaged in volleys with four or five shirtmen who had been surprised in their looting; the shirtmen took refuge behind their carts of pilfered fine furniture.

Our arrival was not unseasonable, we issuing forth to the side of the conflict, so we might outflank the enemy. We fired upon them, and the closest of their number collapsed.

His companion turned to us with surprise — having not hitherto detected us — and screamed, "God damn you, filthy Negro brutes!" and discharged his rifle at us.

Private Jocko gave forth a grunt — collapsed — and the smoke of combat twined with that of arson. I recall my terror — spilling the powder upon my hand —

We reloaded—they reloaded—only fifteen feet between us. Again we fired—one was hit—he swore, bent low—and we began again to load.

I trembled as I tore a cartridge with my teeth; but our antagonist and his friends, outnumbered and outflanked, were beating a retreat, ducked low, into an alley. We got off another round, but it did no damage.

Corporal Craigie was full of urgency and outrage, demanding which of us knew the science of *tying a bloody tourniquet, ilk of ye— by God, the man was dying while we gaped.*

None of us was possessed of this necessary skill—and all of us regarded each other with astonishment until Corporal Craigie began calling names and orders—adding, "By God, the villains are escaping"—demanding the rest of us rush forward to harry them and bring them back prisoners.

By his order, three soldiers remained behind with Jocko to claim the crossroads while the rest of us formed (we having lapsed into some confusion) and at a trot rushed after the enemy through the alley.

The Marines sought also our adversary; they were fast upon our heels, letting forth fearsome cries.

Come to the next street—a broad avenue with no commerce now in it—we saw that the rebels had turned in their course to flee off to the left, and we pursued them, grim in the knowledge that if we allowed them time to load their rifles, they should make unhappy work of us.

One more street passed, and we had lost them; the Captain of the Marine company called to Corporal Craigie and demanded that we divide two lanes between us.

To this, our Corporal complied. With some apprehensions of our hazard, we marched between houses.

The lane was of no great width, unpaven, and was filled with smoke. We passed down it with care.

We came upon an old woman sitting in her garden in a wash-tub like Diogenes. She was clothed, her dress soaked from the water in which she had sunk herself; she wore a calash upon her head.

She berated us with a steady stream of invective and imprecation for as long as she could see us; calling us murderers, barbarians, and every other name she could devise; informing us that she should be safe in her tub when we were burned to cinders.

We left her by her withered hollyhocks and sought onward.

❧ Through gardens hushed, past vacant houses we marched, and each blank window filled us with alarms.

The only sounds which came to the ear were flames, from which a continual haze was thrown.

"De'il ta'e their damn impertinence," swore our Corporal; and we had almost give up the chase and returned to our fallen comrade when the smoke along the street for one moment lifted; and we saw the enemy detachment marching unaware past, one block along.

We did not have to be told; but as Corporal Craigie hissed, we lowered our muzzles—and, his signal given, fired.

There was a great noise of shot, but none hit; and they turned, startled, and fired at us—as we struggled to reload.

The smoke blew past.

They rebel dogs were gone, as were they fetched away by sorcery.

The Marines rushed before us on the cross-street, following upon the rebels' heels.

We stood in confusion; and might have continued in that way for longer, had not a door thrown itself open, and a rebel appeared before us.

❦ He was of the militia, and had a musket hanging upon his shoulder. Back to the street, he yanked a handsome clothes press out a door and conducted it, thumping, down the building's brick steps. He looked about him, saw no friend — saw he was abandoned — saw only the muskets of direst enemy — smiled, and offered to sell us the clothes press for a guinea.

Corporal Craigie demanded he lay down his arms.

The rebel said, "You ain't going to find excellenter workman-ship, boys, for that sum, a guinea. Look'ee, pray, see the dove-tailing of the joinery. Give it your eye."

We bid him submit to his King.

"Boys, that ain't here nor there. I'll take an even pound sterling, in the light of circumstance. Look'ee, sirs, fine as Hepplewhite and Hay."

We presented our bayonets.

The rebel nodded sadly; then gestured back at the house from which he had just issued forth. "There's a fire-screen painted with wigwams I ain't stole yet that I'd be willing to part with for a skip and song. A master's brush."

Bono stepped forward to bind the man's arms.

"But mayhaps," said the man, "you ain't fanciers of true quality."

We tied his wrists together.

Corporal Craigie posed interrogation: "Who set the fires?"

"You did, as I reckon."

"Who set the fires?"

"You did, my Scottish love."

"On thir street, man. Who set the fires?"

"Look at your own hands."

At a nod from Corporal Craigie, Charles held his bayonet to the man's neck.

The Corporal asked again, "Who set the fires?"

The rebel answered, "When a man sits starving and he watch the citizens of a town lick His Lordship's black arsehole like a cur with hopes for stroking, a man starts to resent their flattery and groveling, and maybe if a man sees His Lordship's going to light a little fire, a man reckons, *Maybe as I should light a little fire myself.*"

"Vauntie birke, ye are," said Corporal Craigie.

"A man reckons, *Here's a little payment for all the time we spent waiting around our fire-pits Christmas Day.* A man reckons, *Here's showing Norfolk our high opinion of people who don't love their country-men as much as they love despotism.* A man reckons, *I'm drunk and I don't care a fig.* A man reckons, *We do this, and we ain't going to get the blame anyways. Because Lord Dunmore, Governor of the Negroes, started the burning. So when they say, 'Who burned Norfolk?' ain't nobody going to answer nothing but, 'Lord Dunmore and his Ethiopian Regiment.'* Welcome, boys, to the annals of tyranny."

The Corporal ordered we should gag him; and gladly we did, to stop up such filth.

Corporal Craigie ordered we should return to the square where we had left Jocko dying, and the others of our detachment.

We turned about, two guarding the prisoner. He stepped along, jovial of eye. The flames were reflected on the quick of it.

Thus arrayed, we returned to our fallen companion.

✤ The flames now were more impudent in their motion, and one street was impassable for them. We arrived back at the square with all possible expedition, our nerves in no settled state.

One of our number stood guard there, while two of the other soldiers had busied themselves in binding Jocko's wound and preparing room for him on the rebels' abandoned cart; which conveyance was emptied now of all but some sacks of grain and a few hogsheads of dried fish.

We coming to them, Private Harrison rushed forward to greet his grievously wounded friend, calling, *"Jocko! Jocko!"* But it was evident to all of us that Jocko could not hear himself hailed; that he was wandering already upon the foothills of a country where there are no names.

Corporal Craigie stood above the wounded man; cried, "He's all over his sark!"; and asked if any among us knew better how to bind.

Months ago, I applied a tourniquet to Dr. Trefusis after letting him blood; a scene which does not speak impressively of my skill in this art; but now I stepped forward and offered to tighten the bloody sash tied about Jocko. Bono and I did what we could, the first desideratum being rum, which we poured between his lips; the second being a steady hand in retying the cloth, which operation I undertook as the insensible patient twitched.

The strip of stuff had not been placed well atop the wound, and I shifted it so that his belly would be better gripped. I feared my inadequacies; supplicated Bono to yank tighter, which he squatted and did. Jocko's head lolled, and I could not but recall that awful vision, the insensate head of the dead sniper upon the stairs, cheek pierced by our musket-fire.

We bound Jocko as best we could. The wound was deep, however, and he bled copiously; his breath was weak, his eye empty. We lay him upon the cart, tied the prisoner's rope to the axle, and drew them along after us in our dismal parade.

We quitted the scene, leaving behind us a toppled parlor on the dirt street, table flung with arms wide, clock facedown, chairs jumbled on the ground.

☥ So our march continued.

We came upon a church on fire. The impious wretches had lit the house next to it, and now the steeple burned fiercely. The portal gaped, and a congregation of flames issued forth.

We came upon a carriage abandoned in the street, the door open, a horse dead before it.

We came upon a gown in the road. The arms were spread, beseeching.

✤ At a place where three roads met, we came upon a father huddled with wife and three daughters; the father placed his body between us and the girls. When we challenged them, the man sobbed, "God save the King . . . please you . . . or whatsoever . . ."

We left them where they stood.

We came upon a mad dog which growled, then ran at us; Slant flinched, but Pomp jabbed at it with his bayonet until, it skipping and leaping, the dog was impaled, and collapsed; and we marched on.

We came upon a street that was a scene out of the infernal regions, each house afire, a lane where demonic citizens might walk, capes black, bonnets bulging, baskets filled with mewling roots.

There was no passing down it; the flames billowed from each side.

We came upon a another detachment of rebels espied down a far street, obscured by smoke. They fired upon us; we returned their volley. When the clouds cleared, they were disappeared.

We came upon a fire engine in a neighborhood of flame.

The tank was empty of water. Two men, blackened with soot, sat upon the wheels, and smoked pipes. They did not bestir themselves for us, but watched as we passed, dragging our cart, Jocko motionless behind us on his berth.

❧ Whichsoever way we turned seemed to be flame. The houses were consumed; the bricks of houses still standing were blackened; the air so thick with soot that we now all coughed and gagged at every step.

From every side, the roar of conflagration; the air was mobile with sparks and gentle black ghosts of ash. We feared for our powder.

All was acrid — down side-alleys, vistas of flame — walls collapsed — steeples burned — trees were reduced to hands of fire, plucking at the roofs — a distillery or magazine exploded distantly with a great roar —

Down a street, a detachment of the 14th marched, their red coats rippling in the scarlet heat.

And we stood at the center, so it seemed; black men, blackened cart; white, smudged prisoner and officer; viewing the world turned to fire.

✦ Heraclitus believed that all the universe was fire, a conflagration never doused; and the Collegians in some wise agreed — speaking of the subtle fluids, the atomies and energies, that made up matter; and standing there upon the street, how could one believe otherwise?

I could not determine what was darkness and what was light; but all was energy, as if each stable thing had given up its wonted solidity; for matter itself rippled; light melted and ran; and we were not solid, but our bones themselves were energies, involved ever in exchange; our skin spat forth its superficies; a face, burst with musket-ball, bled; a body on a cart loosed its spirit; and we were bombarded always by the æther.

"From a fire which never dies nor sinks, how should one escape?" asks Heraclitus — and so I felt then — for all around me was the buzzing of that energy — as Mr. Sharpe's foul image of a universal

use—all things engaged in the devouring of each other—and I thought, never shall the woodland seem like woodland—never shall pasture hum with bucolic quiet again—but only the cicada-call of frying—as all objects seek their stoking, their fuel—striving against one another—man to wrest nutrient from animal, animal from herb, grass from the sun—the center still of our system—that vast body, profligate of energy—which we struggle to imbibe, and kill to enjoy. There is no respite, no surcease; for we are always burning, always absorbing—sparks flaring briefly in this vast system of need and theft, this insubstantial latticework of flame, this tireless inferno, this monstrous riot, where all, at last, are consumed.

> *"There is exchange of all things for fire and of fire for all things, as there is of wares for gold and of gold for wares."*

We stumbled forward with our cart, our prisoner, our dying friend in arms.

♀ I was roused from my reverie by the sound of a drum commanding retreat.

We had, previous to this, directed our steps back toward the quays, we being sensible that the town was become ever more treacherous as the flames spread, and there should be fewer and fewer routes that could be followed to safety. Thus, it was a matter of only some five or six streets until we reached the main square on the waterfront, where stood our colors and the Regimental drummer, who resolutely beat our retreat.

We delivered our prisoner and the stores we had collected to our Lieutenant and boarded our transport. Jocko was removed to the hospital ship.

All that night, the city of Norfolk burned. At some hour, I awoke to the sound of the cannonade renewed; others slumbered still, clutching their heads to impede the sounds of detonation.

In the dark of the early morning, I rose and went above-decks to watch the city's continued destruction. On the town's far rim, the enemy still rejoiced in lighting their fires, still drank and looted, whatever their officers might forbid in word; for oft the commission in the word is not the order in the eye; and officers of angry men may wink at much. The town cast its light across the water, the ruddy embers slipping across the waves. All smelled of smoke.

The *Dunmore* hurled more carcass shot at the broken wharves.

I returned to my bed.

Thus ended the first day of the year 1776.

[VII.]

MOTHERLAND

═══════════

drawn from the
Nautical Diary of
Private *Octavian Nothing*

────────

If Buttercups buzzed after the Bee,
If Boats were on Land, and Churches on Sea,
If Ponies rode Men, and the Grass ate the Cow, . . .
Then All of the World would be turned upside down,
Down, derry down.
Then All of the World would be turned upside down.

— Traditional

❧ For three days, Norfolk burned. After a time, the fires were more isolate in their devouring; the town presented a spectacle of black chimney-stacks and scorched ruin as far as eye could see.

Lone shirtmen crouched upon the shore, firing at the fleet, then falling upon their bellies and disappearing before there could be answer to their impertinence. The great billows of smoke veiled their audacity.

At night, we might still hear them reveling in the ruins, disgraced by drink. They shouted in the burnt alleys.

Now the town hath fallen silent.

Over all hangs the cold brume of char, drifting across the water, lying still upon the decks of ships.

We go about our business in the sight of the desolation. The column of smoke does not break, but hovers above the city, as above the Cities of the Plain when smote for their sins.

There is much speculation, as might be imagined, as to whether we shall remain at Norfolk, now that it is razed, or whither we might go. If our officers have heard of the approach of troops sent down from Boston, or the march of our Indian allies to the north, gathered into war-parties to aid us in this our uneasy situation, they have not seen fit to tell us of this glad news. We await word of our next movement; none comes.

Men, when they speak, speak bitterly. Several tug at the stitching upon their shirts—*Liberty to Slaves*—which they believed talismanic, as the inscriptions of the African *mallam*s are said to protect against all injury. They complain that they think ill of Lord Dunmore's skill at sorcery.

The *Crepuscule* is becoming sickly. Several of our men have taken fevers, afflicted with some distemper which fell on the other ships and now visits itself upon ours. We await word of Jocko, but fear that he hath met his final reward. We tend our sick as best we can.

We sleep heartily both by day and by night.

January 5th, 1776

We cannot rid ourselves of the stench of smoke. There is little talking in our dank hold.

Upon Twelfth Night (saith Slant), masters upon plantations here bid their slaves heap the tobacco plots with brush and trash and light the plots on fire; the ground burns all night. The next day, when the ashes have cooled, *you rake the ashes. You rake in you tobacco seed.* Later, when the sprouts have come up and are strong, they are taken from these beds of ash and transplanted, each to its own mound.

Says he of Norfolk: "It's a New Year's . . . burning. You got to burn, to grow."

Quoth Bono grimly, "Glorious, glorious. That is a pretty sentiment."

January 6^{*th*}*, 1776*

Several fellows of our Company were today detached to be taken up the James, that they might secure provisions. We wish them luck.

Several of the women of the *Dunluce* were rowed to our ship this day to call for our laundry, which they propose to beat and boil in the galley of their ship, that it might be rid of the grease and smoke of battle, which contribute not a little to the oppressive fumes of our dark hold.

I record only this fact, *several women come aboard,* but Oh! how much might such an unassuming phrase conceal from the ignorant or convey to he who wrote it; how doth the heart, barely able to wish, sing in such constrained phrases; and how oft doth beaming hope come masked by daily round.

Miss Nsia was in the number of the washerwomen, and, with confusion of humility, came to my side and inquired whether Private Nothing wished his clothes washed; to which I assented gratefully.

Then transpired my confusion, for I wore them, and knew not how with delicacy to change my dress with the ladies present.

She awaited my clothes, and I, without a word — unable to refer with propriety to undress — stood hapless and motionless.

At length, she prompted gently, "If Sir wish his clothes washed, he must needs give them to me in my hand."

"Prince O.," said Bono, coming to my side, "you look like you been slugged with a maul." He bowed to Miss Nsia. "But who wouldn't be stupefied by such charms and excellences?"

Still involved in my perplexity, I exclaimed piteously, *"I am wearing my shirt."*

They both regarded me; after which Bono, who knew not the cause of my consternation, granted cautiously, "That you are, Prince O. Yes, indeed." He explaincd, "This boy is a rare genius, proclaimed by all the gentlemen of Boston. He recognize his own breeches, too."

She smiled; this did I see. Anger flared in my breast at Bono's jesting, for I perceived the glint of the knife-edge in it; and I said, "I am — I apologize, Mademoiselle — I am confounded — I — as to where to change my dress that will not offend."

Bono took my arm and pointed back at some casks, where I saw dim movement. "There's men removing the old garments behind the pork, Prince O. Why don't you repair there and change and I'll engage this fine lady til you return so she don't become listless a-waiting."

I took my leave of them, my breast a welter of shame, longing, and pique; before I was three steps away, I perceived, Bono was already well on his way to introducing a relation of his heroism during the late assault. "Our clothes," he said, "got somewhat fusty in the rebels' little New Year's callithump. They're rowdy boys, and I reckon they knocked down a candle during their celebrations."

He talked on while I retired.

I returning in my old white shirt, with my oznabrig and breeches in my hand, I found the two of them engaged in lively converse.

"So I held my bayonet at his throat, and he submitted," Bono said. "I tied him to the wagon."

I bowed again to announce my return.

Miss Nsia said, "Private Williams been telling me about him and you in the fires. How you tie the bandage for that man."

[305]

"Without expertise, I fear, which might have proved fatal."

"I am sorry," said Miss Nsia. "But you still brave for to try."

"Sweet Saint Pete," exclaimed Bono, "do I see velveteen breeches?"

"I had no other," said I. "'Twas these which I wore when I listed."

Bono commenced to laugh. "Velveteen," said he. "That's fine. That is very fine, Prince O. A city is burning outside, we're on a ship sending over bombs, our artillery been repulsed, the whole town is one big ruin, and our friend, he's dying on the hospital ship—and then comes you, ready for a minuet at Ranelagh." He explained to our lovely companion, "In London. Ranelagh."

"I wore them," said I, "when I played the violin with a band of music in Boston."

Bono could not conceal nor restrain his mirth. "Daintily done! Daintily done!" he said, and Miss Nsia smiled at his horse-laugh.

"I have," said I with dignity, "my garments here, and I thank Miss Nsia for her assiduity in arranging for their washing at a time when to travel between ships is a matter of some hazard."

"Prince O. is a very fine talker, when he talks and don't just stare."

"I am sure he is," said Miss Nsia. "I come here back with the clothes on the morrow, if the boat come."

"You can hope there ain't a sortie tonight, Prince O. Or if there is, you can pirouette after the enemy to fright them."

With this, we bade farewell to the damsel, and were left to each other's company.

"You were not wrong," said Bono. "She is a tearing fine specimen. She got excellent reserve. Not so confounded get-at-able."

His coarseness repelled me; that she who I worshipped as a being almost celestial, whose music had so deeply touched the springs of my being, should in turn be valued by one who could not comprehend her merits, was a matter of strangulating distaste; and I could not bear to be near my friend. There was no place to go, though; no motion possible in that straitened space; and so I was suffered to sit nearby him as he mocked my breeches further and regaled our companions with tales of how I had once been preferred in the College of Lucidity, a tale told with all the trinkets of endearment—"sweet boy," "my friend," "this dear lad"— but conducing only to my shame as I observed Private Harrison's smirk, the merriment of Charles and the others who did not think it cruel, their relief at diversion.

The air still smells of burning.

January 7ᵗʰ, 1776

This day, unwanted idleness. The smoke hath cleared from the ruins of the city; we can perceive small people to be touring the empty lots and shells. It is desolate.

I cannot abide this inaction; surveying the shore, I take each destructive role I might: I wish at once to be soldier and commander; in my fancy, I invade by land and sea; I calculate the angle of artillery and adjust the quoin to fire; I fire musket-volleys; I wish to prove myself against our enemy, to feel them run before us. I vow we shall tear through these scoundrels — and we shall see true liberty unleashed, as hounds strain first, and rush their prey, and then, sated, curl before the fire in utmost docility, twitching and smiling at their dreams.

Jocko is gone from this world. We received word this day that he hath died of his wound. No one wishes to speak of it.

In the midst of a long silence, Will asked our mess *whether, if we win, the slaves down in the Sugar Isles going be freed.* No one ventured a reply. He pursued this dolorous inquiry, asking how one might again find someone shipped off down there. When there was no further response, he laughed without mirth and said that *it was a funny name, the Sugar Isles, because it sound so sweet.*

Again, we none of us could find heart sufficient to answer him.

Little else has transpired. Many on the ship are poorly. They run fevers, and I like not the look of it. The *Crepuscule*'s crew protesting the proximity of the sick, we have dragged the pallets of the afflicted fore. Our Company lie between the fevered and the crew.

We all fear the distemper.

January 8th, 1776

My spirits have been in an impossible ferment, as were they corked.

Two of the women came today to return the clothing removed yesterday. Though Nsia was not among their number, Dr. Trefusis had clamored for a place aboard their skiff, that he might come and inquire after our health and our part in the battle. I narrated its events, not stinting Pro Bono's actions therein. We then read Greek, and it was most welcome: Dr. Trefusis has set me upon the *Voyage of the Argo;* in which I recall those tales of heroism for which my fondness was so great in childhood. To read these ancient episodes is to be returned, as 'twere, to myself; in lost antiquity, I seek my restoration. And so with gratitude did I con out the tales of Jason and his brethren plagued by the screaming race of harpies; or stranded on the infinite beach of Libyan Syrtis; my fancy conjuring up not simply the gray plain, the mist, the ship tilted in soft mud, not simply the scenes of battle, but also my chamber back in Boston, where of an evening, in my childhood, I would sit beside my mother, a fire in the hearth, and dream of spear and claw. They are a gift, these tales, the milk of solace, and he knoweth well who teaches me, that he grants a boon in thus recalling me to former ages.

Pro Bono, however, mocked us when he came down from his exercise on deck, and jested — I recall not what raillery — at our bookishness, that *we were fine gentlemen to be studying at such a time* — this, when he himself and Dr. Trefusis, but a few weeks hence, were waggish in confederation like smirking schoolboys as I looked on.

Dr. Trefusis was, I'll warrant, not unriled by Bono's jests at his expense, and protested with some pride that there were excellent reasons to study the ancient texts in time of war, et cetera; to which Bono replied that he had just apprehended news, would give us little appetite for our dainty repast of Greek tit-bits.

"Which is, sir?" said Dr. Trefusis.

"You told us of an agent who rode up to fetch down the Indians and such? To aid us?"

"One Connolly," said Dr. Trefusis. "Lord Dunmore dispatched him with the highest hopes for his success. He is to gather a force to supplement the—"

"Aye, he been taken."

"What do you mean, 'taken'? By the rebels?"

"By a Funktown hatter."

"I see."

"Man knew his head from hatting. Recognized him. Committee of Safety took him. He was real insolent to them and they threw him in jail. Just heard about it on deck. They're all squawking on the fo'c'sle. Lord Dunmore, he got a letter from him. The agent."

"Connolly."

"Is that the name? Well, it's all up. No one's going to the Indians. The agent's in jail and the rebels has published the whole plan as an example of, you know, perfidy."

Dr. Trefusis scowled and swore. Bono crossed his arms in satisfaction at our discomfiture. My faculties could not encompass the news; for though I was not insensible of our perilous condition, I must own that my thoughts gnawed primarily on Bono's pride in relating disaster, his satisfaction always in *knowing*. My idol wished always to be first in the telling, to regale others with the story in its fullness, from beginning to end, from miller's hut to crown and castle. I considered, my choler rising: He was that nature of personage who, when they laugh, make all who don't laugh feel prim; and when they are solemn, make all who have been laughing sensible of the chill of silence and the feebleness of gaiety. How doth the voice of one determine the pitch of the others!

And so, to my shame, I felt only insolence toward my rival when I should have meditated upon our difficulties, the danger that, without allies, we might be overwhelmed and tried for treason, slain, or sold to the Sugar Isles.

Dr. Trefusis, from the distraction of his countenance, clearly thought on our straights, and found little comfort there.

"We ain't going to yield," said Bono. "You look at the ships — we're a force, sir."

"That you are."

Bono and I both noted the "you"; Bono looked at the philosopher and said, "You'll hang too, sir."

"Indeed." Dr. Trefusis gave a wan smile. "I won't make as fine an ornament as you, though."

"That's the truth. I reckon they're hanging me in effigy right now just so as they can have my face around town more. Special ladies' request. 'Hang that William Williams again. When his eyes bulge out, they seem to look at my very soul.'"

Neither of us laughed at his jest; Dr. Trefusis was sorrowful at the news, while I endured the lashes of irritation as well as, in some confused wise, the murmurs of desperation.

"Gents, I'm sorry I called halt to your boat story. I just reckoned you might like to be apprised that we's alone in this battle with no aid coming and the rebels all around us. Now back to the Greek. I hear it repels grapeshot real fine."

But indeed, we had no stomach for our Greek dainties, once he had delivered his bitter mouthful.

� It is the night. I have lain in my hammock for some hours, my arm within striking distance of Pro Bono, and revolved thoughts of that most provocative of mentors, and how he urges me onwards with leading-strings, and how he tugs me back so I should not toddle too far beyond his ken; and at once, my soul moves its several ways: Indignation, rising hotly from her throne, remonstrates that he acts toward me as one would toward the most incompetent of younger brothers; that his superiority of address can in no way be tolerated —

And then comes soothing Humility — who scolds me — *He treateth thee as an infant because that is what thou art; thou art the least practical of youths, a flimsy, insubstantial thing, little adapted for this world, knowing only the languages of vanished places and the pretty fiddling of idleness, when all around, the kingdom burns.* I might resent his censure; but I deserve it, for I am incapable of action, at best a digger of ditches, at worst, the spoiled poppet he imagines me, unable to speak with my fellow man, viewed by those around us as a prating fool, my speech incomprehensible, my manner stiff; while Bono is possessed of natural charms and social graces to which I never can pretend.

And yet Bono was kind to me in my minority — and yet even his kindness was vanity — and yet he had none of my advantages — and yet — and yet … And so my thoughts ran on as I lay cramped in my hammock; and so they run on now, as I crouch next to the hearth in the galley; as I write huddled here, thinking upon my mentor and tormentor.

January 12th, 1776

Several men, Charles among them, are taken with a fever and a vomit which appear perilous; most so, as they require water at all hours, and we have not as much potable of that necessary element as we might wish, though surrounded by its lapping.

We walk among the sick only when tending them. There is no doctor attached to our Regiment, so we minister as best we can. Better Joe hath suggested some specific remedies, which Isaac the Joiner decries loudly as the cant of heathenish superstition; and indeed, one wonders at the applications of bone.

We none of us can abide too much longer this containment, trapped here as we all eat our diet of galling news and the smoke of ruin.

I cannot abide here longer. I have requested to be sent on one of the foraging parties.

The final sundering came in this way: Dr. Trefusis, hearing word that the sickness was general over the fleet, recommended that the bedding of the sick be washed with more regularity, as the folds of blankets might contain miasmatic gasses and the crumbs of animalcula which contribute to contagion. This proposal met with indifference one way or the other from Major Byrd, the commander of our regiment; but indifference is not condemnation, and once Dr. Trefusis continued in this vein so tirelessly that some of the women who found it not impossible that disease should be caused by beings invisible to the eye took up the cause as well, it was decided to attempt his palliative measures; and so the washerwomen undertook to circulate among the ships and douse the sheets.

Need I say that I greeted with a silent jubilation the return to our ship of Miss Nsia, who had not accompanied the return of my uniform; and that I felt particular pleasure in the opportunity to work at her side aiding the sick, flattering myself that there is no sweeter connection between man and woman than that forged in mutual assistance of another — thus, in my gross vanity, making selflessness but a stage for selfish display. (Foolish heart!)

We helped the sick to their feet, and to them donated our own bedrolls, consenting to go without blankets for one night. Nsia smiled upon me as I spake gently to those laid low, and as I took their hands.

Bono, seeing her present, came to our side, however, greeting us both and proffering his help; and I could not mistake the bashful confusion upon her face at his appearance, the admiration in her eyes at his superior gifts of charm and form, his easiness in his limbs, his settled compact with the world.

It was no surprise that she was taken with him; and yet, it burned in my vitals, as it burns now.

He assumed the bulk of work, speaking more companionably with the men, with Charles than I might, as he was Charles's sworn friend; he clucked at the children and squawked, bringing forth their shy laughter, whereas I could only speak to them gently, but could not make comic sounds, as I am not of a comic disposition. And all of this conduced to convince not simply Miss Nsia of his superiority to me in every way, but me as well. I could not evade it; I was and always would be a lesser man.

The women washed the sheets in the galley and wrung them out, and we hung them to dry upon the rails, so our ship flapped gray in the winter breeze.

Thereafter, the ladies joined our supper by way of payment for their services, and we sat below and held a more somber feast than our last musical festival, before Norfolk had burned.

Our minds were turned, I suppose, to our fates, should our expedition fail, and to the torments that awaited us; and thus our conversation turned upon the dismal subject of punishment. Some told stories of wily crimes which elicited much laughter: slaying a master's goose to get the meat, or theft of pewter trinkets. But most of the tales were grim. Better Joe spake of how, one day out of the Bight of Biafra, there had been an uprising upon the Guinea-man which carried him to the New World; that three men, having coated themselves with a spell that should have ensured invisibility, escaped their chains and attacked the purser; but still were solid to the eye, and were captured; and were then, in the sight of all, decapitated, their bodies and heads thrown from opposite rails of the ship, it being believed that such a death would mean that their spirits could not find their way back to Africa; and all knew, in that moment, that their home was lost, and that their gods could not find them; and that upon these shifting waves, there could be no safety, no village known, no family to grant a name, no ancestor to provide a comforting word of advice from their burial ground; *no village more, no god more, no old father more, no old mother more, no name more; for buckra god give buckra power over all the sea; buckra god have the gun; buckra god, he crush us.*

They spake of tortures which rent my heart. A man talked of seeing his wife pinched by children who he could not scold nor wave away with his stick, but must suffer them to torment her as she stood, eyes closed, twitching. Several recounted tales — agreeing, "Aye, that, that, worst, aye, that" — of being tied up and whipped, and then (by order) boys applied to scouring their backs with hay, and salt water poured over the wounds — and I could no longer bear to hear them without tears; which I shed not simply out of my sensibility of the pain, but at the thought that men could inflict such calculated agony upon each other blithely, with sport and fascination, and that it should be done for the continuance of nugatory pleasures, so that they might enjoy luxuries: a finer metal in the instruments of their table, or a room in which to half recline separate from the room where they reclined fully. I am weak-hearted, and I wept.

Nsia saw me, and inquired whether I was well.

I began to reply, "Miss Nsia must forgive my weakness, for when one can —"

"Prince O.," said Bono, "is a little tender. It's all new, ain't it?"

I could not speak, so galled was I.

Ever louder, his voice attracting the gaze of the curious, Bono explained, "Private Nothing was raised up in a thimble of luxury. Worst they done to him, most terrible thing ever, they told him he couldn't read whole Latin books no more. That sent him into a mope for maybe three years."

I was aware of the eyes upon me, the eyes of those for whom I wept turned impassively upon me; I averted my own eyes and wiped away the late evidence of my weakness.

Bono said, "He's a tender one."

"Bono," I protested.

"You are, indeed. You are a tender one."

"I beg you not to animadvert to the —"

"Animad —, see? That's what they taught him. Poor little Buckra here. He never knowed the whip."

At that, I began to protest that I had known the whip — an absurd object of pride — but Bono spake over me, explaining to all, "Prince O. never really known what it felt like, til one time when he was ten, and he and his mama acted like no one'd ever been whipped before. They got a sofa to sit on like they was having tea. It was the properest little whipping I ever —"

"Bono, I would ask you not to —"

"Private Nothing, he lived in a sweet, fine dream where he was a princeling of quality, except I would pinch him to wake him up." He reached out—as he had done years before—and clamped his fingers upon the flesh of my arm, squeezing as I protested—and our companions, startled, laughed at what they believed a show of fraternal rivalry—while Bono squeezed to bruise, and narrated, "I pinched him thusly, and told him, 'It is the hour you better wake up.'"

"Stop!" I cried out. "Bono!"

"I said to him, 'Rise up!'"

"Bono!"

"I had to wake him up. *'For my mercy endureth forever,'*" said Bono, and he loosened one hand to slap at my head in play; but there was no play in his eyes, only fury. I saw Nsia watching us, bemused, and could not abide her gaze. I pulled upon my arm, endeavoring to withdraw it from Bono's grasp, and he drew me close to his face, and I once again protested that he should stop, and he with a look of mirth, wherein there was no mirth, patted my head, smiled into my face, and said, "Your mama ever—hey, don't pull—for my mercy endureth forever."

"Hold!"

"*'For my mercy endureth forever.'*" He kicked at my shins. *"Ha! 'For my mercy endureth forever.'"*

"Hold!"

"*'I have slain great kings—for my mercy endureth forever. For my mercy—'*"

"Bono!"

He twisted my arm behind my back.

"Your mama ever tell you that you—"

"Don't you mock her!"

"Your mama ever tell you—"

I pulled free and shrieked at him — my voice hoarse and high with anger —

"She is dead. She — is — dead."

(A childish shriek — awful to recall — the petulant — never again —)

He stared at me, astonished. All were silent.

"I saw them cut her up," I said, "to examine the nature of her skin."

With that, I took my leave, and stormed up to the quarter-deck, for I could not abide the stares among my company — could not — and so crouched by the bulwark above, trembling, wishing to press myself into wood and so cease.

The storms of passion — the heart — I cannot describe the like — the calamity of all my spirits —

I hated him; I despised myself more, my pettish voice squealing its misery — I hated the ship, the shore, the river — I wished nothing more than an end of thought — I cannot describe it — I cannot.

And he was there beside me on the deck.

I stood.

He said, "Oh, Octavian. Octavian."

We stood side by side there in the near-dark; I could descry the fear in his eyes, the discomfort in the mouth.

He could barely speak. "This true?" I did not answer, so he said, "How she . . . How she go over?" He asked it gently, but with fear, for he did not wish to hear the answer.

He was not prepared for my blow. My fist caught him full in the face, and he fell backward, and I leaped on top of him and kept pummeling him, and had known no joy like that for some time, the pleasure of blow after blow; and the greater pleasure of observing that he tried to rouse himself, but could not, save a hand on my throat barely clenched.

With sharp exclamation the master-at-arms and two midshipmen began to beat us with truncheons, crying, *"Heave to, heave to!"* and *"Cease, you Negro brutes, or we'll hurl ye both in the river!"*

Cowed by their blows, we ceased and I rose. Bono had, from what could be seen in the dim light, a great deal of blood flowing from his lip; and when he stood, made a final lunge at me, which was arrested by the swift action of the sailors. They warned us against any further fighting; told Bono to go below, and me to remain above for watch; and that if there was another conflict, they would present the case to our commanding officers, and there should be consequences.

I begged an extra watch; I stayed all night upon the deck of the ship. A great wind blew upon us in the early part of night, which forced us to remove the sheets from the ship's railings before they should blow away. One eluded our grasp and toppled through the dark, a thing flapping, but too ungainly to fly. It was engulfed in the water and slowly crawled into obscurity, a beast either skulking or stalking.

Then came in the rain, and all froze and was black.

January 15th, 1776

Detached this day upon forage detail to aid in the victualing of the Regiment. 'Twas a relief to remove myself from the *Crepuscule* for reasons which need not stand on paper. My absence from that ship is most conformable to my desires.

Fourteen of us have been removed to the *Plover* schooner and, receiving favorable winds, set off up the river, flying no colors. The pilot is a Negro man reputed to know the river well, which circumstance delights us all, and we spent a pleasant hour in hearing his tales of the river and his account of his master's wrath when he absconded with a boat some months ago — the pilot drifting away from the dock, the white man stranded, shouting after him that the pilot *should not steer so clear of shoals, scudding on the burning lakes of Hell.*

Bono is not present on the voyage, which is a gratifying circumstance; I have whiled the time in speaking to Pomp and Slant. They asked me for an explanation of reading and writing, Slant saying, "You friend Private Williams, he writes too." I replied that Private Williams was no friend of mine.

So I have determined to teach Pomp and Slant how to write. I have removed the final pages of this book as a quire, and it is my purpose to use them to demonstrate the arts of literacy. In this way, I hope to spread among others the gifts lavished upon me for my pains in the College of Lucidity; to loose knowledge from its corral and allow it free pasturage. And so today, I wrote the names of my companions upon the first page of that quire — POMP and SLANT — and they traced them after.

Thus we whiled the afternoon.

We grew apprehensive when another sail approached, but met with no resistance, save a dialogue with the schooner *Doretta,* which vessel stood for us and called out a challenge, by which our captain apprehended that she was for the King, issued a letter of marque or reprisal; and so we greeted her, shouted our commission, and proceeded unmolested. We passed other boats and ships of small draught, but all avoided challenge for fear of tampering with privateers.

At dusk, we hove to and laid down our anchor a bit past Jamestown Island. I take this opportunity to write these lines. Tonight we commence our raiding party.

Last evening's foraging succeeded admirably well. When night fell, we proceeded up the river, there being a reasonable moon. When we were in striking distance of a plantation known to the pilot, we put out in the boats and made our way to shore. My spirits were in a joyful sort of agitation, so desirous was I of activity; hazard itself seemed merely thrill.

We raided the barn and the pond both. It proved necessary that we strangle the ducks, which was not pleasant work, though requisite; we brought away two bags of them.

At the alarums of the chickens, the house was roused, and we soon perceived Negroes making their way for us; but when they encountered a line of us with muskets presented, they opined it was not for them to risk life and limb for their master's hog.

I cannot truthfully report that Better Joe is an effective soldier; he is slow, and his musket seems an object of disgust to him; but he is an excellent driver of beasts, as is Pomp, both acclimated to such employment, and it is through their offices that our endeavor met with the success it did.

We returned to the schooner with our spoils, as we feared that the owner of the place even then sought out his neighbors to repulse us. There was no resistance, however, and it was but the work of an hour, after which our pilot dropped us down the river so that we should not be subject to insult from the shore, were the militia to assemble.

This day, a cold, heavy rain, which makes the sailing difficult, so we are anchored in an inlet and idling until such time as we may either continue to fall down the river to the ruins of Norfolk and the fleet, or fetch more provisions from the shore.

One of the sailors, speaking of the *Doretta,* told us that any man who names his ship after his wife is a fool, for it is sure to meet with some cruel fate, as plague, mutiny, madness, or Algerians. Pomp asked him of the sea's lore, and he told us tales of sea-waifs in cradles of kelp, and the glowing corposants that crawl ship's spars when guilty men keep crimes embosomed.

Such a day is not distasteful; for I find that I am no longer merely an observer, sat upon a dark deck; but I am engaged in the struggle, and this itself brings joy.

January 17th, 1776

Last night, another two raids, both successful.

In the first encounter, we exchanged fire with a white man of the house, son or servant, possessed of a pistol and fowling-piece. He stood by the door and fired while a sister or maid reloaded for him; still, she was untrained in the science of charging a piece, and we found it no difficult matter to fright them from the door and then, Corporal Craigie barking us forward, to shatter the windows with two volleys and batter through another with our bayonets, that the fear might not relent. This treatment being administered, no other opposition followed, and we made off with two cows and a bull, ten swine, a quantity of flour, and a multitude of fowl.

We returned to the ship to find a strange envoy from a man of wealth but two miles down the river. He begged us to give him some small recompense for all that we wished to remove from his plantation, take what we would; explaining that, being loyal to his King, he suffers under constant threat of having his whole property seized by the Committee of Safety, and wishes that we would use these stores to supplement our efforts, rather than allowing them to fall into the hands of rebels greedy for gain. He instructed that he should leave lanterns burning upon the dock early in the morning, so that we might land there and pursue the bargain under cover of darkness.

We approached his dock with trepidation, expecting an ambush, but found no resistance, and indeed an old slave left to lead us to the house. We every minute anticipated some rush at us, and marched up through the paddocks and orchards with great care — our muskets charged — and the ship itself glowering offshore, threatening violence with its small guns if any irregularity should ensue.

There was no deceit practiced upon us. We found the owner anxious and affable; Serjeant Clippinger paid him a small requisite sum for his livestock and an excellent supply of grain. The man then requested that we beat him, so that he might claim he resisted our sortie. His scheme is, now without any goods to his name but with a small sum, to remove himself out of the country entirely and away from the scrutiny of the rebel scoundrels who wait to imprison him; he shall settle in some place to the north, where he shall tell tales of how he lost all in a raid by the dog Dunmore, and shall thus achieve honor little accorded to him here, where he hath spoken too frequently of his service to the King.

The gentleman stood against the wall to take his beating and said, "'Pon my honor. Who'll have at me?"

When none stepped forward to engage in this strange office, Serjeant Clippinger surveyed us; I was struck with surprise when he called out my name. "Private Nothing, he's our pugilist, as you might say." To me, he nodded. "Strike him," he said.

I little liked this commission. I inquired where I should strike.

"Bloody nose, sir?" Clippinger offered.

"Nay," answered the gentleman, "I must have swelling. Swelling or nothing. I should be greatly gratified by a goose-egg above the eye."

Clippinger nodded. I weighed my fist, and observed my target; but I found I had no will to strike the gentleman. He stood erect, eyes closed.

I struck him, but it was as a child's punch. He swore that *'sdeath, 'twas nothing,* and Clippinger bade me strike him again.

"Think on your friend," Clippinger told me. "Private Williams. Strike the gentleman like he was Williams." The Serjeant thought himself clever, and smiled an awful smile in his spotted chops. "Go on, then."

I faced the man again, and could not strike. I was sensible of the restiveness of the others. I felt shame at my failure.

"You was lately so anxious for to strike a man," Clippinger taunted. "Where, pray, did that go?"

Private Cudjo stepped forward and said, "I strike him."

Supplanted, I stepped aside; and felt manhood retreat before me. Upon the deck of the ship, safe upon the waters, concealed by gunwales, protected by cannon, I had dreamed of violence; and now I could not lift my hand against a man who desired it — and "No," said I, stepping before Cudjo. "No — I shall undertake it."

"Whence this arguing, sir?" demanded our host.

"Never you fear," said Serjeant Clippinger. "A blow from Private Nothing is like to a cradle-song from any other body."

Wishing to acquit my honor, I stood firm and handed my musket to Slant, who blinked in soft concern.

We sat the gentlemen in a chair; Private Cudjo held his head gently, and this time I struck him with vigor just above the eye so it might swell shut, and then beat him once with a wooden spoon to assure a lump upon the forehead, so he might claim he lost consciousness.

He swore an oath in pain, then, having recovered, exclaimed, "'Pon my honor — excellent, Serjeant."

There followed a discussion of how we might create the illusion of struggle, to which I did not closely attend, being distracted in my thoughts and anxious for no reason I could own, holding my musket trembling in two hands, the knuckles of one still stinging.

The Serjeant recommended we break furniture; our hostess's wife remonstrated that this was not to our purpose.

Pomp suggested we might tie the gentleman to a chair, conformable to tales of robbery; which suggestion, I may relate, met with no disapproval. Private Cudjo chafed the gentleman's wrists so they bled, and then tied them fast, that it might appear he had been subject to all the indignities of martial harrassment.

Once tied down and paid, he was exceeding pleased with the whole proceedings, and merrily instructed us where we might find his cattle and pigs. We were assisted by his Negroes, one of whom wished to depart with us, but was forbidden by his bound master. Slant, kind soul, whispered that the man should simply hide himself aboard the transport; but was detected in this subterfuge by Clippinger, who berated him for thus abusing a gentleman who had dealt so openly with His Majesty's forces.

As a final favor to the planter, whose wife provided us with tea when we had completed our labors, we set two hayricks and his drying-house on fire and released two volleys of shot into the air before we set off into the night.

Following this second raid, we perceived that the countryside was roused against us, and slipped down the river once again.

This morning, grim work. We have fallen upon a plantation down-river with infinitely less gentility and infinitely unhappier issue.

We landed with our full force and, knowing from the pilot that this was the house of a rebel, offered no terms for conveyance, but rather made straight for the stores and livestock to pillage. Five of our number labored to remove the fowls and swine to the tender while another five of us stood guard—and soon espied a party of Negroes approaching to repulse us.

They burst forth from the orchard, most armed with scythes and grubbing hoes, one with a fowling-piece. We presented our muskets, and the men, struck with fear, held back.

Serjeant Clippinger urged them to join us; but they did not respond. Clippinger then requested us to urge them to throw off the bonds of slavery. "Tell them, boys."

There was a mighty silence, in which both sides awaited attack from the other, the protests of the cattle heard down by the river. We regarded their array: men with blades, men with guns.

Said Isaac the Carpenter, "Join our number, brothers."

But they did not move. They blinked; and one lifted and dropped his elbows; but they stood firm.

And gently, Slant said to them, "The bodies, the bodies facing that way is free. The bodies facing this way is slaves."

We were all, slave and free, struck with the oddity of his statement; it was unclear what this pronouncement signalized; but Pomp, seizing upon our friend's meaning, said, "He right. You step over and face that way, you is free. Look at your persons." Our enemies eyed their weapons and rocked upon their feet.

Impassioned now, Pomp urged them, "You just turn your foot a little bit—a few inches—you free. Turn your hip, and you free. Move your leg so three toes face that, that apple tree, and you going to feel the wind in your face."

They did not stir. At last, he pled, whispering, "Just turn on the grass. Like a child in the morning."

They looked at us uneasily, and Clippinger addressed them: "Step lively away, boys, or we must needs fire." They did not move; and so Clippinger ordered us to ready our arms—unneedful, as we already presented; and still they stood strong for their master; and Clippinger shook his head in a show of distaste, and our hands shook upon the triggers, and we all knew that we would fire, and they would die.

And then, the man with the fowling-piece discharged it at us, and several of the others rushed forward. Clippinger instanter ordered us fire, which we did, having no choice—we fired right upon them—and one fell—three reaching our line, the others, following the blast, retreating.

Bayonets made short work of two who reached us, Clippinger dancing about with his hanger. The other, wounded, fled.

We watched them scramble through the orchard. There was no utility in firing again; Clippinger accounted it little worth the loss of powder and shot. Our spoils were below, and to the river-side we repaired, there to embark. We could not speak.

No more resistance was offered us. Some fifteen minutes later, our launch set forth on its final leg, leaving dock and bloody ground behind.

The boat gained the ketch and we climbed aboard.

We were unharmed; we left the bodies of three of our brethren upon the brown grass.

As we left the scene of this massacre behind us, my thoughts were engrossed with visions of Bono, known to me since before my breeching, and our desperate feud, our tussle in the dark. First, a sorrow at our division; a confusion that we should come to blows; and then anger: I am no longer a child in pudding-cap and skirts to be pinched and teased; and if he demand the awed obeisance of the babe I was . . .

At noon, there was a wind upon the river, and we shivered upon our deck.

Later

We are returned to Norfolk's ruins and the *Crepuscule*. Our raid is applauded as a success; the choicest of the meats have already been disbursed among the galleys of the wealthiest among His Lordship's supporters.

Now returned, I avoid Bono as best I can, though his smoldering gaze often lingers upon me. When I departed, his eye was swollen so large it was almost shut. I fear our intercourse cannot be other than filled with animosity.

None of us who were out upon that foraging raid have much taste for company. We do not recount our adventure. A gloom has settled over us all. We avoid even our own society, so much as may be avoided when we must sit knee to knee. We do not speak. Slant watches over us all; Charles feigns sleep.

In the evening, I could little abide company, and when we were admitted above for our period of exercise, I removed myself from the others. Standing upon the fo'c'sle deck, I surveyed the black ruins of the town and the small duties carried out by light of sunset and cresset on other ships: the watch upon one whistling, another engaged in holystoning the deck, and on the *Peace and Plenty,* women in wide beaver hats taking the air.

Bono came to me. He came to my side and stared out across the water. I would not look at him.

We did not speak, but watched the small waves and the gentle protocols of falling night.

At length, he whispered, "Her name was Morenike."

And then he went below.

January 19th, 1776

This day, heartening news of the situation upon the shore: Two prisoners were taken Thursday last; they have been questioned, and admit that the enemy is as distressed in their lodgings as we are in ours; that they are cold and sickly and, being militia and thus little used to campaigning, they wish to return to hearth and plow. The fire spread far into the countryside, and now the rebels are huddled in the blackened ruins as fitting punishment for their incendiary havoc.

Though there has been no word between Bono and myself, there is communication enough as we pass; the sight of his still-bloated eye serves as apt reminder of our struggle.

Today he came to my side with one of the drummers of the Regiment, which sturdy youth I have seen perform most astoundingly in the course of our dances. I had not seen this youth upon our own ship before except in time of festival; he was not of our Company.

For a long while, Bono and I surveyed each other, both, I'll warrant, with some sullenness in our countenances; and then Bono said, "I present Private Olakunde. Private Nothing. Olakunde is of the Oyo Empire. He may be able to . . ." Bono shrugged and walked away.

'Twas an offering for peace; a palliation of our enmity; for Bono knew how this should please me, for I sought always word of Oyo, my mother's country.

I greeted Private Olakunde and praised him for the excellence of his performances upon his drum, for which he thanked me. I noted to him that I had not seen him before on the *Crepuscule,* save

[335]

when he had come once for one of the palavers; and he indicated that several of his Company had been transferred to this ship, for his ship's captain *say, no more they stay on he ship; very sick, that ship.* He made a noise of disgust and regret with his tongue and teeth.

We spake for some moments about his drumming, he informing me that he had learned to drum praise in his own country, which was the empire of Oyo; that there, drummers beat out the praise of those who pass upon the streets or in the great houses; and that those flattered by their report place coins upon the drummer's forehead, and that this was the profession in which he had excelled before, three years ago, he was taken out of that land. He hath two drums now, one of his own making, and one issued by the Army, upon which he beats out the music and signals of the white men, our officers.

Upon inquiry, I found that English was the least of his languages, preceded by his own tongue and the speech of the Mandingoes. Thus, his English was not of the best; and I, in faith, could not speak any word of the language of Oyo. So though we had great will to speak to the other, we were constrained in our discourse; I fretted at my ignorance.

It was then, with infinite care, that I introduced the topic of my mother, and told him that I wished to know more of her country. He awaited her narrative, and I told him what I knew: that she was the princess of the Egba people in the Oyo Empire, and had been seized in a battle, and the other scraps I recalled from the stories told me as a child.

I pressed him: "Do you know of the Egba?"

"I know Egba," he assented. "South from Oyo City. From Ake, Kemta, Igbore."

My heart rejoiced at this hint, and I pressed: "Then you have perhaps heard of their king? You have perhaps heard of the fate of their king and his daughter?"

He looked at me with discomfort. "I don't know no Egba king. I don't know Egba too many."

I pled, "There is no word of their sovereign family? Or a raid made upon the royal house of the Egba?"

These questions but increased his uneasiness. "Maybe some king I don't know."

"Please pardon these importunities," said I. "I fear these questions cause you some secret uneasiness."

He judged me with a look; and then owned, "No king. Egba people, no king."

I heard him with astonishment. "Now? Perhaps the King was dispatched—overthrown—at some time. Seventeen or eighteen years ago."

"Egba people, people in Egba Forest, each town rule by they *Ogboni*—many old men together, many old women. *Ogboni*."

This account of some species of republic among the Egba was unwelcome as gall; providing the bitterness of doubt when I longed for the balm of reassurance. My mother had not been unspecific when she spake of her royal Egba parentage and my birthright.

Olakunde saw my evident distress; and he rushed to soothe: "No, maybe some king I don't know. I don't know Egba people too many. Maybe you mother father, he sent by Egba people to Emperor of Oyo. He sent like a king to Emperor house."

I knew not what to think.

"You mother, she have"—he indicated lines upon his face.

"She have three . . . ?" He drew his fingers across his own markings.

I replied that she did not. His uneasiness at my reply led me to suspect that, had she had the scars he inquired after, the proof of her nobility might have been made more sure. As 'twas, he could neither affirm nor deny her account of her childhood.

My face must have been expressive of my uncertainty and the disappointment of frustrated hopes for confirmation, for perceiving my confusion, he rushed to mollify me, either through the ministrations of truth or the gentle balm of lie. He averred (thought I, over quickly) that perhaps my mother's parents — *she father, she mother* — had been waiting for her nuptials to apply the scars.

"You mother name," he asked. "What she name?"

I replied, "Morenike."

"She have more name?"

"I know not other names."

"Three name."

"I know not."

The one name revealed little, for, said he, *Morenike* was but one name of three, and said nothing of her family.

He has, however, told me of its meaning.

Her name, *Morenike,* signifieth, *"Now do I have one to pet."*

January 20th, 1776

Sick with the fever. I cannot hold the least thing in my stomach.

January 21ˢᵗ, 1776

Sick with the fever. I cannot perform my duties. Where I am lain, there is no light to read by, so I must add dullness of mind and fatigue of spirits to discomfort of body.

Others rally and improve.

Later

Some action is undertaken. I awoke to a heavy cannonade, startled, sweating — and found that the lively among us were swarming up the ladders to see what transpired — shoved back and warned away by the sailors above, who shouted that we must remain below.

As I write, we hear the thunder of cannon-fire. We know not what it signifies.

⚑ In the quiet following the bombardment, I have received a visit from Pomp and Slant, who have hitherto kept themselves away from the sickly end of the deck, sending as their envoys only looks of compassion and, in the hours of my waking, waves of the hand. They came now to my side, cloths wrapped about their faces to repel the contagion.

"Never thought it would be so slow," said Pomp. "War. I did think hazard. And I did think blood. I think, 'Boy, you going to have to show some bravery now.' But I didn't think just it would be this waiting. I didn't think just listening. And all the sick."

Slant could not speak for anxiety. He did not want to open his mouth near the ill, for fear something would leap in.

Awoke today to find Bono and Olakunde at my side; Bono has told Olakunde of my fiddling and spake in the most flattering terms of my abilities as a musician. Olakunde and I talked of music, though with little success, me knowing none of the terms of Oyo musicianship and he knowing none of ours, save those few learned when he was taught to coax a British drum to speak in the English military style by the drummers of the 14th.

He did tell us of the great orchestra which played at the court of the *Alafin*, the Emperor of Oyo, for which Olakunde's father had played the fife. Olakunde explained, "*Alafin* of Oyo a very great man. He so great man, no man ever see him sit or see him stand. No man ever see him eat. No man ever see him talk. When he wish for talk, he whisper, he whisper him thought, and he eunuch men sing it out to every body. He hold the *iru kere* over him mouth and whisper through it."

Bono inquired what the *iru kere* might be.

"Cow tail," said Olakunde. "Holy. He hold it over him mouth and whisper by it. We call it *iru kere*."

"Sure," said Bono. "Our King also speaks through a cow arse. We call it *the Prime Minister*."

I thought this jest low; not least because it merely confused Olakunde, who understood it not, and he delivered some looks of confusion before I reassured him and bade him to ignore Bono's whimsies.

I asked Olakunde to describe the country of Oyo, as I had begged my mother when she lay upon her sickbed; and he replied with some confusion that he did not know what I wished him to recount; to which I replied that I wished to know any fact of its solidity: the nature of its cities, the smell of its dirt, the diurnal round of its people, any small chore my mother might have engaged in. And so I asked questions and he spake as Bono sat by soberly and listened.

Olakunde told me of the cities, that they are moated and have great walls, and are surrounded by rings of forest which are designed to repel the incursions of horsemen; and he spake of the mansions of that place, where many families of one geniture live together around one fine *atrium*. He told me of the language and its singing, as had my mother when she lay close to death, her one final gift to me.

He related that the manner in which one sang a word designated its meaning, so that *ilu*, a word for *drum*, might, sung differently, signify *a town*; that *ayan*, a cockroach, might, differently lilted, represent some smell; and so with *iya:* which was at once, depending on the singing, a mother or a separation.

When Olakunde had left to receive his meal, Bono said to me, "You find out what you need to know?"

I considered, but did not speak.

He asked, "When will you know enough?"

"When, for the first time, I finally know and understand her."

"Then it's a long time you will wait."

"I do not understand the least particle of her."

He said, "Who understands any other body?"

"Do you understand your mother?"

"My mother ain't one of the world's great mysteries. She likes a good lot of butter and prefers sons to daughters."

I nodded, and laid my head back upon my blanket. He observed that my gaze was fixed absently upon the stanchions, and after a time grew tired of waiting, and asked me what I thought of.

Said I, "Is not a mother always just a separation, differently sung; for is not our exit from the womb the—"

"Sweet mercy in a firkin!" swore Bono. "Not another word of your damn metaphorizing! By God, don't you have vomiting to do?"

"I was observing merely that—"

"You wax philosophical and I'll shove my elbow in your mouth."

And thus Bono cajoled me into smiling. He told me of some altercation on the deck, a comic encounter in which "the spotted Serjeant Clippinger" faced off against one of the corporals of the Queen's Own Loyal Virginians and was forced to retreat with apologies. He enlivened an hour, and then departed to mess with our fellows.

I write this sitting up upon the flock-bed I have been lying on with the sick. I have every hope for a quick recovery.

I have been, since my interview with Olakunde, in a state of considerable ferment, painting for myself the land that would be mine, had my mother not been torn away from it. This evening, I related to Olakunde the full dimensions of her tale, or I should rather say, the story she told me: not simply the tender prince, the cruel rival, the battle, but also the residence among the Collegians and their cages, charts, and paraphernalia.

He thought upon what I had told him; and in return, he has told me this tale, a tale of the Venus of my mother's people, their Aphrodite, the goddess Oshun.

❋ THE TALE OF OSHUN ❋

In long time ago, in Oyo, they a beautiful woman, she name of Oshun. She beautiful past all other lady. She beautiful in she face. She beautiful in she hair. She beautiful in she mouth, in she eyes, in she hands. She walk, and all the Oyo mens, they love her in they belly; they want her in they arms.

But Oshun, she too fine for mens of she own Oyo country. The gods above, in the sky, the *orishas,* they has big want for Oshun too. Oshun say, "I marry some *orisha* god, then I never want nothing." She take Shango for husband, Shango, *orisha* for lightning. When Shango talk, there fire in he mouth. Them days, he King over Oyo. She take him for husband. She think,

"This fine, for true-true. My husband, he King of Oyo and *orisha* for lightning."

Then she see Ogun, *orisha* of iron. He say to her, "Oshun, woman, you leave Shango. You hark here: I the iron *orisha*. I make for farmer can hoe. I make for slave can scythe. I make for butcher can cut and butcher can chop. I make spear. I make Dane gun and I make fetters. I make chain. This a world of iron, Oshun, and I is the master of iron. You take me, sure."

So she leave Shango and go to Ogun, and then she Ogun wife. She live in a iron house.

Then all the *orishas* see she leave Shango, and they come and love her, and say to her, "You with me," "*Ki!* You with me!" And she be tricked, and lose her ears, put them in a soup, and she be tricked, and lose her hair, and must has to wear a great wig, straw wig, and always, the *orishas* want her. *Orisha* arms reach for take her. *Orisha* mouths try for kiss her. *Orishas* all around her.

Then all the *orisha*, they quiet, because a noise in the forest. Out of that forest, out of that forest come Sonponna, *orisha* of the smallpox, wrap in red cloth. No body see him face, him hair hang down over him lips. He carry him arrow. He carry him red club. Dogs come with him and wind and devils with whips. He don't say nothing to Oshun. He take she hand—no word—and he take she throat, and the other *orishas,* they watch.

He start for lead her back to the forest.

Then, the other *orishas,* they talk loud: The medicine *orisha* grab she arm and say she his, he save her from Sonponna; and the *orisha* of *[Here Olokunde sought a word of me.]*

[*347*]

fate—the fate *orisha,* he grab she arm and say, "You come with me, and nothing ever change. I tell you all the thing that going happen," and Eshu, the *orisha* of changes, he meets she on the crossroads, and he say, "You come with me, and everything change, all games, all tricks," and one *orisha* on she left, and another *orisha* on she right, and *orisha* in the tree, and *orisha* in the dirt, and all for to hold her, all for to kiss her, all for to make they children.

And Oshun, this beautiful Oshun, she can only see eyes. She can only hear they shouting. So mighty palaver. In every place.

She don't say no word. She tired. Oshun tired of they eyes, the *orisha* eyes. She tired of they hands, the *orisha* hands. She tired of they mouths. She leave them *orishas.* She take off her hair. She go down to Oyo town.

Oshun leave the *orishas;* she tired, oh, very tired, tired. Oshun lie down and become a river. She rest in that river. Last thing, she close she eyes and rest.

Oshun, now she still a river, run through Oyo City. Every body can touch she hand, but no body can hold it. Every body can touch she hair, but no body can take it. Every body be in her body, but no body be in her body. She go on past. A thousand years now, she done run through Oyo City.

And the Oyo girls, they sit by that river now, and they looks at it for they mirror and sees them selfs. They laugh, them girls, they laugh in the river, and they fix they hair for beauty. They want for be just like Oshun. ✳

Thus, Olakunde's tale of the Venus of his people; of my mother's people; of my own. I wonder whether she knew this tale, and if she knew it, whether she told it to herself as she lay upon that pallet, requesting fairy tales of me; while in the house, Mr. Gitney, infatuated, prepared his fatal treatments.

I wonder if she knew this tale.

January 24ᵗʰ, 1776

Last night, a relapse by three of our mending number; they are taken again with a new fever. There is a great fear that one fever hath become the avenue for a second — and that this new fever is a greater one. I am afraid for myself and for all of us.

Miss Nsia says that upon other ships, men have died. They have been laid to rest in the river, without ceremony, in the dead of night, lest the enemy perceive our weakness and rally in their own sickness to strike us while we ail.

Dr. Trefusis hath arrived today on the boat with the women, clutching his wet, torn letter of passage, that he might come below and inquire after my health, which he heard was not of the soundest.

I averred that I mended, though others sicken. Now there are ten of us here upon these mats and the flock-bed of sickness, which stinks most revoltingly of our illness.

He and Bono sat by my side, though clearly their senses were assaulted by the noisome sheets and the breath of myself and those around me. Bono hath been highly solicitous of my health, showing me all the kindnesses of which he is capable.

"Bono hath informed me," said Dr. Trefusis, "that you met with a young drummer of Oyo. I trust the discourse was fruitful?"

Being exhausted, I knew not what to answer.

"He asked him about Princess Cass," said Bono. "They talked a real long time."

There was, at the mention of her name, a silence among us; none wished to speak, as would further words disturb her lingering spirit.

I said to Bono, "You will perhaps accept my apologies for my deception."

Bono nodded; then shook his head. He offered no absolution, nor any rancor.

He asked, "You ever going to tell me that story? You want to tell me how she . . . ? You wish to . . . I would be gratified to know."

Dr. Trefusis shifted uneasily, little relishing the discomfort this inquiry occasioned.

To Bono, I said, "I will tell you now."

"It would," admitted Dr. Trefusis, "perhaps be salutary for you to recount it."

And so I began.

I have heard others' stories and recorded them in these pages; there is no need to animadvert to my own. Though Bono had, it transpired, heard the general outline some days before from my tutor, this was our first true rehearsal of its particulars and the stripping away of the lie I had told him when first we met at Great-Bridge; and so, again, she danced the minuet in Canaan and she fell; she lay sickening; she demanded fairy tales from Ovid; she was practiced upon by the ineffectual cruelties of the scientists, heated and cooled; and at last, expired.

Dr. Trefusis listened to us both; and Bono asked the questions he wished to know.

He posed a few inquiries with anger to Dr. Trefusis, demanding to be told of who conceived of that grim — I write it — that grim autopsy.

Dr. Trefusis allowed as it was Mr. Sharpe; and protested that he himself had argued against it in the strongest possible terms, but that Mr. Sharpe would not be turned from his path, and Mr. Gitney's spirits were sunk too low, his mind too dejected, for resistance.

When the story was complete, Bono appeared harrowed and gray.

"Tell me, sir," said I to Dr. Trefusis, "tell me of her youth."

"I know nothing of it," said he, "save what she told you."

"When she first appeared at the College."

"I was not in residence there at that time," said he. "I know only that she was big with you and spake almost no English."

"When," I asked, "was she discovered for a princess?"

"As soon as she could make herself understood by her captors."

"By which term you intend Mr. Gitney."

"He was indeed her captor," said Dr. Trefusis. "As was I, later. As were we all who resided there. Though Mr. Gitney owned her until the end."

"No one owned her," said Pro Bono. "No one could ever own her."

Dr. Trefusis concurred. "Your mother walked with the stars in her hair. The rest of our company squatted around her and picked out equations in mud." Smiling with melancholy, said he, "'*Rara avis in Terris, nigroque simillima Cycno.*'"[4]

When he had gone, Pro Bono lay with his head back against the planks. "Prince O.," he said carefully, "I heard a story."

I asked him to relate it.

He said that Aina, the cook, had told it him; and that she had heard it from another woman who had lived at the College of Lucidity before Bono had come to reside there.

"I vowed to myself I wouldn't tell it you. I thought I never should. Prince O. . . ."

I begged him tell me; but he betrayed some confusion. He would not relate the story; he says he shall when I am well, when I am strong. One final story which he knows.

And so, with trepidation, I await my full recovery.

---

4 "A rare bird upon the Earth, not unlike a black swan." — Juvenal, *Satire* VI [Editor's note]

Dr. Trefusis again this day.

He inquired after my health, and being told that I mended, he was satisfied.

"Sir," said I, "I am still apprehensive of my health, lest this new fever spring into the place vacated by the old."

With some discomfort, he looked upon me, and replied, "Thou hast nought to fear."

"The men around me are all afflicted," said I.

He placed his hand upon my brow. "Rejoice," said he, "for that is not thy lot."

I could not comprehend his assurance.

"You cannot fall ill of this new disease," said he. He placed his hand now upon my hand. It may well be imagined, the sensations I underwent when he told me, "It is the smallpox."

January 28th, 1776

More have fallen prey to fevers this day. We receive reports of other ships in the fleet where the illness is much more advanced upon the people; the sores have appeared upon some.

We await this unwelcome development.

I ate a full supper this day, and my head is again clear. The others who have shared my pallet these last days worsen. I pray God they may be delivered of the worst of the disease.

Today a word from Slant, delivered by Pomp, as Slant will no longer approach the flock-bed of sickness. Pomp came to my side, and said just, "Slant ain't had it."

In that, a world of anguish. I watch him down the length of the ship; he grimaces and works his fingers backwards and cannot sit; and none of us can walk about, or breathe any air untainted.

I resumed my usual hammock last night. I am embarrassed by my health.

Slant's anxiety is awful to observe.

"Is it . . . by breath?" he asks, jaw working.

I own that such is not known; but that indeed, the scholars of the College believed the disease was caused by the inhalation of truculent animalcula.

Pomp asked I explain myself; which I did, but it was no comfort to Slant. He looked up and down the deck at the folded and stricken bodies; and he said, "When does a body know he has it?"

I answered miserably that the disease hath a period of quiescence before it blooms.

"You mean it might . . . already be in me?"

"I am sure you are uninfected," said I.

"How long it take?" asked Slant. "To . . . show?"

"Two weeks," said I. "With us, it waited two weeks."

He shook his head and covered his eyes with the heels of his hands. Pomp begged him to rally, for there was no cause yet for uneasiness; but Slant merely whispered, "I may be dead already."

I look with Slant's eyes down the length of this dark hold, and I see men involved in speech and exhalation. Any word releasing breath might be the sentence of death; any word inhaled, be it "is," or "sweet," or "the." I see soldiers conversing in the gloom. Their every phrase is embroidered upon a flag, as in satirical sketches; but the letters cannot be read, for they are not of our alphabet, but of the speech of the dying; and we fear to know who next shall con its lessons.

This day, Bono's revelation. There is nought but this to report; nought to consider. I approached him; I inquired. He wished to wait. I importuned. Some hours passed. We ate. He came to my side.

He inquired as to whether I remembered Beth, a *fille de chambre* at the College in my infancy, though in that time, called Miss 22-05. I replied that I did not remember her name, but recalled her number, and that she was a pleasant woman of perhaps two-score years.

"She spake the tongue of Oyo," said Bono. "Your mother, she cried when she was first come to the house, and Miss 22-05, she comfort her." He relucted to continue; and yet, I waited, and so he continued.

He related—

There is no virtue in concealment. When the earth is rendered chaos, regulations of speech and propriety are rendered impotent, just as city may become desolate, and street, battleground, and flesh may become fire.

O Lord, we are vile; have mercy upon us—have mercy upon us—

Or rather, have no mercy upon us—none at all—but bring the full arsenal of Thy savagery to bear upon us and extinguish us utterly—for there is no one worthy in Thy sight.

☙ As Bono heard the story: In my mother's first days in the house when a girl, she could not cease weeping, not yet having assumed the terrifying reserve and governing dignity which were her portion; and in those days, finding that Beth spake her tongue and offered a bosom to cry upon, my mother, whose name was still Morenike, had recounted through her tears that *quanquam in nave tanquam pælex designata ut nautas lascivientes satisfaceret. Repugnavit, quisque eam stupravit cæteris spectantibus.*

Quae facinora Deus avertat! Quam sordidum animal est homo! Tuam misericordiam non peto, Domine, sed potius precor ut iratum nobis omnibus te præbeas. Nos penitus everte, Domine, tanquam tui aspectus indignos.[5]

It was shortly after this revelation to Beth that my mother announced her royalty and prevailed upon the philosophers to train her and her son as royalty should be trained; and within three more months, she did not speak to Beth at all, save to deliver her commands.

---

5 "... upon the ship, she had been selected as a concubine to satisfy the lusts of the sailors. She had resisted, and they had fallen upon her, each committing his indignity in the sight of the others. God forbid such atrocities! How vile a creature is Man! I do not ask Thee for mercy, O Lord, but that Thou turn upon us the full savagery of Thy wrath. Destroy us utterly, O Lord, for we are unworthy in Thy sight." [Editor's translation]

✣ She was a child; and I am her senior by four years or five.

She was the daughter of a King in Oyo, and stood in her father's train before the great stool of the *Alafin,* clad in precious raiment; or she was a girl in a village undistinguished by royalty, a place by a river, her father a herdsman.

She was snared by an invading army as her city burned and men fell beneath the spear, taken to the coast in a long coffle of her playmates; or she was taken by guile in the woods, men who lured her too far from her village for her screams to be heard; or she was sold for some debt or some forfeit; any of these.

She was given over to the European slavers at Whydah, and well may I imagine her terror at her embarkation — the grins of the white devils so oft described to me by those who, until that glimpse upon the ships, had never seen such pallor except on some few uncannies as had been touched by spirits.

She was imprisoned for some time at the island fortress of B—; I cannot venture any more speculation upon the rigors in that dungeon, except to aver that the perfume of flowers, the gallantry of the harpsichord—those two things she spake of most in connection to that vile place—were never smellt nor heard there, deep within those vaults of stone.

She was taken upon a ship, the *Incontrovertible,* Captain Julian McFergus, Master, for whom I prayed, by her instruction, many nights. I wonder now at these prayers: for mayhap in the course of that voyage he interrupted the indignities practiced upon her person; or—and this I fear to name—mayhap he was captain of her woes, and she bade me pray for him, that the villain might be scathed by her kindness, that he might be reformed by her sardonic benisons, cast at him night after night from a distance of leagues and years.

Assaulted, imprisoned, taken forever from her family, that fount of all comfort, abandoned by her gods—doubtless sick—wretched—enchained—and then—

I saw her now arrived at Boston, she but a girl of thirteen years, a child with a child showing in the womb—Morenike, I shall put my arm around thee and lead thee as a brother might his trembling sister—

Taken to that strange house—her spirits disordered from months, seasons, perhaps a year of calamity and uncertainty—who may tell the secrets of that bosom—what clash?—she at once an object of universal despicience and awful desire—cast down and yet, by motherhood, made the center of another being's petty world—beset upon by shame and by pride—by anger and hatred—by fear—allowed no identity conferred by parent, village, or local god—

What matters it if she concocted some girlish story of royalty? What signifieth it, if it be childish lies? Who shall hold her accountable, given these tumults, for pleading her belly to delay the fall of the terrible sentence?

If it was an imposture, it was perhaps a blessing that she could not at first speak the tongue of her captors excellently, for I suspect, had she been capable of running out some whole tale at once, she had been detected; but instead, she learned the tongue as she learned how to play upon the susceptibilities of those around her; and taught herself the tale she needed to tell, truth or no.

I see the years draw on, and she gains in fortitude and dignity; learns to cast off any memory of that past, with its perilous glimpses of nightmare (the stone of the basalt crypts, the shrieking of lamentation); either thinks not upon the years before her abduction, or plays them out upon a stage so buried in the ventricles of the brain that it never can be detected; and her attentions are drawn to fine gowns and the addresses of people of the first quality. She is procured lush wigs of white hair from pensioners' homes in Prague, and moves her hoops with such delicacy that a countess might envy her.

There is much which remains closed to me. Perhaps I shall never know whether she felt the tenderest of affections for Lord Cheldthorpe, or simply dissembled; and perhaps she knew not herself, for acquisition and station are delightful; offered riches and ease, who would not love? I shall never divine what passed between them, how adoring or how calculated; but it requires little insight to appreciate her fury at his insults, and the defiance with which she battered at him—delivering us, after all her efforts, into common slavery.

For many years, once I was sensible that she exaggerated or fabricated the tales she told me, I bore the humiliation of this mark of her disesteem. "Recall," she would say to me, "that you are a prince"; and I began to doubt her reiterations and resent her impostures—the tales of orchid thrones and panther steeds. "Tell me one true thing," I demanded at her extremity.

But I see now how sedulously she labored to create her illusion; for she knew it should protect me only so long as I believed it. The tale of my royal parentage was all that kept me from abject slavery. She spent her life weaving it, in comfortably deluding me, that I might wear the lie as proof against all injury.

Present or no, the royal blood of Oyo, of the Egba, was not the great birthright handed down to me. It signifies little, whether I am scion of a noble line.

Her lie was her last gift to me. It was not a rebuke or a mark of ill-favor.

The lie was my great inheritance.

✣ And if there standeth my mother in a gown of China damask, and beside her, her tiny little son, twig thin, regarded by the whole of the company as he playeth solemn tunes upon the violin, applauded by all assembled — then see there, back against the wall, Pro Bono, some eleven years of age, dressed in livery, taught the lessons of silence and obedience. He hath been sold at eight from his mother's side, and now must daily watch another boy enjoy coddling, plaudits, and idleness. He must serve the tot at table; he must rise and see the princeling is dressed in finery; he must listen to the mother's fatuous tales of Africk royalty, knowing that all that debars him from these pleasures is a story likely knit out of fancy; keenly aware that the darling of all eyes is no more or less than he.

Now know why he might pinch that child upon the arm when no one observes. Now know why he might wish to offer his protection, and at the same time, revel in the look aghast in those wide eyes as the full dimensions of their prison are revealed.

I lie upon my mattress in the night and listen to the idiot slap of water against the hull.

"Bono," I pressed, "do we know absolutely that—the scene of my conception—?" (My mouth could not utter the words.) "Might she have been pregnant before she was taken upon the ship, as she always averred? Did she speak to you ever of my parentage? Whose child I am?"

He was not easy with this questioning. "Reckon I don't know," he said.

"She told me my father was a prince."

It was shortly after the bell rang for the close of morning watch; we paraded the deck by company for the exercise of our limbs. The sky was dark: gray clouds above black ruin.

I owned, "For some years, growing sensible that some part or whole of her narration was not founded upon the firmest bedrock of veracity—"

"Ha," said Bono.

"For some years, I feared I might be Mr. Gitney's child."

"Now, that is a fate worse than death. If that be true, you should consign yourself to the waves this same moment." He gestured carelessly over the rails. "Especially if that nose come out late in life." His jest made, he amended, "You ain't Mr. Gitney's child. Understand? Dr. Trefusis says she was big with child when she arrived."

"Which signifies what? Six months following conception? Seven?"

He shrugged his shoulders, saying, "Don't rightly know. She was a skinny little thing; could have been three months and she was already big with child for aught I know."

"You calculate it could have been as little as three months?"

"But the College could've boughten her at any time after she showed: seven months, eight, nine. Any."

"How long lasts a transit across the Atlantic?"

"Sweet mercy, Prince O., I pray you, don't torment your own self. You ain't going to find a father through numbers."

"We know not what transpired while she was immured in the slave castle."

"I reckon it takes like to two months across the Atlantic, but that's from England, and no stopping. Your mother, she went to Jaimaica or Barbados or such and then up the coast. So longer. What does that tot up to? And then there's winds. I can't recall, but it's faster going the one way than the other. Because of winds."

"So I could be the child of a sailor."

"Or a jailor. Or another captive. Or a prince. Or a king." With a great look of sympathy, he pleaded, "Don't worry your own self this way, Prince O. I am asking, because I will tell you, you ain't ever going to know the answer. First moment you'll know who made your body is when you leave it behind and can pose a few sharp questions in the avenues of Paradise."

With an anger my companion little deserved, I replied, "I wish to know who I am."

And with some irritation, he responded, "Then recall that you enjoy the fiddle and Scots tunes and them Italian trumperies and you enjoy treacle tarts and, when it rains, books where men in fine dresses throw spears at each other's feet. Recall you got a friend you once called Pro Bono and you got companions you call Slant and Pomp and Will, and they call you Buckra, and in the enlistment rolls, you're named Private Octavian Nothing. Because we ain't anything more than a name and some likes and some distastes and a story we tell about ourselves."

"And what others say about us."

"If you want them stories heaped in, too, then you're welcome to them. And we're a body; and sometimes the stories and the name, they live on after the body — and sometimes the body lives longer than the name or the story, though that ain't for aye, especially if"— and here he raised his voice—*"a set of FOOLS confines you to a ship rotten with PLAGUES."*

We circumnavigated the deck in our rows.

February 2ⁿᵈ, 1776

Last evening, a cannonade from the ships; to what purpose, we have not been told. We can divine no meaning nor strategy.

This day, the first smallpox sores appear upon the sick.

The day was consumed in bringing water to the afflicted. There is a miserable shortness to our supplies of that indispensable element. Pomp, who suffered the sickness as a child, circulates with me among the afflicted, bathing them comfortably and urging them to resist scratching and worrying at the sores, lest they rupture.

I recall too well the stench of this affliction; it resembles no other smell. It recalls me intolerably to those final days in Canaan.

Slant is in great anguish at the apprehension of the fever. He moves in perpetual agitation.

Suffering a head-ache and a poor stomach; we are all besieged by petty illnesses, trapped as we are upon this ship.

For nigh on two weeks, our clothes have seen neither water nor soap, and they are now considerably enstyed by the muck of the deck and the contagions of the air. Thus, 'twas with general acclamation that we greeted the arrival of two women to collect our laundry this day. Though I harbored a desire that I might see Dr. Trefusis as a result of this necessary visit, and spend an hour indulging in book and debate, he was not permitted to accompany the washerwomen; my disappointment being most agreeably mollified, however, by the appearance of Miss Nsia.

Private Draper's child, who hath for several days been quartered with us upon the *Crepuscule,* would not remove his shirt for washing. I was down upon my haunches, speaking what reason I could to him — *Master Thomas, I pray you remove that shirt and put on this* — a debate wherein I argued that *he did not want, did he, to be a mere frigate for mites and chiggers* — and he replied that *'twas his best shirt and he weren't giving it; he didn't mind no mites; they was his mites;* and so my coaxing turned to pleading; and his complaining turned to obduracy — at which juncture Miss Nsia and Pro Bono appeared at my side, and I was confounded in silence, abruptly sensible of how my head-ache dulled my wits.

"He won't yield up the shirt?" said Pro Bono.

I shook my head, and half rose to deliver a bow to Miss Nsia, but could not fully rise nor fully sit; and so gave over and squatted as I had been.

"He is," said I, "on most days, a charming child."

"'Cepting he probably brought the mites on board with his mama," said Pro Bono. "That's what I heard." He said to the boy in play, "It's lucky you're so prodigious sweet-faced. Otherwise we'd all feed you to them sharks for introducing fleas."

"Where's the sharks?" asked the boy.

Pro Bono pointed aft, toward the sailors; Master Tom swung his head in delight and horror to observe the most dangerous of fishes; at which Miss Nsia swooped down, seized upon the child, and commenced tickling his sides, whispering, "A fingery bite! Them sharks has a fingery bite!"—to which the boy squealed and laughed—she growling, "They got wiggly teeth and loves that meat under the arms! 'This boy eats fine! Most well-tasting child I eats for three weeks!'"

"It's owing to he's garnished with lice," said Pro Bono. "They makes a fine *amuse-bouche* for the king of the sea."

My heart swelled at the sight of Miss Nsia's considerable powers brought to bear on this giggling child; and it was with delight that I watched this tender and familiar scene, in which natural compassion was so leavened with sportiveness. But no sooner had I entertained visions of this delightful charm being brought to bear upon me, than I realized that Pro Bono and Miss Nsia, now struggling the child out of his shirt as he writhed like a fish, were grouped like parents; whereas I sat apart, my head aching, my adoration unmatched by any powers of persuasion or address.

Tom Draper was changed into a wide, long shirt that trailed upon the ground. His other, stained, was in the bundle of laundry to be washed, and he, delighted with the game, was running through arched legs to find his father.

Bono noted my sadness; he watched my eyes upon her.

Together, the three of us collected the shirts and breeches from such as were afflicted with sickness, all lying together in the stern. They were slow to move and shivered in the cold before we wrapped them again in blankets. Miss Nsia turned with nice discretion as Bono and I lifted off their smocks.

When she bade us farewell and retired, I entreated her to forgive me my lack of animation, adding that, between illness and fear of illness, I was not in much countenance to speak fluidly; but that the restorative powers of her presence had rallied me.

"Private Nothing," she said, "you makes a pretty little speech right there."

When she had gone and we were alone, Bono adopted a tone of utmost seriousness, and said to me, "I withdraw all claim upon her, Prince O."

With some misery, I prayed that he should do no such thing, for in her looks and speech her admiration for my companion was clear.

Bono shook his head. "I would truly like to see you dew-eyed in love," he said. "'Cepting you'd be lyrical. All hollyhocks and wee folk skipping in the barley and ain't it like what Plossitossitus says about the return of spring." He put his hand upon my shoulder and rose. "In earnest, I withdraw my claim," he said.

Said I, "It is not for us to decide."

He thought upon this. "A true word."

"She hath made her determination."

"You don't know that, surely."

"Her eyes speak of her favor."

He argued not, but brooded; he was as sensible as I of the marks of her regard. I should perhaps have found gratifying a little more polite resistance to my observation, but he offered no feint; he denied not her favor and accepted his lot with alacrity. Had I not been beset upon by other anxieties, I would have been more galled by the speed with which he laid aside his professions of equality in the contest; but being consumed with exhaustion at our ministrations, I merely observed in defeat and humiliation his assumption of the bays.

He looked fore, toward her retreating form, and said, "She is monstrous fine."

I nodded, my head beating with its ache. "Private Williams," said I, "there are more sicknesses than the smallpox, and we endanger ourselves by resting in the vapors."

"Aye," he said. "I don't cut so excellent a figure when I'm vomiting. I bend from the waist, and it interrupts the line of beauty."

Thus we removed ourselves as best we could from the ring of contagion.

Today, I instructed Pomp, Slant, and Olakunde in reading and writing. I do not regret pulling out the leaves of this book to make a lesson-book for my friends, though I approach its end: Their pleasure and assiduity repay me. In the last several days, in our idleness, Pomp and Olakunde have learned the better part of the alphabet; and Slant, though he hath not brilliancy of parts, excels in generosity of spirit and humility of demeanor, which makes him a ready student.

This day, when we were finished with our lesson, we swapped the tales of Africa and Europe: Olakunde told us of Ogun, the god of iron, beloved by smiths and warriors; which potent deity was despised by the other *orishas* for teaching man the mysteries of the forge and smithy; and I in return told them of Prometheus, similarly condemned, and of lame Hephæstus, blacksmith of the gods, toiling in his Ætnan gulph.

For Pomp, who begs tales of horror and enchantment, Olakunde recounted tales of the red monkey who with withered lips enounced sacred knowledge to the oracles of Oyo. He spake of the cults of the forest demons, whose wails could be heard in the bush when the brotherhoods met in convocation. He spake of the ghost societies who worshipped the dead, which spirits returned, said he, caparisoned in the feathers of many birds, and speaking in tones too low for mortal throat; or faceless in grave-shrouds, walking between the huts and crooning of judgment. In such a humor, he told us that his city was oft called Oyo Oro, "Oyo of the Ghosts," and so it seemed to us as he spake: empty alleys of mud, tenanted only by the gray dead and the frigid moon, as the living lay slumbering in their houses, or shivering in corners in the greatest transports of fear. And as he spake of these things — the crying in the woods, the dead returned — one could observe Pomp's pleasure in the fear of it, as he painted for himself the swamp where once he had kept cattle, and peopled that desolate bogland with horrors.

And I rejoiced to hear of this city too, for hearing these nocturne tales, I might glimpse the place in daylight, too, this capital of my mother's land, half heard of in trivial mentions, unadorned and unmajestic: women in the marketplace; goats tied to the camwood tree; the pepper stews for which Olakunde yearns; groundnuts and cassava; the sun-graced courtyards where livestock brays and where, in the morning, the head of each household greets his patriarch by prostrating himself, touching cheeks right and left to the dirt, as women recline on their elbows.

These are the tales I wish to hear.

Olakunde narrates always with looks of the greatest solemnity, but raveled deep in his demeanor is his joy in telling these tales, and to an audience so delighted with his testimony.

He tells us also the wonder-tales of travelers from other realms in Africa: of the men of the Upper Coast whose teeth are pointed; of the great cities of the north; of desert Taghaza, where the houses are built of salt with roofs of camel-skin. He told us of a king who fought wars across the Niger by releasing fleets of birds trained to hurl arrows. He told us of the Emperor of the Ashanti, who sits every day beneath a tree of gold, upon a sacred stool of gold, with his feet in a basin of gold, his skin glistening with a paint of tallow and gold, surrounded by troops of royal pickpockets, cats, and a hundred albinos. Olakunde told us then of the yam protocols of the Ashanti, wherein all of the noblemen of that country must arrive in dignity to pay their respects to the Emperor; and as each processes through Kumasi, the capital, he must sacrifice a slave in each quarter of the city, the blood running into holes where the yams last grew.

I expressed surprise, that slaves should be sacrificed thusly; to which Olakunde nodded and replied, "In Ashanti, true. In Dahomey, true. Before, not so many slave kill. Now so much war, the *orishas* so angry in they bellies, and the kings say, for buy slave, only a few cowries, only small gold . . . Now many prisoners. Kings know true price." Thus these rites where slaves are slit, where executioners dance slowly before the Emperors, drumming on skulls with their knives. So learn I of that continent's wonders, and of its terrors too.

Slant doth not speak as we tell tales, for he claims he hath no tales to tell; but he frets away all hours when he is not on deck, certain that he shall inhale some fatal breath, and every occupation for his anxious mind we can offer him is gratifying to him. It is my suspicion that he is too sensible of how words desert him to tell tales in company; but I wish ardently that he should speak freely. He sits with eyes fixed upon the speaker, mouth open, limbs motionless save for the hands, which pace and wheel upon his knees.

On some occasions, Will joins us and listens; but he does not speak ever. He asks no questions and offers no tales, deprived of his antic companion, with whom the recounting of incident was a joy.

And for myself, I lie in my hammock at night and whisper the names to the darkness: *Dahomey, Taghaza, Sankore, Accra, the ancient realm of Songhai.* I know not where lie most of them in that vast continent, but I must reclaim the names I would have heard in stories, had I grown up amongst those cam-wood trees, those wattle walls, instead of that gaunt house in that cold city on the Bay.

There is a power in names. Olakunde told us of *ashe*—the power which runneth through all things, subtle and flexile, which finds its most potent expression in human utterance; so that it is a terrible thing to call down imprecations upon an enemy, or to wish for anything but good, for what is said out loud is forged into truth.

So tonight we sat and told our tales: Olakunde of Oyo, Pomp of marshy cunning-men and revenants, and me of Greece and Rome. Slant and Will listened; and even Bono, when he was by, hearkened some and quipped. What signified was not the tales we told, commonplace or fantastical, but the gestures, the silence of friends as another recounted.

If, through utterance, *ashe* may claim us and make what we say true, then this, in recalling these nights of fable, is what I speak loudest, what I declaim to the listening firmament:

"Oh, how good and pleasant it is for brethren to dwell together in unity! Like the dew that cometh down upon the mountains of Zion: for there Jehovah commanded the blessing, even life for evermore."

Cries this morning in the darkness—a hideous heaving of bodies—something burst within a man—and he writhed in mortal throes—screams and shouts around him.

Within two minutes, he was without consciousness; and though some ministered to him, attempting to breathe life back within his encrusted lips, all assays were vain; and within three minutes, he had paid his debt to nature, and was gone.

Captain Mackay came below and inquired as to the source of the disruption; and finding it, demanded that the body be hurled off the ship in the dead of night, that we might obscure the sickly nature of our fleet from the enemy.

At this, there were great protests; but the Captain was firm; and some wrapped the body in a blanket and went above to drop it in the river.

Olakunde informs me that my people name smallpox *Sonponna;* and that this most fearsome god hath his own votaries; but that none call him by his name, rather naming him by indirection, as "Hot Ground," "Cold Ground," or "Sweetly, Softly"; hoping by refusing to call upon him that he might pass them by and spare them his attentions. Thus also do they place gifts of palm wine in gourds outside the houses and by the sides of the sick and the vulnerable, that he might be entertained and, sated, process onwards without prejudice to those who lie fearing his nailed caress.

My mother had a stoup of wine lain at her side in her last hours—I recall it now, though I did not understand it then. When she was dying, wracked with her irruptions, in the slave quarters of that house in Canaan, this libation sat by her, untouched. I knelt by it when I went to wait with her.

Thus did she lie, without speaking of this rite to me, even some four thousand miles from her home. At the last, she hoped that the gods of her childhood could be charmed as we all were, and delight in company with her, and then, as briskly as we all had, move on without touching her, without knowledge of her, and leave her unharmed.

February 6ᵗʰ, 1776

At four this morning, all at once, at a signal, the rebels — stationed in yards and by windmills, in tanneries and shops across the ruined town of Norfolk — in one moment — set fire to all of the buildings remaining in the district and fled.

There were alarums. We were awakened and scrambled to the ladders. We were not admitted to the upper decks. Across the river, the bugles cried up warning.

We clamored for news and were scolded; heard firing from shore; smelled smoke.

After fifteen minutes, those of us who do not suffer the sickness were admitted up on the quarterdeck with our muskets. We saw the flames; and what gnawed most at our vitals was the message delivered us by that captured rebel: that all of this desolation, this looting and despoiling — all shall be blamed upon Lord Dunmore and us his troops.

It shall not stand as a record of the rebels' inhumanity; it shall not raise indignation in the breast of the righteous; none shall commend us for our efforts; but instead, it shall be noised abroad that these crimes were ours; and we shall be reviled for what our enemies have done.

Nothing is gained.

So we watched that final conflagration on this cold morn. Firing began from the shore, and we were once again ordered below.

I have not seen the sun today. I am not on watch, nor is there any duty which should take me above.

They tell me that the rebels stream out of their encampments by the ruins. They abandon the site forever and leave that useless bauble to their foe.

We are left, our fleet, the last vestige of royal power in this benighted Colony, guarding a town that is ash entire, under siege from none, delectable to none, strategic for none; and we sit at anchor, uncertain.

I can scarcely breathe for anger.

⚚ I am at the end of this book; there are no further leaves to write upon, but the stubs of that quire I tore out to instruct my friends in writing. Thus this record must pause until such time as I come into paper; at which future date I hope also that I shall have more matter to record.

So do I leave us upon this ship anchored by a smoldering, desolate town, where we have been drifting for more than a month, sickly with the smallpox, which only spreads its infamous depredations. I leave us with the country roused against us, and our liberator and commander reviled. And yet, we shall succeed because we must—we have no choice in the matter—to fight or to submit to the greatest indignities and outrages.

I have, strung about my neck (as it were), lockets with the faces of the dead: a rifleman crushed upon a staircase, a wound through his cheek; black men lying upon the grass; the startled look of a Loyalist I struck; and as, some nights, I view these miniatures aghast, I want some comfortable voice to tell me, "My son, my darling son, you have done what needs be done. This is no crime, but rather valor"; and I should believe that voice.

As I close this volume, I am overtaken with an ache that the most charming and accomplished of mothers shall never read my words, and shall never know of our deeds and the actions upon which Pro Bono and Dr. Trefusis and I are embarked.

In my extreme youth one night, she laid her hand upon my head and read me a Psalm on slavery, a lamentation for the yoke which the people of Babylon had laid upon the shoulders of the children of Israel, and I recall her fingers spread wide upon my bare scalp; and I recall that it was as if she directed my gaze — though she could not speak aloud of enslavement, she set my eyes upon a path; and now I have followed it; and it is a circumstance unspeakable that she shall never sit in the garden while Bono and I run to her and embrace her and babble our tales of heroism; that she shall not see me grow to manhood in this conflict, and shall not know that her son was one of the number of a thousand or howsoever we shall swell who won English freedoms for all.

O spirit; lay your hand upon my brow again.

Speak comfortably to thy son,

OCTAVIAN NOTHING
The *Crepuscule,* off Norfolk
February 6th, 1776

[VIII.]

THE HOUSE
OF THE STRONG

drawn primarily from
the Nautical Diary of
Private *Octavian Nothing*

A little rebellion, now and then, is a good thing.
— Thomas Jefferson, letter to James Madison

Gosport, Virginia
May 19

Dear Beetsie

I pray you is Well. The Lord has blessed me with health
thus so far tho there is many in the camp taken strongly
with a flux. The corn shuld be laid down in the Lower
medow now, I reckon it is, Toms a good boy, you tell
him That. Im greeved over the Chimny, it cant wait for
mending. It will fall in. Mr Sawston down Mantapike
owe us some good labour, you Send Tom down to
Mantapike and he shoud say Im calling in the dett, &
its time Sawston mend the chimny.

　　Here the drums of war is beeting. I told you Lord
Dun. burnd the Town of Norfolk and the colim of smoke
gone up for days. if that ain't enow we hear he has hachd
the most diabolical of Schemes wch is he give all his
Negros the Smallpox, then he going to Reliss them
on land and hopes to spredd the sickness through the
Country in a great Plage. God will damn him for this Act.
Surly it is meet and right he is surrunded by Negros in
his little pirat fleet because there is no blacker devil than
Lord Dunmor his self, there is no blacker soul no deed so
dark. if more Negros knowed what this awful Scowndrel

done then they wuld not run to him as they do, and so I bid you tell it out.

Rejoyce your heart now tho Beetsie, we got our cannons and we got our fireboats and Ld Dunmores Negros just sit there in there ships and there camp and we are ABOUT TO MAKE FINE WORK OF THEM. You will hear of a grate fight and you will know tis

> yr loving hulsband,
> J. Wittol

The Second Part of

The ITINERARIUM
of Private OCTAVIAN NOTHING

⚜ ⚜ ⚜

May 24ᵗʰ, 1776

I begin with a departure: This day our fleet set off for Chesapeake Bay.

For months, I have not writ, having no paper upon which to write and no matter to record; our days passing in the tedium of routine, the languor of inactivity, and the terrors of disease. We have encamped upon the shore; abandoned our encampments; and now we have set off, at last, from the ruins of Norfolk.

Thus I begin my record once more, in hopes of more felicitous issue.

Paper hath been more than scarce; it is an article impossible to come by. The paper I now write upon was purchased for me by the most generous of friends, Pomp, Slant, and Olakunde, in return for my lessons in reading and writing. It is a fine bundle of black-edged mourning-paper, purchased of a serving-man upon one of the pleasure ships. It belonged, I am told, to a gentleman whose wife died of the smallpox three weeks ago; he himself succumbed but four days past, joining his spouse before ever he could write of her death to kinsman or friend; and his servant dispensed with all of his property in a phrenzy before we sailed, this envelope of mourning-paper among the rest.

I trust the black border on the page will not prove prophetic.

In these last days, the rebel hath gathered in greater numbers on the shores, emboldened, threatening some insolent move; and so we turn our backs on the Elizabeth River and now Hampton Roads; we leave behind us the melancholy ruins of Norfolk, that scene of desolation: a black labyrinth of cellar-holes and chimney-stacks, rebel pickets smoking in the sockets of meeting-houses.

There has been a word abroad that the rebels have seized upon cannons and dragged them into position at the mouth of the Elizabeth River, which circumstance would have trapped us there had we not quit the place. For the last week, we have seen murderous detachments parading on the shores. Great numbers of militia met together in full sight of our encampments and fleet, that they might spy upon us and confer.

Thus, we seek a new harbor, and a new encampment.

The final departure, two days ago, was a scene of stupendous activity — fully a hundred ships in motion. Though we who are held below could catch but glimpses of the active fleet when called above, even these brief prospects of activity thrilled the blood: warships and their tenders coming about; the schooners of wealth and *ton,* their masters arrayed in greatcoats on their decks, their ladies in silk flying-gowns witnessing the rise and snap of canvas; the herring buss in which some have been confined in utmost wretchedness for a space of months — tradesmen and journeymen and their prentices — rejoicing at the vast progress of sail.

I delight in our motion, though it be flight. We have been for months constrained in scenes of prodigious sickness and desolation; we cannot but feel gratitude that we exchange these sad prospects for new views. The refreshment of alteration is welcome after the staleness of inactivity. Flight is change, and change is pleasurable when fortunes are low.

Our Company are confined below for the voyage, and we can gain no certain intelligence of our destination. Lord Dunmore and his advisors must have seized upon a new place suitable to our purposes—hovered (as I envision them) over a map, debating our Fate, descrying new stratagems; and I pray that their deliberations were touched by a happier notion than those which have guided us for these five months past, which seem to my imperfect understanding merely a galling trial of hesitation and thwarted opportunity.

The motion of the ship is mysterious. We know not what river, what bay, what shore awaits us, and we little care, so it is a place where we may rally and fight.

Neither we nor the ship's crew have received any rations this day, there being some late dispute with the victualers. Hunger is general. Slant chanced upon the sailing master's mate cradling Vishnoo in his arms and rocking him, singing, "I'll eat you, my sweet, from calipash to calipee"; to which the other sailors replied with coarse laughter and cheers, as the tortoise's bewizened head cocked from one side to the other to compensate for the swing.

Slant is greatly distressed by this terrible lullaby; and protested to Olakunde, Pomp, and me, "Maybe he live for one hundred years. They can't go eat him. Another thing can't die. Not one more thing."

Said Pomp, "Vishnoo's the one body on this ship don't deserve to get in a soup."

May 26ᵗʰ, 1776

This morning, allowed above for some minutes' exercise, I saw the great fleet in motion, which is a sight to leaven all the spirits: our floating town spread leagues before us and leagues behind, a vast collection of pleasure barques and bilanders, ketches and hoys.

The fleet passes vast plantations laid upon the banks in unspeakable gentility. We see master and slave alike, confounded at the celerity and ineluctability of our approach, calling warnings — messengers sent on horseback, riding no faster than our progress, posting along ridges, bent close upon their steeds. Boys running from the dairy, the smokehouse, hollering.

"Where we going?" asked Pomp.

Slant pointed at the sun, at the shadows. "North," he said.

Pro Bono came to our side, having inquired of a sailor, and told us, "Up the Chesapeake. Past Mobjack Bay."

I know not why, but at this intelligence, we all smiled; I suppose, because there is so much of motion in it.

Thus, this morning's view.

Just an hour ago, the *Crepuscule* was fired upon from the woods; a bell was sounded, and we were rallied to stand to our arms upon the deck. Below, we could not even hear the crack of the enemy's rifles.

We went above; we formed; we fired a single volley with our muskets. Our ball could not reach the minute figures who annoyed us; nor could their rifles reach us; and so both their aggression and our defiance were but shows of force.

Empty show it might have been, and yet not without anxiety for others in our van, for our fleet is possessed of no firm discipline—ships falling well behind, detained in eddies—and the eye of the passenger, deluded by the convolutions of the coast, can never be sure of distance—and still the *crack! crack!* of rifle fire echoed without cease—the air was alive with it—and pilots could be certain of nothing.

The *Crepuscule* quickly outpaced the guns of impotent rage and continued reaching north.

So we have traveled on, the cries of the sailors above us, Vishnoo trundling between our knees.

Come nightfall, we have found ourselves anchored near an island at the mouth of the Piankatank River; and there we come at last to rest.

We hear that Lord Dunmore has purposed to inoculate such of our Regiment as have not yet suffered the smallpox — a welcome measure, though come late — and that he sought this isle as a place of refuge where this delicate operation may be carried out without disturbance or annoy.

This plague hath ravaged us; three or four die of it each day. Slant continues his vigilant practices against its depredations; but other contagions have settled upon us in its wake. Were our ranks not swelled every day by men crawling through the reeds, families arrived in boats, and victorious runaways bleeding in their shirts, we had been decimated.

Of late, sensible of disease and impending battle, Dr. Trefusis hath convinced Bono to aid him in the concoction of final words. This gravediggers' game they pursue whenever they meet, protesting that a body can never be too forward in such preparations; the one recommending the Style Sentimental-Heroical *(Weep not for me)*, the other the Masculine-Stoical *(I weep not for myself)*; Miss Nsia scolding them both for their fatal wit.

Miss Nsia and Dr. Trefusis are not with us now, being confined to their own ship; I while the slow hours with my own friends, delighted that, after years of solitude, I may call others by that agreeable name. When we are together in company — Slant, Pomp, Olakunde, my own self, even unspeaking Will — we no longer seem broken, as we did; we no longer seem children, but comrades. They did not laugh when I spoke today of the Argive host and the fall of Rome. Slant added that he hath known a cat named Agamemnon. Olakunde told us of my mother's gods; he told us of Eshu, the very spirit of time, deception, and change, an ancient boy who standeth at a crossroads, to which sly potentate Olakunde prays for victory over obdurate fate. And Pomp, hearing of change, mentioned his experiments in the fluctuation of swamp-water in ditches, which he hath conducted in his idleness, but which speculations would do honor to one of our academicans. Olakunde and I quizzed him on the predations of the alligator. And together, we make a fine company.

I envision the future day when this campaign is finished, and we grown older and commenced men of means — with wives of our own, and children, and farms, perhaps, laid about with barns. Olakunde shall be the Ovid of far Oyo, writing the tales of Africk metamorphoses; and Pomp recording his ghost stories for a winter night. I shall write sonatas *en trio;* and Slant perhaps shall be proprietor of his own plantation.

Grant us, Lord, a Thanksgiving feast together in that distant day; and we shall tell our children — *Eat goose? There was a time when we ate tallow candles with a stomach and thought slush and horse-junk well-tasting.* And we shall unfold our old shirts, which tatters shall be darkened with the smoke of Norfolk, and tell them tales of vanquished rebels and Dunmore until the spirit-hours, when they must be lifted and taken to their beds.

Pork-junk again for supper. We hope for better rations soon.

❧ Touching upon our movements, I should relate other news, as painful as it is interesting. While we idled the months away, exerting our efforts to watch over a city of embers and stones, Boston is fallen to the rebels. My dear town is fallen; the city upon a hill. This I must record.

Report relates that the slave-driver General and his rebel army fortified Dorchester Heights, across the harbor from Boston, in but one March night; and once thus positioned, they commenced shelling the town. His Excellency General Howe arranged for an assault upon the Heights in boats and transports, which was to be a victory as costly as that upon Bunker Hill; but the wind came up so strong they could not sail, and the cause was lost. The rebels remained entrenched and victorious.

The Army have removed themselves — one hundred and seventy ships fleeing from the harbor — and the King's power there is no more. The rebels have swept in through the empty streets, the abandoned barracks.

For more than a month, my town was lost, and I knew it not.

They flee as we flee; and everywhere, order is vanquished.

I wonder at the fate there of Mr. Turner, whether he is fled; and whether Sip of the orchestra was removed with the Army and the Tories. The frugal Mrs. Platt, if she still inhabits her sallow rooms, will not be displeased. It will mean meat assured and resumption of commerce.

I think on the Collegians, returned to their gaunt house, which hath, I suppose, been barbarously used lately by His Majesty's troops, and is like to be in no excellent state of repair. I see Mr. Gitney step into his dim habitation, head inclined to take in the broken staircase, the slitting of the Claudian pastoral hung upon the landing, nymphs on the green now darkling and sprawled near gashed fissures and abysses.

The last time thou stoodst there, sir, I stood by thy side; and my mother was with us, and alive. She ran to fetch her mantilla.

'Tis more than a year since then. Mr. Sharpe, Mr. Gitney — stand there upon that threshold. Meditate upon what you have done. Look you well into that brown gloom.

We all flee, in hopes of finding some ground of security.

Awoke this morning to discover that some hours before dawn, a landing party of Marines had conducted an assault upon the island, which is called Gwynn's Isle. They met with no resistance.

We were piped awake at sunrise and mustered in preparation for disembarkation. When we were brought up upon the deck, we saw in ruddy first light the motion of countless launches all around us proceeding to the shore of the island. We shortly followed, rowing the broad avenues through the fleet.

We passing the *Dunmore,* there was a general commotion upon our launch, and hands pointed to the aft of that vessel; where, upon examination, we could perceive His Lordship standing in the windows of his cabin, candles lit around him, gazing out upon the dawn and his assault. He appeared no more than a specter, features indistinct, a white face held gently in darkness.

We grounded our craft upon the western bank of the island. There were, by the time of our arrival, hundreds of men upon the shore, with our drummers beating to form us into companies.

Our Company proceeded north along the shore, a woodland upon our right; then marched along a road that led into the interior of the island, past a sizeable pond and several prosperous farms. At these generous habitations, we halted briefly, that an ensign might deliver word to the inhabitants of our securing the island in the name of His Majesty.

We having marched and delivered fine shew of arms throughout the northwestern quadrant of the island, we returned to our point of disembarkation and commenced our breakfast. Hardly had we begun to eat when we were ordered south to begin work on building a fortification and barracks.

I little relish the thought of more construction.

We set out to dig latrines, while others of our Regiment were put to raising redoubts.

We could see the enemy upon the shore. They were separated from our island by but two hundred yards of water — a channel scarcely sufficient to splash through as refreshment on a summer's day. Their proximity was intolerable. Still, we set to our digging.

'Twas not yet eight when they opened fire upon us.

The Quartermaster-Serjeant who strolled along our lines held up his hand and commanded, "Dig, boys. Pray don't give no mind to the rebel scoundrel."

Nothing concealed our antagonists; they crouched in rustic garb, armed with rifle and musket, in the ferns across the narrows, firing and reloading without haste or concern.

Slant, laboring beside me, ceased to dig and glared across the river at these impertinent curs, a look I had not seen inhabit his features previous: the look of one pressed by continual harassment to abandon good nature for extreme hatred.

We labored on. The fire, however, grew so troublesome and quick that after but a few minutes, the Quartermaster-Serjeant, having demanded we stand firm, called out orders for us to pull back.

We could not proceed with our work until the sloop-of-war *Otter* and her tenders assembled themselves near us in the channel, and began fire from their cannons, which sharp bombardment convinced the rebels to flee from the shore.

The *Otter* remained at anchor near the point where we labored; thus covered, we returned to our duties.

We spent the remainder of the day in constructing fortifications and the rudiments of the camp.

It appears that this shall be our occupation for some days to come.

June 1ˢᵗ, 1776

Last days spent in building fortifications.

The rebels, so close it seems one could shy pebbles and strike, build their own fortifications across the channel. Their redoubt is upon the slope of a hillside, and thus commands a view some ten or fifteen feet higher than ours; and yet no objection is made to our labor, which is constantly transacted beneath their view.

Beneath their gaze, upon the point closest to them, we have raised up a breastwork and a stockade, which fort we call Fort Hamond. Beneath their gaze, we have dug a trench to divide our peninsula from the island, that our encampment may be more agreeably defended. Beneath their gaze, we have cut low forest groves and hauled logs. We have raised up gun emplacements. Beneath their sardonic gaze, at the extreme eastern end of the isle, we build a *lazaretto* which shall receive those afflicted with the smallpox and the flux, which unfortunates have been confined this week aboard the *Adonis* hospital brig. We fear the enemy shall come to know how many of our number are riddled with disease.

Our forces being so sickly, the Marines have been landed again and prevailed upon to assist with guard details.

We are all suffering from our labors. There is no jesting or speech among us. Bono and I labor together, but sit silent at meals. Slant hath an hard, angry look in his eye, which I can little credit when I then see him, returning from our drills, stop to feed the sheep by tearing up grass with his hand, whispering to them with nary a stutter, I'll be bound.

All of our drills and our fatigue duties are transacted under the insolent glare of rebel pickets. I cannot abide their scrutiny. At every moment they stand silently observing us, I am sensible of their scorn for our Africk number, as if we merely play in mud like children while they do the work of men to contain us upon this island and wait to taunt us with ruin of our sand-pile. I wish to prove to them that we have not flown here, so much as settled upon a firm place, from which we shall sally forth. From such an isle, we may storm the land.

I must confess to weariness. How many ditches, in this one year, have I dug? How many revetments and scarps have I raised? And none seem to hold off these devils who wish to belabor us with their tethers and paddles and speeches on the rights of man.

The quarantine camp being sufficiently in readiness, we assisted this morning in the transportation of the victims of pestilence from the *Adonis* to their huts. Many are in the most advanced agonies, and each motion of the carts increases their suffering. They moan most terribly; their encrustations are awful to behold.

How strange (I marvel) that a ship named the *Adonis* should be the place of disfigurement.

The inoculations of those who have not yet suffered the disease shall commence shortly. Among some, accustomed to this practice by long usage in Africa, there is stoical assent; but the most are struck with horror. Old Better Joe endorses the procedure to all who shall listen, saying it is a tremendous charm against the pox; which leads Charles in his contrariety to mutter to Slant that he should *pay that old man no heed, for them gods are left behind,* and not to hearken to superstition, for inoculation can lead only to death. Slant is beset upon by all the transports of terror at the prospect. Isaac the Joiner saith that the Lord shall smite down whom He wishes with His pestilential scourge; that no such vain practice as introducing fevers shall help a man escape Jehovah's wrath.

I spake to Slant of the benefits of inoculation, which hath spared me the full ravages of the disease; to which he said nothing, while Charles replied, "We heard about your mother"; after which, my remonstrance ceased.

The Marines assisting in removing the sick from the *Adonis,* we discovered that twelve of our Regiment had died undetected of the pox while the ship lately stood at anchor off Gwynn's

Island. The command was for these bodies simply to be thrown overboard.

This heartless mandate was protested by my fatigue party, there being a strong belief among my companions — heathen and Christian alike — that when the dead and their burial grounds are abandoned, as in our flight, we condemn the spirits of the deceased to an eternity of oblivious, hungry wandering. The other men desired me, therefore, to write to Major Byrd as an intermediary and ask that he rectify this galling practice.

This I did, the black border on my mourning-paper being sadly fitting; I wrote to the Major, requesting as a sign of his beneficence that the bodies of such as die from smallpox be remitted to the charge of the various priests and enthusiasts of the Regiment, who should take care that the dead be disposed of according to the custom nearest their own dispensation.

Major Byrd replied to us favorably, if somewhat tartly, that we should find little resistance to a claim on the corpse of a dead, disease-riddled Negro, that being an object not universally relished; and that we might bury our dead as we pleased.

This word the Ensign delivered when we were at our supper. What followed then was debate upon how the bodies should be laid to rest, it being interdicted by ancient African practice that we should bury any victim of smallpox with other dead, and it being impractical to dispose of them as any African custom demands, either by depositing them in a forest or rendering them up to priests of the several smallpox gods. Thus, there gathered a loud convocation of such of our number as claim familiarity with appropriate rites of burial — a meeting of palaver-men, Christian New Lights, *obeah* priests, and new-made cunning-workers. There was much argument, and those sensations of fraternity and comity which at first brought our Regiment together at our dances gave way, I fear, to anger: *"What signifies that?"*—*"He don't remember."*—*"He god no god at all."* Men muttered in small cabals or threatened one another by the fireside, cutting each other with their eyes and hissing, vaunting superiority in their familiarity with the Unseen. All claimed to recall a better rite, and none would brook the others'.

I feared there should be violence. Better Joe rose up and, his eyes closed, his arms out, began to cry curses in his own language.

It is a testament to our confraternity, however, that a curious ground of agreement was eventually reached: the necessity of concealing all mourning at the smallpox burials, and displaying only dancing and festival triumph.

This agreement struck me at first with astonishment; but when 'twas explained to us by Isaac the Joiner, glowing with compromise, I saw its rectitude, and the confluence was so appropriate in its measures that I was deeply moved: For those of the Regiment who maintain that the disease is spread among us by pestilential spirits, funeral celebrations are necessary to deceive these malicious beings into believing that we think them of no account, that they might pass on and leave the rest of us unharmed. For those who believe the smallpox is but the expression of the Christian God's will, there is no cause for aught but celebration in a death, which is a liberation from this flesh.

And so, tomorrow night, we shall hold the first of these grim fêtes to inter the dead and trick the gods.

June 3rd, 1776

This day, in the evening, we held our funeral games.

There was, it seemed, more reason for merriment than the deception of malignant spirits: This day the women were rowed ashore from their ships, and have taken up residence with us. Anxious to be reunited with our friends, I accompanied Pro Bono to the shore, and was treated to a fine sight: the fleet at anchor there, one hundred or two hundred ships, lit red with the sun as it flickered upon the water, as the women were rowed toward us, waving and calling out across the shallows.

Dr. Trefusis accompanied them ashore, and 'twas my pleasure to escort him through the rough terrain of flat stump and loam we have made of the forest, down to the peninsula and to our tent. He was merry to see us, but his gaiety ceased when he saw our situation. He sat by our fly, casting looks across the channel, up toward the hillside where the hundred cook-fires of the enemy light up the night.

Come darkness, we took fire-brands and crossed the isle to the far shore, away from the scornful gaze of rebel and Redcoat alike. There we built our bonfire, and Olakunde and the other musicians began to make their music for the dance.

'Twas a strange scene, for most were delighted at their reunion with spouse, friend, and child; and others, the grieving, were asked to impersonate mirth to bewitch malign gods.

We dug pits by the shore and the lapping water, which place was held proper for tainted burials such as these. The corpses of the dead were laid upon the sand, and around them, those who knew the rites began their dances and grinned in simulated mirth.

The families of the dead, the friends, were instructed to show no sign of grief, none of the lineaments of sorrow.

Those who wished merely to drink and embrace were prodigiously discomfited by these uncanny shows, and moped, and glowered, and some moved off a space so as to give the mourners room sufficient for their ghastly levee.

And so there were two fêtes tonight, in neighboring groves: in one, mirth; in the other, mirth personated; in one, the transports of delight; in the other, the delights of despond; in one, the celebration of arrival; in the other, the rites of departure.

For a while, I observed the funeral games. The mourners leaped in the light of the fire and sang. All laughed, as if in jest, but the laughter was without joy; none wept, but the eyes were deranged with sorrow.

Will, silent Will, stood by my side and stared upon the graves, as if he wished himself therein.

Looking upon that scene—the full moon above, the flames below, the dancing bodies of the mourners, and behind them, the vast expanse of Chesapeake Bay—there could not be a scene conducing to greater sublimity. We stood there at the edge of land—seeing, beyond the graves, the bay, the distant, invisible sea, dark and yet illumined, profound and yet quiescent—our thoughts turning naturally to that final deep from which none return.

Beside us, men shaved each other's heads in grief.

When I had taken my fill of this strange draught, I made my way through the pines to the other convocation. I urged Will to come with me, believing it did his wounded soul no favor to watch more exertions for the dead. At this second scene of revelry, we found Slant and Pomp sitting silent upon the ground. They both inspected their own hands. I sat by them.

There was much talking and laughing, and a pleasant music played by an old man upon a hoe with finger-rings of lead. Charles and Pro Bono and their ilk sat about the fire and smoked their pipes, speaking of strategy, Miss Nsia among them; while near us, soldiers played a game, measuring out seeds in divots in the dirt, as others around them squatted and offered advice for leaps and tags, chewing upon sticks, drinking flip.

Olakunde, his drumming complete for the evening, came to our side. Slant seemed uneasy, and craved diversion; I presumed his melancholy air was occasioned by the inoculation to come and the grisly rites just past. So we sought to enliven our own gloomy wits as we ever do through conversation.

Watching the sparks and the fireflies, we told tales of flight: Olakunde told us of dead souls flying to freedom; and Pomp told us of live men rising from the fields, light as thistledown upon the wind, hands outstretched, yanking children from the tobacco weeds, lifting them, hauling them up onto shoulders lighter than air, great hordes of them disappearing across the seas. And I told them of Dædalus and his son, slaves imprisoned upon Crete by the walls of the Labyrinth that their own labors had built—father and son fleeing bondage on waxen wings.

In the midst of these tales, Slant wandered away from our number; and I was about to inquire after his sudden departure when Bono, Charles, and Private Harrison came to my side and demanded of me: "Draw the Colonies."

As I sketched on the dirt, Bono said, "See, we're bunged out of Boston. We have New-York still. General Howe sent a force down to tame the Carolinas. And what I say is, they're fools to fuss with the Carolinas. Faith, Prince O., that ain't where Maryland goes. You got it spang into Pennsylvania. See, what I'm saying is that whatever species of idiot is commanding this effort should focus his self on Virginia. They take back Virginia with us —"

"Food for New-York then," said Charles. "Pork, ham."

"Corn," said Private Harrison. "Plenty of corn."

"Wheat and such," agreed Bono. "Instead of they're supplied by Halifax or Cork."

I opined, "I believe Halifax is closer to New-York than is Virginia. If you'll excuse me, Slant seems melancholy, and I should —"

"No one excuses you," said Bono, who despises correction. "Apply yourself to Delaware. It looks globby. It ain't that globby in life. Listen, if General Howe stops sending troops down to the damn Carolinas, and sends them here instead, we will conquer Virginia again, and gentlemen, Virginia is the Pope's nose of colonies. I tell you this: I do love my old Boston-Town, with its fine six shades of black breech, excellent dead fish in the alleys, and a nation of hymnody all Sunday long, but Virginia is the — what's a gem? — ruby. Virginia is the ruby among governments — first in fashion — where the real genteel come to whip horseflesh and spit. We secure Virginia, and all the rest will drop."

"General Washington," said Charles, "he hear we take Virginia, he come back down, defend his house, his land, his all these thing."

Slant was back, but there was vomit upon his shirt. His hands were sticky with it and his eyes expressive of guilt.

"You reckon we can draw Chesapeake Bay and the Kingdom of Accomac?" Bono asked me, squatting beside me. "Together?"

Seeing Slant was in some distress, I rose and I replied that I was gratified they had applied to me, but begged them continue without the imperfections of my cartography. Slant protested that I should stay, bidding Pomp and I good night. I inquired if all was well; he replied he had vomited, and believed he had a fever.

Pomp and I led him back to our tent. At the mere suggestion we could take him to the quarantine camp, he demurred in the most plangent tones, saying, "This ain't the smallpox. I ha—, ha—, han't had the— ... smallpox. You don't take me there. You don't take me—they all has the smallpox there. This ain't no smallpox."

Pomp and I watch by him while he sleeps.

June 4ᵗʰ, 1776

The King's birthday. Great cannonades and twenty-one-gun salutes from all the ships of the line, and a flourish of detonations from Fort Hamond. From the *Fowey,* we hear distantly a choir of seamen singing a *Jubilate* in harmony.

Today, all those who have not had the smallpox were removed for inoculation and sequestration in the hospital. Slant was detected in his illness; though he protested, none know what his fever might be; and so they removed him with them.

This evening, I attended Slant in the hospital to quiet his distress. There are soldiers by the camp of the sick who question closely as to whether we have previously suffered the smallpox. I showed the mark upon my arm and was admitted. I spake comfortably to him and fetched water both for him and for those around him, who had not received succor all day. I asked Slant whether our officers visit the dying, which is their duty; but he said that none will enter the Negro pest-house. I watched by his side until a regimental doctor—sent from the 14ᵗʰ, as we have none of our own—came by with febrifuge.

The ravages of the sick are become inhuman. Among those fully afflicted, the skin boils and runs with yellow matter. Trains of sores encircle the eyes and gather at the lips. Some are distempered out of all reason and nature, and grasp at all who go by with hands emaciated by the deprivations of fever. Some of the sick lie without motion, suffering an entire stagnation of the fluids. Equally pitiable are those such as Slant who display the fever, but who have not yet come into pocking—for they wait there on pallets amid the stench and disfiguration of their brethren—eyeing each minute the tears in the flesh, the dissolution of form and distemper of mind which may soon be theirs.

The women and children are not exempt, and the heart cannot be moved to greater pity than to see a child, stubby of leg, working his way along an aisle of mattresses, his lips aswarm with sores, as the infant Plato is said to have drawn bees to his mouth by the sweetness of his breath. Now that I am returned to my own tent, the mind relucts to recall the wailing anguish of these children, the manner in which they bat at their mothers and their own irruptions.

Many, of course, have escaped, the fever having run its course. The scabs harden and, at length, fall off; and gradually, the mind reasserts balance and health.

Others succumb, and in squalor see their last vision of Time.

Slant and I had spoken but twenty minutes when, hard by us, a youth who had held still for too many days suddenly burst forth with a scream of fury, half stood, and began scratching at his whole body with his fingernails, raking open the pocks, his entire frame shaking, yelling in ire at his own disordered flesh. His blood ran out copiously, and he sought to worry himself—thirsty for damage—even as we tugged on his arms.

We quieted him; I washed him with water as he wept. Slant, lain back down beside him, was in an excess of horror, but I was not at liberty to remain longer, and so, with anxious blessings, I made my exit.

I returned to my tent to find Miss Nsia sitting with Bono. He endeavored, while they conversed, to tie her hand to her foot with twine as a jest. She spied his design and pulled away her wrist. ~~It is no time for~~

I fear there are some who, themselves immune to terrors, are too deficient in compassion to—

Even now, they laugh.

It becomes us to forget the seductions of Venus when Hygeia weeps for want.

I wished to go again tonight to view this evening's funeral games for the dead, to observe again the dancing and grinning; but when Bono and I requested leave to do so, we were denied. Thus we spent the evening by our cook-fire in idleness.

Shortly after the cannon marked the evening, Captain Mackay sent his aide, requesting we go forth and pull Serjeant Clippinger from his amusements. We sought the Serjeant out; and Bono and I came across him sitting with white privates of the 14ᵗʰ, singing bawdry which I shall not repeat. We lifted him to remove him from their presence, and he protested that we were too monstrous ungentle — *boys, boys, look ye — boys — the brave lads of the 14ᵗʰ was going to chivvy me out a woman for a little kissing comfort.*

We delivered him to the Captain. Bono and Miss Nsia spent the remainder of the evening in making lips with their fists and puppet-courting as Clippinger and mistress. Bono pressed his hand to the dirt, that his fist might be pimpled and scarred.

I fear we none of us have much respect for our commander.

[Anonymous song]

How pleasant to join the King's Army!
How brave, sir, to march on our way!
When we limp from the plain
In most grievous pain
And our legs are both broke
And they're spattered with brain—
Thank the Lord, sir, for eight pence a day!

How pleasant to join the King's Army!
How brave, sir, to march on parade!
With the pox and the flux
And the year's only fucks
Are straight up the rear
From a Welsh fusilier
'Tis no wonder we listed and stayed.

How pleasant to join the King's Army!
How brave, sir, to do as you're bade!
To freeze and to fry
And to fall and to die
While the author of war
Is home thrumming his whore
And prinking his hair with pomade.

How pleasant to join the King's Army!
How brave, sir, to march on parade!

June 8th, 1776

Some startling news this day.

I visiting Slant at the noon hour with Pro Bono, we came upon Miss Nsia, who was carrying water to the ailing. "A ministering angel," said Bono, and pressed her free hand to his lips.

"Ha!" she scolded with a laugh. "You shut you devil mouth." She pulled away and flicked his cheek with her fingers.

"We has news," Bono announced to me, and the unwonted shyness of his manner conveyed his news faster than word.

Miss Nsia said, "I am the greatest fool that ever walk on mud."

"We is getting married."

My thoughts were in a ferment; I barely knew what to say.

I wished them hearty congratulations, and enlarged upon the importance, at moments of great strife, of the forging of those bonds which unify human variance and align individuals in amity, providing safe haven so that the tenderer of sentiments might once again bud and flourish despite the incursions of violence.

"You give him some water and a rasher of bacon," said Bono, "he'd go on for some time in this vein."

Their delight was too great to note that their announcement may have occasioned any uneasiness in me, though I stammered, and imagine I blushed. Confronting their joy, once I have settled my wits, I am sure I shall feel joy in sympathy; Bono would do so for me.

I pray to remember the pleasure in other's triumphs. We must endeavor to smile not just with the face upon the sweet felicities of others, but with the heart.

This afternoon, we were returned to our details. I spent hours neck-deep in a hole.

Today—I can scarce write it for ire—today as we shoveled dirt into barrels, to erect a mortar emplacement, I happened to look down the shore of the island, and there I perceived a body of Negroes engaged at digging an artificial harbor. I believed my senses deceived me—for one was Slant.

We being released for our dinner, I ran to the place where they dug.

Slant, hands red and wet with sores, stood shirtless in the pond, great masses of insects swarming about him.

I fear I swore—I choked back horror—I asked him why he toiled there, when he should rest.

Said he, "Lord Dunmore ordered it."

"The sick?" said I. "To dig?"

He shrugged and said, "Most of them ain't sick yet. The . . . inoculated. They're waiting. To be poorly. They ain't sick yet. Most of them." In such meandering repetitions did he speak. The mosquito-flies delighted in the corruption of his flesh. Its smell was overpowering in the heat. He swatted too slowly for insect eye at the swarms around us. His arm was sluggish. He did not complain.

I reeled at these revelations—and let it here be recorded: By Lord Dunmore's order, that work is undertaken by a force assembled from all those who have smallpox and who can wield a shovel—and by the slaves of Loyalists, which force His Lordship has pledged to leave in bondage—for he promised freedom only to the slaves of rebels.

Slant could not close his mouth. His head twitched nearly to his shoulder with the bites. He stood, socked in grime, without a shirt upon him, in his wet pit.

"Slant," said I, "feign collapse."

He looked upon me with confusion, and I demanded again that he fall and wait to be led away as unproductive. "Once I am gone," said I. "I will protest this in a letter to the Regimental commanders."

He did not respond but with a nod, signifying no steady purpose nor comprehension. With this, I quit him and returned to my detail, where I made complaint about the circumstances.

I have spent the remainder of the day, when unengaged, in complaint, each officer chiding me and sending me away. Corporal Craigie revealed a humane disgust at the practice, but said I should speak to the Serjeant. As might be expected, Serjeant Clippinger had no interest in the case, and enjoined me to cease my prim bickering. I wrote a letter to Captain Mackay, to which I received no reply. I wrote a letter to Major Byrd, which was returned to me by his aide-de-camp, who regretted that the Major was accepting no letters from *that vile, pox-ridden band of Negroes* that was not first dipped in vinegar. I have no vinegar. I wrote a letter to Lord Dunmore, which I saw read by its messenger and ripped in eight before my eyes.

I have run from end of the isle to end. When I returned to our fly, evening having fallen, I found Dr. Trefusis applying cold tea to his sunburns.

Unable to contain my anger, I recalled the encounter which had transpired by the officers' pavilions.

"Lord Dunmore," said I, "cares not a whit for us, does he?"

Dr. Trefusis regarded me with care, then replied, "I fear generosity toward thy benighted race is not, perhaps, first among—"

"Tell me."

He admitted, "Not a groat."

"We cannot look to him for safety."

"You can, so long as your safety is a strategic necessity."

"We have hazarded our lives for his cause."

"I fear, Octavian, you often do not account for self-interest. 'Tis only self-love and self-interest which actuates animals."

"Which animals?"

"Mammals with titles, *par exemple*. The wrist-chafer."

"Do not speak to me of his wrists. He was our hope."

"A pity," said Dr. Trefusis. "We do not need a hope, but a hero."

This evening, in our fly, word that the rebels bruit abroad that they shall proclaim the independency of the Colonies. I feel in my soul only a weariness at the continual braying of their vanity, their outrage at small sufferings when greater are to hand.

Tonight, I observe the fires of the rebels upon the shore. We all call their camp *Cricket Hill,* because they swarm so many. As I watch them, I think of a tale taught me by Dr. Trefusis in those days following my first whipping, when he tutored me upon antique slavery and its discontents.

When the pirate-king Sextus Pompeius led a force like ours, of slaves who had thrown off their shackles of bondage, his raids were productive of such terror that the very rulers of Rome sought to treat with him; but he would not walk upon the land to meet with them, for fear that his people should be taken and returned to slavery. The water and the shifting waves, that element most known for its mutability and treachery, was to him the sturdiest and most familiar field of operation; the land, immutable, was the site of betrayal and uncertainty.

And so when the rulers of Rome sought to parley with Sextus Pompeius, he demanded they do so thus: each party situated upon a floating platform, shouting to each other across the waves.

I think upon this when I view the activity of our enemy, so close across the bay that we might hail them with barely a raising of the voice.

I watch their fires, the sound of them upon the hillside like locusts; I look out at the *Dunmore,* the seat of our Governor, floating serenely amidst its city of ships, and I think of the pirate-king and the rulers of Rome upon their buoyant platforms. Is it not ever thus, the attempts to parley between master and slave, and perhaps between all men — is it not always words shouted across the shifting flood, torn away by wind? Each hath his element; each is wary of brigandage; and a gulf roils between us all.

Everywhere, the depredations of sickness; nowhere, even within our skulls, is there ease. The Regiment does not rest upon this island.

This hour I have gone to the east side of the island with Charles and Bono to watch the celebration of the funeral games; three were to be buried. Tonight, however, there was a mood of danger there. We found men guarding the dance jealously. Private Morris debarred our passage with his arm.

Isaac the Joiner stood watching the group of them. "They are raising demons," he said.

We stood by him and observed. The crowd was small and selected of the greatest enthusiasts among the Regiment; they played upon cookware.

Then I heard great cries, and I saw that two danced and shuddered in the midst of them, throwing out their limbs, calling, and hissing; one of these rapt individuals was Better Joe, in a mask he had fashioned out of cloth, crying as if the god were upon him.

"They made a drink," said Isaac. "Some recipe out of blood and dirt dug from the graves. They're swallowing it." He put his hand over his elbow and said, "It's the sport of idolatry. A new covenant with their damnable gods. To reverse the crippling enchantments of Europe with their deviltry. To defeat the magical power of the white man." He looked down. "And I can't blame them," he said. "I cannot blame them."

I watched Better Joe's gyrations in the mask, while all around him stood back and watched his hissing. I saw potency there, and eternity.

Isaac closed his eyes and muttered, "By the power that is within me, in the name of the Lord Jesus, I ask, Lord, I ask that this wicked spirit be cast out, that Satan's work be confounded, that this unfortunate Africk energumen be freed from the shackles of diabolatry as he was of slavery."

Better Joe looked out into the night — with a great commanding croak, pointed at Charles, and through the crush of devotees, bid him approach. He waved with his old arms and spake in the language of the Ibo.

Charles frowned and turned away; he walked back along the path we came upon. Bono and I rushed to follow.

Bono said, "If these incantations move them to fight better against the rebel, I can welcome it. But if they take up arms against our own officers, I am telling you true, there will be a sure work of cruelty, for we ain't no equals to the regulars, and they won't recognize no distinction between us if there's a revolt."

Charles did not speak to him in return.

Near the farms, some piles were burning.

"What is a ma—, a man worth?" Slant asked me today, his lips enjoying but slight mobility.

Before I had thought sufficiently upon his question, I answered gently that I did not know, but reckoned it at forty or fifty pound; there being no natural price for a man, as it fluctuated according to the tobacco crop, rice, coastal storms, and other several factors; that there is no security in such tallies, all prices hanging upon other prices in a complicated rigging.

Having proceeded this far, I ceased, and saw the unenlightened look in his eye.

I began again. "There is no price for a man," I answered passionately this time.

He did not heed my foolish reply. "I thought we was going to . . . fight," he said, his ravaged face twitching. "I thought that's war. You fight."

"We will fight, my friend," said I.

He nodded, as best he could. "You will," he assented.

June 14th, 1776

For two hours today, I stoked a fire to burn barrelfuls of pork we found blighted with rot. Thus my employment.

Dr. Trefusis, who went to minister to Slant, delivers word from the sick-camp that one of the inmates of that place has refused food. Against orders, he left his mattress today and walked to the eastern shore of the island, followed by a crowd of devotees; and there, he knelt upon the dirt of his brethrens' graves, and began to eat that dirt, shoveling it into his mouth.

He says he commences a ghost.

June 15th, 1776

This day a soldier of our Regiment was discovered stabbed to death in the ditch by the encampment. 'Tis not known who killed him. The ghastly deed was done between the hours of three o'clock and five o'clock in the morning.

Rumors of gambling debt and magic both abound.

In the night, Isaac the Joiner had a dream in which we all hung with wires through our bodies, and pigeons made their homes upon us, even as we died suspended.

He claims this dream to be divinely inspired, and fasts this day.

Better Joe is seized with horror, and walks with a blanket wrapped about him.

June 16ᵗʰ, 1776

Slant is dead. Returned from our field exercises, I paid him a call at the hospital. He was not upon his bed. I found him shrouded in the wheelbarrow.

Thus informed by the sight of him covered by burlap, I set out from the hospital and returned to our camp, where Pomp swept out our tent. Upon my appearing, he put by his whisk and asked me how I fared.

I went to my pack and removed my razor. I gestured he should sit; and he knew the truth of it.

He sat before me without tear or grimace, and in silence, I shaved off his hair.

When I was finished, I sat, and he performed the same office for me. We both, I believe, thought upon that dream that one day we should all sit at the same table on Thanksgiving; that we should show our children our shirts, and tell them tales of when we were young.

It took Pomp some time to complete the shaving, he not being accustomed to that work. I welcomed every stumble, for it brought blood.

Bono came to our fly, bursting full of news; but seeing this tableau, he stopped up his tongue. He observed us in this rite, and though we shed no tears, he did. He whispered, "Liberty to Slant. Liberty to Slant."

Slant was one of six to die this day. We took him in the evening down to the waterside. Isaac declaimed a prayer of his own devising. Olakunde, versed in the praise-song of Sonponna, spirit of smallpox, beat upon the *dundun* drum and sang of how the god could not dance, being lumbered with a wooden leg, but still could watch the dancing of others in his honor, *O great one, Cold Ground, Hot Ground, Father in the Forest, Wind Like a Man, Peace to the Afflicted, Sweetly, Softly*; and then we lowered the bodies into pits near the lapping water; where Slant's blotched face was covered with sand, his gray eyes blinded with mud, and his limbs, finally, hidden forever from the sun. The last I saw of him, he lay on his left side, an amulet in his hand to guard against deviltry on his last, long journey.

Then began the awful crooning, the grimaced smiles, the mothers clapping for the death of their children to deceive the god. The shouting was loud tonight, and I thought on tall Slant, ill-toothed, slow of speech, gentle of heart. Before me, the crowd of twenty or so surged along the brink of the pit. Women courtesied with kerchiefs in their hands. Men lamented in joy and wailed in exultation, while others slapped juba upon their arms and thighs.

Bono took my hands; he drew me forward. I resisted, for I knew not the measures; but he insisted, and I followed, and found myself next to Pomp in the dance, next to Bono himself. Miss Nsia stood by the verge and watched us; we were among the others, and I knew none of the steps they assayed, but still I moved with them, my teeth clacking with each step; a leg unused to vivid motion, an arm; our bodies roiling above, Slant's inert below, and we all beat time, we all bowed low, we all spun in the night, and paced in lines, and clapped.

For the first time, I danced.

A LAMENT

translated by Olakunde and set down in the language of his oppressor

Death sit in the house.

Death sit in the field.

Death sit in the river.

The house is full of smoke,

But the field is full of sun.

Go now to the heaven of breezes.

Walk to that heaven.

We will not kill the antelope,

We will let the antelope run,

Until you there and gone.

June 19th, 1776

I cannot abide this camp longer, and have requested I be sent out
upon a forage expedition; which request has been denied.

June 20th, 1776

This day we hear that soldiers have been deserting the 14th Regiment and fleeing under cover of darkness across the small space between our camp and the enemy's, there to take up arms and join our opponents.

And why should they not?

When, a few days past, the Articles of War were read to us all, great shew was made over those words devoted to the punishments for soldiers who dare desert.

'Twas, it is certain, a warning to us that if we of our regiment consider flight, or action through uprising, taking up arms against our officers, we shall die.

I spake of this with Bono; who replied, "Fools. Where they think we going to run?"

June 22nd, 1776

There were no drills this day, nor no digging of earthworks. His Lordship hath no use for us.

No one speaks of Slant.

A cult of suicides hath grown up by the burial ground upon the east side of the island, a communion of willed starvation. Dr. Trefusis and I today walked to that melancholy place, to view the suicides' pitiable condition and inquire whether we might in some wise offer succor.

They wait to die amidst the grove of red pines, sitting naked, leaned against the scaly flanks of the trees. They refuse all sustenance, as they do benefit of liquid. They are slow in their motions; most are afflicted with the smallpox or some other distemper.

They will not speak to any. The officers will not walk among them. We watched one crawl to the graves and begin to eat the dirt, coughing and gagging all the while.

I offered assistance to one, lifting him from the ground; but he filled himself with heaviness, until all my efforts could not support him. He being placed again upon the pine needles, he curled and put his hands in his mouth; his lips were dry with clay.

In the midst of sorrow comes joy. Today, Pro Bono, called Private William Williams, was married to Nsia Williams.

Marriages between Negroes being celebrated in this Colony with no priest nor legal binding, they were free to marry as they pleased, which they did by passing a cup of wine, and, amid applause of all the guests, pouring the lees upon the ground as libation, after which, they met in a kiss.

It was a most affecting occasion.

The homily and marriage sentences were said, at Bono's request, by Dr. Trefusis. They ran somewhat thus: "It is with unutterable pleasure that I present to you today young Private Williams and his bride, whose beauties of person are equaled only by those of her merits.

"I first knew Private Williams"—and here he could not forbear shedding a tear, his voice clutching too tight for words—"I first knew Private Williams when he was but a child, a reprobate little nursling of eight summers, a charming wag we called, out of our deep affection, 24-06.

"I tell ye, my friends, there was a look in 24-06's eye that spake instanter of his wits and acumen. I recall the first instance where I fully credited his quick parts: I observed him blacking his master's shoes. One may apply blacking as one will—for it is not in the application, but in the buffing, that the art of blacking lies. And yet, I perceived that the young 24-06, denied most materials for expression, daubed pictures upon his master's shoes. They were faces, as I recall, with tongues out or rapiers thrust through the heads. They were the very spirit of insurrection and glee.

"Then, without remorse for the passing of his figures, he took up the cloth and began his buffing, which obliterated each face in turn as he whispered, 'And then he died! And then he was kill!' He brought the shoes to an admirable sheen; and yet, I could not ever after look at my friend Gitney's shoes without seeing those faces hidden there, invisible as the phiz of the pixie, gaping out, mocking all routes walked by the boy's master, making all business of that great man inane, for the clucking of the shoes.

"Mr. 24-06, Private Williams, still brings to all he touches an admirable sheen; and yet, he cannot improve upon the polish of his bride, Miss Nsia Randolph of Chesterfield County. In Nsia combineth the modesty of feminine grace with the forwardness of moral strength. Employed in this Regiment initially as a washer-woman, Miss Nsia hath become a help to the afflicted, working tirelessly with the ill to bring succor and relief. Far too often, the voice of an angel proceedeth from a breast too little angelic; but in this instance, angel coats the throat and cradles the heart, from which emanate all kind virtues."

Here Dr. Trefusis stopped and reflected before continuing, so moved was he by the direction of his own oratory. Said he: "When one comes to the end of one's days, one looks about, exhausted by the blasts and eddies of fortune, and longs for the quietude of annihilation; and yet, 'tis not simply that: for the sight of lovers such as these recall to us the sweetness that we may find here upon Earth as well—and looking upon them, I am transported by a sensation of all the multitude of things that shall remain closed to me in this one, little lifetime: the languages forever unknown to me, in which I might, on some summer evening, have spoken of love—the huts beside some riverside, in which I might have heard tales unimagined—the volcanoes I wot of distantly—the castles in Turkish crags I shall not lay eyes upon— ... See ye? All the ... Yes. Indeed.

"And like a child who hath been spun upon his father's shoulders, the whole while screaming and protesting, who now, sensible of the ride's end, feels the hands lain upon him to set him down from the vomitiginous swirl of motion—calls, 'Pray, again! Again!' and wishes to start the game anew—so do I feel, seeing these two standing before me. I wish, as the gods of the *Hindoos,* to sprout a thousand faces, each one peering into a different life; a thousand feet to tread different soils; and a thousand hands with which to practice compassion.

"One cannot, however, return to this place; for *nolens, volens,* we are all headed for that last great river where all is forgot. So I bid you, my dears, my loves: Live fully in thy single face, with it pressed deep into the world; walk with strength and dignity, dance with joy, for all those who lie in the dirt beneath thy feet and dance and walk no more; and stretch out thy hands to take another's, to embrace as many as thou canst; as today, you do.

"And so ..." Here he raised his own hand. "And so, now, in the eyes of man and the empty void around man, by the power invested in me as a bitter, sentimental old splenetick, I hereby name thee, William Williams, and thee, Nsia Randolph, man and wife, to have and to hold; may ye find a joy in each other as senseless and complete as the death that shall eventually sunder you. Amen."

He clasped their hands to his chest, overcome with tears, and there was general acclamation.

Following this, we retired to the wedding feast, which, there being no meat for the Ethiopian Regiment for two days, consisted of pork bones boiled in water.

Bono embraced me, and I him, and we did not, for long minutes, release each other. When I did step away from him, I saw his face wet with tears, and he whispered to me, "I would my mother was here."

"When this is over," said I, "we shall find her."

"We won't find anyone," he said, turning. "And this ain't ever going to be over."

He went back to his feast.

❦ In the wake of the festivities, we watched the Regimental children play, running about the pasture and fancying themselves captives in the great oven of Nebuchadnezzar. They leaped and schemed escapes, producing doors from air.

Observing Miss Nsia — now Mrs. Williams — smiling upon their antics, Dr. Trefusis asked whether the new pair wished soon to have children. Mrs. Williams replied that she did not wish to at present, given the hostilities; but that Pro Bono desired to as soon as they might. "He wish a boy. I tell him, 'You just want to see you own face on more people around our house.'"

I owned that I was somewhat surprised to hear that Private Williams was so much in favor of reproduction, when his views of our future were so grim.

Mrs. Williams laughed. "So he says. But Private Williams — he is a big hank of sentiment." She turned to me and asked, "Private Nothing, you ever wish for to marry?"

I hid my confusion at this inquiry, little desiring to meet her gaze (she who I found so perfect and artless) nor that of my tutor (who should sound out my discomfort); and I replied that I did dream of retiring after the war to a cabin by a great, silent river with a fair one who might join me in such solitude, that we might together make music, merriment, and a nobler generation.

"Someday soon, you find that fair one," she said in mollifying tones. "You a handsome man." She patted me upon the arm. "When I met you, I thought you was very handsome, excepting you wasn't interested." She laughed. "You was more handsome than that fool," she said in tones of delight, watching her husband scamper across the field, tilting with the children, playing the Babylon King.

I nodded; and presented my regrets that I had to step suddenly away upon an errand. Dr. Trefusis watched me go, as the children, screeching with delight, were beset upon by lions.

June 24th, 1776

This day a dispute broke out among our Regiment.

It was occasioned by the cult of dirt-eaters, which despairing souls grow in number upon the far shore of the island, smeared with loam, destitute of movement and lost to all sensation, encrusted with dirt, begrimed with misery.

During supper-time, we heard shouting from another Company — curses the most furious — and, wondering at this outburst, we abandoned our plates and rushed to witness the argument.

It ran thus: Speaking of the dirt-eaters, a soldier of Coromantee blood had said this slow self-murder was nothing but *fool Ibo weakness,* adding that *he ain't never met an Ibo man, but they cried theyselves to sleep;* and *soon as there's any hardship, they stringing up they noose.*

At this, those of Ibo blood were greatly affronted, and rose to protest; the Coromantees jesting further; one of them recalling when he was new off the ship, unseasoned, and *all the boys was took for to be branded,* that the first Ibo boy having the scalding brand pressed into his shoulder screamed in pain; and all the other Ibo boys, in the transports of sympathy, began to wail, to moan, as if had they themselves been seared — *like some parcel of girls, so affrightened — oh!* Whereas, said he, the Coromantees danced up to the *buckra*-men and offered their shoulders; they laughed when burned — "Now, they was men, not Ibo girls."

And at that word, the men of Ibo blood, pressed to defend their honor, fell upon the Coromantees, and began to strike them; an Efik man still recounting how his father had told him of conveying

[440]

those blubbering Ibos for sale at Old Calabar; and hearing this, Charles, who cannot abide an Efik, plunged into the fracas and began in earnest to try to crush the life out of this vaunter's lungs. The combatants had hard work of it to avoid the embers of their small fire, engaged in their melee at its side — plates rattled beneath their heels and there were dim cries of pain. The scene was pitiable — the violence earnest, but with all the lassitude of the starving, peered down upon by triumphant rebels, Olympian in the dusk.

Into this skirmish stepped Isaac the Joiner, crying, "Dear brethren — peace — dear brethren — for the sake of Christ our Savior — " until the rest of us, roused from the stupor attendant upon shock, slipped in to divide again the Gold Coast and the Ibo uplands — heaving men back by their arms — glimpsing, among us all, not simply fists, but knives.

At this interesting juncture, a white lieutenant, hearing the cries, approached shouting; at which the scuffle evaporated entire, and left only men standing ashamed around the ruins of a fire; returning to their own suppers; facing away into the night.

Above us, from Cricket Hill, came the sound of applause.

June 29th, 1776

Our Company is assembled this day for foraging raids upon the Rappahannock. We set forth in the *Crepuscule* shortly after dawn.

Pomp and I were pleased to discover that Vishnoo was yet uneaten, and we spent the hours of our voyage reclined, with the tortoise corralled between us.

At noon, we sent word at a plantation chosen by what means I know not, requesting they should deal with us fairly and present us with corn, livestock, and other sundry provisions. Seeing our numbers drawn up with muskets upon our launch, they did not hesitate to comply, though 'twas said they were rebels.

We are newly arrived back at the sloop, having brung off a quantity of sheep and three cows.

Olakunde tells me he shall teach me an Oyo tune upon the pipes.

[A memorandum to Captain Mackay]

June 30

The *Crepuscule,* off Gwynn's Island

Captain Bryant of the *Crepuscule* sloop-of-war presents his Compliments to Capt. Mackay and wishes to make known he shall appear presently to inform the Captain of the Loss of 7 Privates & one Officer in their late Raids upon the Rappahannock.

On the 29th in the Evening, about 6 PM, we anchor'd near Fairweather Creek on the Advice of Lt. Bryson & sent a Party of 21 Privates & their Serjeant ashore. There, the Enemy engag^d with the Party & in the Affray were captured or slain 7 Privates & Sjt. Clippinger. A full List is appended to this Memorandum.

Following this Skirmish, the remaining 14 Pvts. were brought aboard. We sent warning Shots to annoy the Rebels, but received no Reply. One Half Hour later we sent a Flag of Truce ashore to demand Return of any Taken & any Dead. The Rebels w^d not treat with us; they had abandon^d their Post of Ambush & could not be Found.

We waited until 10 PM (some 4 Hours) but Sjt. Clippinger not returning, we weigh^d & set sail.

We fell down the River toward the Bay.

We may supply more Details as necessary. This Memorandum to notify you of the Circumstance.

Capt. Bryant of the Crepuscule

Gwynn's Island
June 30th, 1776

To His Lordship the Earl of Dunmore:

YOUR LORDSHIP shall forgive his correspondent for troubling him, but I am in a most anxious taking and I do exist
in hope that Your Lordship might in some wise amelio-
rate my concerns. It is a vexing matter of some note that
when the foraging party aboard the *Crepuscule* sloop-
of-war returned this morning, they reported they had
lost several of their number in an engagement upon the
Rappahannock. There were two Privates of especial
interest to me assigned to this detachment who were not
among those who returned. I wish to hear with all celerity
of their location and the manner in which Your Lordship
proposes to assure their safety. Such word shall do much
to soothe the troubled mind of

thy most humble & obedient servant,

Dr. J. Trefusis

[444]

Lost, presumed dead or captured in Saturday's action
upon the Rappahannock:

    Serjeant Thᵒ· Clippinger

    Pvt. Wᵐ· Harrison

    Pvt. Pompey Lewis

    Pvt. Wᵐ· Williams

    Pvt. Jemmy Baron

    Pvt. Octavian Nothing

    Pvt. Cæsar Ackerman

    Drummer Jack White, called Ollickundy

The following *Promotions* are made by His Lordship
until His Majesty's Pleasure is known: Corporal Wᵐ·
Craigie is to be Serjeant *vice* Thᵒ· Clippinger, lost.
Private Jacob Tye is to be Corporal *vice* Wᵐ· Craigie,
preferred. Private Quash Miller is to be Drummer *vice*
Jack White in the Regimental Musick.

GOD SAVE THE KING.

Gwynn's Island
July 1, 1776

To His Lordship the Earl of Dunmore:
Having received no answer from Your Lordship to my letter of the 30th *ult.* I write again as I am in the utmost distresses.

I demand to know what measures you propose, sir, to recover those taken prisoner last week. I demand to know your intentions regarding this unspeakable affront to the dignity of His Majesty's troops. An army sits idle here. Perhaps Your Caledonian Excellency might put them to use. That is, I am to understand, what actual men of honor do with armies.

But perhaps fondly mistaken is

thy servant,

Dr. John Trefusis

[A letter from Lord Dunmore to Dr. John Trefusis]

Aboard the *Dunmore*
July 2ⁿᵈ, 1776

Sir You are a doctor and I wonder at what school you learnt impudence. I am not accustomed to receiving scoldings from men the most debased, liars & degenerate rogues. We shall in no wise exercise ourselves for the loss of a few Negroes, which action would be on all heads impracticable & fruitless. They are most likely now sold again or executed and an expedition would be the height of absurdness.

I regret that you lost your especial Negroes. If you would wish to purchase more, Mrs. Daunting aboard the *Pleasure* schooner wishes to sell five.

If however Dr. Trefusis wishes a topman's view of the surrounding country to espy his dear black friends, I shall happily suspend him from the yardarm by his neck if he send another missive like his last to

Your Royal Governor,

John, Earl of Dunmore, Baron Murray of Blair, &c., &c.

[447]

Gwynn's Island, Virginia Colony
July 2nd, 1776

My dear Fruhling —

My news is the most dire. I cannot express the like. I know not how I shall deliver this billet to you. Though coasters depart from our camp here daily, they do so with an eye not to stretching north, but for brigandage about the Bay; and in any event, did they arrive at some northern port, no letter they deposited should be received by you, ensconced as you are in the heart of lawless usurpation and rebellion. However, in times of tumult, oft expression supersedes — by God — no matter —

They are gone, Fruhling — my boys, they are gone.

Octavian, of whom I have written, and William Williams, another servant of the College of Lucidity in the days of our ascendancy, set forth seven days ago with a foraging detail navigating the Rappahannock River. The next day, the sloop-of-war upon which they sailed returned, and reported the melancholy news that they had met with resistance at a rebel farm, and that eight men were lost. Among the number who could not be accounted for were both Williams and Octavian.

'Twas said that at the farm, the rebels lay an ambush and divided the landing party; and having so done, fell upon the smaller of the parties, killing some and taking others captive. Did they survive, a fellow soldier explained to me without remorse, they shall by now certainly be hanged or brutally used in some other manner. I have gone to each officer of that Regiment demanding that they send a retributive expedition, but none evinces the slightest interest in the undertaking. Lord Dunmore himself will not admit me for an audience.

Here, all is in chaos: The Governor of Maryland is fled Annapolis, brought by the *Fowey* man-of-war to our camp. He hath been ousted from his seat. He joins Lord Dunmore here. All royal authority seems to have ceased on the land, and the governors preside only over their floating town and this sickly island. The rebels crowd so thick over the shore that they resemble the locust.

Shortly before he set forth on this final voyage, Octavian, my dear Octavian, spake to me of writing a treatise upon government. I inquired of him what should be its salient points, and he replied: "It is a fact easily discernible that governments are instituted to commit the crimes that their citizens require for gain, but cannot countenance committing privately."

I intervened in this piece of charming youthful *désespoir*, countering that some philosophers say governments were instituted to protect the *natural rights of the*

[*449*]

citizen; to which Octavian said that *nature recognizes no rights.* "Our rights are unnatural, or we should need no government to defend them." I protested; he insisted. "Look abroad in the fields," he said. "What may kill, kills; what may eat, eats. All things are born unequal, and there is no law but that inequality."

I did not disagree, but I was uneasy at the savagery in his address. "You would say yourself," I reminded him, "*'Blessed are the meek, for they shall inherit the earth.'*"

"And you would say yourself," he replied, "*'The world is the house of the strong.'*" Thus ended our protreptic discourse.

And yet, the same day, as we fetched water, Octavian observed a small child of two or three summers, the child of one of our soldiers, wash her father's face imperfectly and laugh; and as Octavian observed this fumbled cleansing and the father's smile, I saw that he wept for the sweetness of it. This is the boy I know — soft-hearted and solemn — not he who speaks of natural rights being nonsense; not he who declaims there is no law but power and profit; not he who declares the inheritance of the meek to be void and entangled in probate.

What soured thee, my child? This I know — for I did. Thou speakest like me.

The world is indeed the house of the strong; and we are indeed a terrible animal. We are granted gifts of intellect almost god-like, to raise ourselves out of the burrow and ditch; and yet cannot enjoy these excellences, for no sooner does one establish the work of his hands and plow the field, than some other, deranged with greed, sweeps in to plunder or to expand their own holdings through act of law or canny dealing.

Speak not to me comfortable words.

We are a foul animal poisoned in all its springs and motivations, a beast of snarling ferity that parades itself in silks and calleth itself an angel, while gnawing upon cattle, seizing upon fowls, ransacking the earth and the seas, clawing our neighbor to provide for ourselves small trinkets to lay in our nests where we curl in bloated slumber.

Do I possess hope for the future? I may reply, I do have hope, in that I do not believe our race shall perish. We shall, in two hundred years, in two thousand, yet be flourishing, the strong oppressing the weak, telling tales of why they must; we shall yet be starving each other, maiming, whipping, killing, raping, sacking, burning, scorning, despoiling, savaging, and congratulating ourselves on our superior nature.

Do not speak glibly of virtue. Nothing shall change — nothing — so long as each individual awaits preferment rather than embodying beneficence in himself; so long as we wait upon the edicts of a government ruled by invested and interested men looking to their private purses; so long as we idle in expectation that all shall be healed, and that we shall somehow be stopped in our career of plunder by an eighteen-hundred-year-old mummy, scarred with the wounds of torture, falling out of the sky or stumbling out of the desert, eyes filled with the tears that we should weep ourselves.

Send me my boys back. Send them back to me, safe and sound, and I shall grant anything. Do not permit me to wither and die alone. I ask only this one thing.

So do I await news of them. I sleep not in the night. In the day, I minister to the dying in the quarantine camp, which hath a sweet miasma so foul it can scarce be borne. Hundreds die now.

In my other hours, I have taken up again the pen of the naturalist; it being my purpose to supply an entry lacking in the *System* of the great Linnæus. It hath always struck me oddly, that the man categorized all of the animals and birds upon the globe, and yet provided no entry upon the creature which produced this plenitude; for which reason, it hath been my steady purpose in these last days to write an addendum to Dr. Linnæus's monumental work, upon that first Mover and Progenitor of all the rest, which species I have given the Latin name *Deus omnipotens*. I have scoured the Testaments Old and New to determine its behaviors and diet; such scraps as I have gleaned according well with what we read described by the *Hindoos* and the authors of pagan antiquity.

The form (limbs, markings, fur) of *Deus omnipotens* is as yet unclear to me. Aristotle maintaineth that God hath no shape, being but the limit of heaven; Epicurus claimeth that it appeareth to be a man in shape, though one of such great blessedness and incorruption that it is uncomprehending and indifferent to the plight of mortals. Pythagoras taught that God is a number; Xenophanes that it is a sphere, passionless and consubstantial with all things; Parmenides that it is but the confluence of earth and fire.

In its habits: It appeareth that *Deus omnipotens* reproduceth not with a female of its own species, but by engendering young upon a female *Homo sapiens* of a tender age, *viz*. Europa, Leda, Semele, Alcmene, and the Nazarene girl, much as the cowbird, first in deception and violence, doth force the female of other species to hatch its young. The offspring thus produced from the conjunction of deity and damsel hath a nature intermixed, the two species commingled, and perhaps, like the mule, is incapable itself of generation.

Some several points remain to be determined: as to where the creature maketh its burrow; how many specimens yet subsist; whether it did, when numerous, hunt in packs; whether it is territorial, jealously favoring the desert wastes and snarling at any that approach, or keeping to the forests of the New World, the denizens of which now claim it as their own; whether it molt; whether it excrete; and most, of great consequence, whether, as some authors claim, it adoreth its children and guard them zealously; or whether, like the scorpion *(Scorpiones Buthidæ)*, it awaits their fall, and then devoureth them.

Your humble & affectionate servant,

Dr. John Trefusis

'Twas but a few hours after I had written my brief entry upon our first raid that we anchored by a bend in the river and were again sent ashore, that numbers and arms might impress with force.

The day was an excessive warm one; the dirt itself smelled of heat when we landed; and, as if distempered, the skies began a sickly-warm drizzle as we formed upon the dock.

We marched up athwart a hillock toward the house, Olakunde beating our step to better impress upon the inhabitants our seriousness of purpose. This drumming could not outstrip that of the heavens, which opened up upon us with tattoo of rain so furious that it seemed to bring on night.

Serjeant Clippinger called a halt before the house, and, standing beside Olakunde, had begun to entreat the inhabitants to show themselves, that we might deal with them fairly, according to the King's intention, when detonations flared in all the upper windows and we found ourselves in the midst of a very fierce fire indeed.

There was no need to call retreat — for at the intensity of that first volley, we had stumbled backward — and now we found ourselves split into two parties. One ran; one held.

Clippinger ordered us to stand and fire — which we attempted — but our powder was so wet that a full two-thirds of the muskets — mine among them — produced nothing but a hollow click — and still the rebel shots blasted out through the windows.

It was at this moment that three more rebel muskets discovered themselves in the dark of the barn, and fired at our flank—causing great confusion, though I believe none was struck. Our other party, fleeing, made an uneven retreat down toward the launch—Clippinger, still by our side, calling across the lawn to them to *stand—stand and fire, cowards*—but nothing could induce them.

Our small party remained—Bono saying, "We perhaps flee, sir?"—and Clippinger swearing and looking in a panic. He assented to flight, and we turned and fled in a disorderly rout.

Now came, however, the boys out of the barn, and they descended upon us with sickle, froe, and scythe. We running, Clippinger ordered still that we affix our bayonets, which I did with trouble, the metal slick with rain, my fingers skirret-stiff with fear—and we found our van overtaken by the brutes. We turned to fight, thinking ourselves rather fine with bayonets—and this did indeed at first startle our pursuers—

We stood our ground now and with great shouts and menace, advanced upon the enemy, who were engaged in full combat with the last three or four of our number. Clippinger stood by and shouted I know not what through the devilish drench and I saw then that the rest of the detachment had still not halted, but had continued their flight down to the shore, and so we were alone, the few of us.

No sooner had this I seen—and queried to myself as to whether a whipping for insubordination attendant on flight was preferable to engaging in the chaotic affray before me—me standing at some fifteen foot distance from the combat—no sooner—

Olakunde ran past me—and Clippinger cried, "Flee!"—and two more soldiers hurtled by me—and then we were all fled, and coursing down through the fields and shrubs. I followed Bono closely and reasoned that soon should I be once again in the *Crepuscule*'s berth, reclined in that smoky, stale, yet familiar atmosphere, drying, able to sleep, the guns of the ship ringed and crowning us like laurels.

I looked back to gauge the progress of our pursuers, and whether they followed — and 'twas then I saw that Pomp had fallen behind the rest of us, cut off.

He was at some several hundred yards' distance from us, alone in a paddock, running back and forth, followed by a clutch of men.

It appeared a children's game: the running boy, the others circling to meet him.

I ceased my flight; and he turned this way and that, darting to elude them until he was surrounded.

He raised up his bayonet. They sliced at him with their blades. ~~He did not. The fool.~~ He did not resist them, but simply dropped his musket — and a blade ran across him. He squealed high and shrill, and I saw the blood spread upon him.

Clutching my musket, I ran back toward him; and was stopped in my progress by Pro Bono, who, sensible of the pause in my flight, had returned to see what delayed me.

"You can't," he said to me. "You can't, Prince O. There's twelve of them or thirteen."

They were lifting Pomp between them. Others stalked away, in search of more prey.

Bono dragged me back behind a great bush and swore. I maintained I had to return and aid my friend.

"You ain't going." Bono held my arms.

"I have struck you before," I said.

"Let us get reinforcements," said Bono; which now I see was but his way to distract me from my course, but which then, in my disordered state, seemed excellent advice.

And so we ran, loping past paddock and hedge.

Down upon the dock, some twenty of our Regiment were in the two launches waiting against the Serjeant's return, with, every few moments, a figure running across the slats from the shore, dimmed by the rain.

We reached the water, though well upriver of the dock. I was in close pursuit of Bono. We saw Serjeant Clippinger in the bushes before us. I followed upon the others' heels, the last in our line, and we cut along the shore toward the launches.

'Twas then we saw the force of men from the barn step forth from the parterre and proceed to the end of the dock, standing, a terrible brood, with their weapons raised. They stood between us and our boats. They had not spied us, but they knew we lingered, and they blocked our route to safety.

One of the launches pushed off and hung in the waters. Someone upon the boat called for a volley, which offensive yielded no results, the powder now being soaked beyond all ignition.

The band of rebels stepped forth upon the dock, and the second launch lit off from the shore, hanging close, lest Clippinger should reappear.

We were now gathered, a small group of us — Bono, Olakunde, Clippinger, Privates Harrison and Ackerman — hanging back amidst some bushes; and Clippinger said, "Mark, the *Crep* will fire her guns and make short work of these ruffians." He nodded his head at the rebels. "Speak you to a nine-pounder, my friends."

We waited in the rain, and the two launches drifted upon the Rappahannock, and still the *Crepuscule* made no move to aid.

"He is alive," I said to Bono. "He was wounded, but I vow, he still lives."

Bono bade me hush; but nothing in my breast permitted me hush.

We crept some feet forward toward the dock and there waited. We were not awarded with any comfortable view, for the launches put forth their oars and made their way back toward the ship.

We were abandoned.

I presented to Bono that we must return up the hill and liberate our friend; to which he replied that I would be no such fool. I would not be denied, but set off; and found Bono following, hissing warnings at me.

We had not gone far — Bono all the while expostulating and decrying me for an idiot, would get us slain — when we perceived that we should have to expose ourselves to cross the paddocks and reach the spot where last we had seen our companion. We made our way around the edge of the meadow, keeping low, and saw, with the lessening of the rain, men moving about up at the house. We could not espy Pomp, living or dead.

We were spotted then; there were shouts and calls, and we retreated down toward the shore, pursued.

We rejoined Clippinger. We hunched there half-hidden, the six of us, as the *Crepuscule* stood inactive on the river.

The men gathered at the farm were begun a sweep to ferret out any who had not regained the launches — we could hear them call to each other. One unfortunate they found — I know not who—and we heard him begging for mercy as they led him away. We heard them approach, and fled along the riverside, stepping through high grass and bramble.

For perhaps half of an hour, we fled thus. A state of greater wretchedness could hardly be imagined. I thought of the wetness—always the wetness—which pervaded all; that was foremost in my thoughts; for in times of greatest strife, the mind oft relucts to animadvert upon things most awful; and so, the chilly scald of my shirt hung across me, the reek of metal in the air, the slap of leaves across my face—these were the objects of my notice.

We came to a tributary of the river—we knew not its name—surrounded by a great area of marshy ground, and with difficulty made our way along it, often sunk to our knees in mud and brackish water.

'Twas then we heard, as from a distance infinitely far, the crack of the *Crepuscule*'s guns, too minute to serve us to any purpose. We squatted in the mud and rested. We did not speak, the six of us, but maintained a gloomy, shuddering silence.

In—I know not—an hour, perhaps two—we heard dogs come to tear us out, and once more rose and moved. 'Twas a warm evening, and we were now so involved with the rain that it no longer cloyed. We felt naked to the elements.

At some time, the rain ceased, but now all was black, and our progress slow. We tripped and could make little headway, and sticks cut at us and the mosquito-flies now encircled us mercilessly and ate at us. We fell and rose and wandered on.

They came for us through the woods—lanterns and dogs—and we ran as best we could. The dogs tumbled across the hummocks and cried out for our blood. We could not see them but their Cerberus tumult filled the black wood and wearied us still more.

We were trapped by them, and each ran our way through the tall grasses; and I saw a faint gleam as two bodies charged past me, and Bono darted the other way, and I perceived that Bono had leaped into the tributary river to cross it. This I did too, with my musket clutched absurdly in one hand, and clutched in my head, the fevered hope that once crossed, the river should absolve us of scent, and the dogs lose us.

No sooner had I plunged into the river and, with convulsive strokes, my hand still holding my musket above the water, set out to cross it, than I saw Olakunde following Bono. He being unable to swim, he was holding tight to his drum, which held him aloft, while Clippinger thrashed at the water beside him.

We swam behind Bono until we had crossed the river, and then drifted silently, heads only above the water, bodies below crouched and twitching along the mud floor. We heard the dogs flood up and down the far shore, where we had stood.

I do not know what became of the other two who fled. I have not heard of them from that day to this, whether they found their own escape, or were taken by our pursuers.

May God have mercy upon them.

And so Bono and I, Clippinger and Olakunde lay that night in the mud of the marsh, flies thick upon our heads, roots around our fingers, guns lain in leaves upon the shore. We were sundered from our party, lost even to those who were lost upon their island fastness, and the country was alive with those who hated us, and wished nothing more than to teach us of our subordination.

꙳ We hid beneath trees in the marsh. We could not cease shaking.

We had nothing which had escaped drenching: no victuals, no bedding. The flies and mosquitoes bit at us mercilessly.

And I could only reflect, that were Pomp there, he should know of the ways of the marsh, and tell us what might save us from their sting.

❧ *On Midsummer Night,* Pomp once related, *on Midsummer Night, you can find out who going to die soon. You know this? This is true. You take yourself down to the church-porch, and you sit yourself there, and at midnight, all the spirits of those people going to die during the year, those spirits all come to the graveyard and knock on the church door. The first spirit who knock, he the first to die, and the second to knock, he die second. They all stand in a line, like for rations. Truth.*

Truth? I said. *Absolute truth?*

He laughed. *Truth!*

Pomp declared that a man of his parish — a youth well known to him — undertook this summer frolic with two maids upon whom he doted; the amorous youth believing that such a scene of horror was well calculated to draw one maid or the other into his arms. But he saw not the spectacle; for come eleven, he had fallen soundly asleep, and was insensible; and come twelve, his two giggling companions fell silent and gaped in awe as his own spirit rose and knocked first upon the door.

There it is, his own ghost — tap, tap, tap. *And he wake up, all frowzle-headed, and ask why those girls disturb him. He says, "Why you wake me up with your tapping?"*

But they can't tell him. And the ghosts, they is all disappeared. So the girls don't say nothing, staring at each other all affrighted.

And a month later — this is true — month later, he was dead of a putrid fever.

I tell this tale in memory of Private Pompey Lewis, friend Pomp; who I still ardently dream shall sit beside my grandchildren and speak of kindly horrors.

⚘ Grasping at my arm, covered with twigs, he spake to me; I heard the violin all around us; I awoke.

I lay upon the ground. 'Twas still night. To Bono I whispered, "We must go back and see whether he lives."

"They are gone," said Bono. "Pomp, Harrison, they are all gone."

"We can return."

"Prince O.," said Bono, "he ain't there anymore. You know that. They took him somewheres. They have their places. The lead mines, out in the west. That's the new fashion. You know it. The Sugar Isles."

"They might still be stationed at the house."

"They ain't at the house. And this ain't one of your romances. You go back there, you die or you get caught."

I knew he was right; and yet, I could not quiet my fancy: We burst into the barn and held their fearful guard at bayonet-point until they surrendered Pomp's location—we sought him out, crawling blue through the night—the crows called warning—then the sortie—his face full of delight as we hacked off his chains—gladdened—the flight back to Gwynn's.

And instead, I thought of him in the mines which have been decreed as our fate if we are caught. He may shovel there in that interminable dark, unable to stand; otherwise, crouched upon his knees, sliding upon his belly, with no air to breathe; he who should be at our side.

And this I thought: *Dear God—protect him—bless him, for living or dead, he shall soon be beneath the earth.*

And I myself could not breathe; I choked; I rose; I could not find air in that clenched tunnel, that throat of stone.

O Pomp—chief usher of horrors—you who sought out death in tales, you who relished death most—now you are engulfed by your own terrors—and I, who am helpless, pray for thee.

✿ We rose before the dawn. There was little sleep had by us.

Our course was clear, without Serjeant Clippinger declared it:
We could not seek out the fallen; did we wish to remain at liberty,
we must find our way to Gwynn's Island; and did we wish to
return to the Island, we must seize upon a boat. No other mode
of conveyance was practicable, the whole of Gloucester County,
across the channel from the isle, being invested with rebellion.
They gathered there thickly to oppose our Regiment, and 'twould
be mere folly to attempt to pass through them. A route by water
was our only expedient.

I suggested that we had, in our flight, run west; and had then
stumbled to the north as we fled through the swamp and its tribu-
taries. We could not hazard making our way back along the shore,

eastward, toward the mouth of the Rappahannock by foot, for we should have to return through the farm where we had met with the ambush. Clippinger, confounded by the geography, had begun to curse and batter trees. Bono, Olakunde, and I determined we should progress left, to the southwest, that we might meet with the shore of the Rappahannock upriver from where we had disembarked, upon which banks we hoped to come upon some craft which should serve our purposes. The Serjeant received our recommendations without comment.

We began our march.

We soon perceived, however, that we could not long continue in our present state. The first instance of a road, we stepped forth and had no sooner set to walking upon it than we heard distantly a team of horses approaching. "There is times," muttered Bono tartly, "when you wish your shirt don't say, 'Liberty to Slaves' in great letters on your chest."

Upon this head, nothing could be clearer. We retreated into the woods.

We could progress no further as we were without drawing the eye of suspicion. Serjeant Clippinger was in great confusion as to how we should proceed, remonstrating (when any suggestion was offered) that we had brung him to this pass, and we should keep silent while he thought. Reluctantly I admit that I can give no superlative portrait of his powers of command, and lament that for the verity of this record, I must, on the contrary, record instances wherein Serjeant Clippinger did not show himself as ready and honorable an officer as his superiors might wish.

Nonetheless, he was our commanding officer. We awaited his orders, a force greatly reduced and impatient for activity. Delay yielded only his intelligence that *Death, death, we might as well skip across the moon as walk through town without a challenge.*

To this, I proposed that we take up a ruse suggested by our fellows in the Regiment when they had fled to His Lordship's service: that we should array ourselves as if we were escaped slaves being led to justice; in which deception we should be infinitely aided by the presence of a white man. I expatiated upon the virtues of this measure: We should be able to walk with impunity through town and past plantation without exciting suspicion, and so make our way south, back to the banks of the Rappahannock, where we might secure a vessel to make good our return to Gwynn's Island.

This plan was not thought entirely without merit by our number, and we spake of how best to effect it.

Bono, Olakunde, and I removed our shirts immediately — garments thrown off so with such celerity, when once donned with such pride. Stripped now, half-naked, we did not look conspicuous, being no more indecent than many of the slaves who labored in the fields around us. Our breeches were our own, and varied, and did we walk without shoes, we could pass as a miserable coffle being led back to captivity or to some new scene of degradation.

The habilement which posed the greatest challenge to us was Serjeant Clippinger's, for his uniform was distinctly that of an officer of the King's Army with some scant Regimental trim fastened upon the facings to mark him as attached to the Royal Ethiopians. In no wise could he proceed out of the woodland dressed thus.

We cast about through the woods, noting the disposition of

houses around us. One had a great array of slaves; and at length, we decided to approach one, claiming that we had newly run away, and request he bring us clothing. Serjeant Clippinger hung back, for the presence of a white man would do nothing but alarm a slave queried in such a manner.

The slaves were engaged in the tobacco fields, weeding. Bono and I crawled along a row and put ourselves in the way of one man who stooped there, suckering plants.

"Brother," whispered Bono, "look'ee, brother . . ."

The man regarded us with a look of anger. "An' you run now," said he, "I don't shout for the overseer."

Bono begged, and the man raised his head and put his hand to his mouth, awaiting some move to holler.

We left precipitously, and he, glaring, turned back to his work.

We were sick with fear. We hid for more hours in the wood, our bites swelling.

Later, we sought out a house where a man lived, it seemed, alone.

He was a farmer of small means in a modest house. We could not risk alarms, and he resisted, screaming murder; we threw him down when he attempted to close the door to us, and Bono held his bayonet ready to prick the man's eye and warned, "If you cry out again, sir, we shall kill you.—We shall kill you.—You cry out, and I swear I will stab you through the eye and into your brains. You listen."

"We'd be fools not to kill him anyhow," said the Serjeant. "If he raises the hue and cry, we's dead as a dog in ditch-water."

The man begged our mercy.

"No need to kill him," said Bono. "We'll tie him and hide him."

We having fetched breeches and a plain shirt, I tore another shirt into strips and bound the man's hands.

"No one will find me," he pleaded. "Don't. Ain't nobody comes here."

"A gag," said Bono.

We gagged the man and hauled him into his loft, where we left him lying, entombed by heat, eyes expressive of the greatest terror.

But my conscience would not allow me to leave him thus. A day or two, and he might be dead.

Against the impatient expostulations of the Serjeant, we brought the man down from the attic and dowsed him with water, that he might not suffer so greatly from the heat. We left him beneath his bed, bound tightly to its legs.

How awful it is to contemplate the accidents that determine one's fate. But for breeches and a plain shirt, this man's life should not have been at hazard.

I see him still, begging, "No one will find me."

We did what we did, and I shall not linger on it.

While Clippinger changed into new breeches and shirt in the little house, we went outside to search for rope; and finding a length, Bono tied Olakunde and me together.

Thus arrayed, we set out again: two captives, a master, and his man.

⚥ All night, we walked as a coffle of the dead. Olakunde and I were roped together, our hands bound, and Clippinger and Bono behind us, driving us. Our muskets were slung in a sack which Bono carried. We wore no shirts nor shoes.

We walked now upon the road. We passed through villages.

We came upon torches and a crowd of men who blocked the road — slave patrollers seeking runaways. They were fortified with drink and incendiary slander.

"Where's you headed with your Negroes?" asked one of them.

"Nansemond County," the Serjeant answered. "They run away from home."

"See that. Long way from home."

"They was seeking Lord Dunmore."

It seemed an innocuous excuse; and yet, it spoken, the man took a greater interest in us, stepping close and glaring into our faces.

I dropped my head so I did not look upon him.

He examined Olakunde, and then said, "Cut-face son of a bitch."

Olakunde returned his look.

"You put down your head," the man demanded. Olakunde would not budge. The man reached out, gently cradled the back of Olakunde's skull, and forced my friend to look down, and then to fall upon his knees. As we were yoked together, this forced me down as well.

When the patroller retracted his hand, Olakunde did not lift his visage again.

The patroller resumed, "Run to Dunmore?"

Clippinger nodded.

"Then you gots take them to the Committee of Safety. They pay you."

Clippinger, sensing the danger of an escort, did not argue, but replied, "Where do I go? For the Committee?"

The man gave us directions; and told Olakunde and me to stir a bone and get up — we had a real long journey ahead of us. With that blessing, the patroller bade us all a jeering farewell.

As we passed through the knot of them, men mocked us. "You pleased now, honey? You real happy now?"

We traversing a mile farther along the road, Serjeant Clippinger began to press upon us a new plan. "This, boys, is what we does. I delivers you up to the Committee, and get the fee, then tomorrow night, I hies you out of the jail. Then we has a guinea or two to show for our trouble."

"No, sir," said Bono simply.

We walked for a ways in silence. Clippinger at this point continued, "You ain't in any danger, because even if they try you and ask you who your master is, you can't give testimony. Y'ain't people. You can't turn evidence against yourself. I tell you. You can't. No more than a barrel or a dog or such-like. And no one else knows you, so no one else can turn evidence against you. So they hold you, and then I slips in, look you, I slips in at night and I frees you."

"No, sir," Bono repeated. We walked farther.

Serjeant Clippinger said, "I'm your commanding officer."

"Sir, if you do persist in recommending this," said Bono, "I shall kill you."

Following this, we walked onward without speaking.

When we stopped to rest in a copse, we did not all sleep, but one at a time stayed awake to watch the Serjeant and make sure he attempted no act against us.

We awoke before dawn to the sound of horns blown on plantations to call the slaves to toil. We began again our march.

❦ The road passed through tobacco fields. Our stomachs complained mightily of hunger, for it had been two days since we had eaten. At every approach of horseman, cart, or carriage, I turned fearfully, certain I should see some minister of injustice come to enchain us.

I schooled myself to face forward with greater looks of despond, that we might not be detected in our imposture. We practiced the slump of the shoulders born of defeat, the shuffling gait of those who knew that there was no pleasant or agreeable end to their pilgrimage. Riders passed us without challenge.

The sun burned through the morning haze, and we all were sensible of thirst and weariness. I ventured to ask how long we might have before the farmer we'd tied beneath his bed was found and released, and might convey an idea of our number and appearance to the slave patrollers.

Serjeant Clippinger, in preening tones of pride and satisfaction, said, "Now I warrant y'art sorry you didn't hearken to your Serjeant and kill the man outright. Tell me, lads: Don't you regret you didn't listen to my word, but you left the dog to be found and to tell the story of who we is?"

Bono said, "He ain't going to be found too soon."

"Don't fear anyway," boasted the Serjeant. "He won't escape. I killt him."

This news was received with horror. I could not feel my hands. We could not continue our march; but stopped in the midst of the road, and all swayed, as were we confronted with some great gulf or precipice before us.

Bono said, "You *killed* him?"

"After I dressed. I put my bayonet through his skull like you said."

I found myself shaking my head slowly, as if to clear it: I painted for myself the man lying beneath the bed, trussed amidst the curls of dust, certain we should soon be gone, and he calculating how many days until friend or neighbor sought him out; envisioning already his freedom, the tale he would tell, pointing at the road and the wood; and then Clippinger's shoes by the bedside; his knees as he knelt to locate the quick of the watching eye.

"Sweet God," swore Bono. "Sweet God."

"He would have roused the whole country."

"A shirt and breeches. We stole a shirt and breeches. You *killed* him?"

"Him or us, lads." Clippinger pointed before us. "March on."

I could scarcely move for disgust. Olakunde's tripping steps dragged me forward — and Bono spake for all three of us when he continued to whisper, "A shirt and breeches. Sweet mercy. Sweet mercy."

We passed on a causeway over fields. Slaves watched our dolorous procession. A child threw stones at finches.

I heard hooves and was certain it was a patroller seeking out the murderers; but it was a youth who rode past without so much as marking us.

We marched on through that hostile country.

✹ The day grew intolerably hot. The air was thick as syrup. In the long rows of tobacco mounds, children stood in the sun and watched the turkeys eat the hornworm and the devouring beetle off leaves.

We passed a manse where two white women, dressed in brilliant sacques, walked arm-in-arm among the blooms, commenting upon the excellence of the sweet peas. Their silken shoes scraped and rattled on paths of oyster shell: handsome women of forty years, speaking of the world as gardeners stooped around them, and, in the distant fields, their bonded farmhands shouted out ragged calls across the furrows.

We marched through village and forest.

We passed farms and mills; we passed slave quarters where goats wandered among the huts, and corn was laid to dry; and there was a spreading oak tree hung with jugs, which spake softly in the summer's breeze.

Women walked by us with baskets of corn upon their heads; men mowed wheat with scythes, followed closely by teams of gatherers. A boy, all but naked, squatted upon the ground, sooting fruit trees to protect them from some scourge.

We passed a great house of some Loyalist where a crowd stood gathered, and all the house's things were arranged upon the pebbles of the street, and animals were tied in the yard, ready for vendue or lottery.

We made our way through the crush, our visages cast down, little liking the press of people.

Farther along the road, we saw a black man sitting in an odd attitude by the side of the road, and smellt an awful smell; and when we reached him, we discovered him dead.

My eyes could not be drawn from this terrible spectacle; they sought it again and again for confirmation, that the body might be so rent, the face thus disassembled; reason would not countenance it, and nature rebelled against it.

It was but a quarter of a body torn from the rest: unseeing, gaping head and lolling arm with shoulder and ribs to join them, impaled upon a stake, and much busied with flies. The stench made breath difficult.

We proceeded past it retching, Olakunde muttering prayers.

'Twas not merely the violence of the death which caused our hearts to quail; not merely the disgust at decay; but the horror that he was set there as a sign to such as us.

We walked on for some time after this without speaking a word.

'Twas Bono, eventually, broke our silence, speaking low. He said, "We shall reach Gwynn's Island. No way we ain't. I am going to meet Nsia again. I am going to press her to my bosom. You mark me, few years along, war over, we is going to have some sturdy little children. And Prince O. is going to sit by our fireside, reading Homer. I vow it. I do vow it."

He said it with such firmness, we knew his words were laid plank on plank to obscure the marker we had seen. He built a barricade as best he could.

We marched.

❦ We slept again in the woods, if our uneasy watches, gruesome dreams, and hours plagued by bites and bleeding feet might be called sleep.

Come morning, we rose and set out. Come noon, we arrived at the Rappahannock and walked along the road by its banks until we came to a house where the grounds were not full of activity. We determined that we should make our way to their dock and steal whatever boat we might find.

The place was, we swiftly perceived, a plantation recently sacked and brought low. The plantings in the gardens still retained their linearity and rectitude of bloom; but a chicken-house was mere ash, and the windows of the mansion were broken.

We found the dairy empty. No one was in the stables; no horses, neither. A phaëton still stood, the traces at the ready, as if prepared for flight.

The kitchens stood at a distance from the house, and it was to this building that we repaired with hope of some new sustenance.

Within, there were the remains of a feast: a ham and bread. We waved off the flies and tried some of the flesh. Its taste was acute and sweet, and we quickly spat it out.

Our investigation of the kitchen being done, we determined to enter the house. The door was open.

"If it is empty," said I, "we should wait here until the evening and set out then upon the river once it is become dark."

"This is not making me easy," said Bono, indicating with his head the lawn, the open door, the window-glass.

"You boys enter," said Clippinger. "I shall stay without."

We posted Olakunde as a guard with him, saying he should not be safe alone; though in truth fearing that he sought an occasion to flee us. We took our muskets from the sack and affixed our bayonets. Olakunde and the Serjeant flanked the door.

Trepidatiously, Bono and I held our firelocks and stepped within. The drone of cicadas in sun and the cries of birds gave way to silence and coolness.

The furnishings in the parlor had been savaged with an ax. We liked not the look of the violence. We frowned to each other and held our bayonets before us.

The next chamber we entered was the dining-room. The table was gone, though chairs remained; the floor was ankle-deep in shards of shattered china plates and bowls. We picked our way through, though with little stealth remaining, for each step cracked and snapped as porcelain shattered beneath our heels. We had no shoes; we feared laceration, and walked with care.

This tide of crockery lay thin upon the floor of the next

chamber as well. The room was dimmed with curtains; it took some time for our eyes to report what lay therein. It was a room empty of almost any furnishings, save a few greasy prints of herbs on the walls.

A woman in a fine cambric gown sat with her back to us, unmoving in a chair. At first, we thought her dead, for she exhibited so little curiosity as to our approach; and then she moved, putting her face in her hands.

'Twas then we saw that in front of her, on the floor, a child was lain prone, facedown, arms spread-eagled.

The woman dropped a hand from her face and scrabbled about on the floor, picking up the broken handle of some earthenware porringer.

She shied it at the child, which lay unmoving.

We could not perceive the significance of this tableau.

"What have you come for?" the woman asked without turning.

"Madame," said I, "'twas far from our intention to intrude upon the grief of any; but believing the house unoccupied, we wished to take shelter here for a few hours before resuming our journey. We shall, of course, remove ourselves, unless there be any way in which we might render service."

She turned and saw us. She pointed at her child. "He won't get up. They took his father."

We nodded.

Bono, at length, cleared his throat and inquired, "Where you wish us to . . . remove him to?"

We heard the clanking of the drabware behind us, and turned, startled, to confront a young man of fashionable dress and perhaps twenty summers. "Who is it?" he asked.

"Some Negroes," said his mother. To us, she said, "They took all our Negroes."

"When was the assault?" I asked.

"Three days ago," answered the woman. "Three long days."

The young man, her son, inquired again of us, who we were; to which we answered shortly that we were traveling down the river.

"Gwynn's Island?" he asked. "Lord Dunmore?"

We looked at each other for confirmation; before either of us spoke, he continuing, "Take us. The rebels, they took my father."

"We ain't going," protested the child upon the floor. "I weigh a thousand pound."

To the youth, Bono said, "You wish to go down the river to join Lord Dunmore."

"The rebels laid us low," said the youth. "We don't have nothing but broke crockery."

We agreed, therefore, to take them with us. "We do have need of one thing," said Bono. "Which is a boat."

"We shall take our boat," said the youth.

Hearing this, the woman roused herself from her seat. "I must choose what best to wear," she said. "I have only met His Lordship twice." She seemed suddenly beset upon by some frantic animation. "John," said she to the eldest son, "attend me. What think you of my plum watteau?"

"I am sure," said he, "I don't know."

"With a little jacket trimmed with galloon, and that petticoat of tobine. Given the chills on the river." She held her head again in her hand. "I can never determine whether tobine seems it should be light, yet feels stiff and heavy, or seems 'twill be stiff and heavy and then feels too light." She shifted upon the pool of crockery, sending up a great clanking throughout the chamber.

"My skull is staying touching this floor," said the child.

"Are we leaving presently?" the woman asked.

We admitted we were not departing for some hours, until darkness.

"Excellent," said she. "I shall arrange my toilette."

In that ruin of a house, she went about her coquetry, applying her dyes, her pomander and pouncet-box. Once her hair was set, she would not disturb it, and sate sleeping in a chair, that it might not muss. The eldest son bounced a ball against the wall; the youngest remained prone.

Olakunde and Serjeant Clippinger being informed of the situation, Bono and I proceeded down to the dock to examine the boat for its readiness. There was nothing left there but a small dinghy that should barely fit us all.

With this news, we returned to our companions, and spent the afternoon sitting in the garden.

Come seven o'clock, we determined to set forth. At the instruction of the elder brother, Olakunde picked up the younger and carried him without.

"Leave me lie!" protested the child as he was brought down the bank. "Leave me lie!"

The elder son dragged a trunk after him, scraping ruts in the grass. Olakunde deposited the young child on the dock, where he no sooner had stood than he began to scream shrilly.

The mother looked about her garden, preparing to abandon it forever; and bade her eldest coquettishly to fetch her a flower to lay in her bosom-glass, "just peeking out," as she said, "between them two fair snowy hills."

It may be imagined, our impatience at these delays, for our spirits quickened at the sight of the river, smooth in its evening undulations; and everything within us pled to be excised from the ruinous shore and allowed to float free. All delay was torment.

The elder son ran from the shore and brought his mother back a phlox flower, which he presented to her with great show of gallantry. While he performed this office, Serjeant Clippinger, Bono, and I waited in the dinghy, desperate to cast off, with Olakunde standing by to hand them in to us.

They came to our side and prepared to step into the dinghy with us.

'Twas then that we observed the full extent of the mother's gown.

"Why those looks?" she asked imperiously. "You object to the panniers?"

"It is a small boat, madam," said I. "This is no space for panniers."

She turned to her son. "One of them could remain behind. Ask one of them if they will remain."

He turned to us.

"We will not," Bono said.

"Madam," I pressed, "I have it on the best authority that among the finest mantua makers of London, the pannier is no longer the mode."

"Whose authority?"

"My mother's, madam. She was a woman of fashion and exquisite raiment."

"Your mother?" she said with deep incredulity. "What does she wear, linsey-woolsey and a Negro cap?"

"She is deceased."

"That don't hardly recommend the seasonability of her taste. Mind you, Lady Dunmore wears French hoops."

We insisted — and her son now urged compliance — that she remove the panniers. She refused, her voice higher, lighter as a panic rose within her.

"We will need space adequate for rowing, madam," said Bono. "Pulling the oars and such."

"The space is already small," I said. "And the boat will be none too stable when we are all afloat together, madam."

"This is absurd," said the mother.

"If you please, madam," said Serjeant Clippinger. "We wish to cast off."

"You shall do no such thing."

We bobbed, clasping the dock. The boat's draw was greater than I would wish, and with but three of us, the water lapped high on the gunwales, threatening to spill over.

"We shall wait, madam," I said, "while you set aside these ornaments."

"Two of you, step out," she demanded. "The boat is too low in the water."

"We regret, madam, that we cannot remain on shore," said Bono.

Said I, "If it please madam, would she —"

"Step out. Two. One, two."

We said we would not; she demanded that we should not travel one fathom without two of us remained behind. We protested with all the propriety we might. She would not compromise her dignity, and shrieked at us so that we might know it. The son sought to calm her—berating us for troubling her—and now the younger child began his bleating and wailing, that he would not leave his father's house.

The mother declared we should none of us leave, that she would not stir upon the river with such rogues as we; that none of us should use the boat.

And so Olakunde stepped aboard, and Bono and I released our grip upon the wood. The elder son shouted curses at us, calling us *dogs and curs, bastards, sons of whores,* while his mother rebuked him, "Not in the presence of your mother. Not in the presence of your mother!"

We left them behind us on the shore. We drifted away from the ruins of their house, and were upon the river.

❦ The light fell as we were swarmed down the Rappahannock toward its mouth.

For a long while, we did not speak, but were all consumed in reverie.

The farms upon the banks prepared themselves for evening. Maids drew water; boys drove geese before them.

We progressed past forests, pine woods upon the shore; and in their depths, where the dying sun hardly shone, spied a glimpse of a steep rise through the branches, mounded earth, secret paths through red needle and hillock seen briefly, then shadowed. There is no young man whose heart is not led on by such vistas, and doth not ride post before him to sweet, lonesome dells bannered with sunbeams and choired with crickets; then further, to the woods where the great Nations of the Cherokee and Shawnee have their home, so dear in the imagination of romance, hunt, and hazard; then on to the mountain pass, hard won; to the grasslands; to the fabled painted cities of the West in their vast plains.

"We must find a place," said I, "where we can begin anew."

No one replying, I said to Bono, "We must seek a place where we can vow to live in more perfect unity."

Bono said softly, "There ain't such a place."

"Row," said Clippinger.

"I shall find us such a place," I said.

Bono rowed, for his were the oars; and at each draw upon them, water spilled into the dinghy, the lip being so close to the surface of the river. Olakunde and I bailed with our cups and our hands, which vessels were too small to stop the wavelets that splashed over the gunwales and dashed fore and aft, aft and fore, across our feet in rhythm with the rowing.

"Damn this boat," said Bono. He rattled the oars on their tholepins. "It's rotten. The wood's all eaten. Look ye, see when I pull? Warps. You see there? Gentlemen, we is taking on some ugly water."

"Row," said Clippinger.

We could not judge of distance, nor of speed; nor note even the undulations of the shore, since to the eye upon the water, the shore looks one gathered rank, drawing to it all islands and coves so that they cannot be seen distinctly. We could distinguish no streamlet, no jetty, and all distances seemed one. No solid contour was certain, but all devolved with the evening into one crabbed mass, gnarled and dark beneath the moon.

The shore was dark; but the river, bright. As I bailed and Bono rowed, I vainly sought to gauge our passage through the waters, to measure the subtle articulations of current and tide and how they contributed to the flexing of the river's vast musculature across which we slid, rising and falling with that flexion, passing through gentle vales and over knolls which every moment dispersed and regathered, until there seemed no solidity anywhere, but simply the blind will of motion.

Slowly, the boat grew lower in the water.

"I don't know no swim," said Olakunde.

☦ The boat began to founder. The water lapped the thwarts. Olakunde no longer bailed, for fear of the element roiling all around him; he gripped the gunwales and sat inclined as if the dinghy barreled down a slope.

Bono had, through his exertions — the boat being well nigh intractable, now swamped — snapped off the rowlock and a stave of the gunwale, wet with rot. We used the oars as paddles, now, perched on either side of the boat; but the hull would not support us for long.

Clippinger swore at us at first, calling us fools; and, when he saw that this booted him nothing, grew fearful as the boat dipped lower in the current. He demanded we row to shore, there to steal another.

This course was not unwelcome nor unwise; we beat toward the land.

"I don't know no swim!" Olakunde repeated to us; and for his sake, we paddled the faster.

The boat all but sank as we approached the bank. Tripping and lifting out Olakunde and the sack of muskets, we floundered through the water to the grass, captives again of the grosser elements. We drew ourselves out of the river and lay for a moment at rest.

The only course which remained to us was to abandon our late conveyance and seek another. This agreed, we started along the shore.

For ten minutes, we passed through fields in the moonlight.

At the end of that time, we spotted a modest house and made our way toward its dock, where we hoped to find a suitable boat.

We were passing near to the house when a voice hailed us; and we found a man stood before us with a fowling-gun; his daughter stood beside him. He wore a hunting shirt and a look of discontent; his girl was perhaps sixteen, and regarded us with distrust. Her hand was upon her father's back.

Clippinger, considerably discomfited by this vision, exclaimed, "Sir! Good sir! Some supper!"

This exclamation startled us all; but Clippinger repeated his request, and added that he should pay handsomely for a meal for him and his captives, explaining that we were escaped slaves who he transported in the name of the Virginia Assembly, and he begged some small repast for us.

'Twas a small house, likely without servants, but the owner was generous. He assented joyfully, declaring that he should always be pleased to aid the cause of liberty. He suggested that Clippinger tie us up to the hitching post and come in; but Clippinger, with a sharp look at Pro Bono, replied that he should prefer rather to sit with us while we ate, because we was rascals of considerable science and deepness. The man guided us to a lean-to in the yard and bade us all wait while he requested his daughter heat us some mash. Before he departed, he congratulated Clippinger and the Virginia Assembly upon the glorious move to indepedency and a nation free entirely from England's yoke; which bewildering commendation Clippinger had the good sense to nod to without further response.

So soon as our host was gone, we began a fierce whisper, discussing the man's meaning, which was, clearly, that the Colonies were voting to cast aside the King entirely, a thought shocking in the extreme.

"They can't simply *declare* independency," said the Serjeant. "A child don't simply *declare* he ain't a child of his father."

"This is chaos," said Bono, and shook his head. "A universal jumble."

"In Oyo," said Olakunde, "if the King is a good king, yes, good. If the King is a bad king, then *basorun* and people say, 'No more.' He must take poison. Special poison, in eggs. He die."

"That," said Clippinger, "is utter savagery."

"I see," said the gentleman of the house, standing in the door, "that you disputes nicely with your slaves."

"I says they was deep ones."

"Real deep ones," said the man, laying corn mush on the table. He set down a sausage for Clippinger. "You took their bonds off?"

"Don't want to cut them too much," said Clippinger.

[*493*]

"I see," said the man. "One moment, and I has some water." He left us once more.

No sooner had he stepped away than I said, "Something is not well."

"No," said Bono.

Clippinger did not speak, but opened the bag and gave us our wet muskets. We lay them upon our knees beneath the table in readiness.

Clippinger had no sooner distributed the firearms than the man returned, holding his fowling-piece charged.

"I hear word," he said, "that a few miles up that way, they lost some Ethiopian devils."

"These is some of them," said Clippinger. "I found them."

"You ain't who you seem," said the man.

That was all.

⚘ It does not take long to die, nor to kill. A life is present or absent, and it is an instant passed between those extremities.

We made show of force; he resisted. He was intent on fighting and alarming the whole neighborhood. We could not have done other than we did, for he screamed, and in one moment more, would have discharged his piece and thus roused the countryside.

'Twas Bono killed him, I still believe, though 'twas my bayonet, inexpertly applied, which became lodged between his ribs.

✠ When he was dead, we ate. His body lay beneath us. We devoured great mouthfuls of the mush with our hands. We had eaten almost nothing for two days.

We divided the sausage and ate it in one bite each.

Our gruesome repast was completed in two or three minutes; at which point, Bono asked, in a voice abruptly blanched, "Where's Clippinger?"

Indeed, the man was gone.

Bono swore. We took up our guns again, wiping our hands upon the table to rid them of mush. We set out in search of our Serjeant, whispering his name.

The yard was dark. Fireflies played over the field. I progressed down toward the water, believing that Clippinger had perhaps gone in search of a boat. I did find a scow overturned by the water's edge, but could not find Clippinger himself.

I was sensible of the possibility that our Serjeant was fled and had deserted, this being by far the most likely occasion for his disappearance; for, I reflected, he had little to return to, did he travel back with us to Gwynn's Island. He had not our dire incentive for the success of that Regiment—a noncommissioned officer in a hated regiment in a precarious fastness only a few hundred feet from a growing and volatile enemy.

From my first sensations at the thought of his desertion—a relief that we might not have him in our company longer—there quickly followed the transports of uncase, and then desperation, for I reasoned that, did he wish to desert, he should have to deliver to the rebels some token of his new fidelity—and a party of black men who had just committed the murder of a white man would be no unwelcome prize to lay at the feet of our persecutors. This, I reasoned, surely, was why he had slipped away so quickly. So ran my logic; and having seized upon these probabilities, logic gave way to steep fear.

I made my way swiftly back toward the house to find my companions and abandon this place.

Upon reaching the house, I saw that the door into the kitchen was open, and thinking to find the members of my party within, I gathered myself and stepped cautiously in.

Here found I Clippinger. He was with the daughter of the murdered man.

I cannot describe the scene.

She was upon the table, weeping; Clippinger had out his knife, and as he labored with her, he whispered to her not to scream, lest her father hear — though Clippinger knew full well that her father was beyond all hearing.

The girl perceived me in the gloom and cried out. Clippinger turned from his work, clutching his breeches. Observing me, he started; and then, seeing it was an ally, smiled and said a thing I shall in no way repeat.

I said nothing.

Having spoken, he turned back to his prize. Again, the table walked shuddering upon the floor.

I stepped toward him, and he withdrew. He stepped away from the girl. He spake to me again, this time in warning.

I did not reply; he threatened.

I drove my bayonet deep between neck and head. He fell backward, but could not dislodge himself from my weapon. His blood, it seemed, filled the room.

My hands could no longer support the gun with him upon its tip; they dropped, and he fell against the wall and then slid to the floor. I believe he was, by the time he reached the ground, lost to all sensation. His corpse continued to bleed.

The earth of the floor was brushed in pretty patterns; flowers and vines picked out in dirt to ornament the rude kitchen.

The girl and I regarded each other for a moment. Our looks were full of hatred, not for any deed, but for the witnessing of deeds.

I did not speak to her, nor she to me. I turned to find Olakunde in the doorway.

He and I left her. We left her to make her way past the body of him who had assaulted her; we abandoned her before she discovered the body of her father.

We went out into the yard, which was full of flat night; we heard an urgent whisper from the side of a shed, where we found Bono awaiting us.

"Where's Clippinger?" he hissed in fury. "Where is that whoreson?"

I opened my mouth to speak; but only silence issued forth. Again I assayed a response; this time, there was a low growl, a hideous, rasping gargle in the throat.

Bono said, "You seen him?"

I could not speak. Tears or something similar interfered.

Olakunde stepped forward. He said, "Died in battle."

Bono looked from one of us to the other, taking in the full dimensions of this scene. He asked no questions, but came and put his hand on my arm.

In the house, the girl began sobbing and screaming for her father. She believed him still alive. We did not wish to hear her find him.

We went to the riverside, where lay the boat. We set it upon the Rappahannock and cast off. We were free of the land.

Bono rowed us far out into the middle of the river, and then let the current take us. We drifted between the banks.

I saw on the shores all of the farms where slumbered slave and master alike. I observed their ordered fields beneath the moon. I saw the vast systems required for their industry: the river upon which we floated, where ketches carried bricks for the construction of house, dairy, and kiln, and shallops drifted, heaped with hay; and where busied the fleet involved in gathering grain and tobacco and conducting crops out to the Bay and beyond, to the open sea.

As if in a vision, I saw the coasters and Guinea-men upon the ocean, plying the waters for transmission of goods. I saw the West Indies, where bonded men slashed at the cane, that we might eat our sugar dainties; and the East Indies, where sepoys walked the walls of fortresses and Redcoats in full woolens charged a Newar's army, screaming beneath the blaring sun, and thus secured our tea.

I saw Africa, all the places told of in Olakunde's tales: I saw the fortresses of Accra, the forest states of the Gold Coast, the markets of Algiers, the *entrepôts* of the grasslands where translators bartered for Ashanti cloth, for the girls of Mahi, for amulets and Awka metalwork, for kola nut and potash. I saw the great herds of the Fulani; and the camel caravans of the Tuareg, laden with salt, leading slave coffles through the bright desert to the Ottoman kingdoms of the north, sand keening off the dunes. I saw the slave-weavers of the Sudan; the child-warriors of the Moroccan sultan; Efik musketeers scampering at dawn into Ibo villages while women screamed alarm; forest wars declared simply to render up captives for sale. And upon these scenes remote did rum distilleries here depend, and teahouses in Philadelphia, and Carolina rice plantations, the account books of Liverpool and the fine equipages of London, Parisian silk-sellers and the seamstresses of New-York, the Customs House on Boston wharves, the proud estates on the Rappahannock.

All these things saw I; and I saw that everything hath its price, and all are in fluctuation, no value solid, but all cost as they are appraised for use; and there is use for all, and constant and relentless exchange. *How much,* asked Slant, *is a man's life worth?* A pregnant child upon the docks doth cost less than a fine dress she might wear two years later; and luxury is earned by being wrested. (And the women walk upon the lawn, arm-in-arm, as the gardeners stoop before them with blooms.)

And I saw the Earth as the sun rose; and it was a world of fire, of particle, spark, and æther consumed and exchanged, no solid place to stand; and we were creatures of fire, loops and bright coils devouring as we could in serpentine chase, exhausting until ourselves extinguished; and all shed superficies, and clutched to renew, and preyed upon all.

Within me, a small, still voice urged, *It need not be thus;* but what could that signify? For I am hungry, and must devour to live.

We passed down the Rappahannock, and at dawn, came to the Bay.

✤ We arrived back at Gwynn's Island this morning, the 4ᵗʰ of July. When we reached the isle, rowing between the great ships of the floating town, coming to rest upon the dirt of the beach, our return was greeted with no emotion of surprise or elation; save later by our close familiars, who wept to see us again, and wept for those who did not return with us. Nsia greeted her husband with shouts; and then they grew silent. They were too solemn for speech. Dr. Trefusis embraced us, weeping.

Works upon the isle proceed as ever: still the futile fortifi-cations, though the rebels glower high above us from the shore. The *Otter* sloop-of-war is hove to and careened in the channel while it undergoes repair; men crawl upon its belly, scraping at barnacles and repairing the work of the worm. Governor Eden of Maryland pays his respects to Lord Dunmore, exiled from his

Colony, and I hope they made a pleasant supper of the collapse of all authority and safety together.

There is weariness and defeat upon every face. Among the sickly, great numbers are dying. There is scarce time to bury them. There are no memorials to these entombed upon the island, save crosses drawn upon the brown loam, which †'s serve the Christians for hope even when racked; and serve the heathens as a suitable sign of the mountain of the living reflected in the lake of the dead. There are many buried there.

By the graves sit the community of dirt-eaters, now fifteen or twenty in number. They will not take sustenance. They sit or lie upon the ground, arms too thin for human limb, faces too drawn for flesh, smeared white with powder. In their eyes, there is already retreat; they are already in the land of the dead.

Dr. Trefusis informed me that Will was among them.

For three days he hath resided there. Will hath sustained many sorrows, as have we all; and he receiving word of the cap-ture of so many of our Company, he could no longer support such harrowing news, and repaired to the grave-grove, there to die. I cannot with ease think upon him and his friend John, newly fled, telling the tale of their turkey call.

When we made our dinner, I went to deliver some of the corn mash to him.

I found him among the red pines. He sat apart from the rest of the cult of suicides, his legs crooked impossibly. There was spittle upon his chin; and he stared at me without recognition.

I presented the mash; which he did not take; nor, in his sick-ness, did he remonstrate when I held the mash before his face.

I presented it between his lips; but the tongue did not move, and the jaw was without motion. The mash lay in his mouth, or dripped forth, cutting a channel in the soil of his chin.

I reached up and closed his mouth. At this, he could not breathe, and shook his head as might a sleeper. He spat forth the mash, and resumed his empty look.

Determined that he should stir from this deathly posture, this fatal repose, I filled the spoon again, and held it before him as a command.

Once more, he did not eat.

He asked merely, "Why?"

Said I, "Why?"

He nodded, and repeated, "Why."

I held forth the spoon, and answered, "Because Slant of our Company is dead; and Jocko of our Company is dead; and Pomp of our Company is gone. And John of our Company is sold."

"John, aye, sold," he said.

"And they did not fall so that you may sit."

"Aye," he said. "Aye, John."

For a time, we sat together. After a time, he nodded slowly. He took a finger's pinch of the mash, and ate it. He closed his eyes.

"Octavian?" he said.

"Yes?" said I.

"Octavian," he repeated.

At supper-time, I brought him home.

In the evening, I write our tale of this last week. We spake it during supper, as once, at the inception of our Regiment, all told the tales of escape; now we tell the tales of the return of soldiers to bondage. We tell of how our companions fell, and how we are become murderers.

"Ignis pepercit, unda mergit, æris
Vis pestilentis, æquori ereuptum necat,
Bello superstes, tabidus morbo perit."[6]

---

6 "Those whom fire has spared are drowned by water; the man rescued from the water is saved only by air tainted with pestilence; and the survivor of war is ruined by wasting sickness." — George Buchanan, *Baptista* [Editor's note]

July 6ᵗʰ, 1776

"The Lord looked down from heaven upon the children of men, to see if there were any that did understand, and seek God. But they were all gone aside, they were all together become filthy: there were none that doeth good, no, not one." —Psalm XIV

✣ In the night, Dr. Trefusis came to me by the fire, his frame involved in the most violent agitations.

"Pray, sir," said I. "What ails you?"

He could not still his trembling. Said he, "I stepped backward into our tent." He sat upon the ground next to me, and demanded, "Know you my assertion that there is no matter, that all is a void, could we but perceive it?"

I said that I did.

"Aye," said he. "Aye." I waited, and at long last he continued: "But ten minutes since, I stepped backward into our tent," he said, his eyes closed, "and I fell. Then all resumed, and I was standing upon solid ground. But for a moment, Octavian, for a moment, there was nothing in the world. Nothing at all."

When Cretan Cadmus fought the dragon sacred to Mars and brought it down, armed with but his lance and his buckler of lion-skin, he sowed its teeth in the ground at the bidding of Pallas Athena. Then rose from the ground savage soldiers, the children of war, and began without aim or plan or mercy to slaughter each other, their eyes no sooner opened than they set to kill all who they first viewed, all that they might kill before being slain themselves, hacking at those who still crawled from the integument of the earth to slay them before they walked; knowing nothing of the world but blood, bone, and fury; which spectacle Cadmus and Athena observed in helpless dread, seeking to intervene, only to be reprimanded by one tall, gory, muscled child, saying that they must stay back, for they did not understand the rules of massacre; which said, he was felled by a javelin, and the thrower felled by a sword, and the swordsman by a bolt; and thus the battle royal continued.

In a short time, in all that field of butchery, there were but five left, and these, red with blood, looked about them at the bodies of their fallen brethren, born but seconds before and already dismembered and inert; and seeing this, they paused. One took off his helmet and threw it to the ground, and dropped his weapons; and so the others, too, weeping. They spake together, and they made a solemn pact that they should not annihilate each other in phrenzy of self-interest, but live in that place in amity; and thus was founded the city of Thebes.

We might be thus.

And yet: When Jason of the *Argo,* seeking the Golden Fleece, sowed the same dragon's teeth in the plains beneath the mountains of Ethiopia, there, too, warriors budded and rose up in the furrows, crested, helmeted, armed with sword and javelin.

No sooner had they shaken off the dew of birth, than they were murderous, and turned on each other and on Jason himself, slaughtering without reason or mercy.

There was, in the end, none left standing. Their rapacity for mastery had been so great that all were brought to destruction equally.

And we might be thus.

❧ Dr. Trefusis was no longer my teacher; there was nothing left to learn. But still, of an evening, we sat there in a field of fires, looking across the channel at the rebels' hill of fires, and we spake as we could of the day just past.

On this night, as we sat in company, we discoursed on many things; and I told Dr. Trefusis that some weeks before, I had finished with Apollonius's *Voyage of the Argo,* upon which I had a query.

My preceptor indicated that it would delight him to offer assistance upon any point wherein his small powers might prove of use — declensions, verb irregularities.

I said, "I have a question regarding the dragon's teeth." I told of the war-like births witnessed by Jason and by Cadmus, the one crop of souls arriving at truce, the other so involved in its savagery that none was left alive.

"Which," said I, "are we?"

"As a species," said Dr. Trefusis, "I believe we hunt in packs and show our bellies. We are territorial as the beasts of the savanna. We mate for seven years, in which time our young grow to full mobility; and that accomplished, we turn to fornication as a means of further propagating our seed. Oh, we are a delightful guest. That is all, say I."

"Pleased you delivered my wedding sermon," mumbled Bono. "Can double at my God-damned funeral."

"There must," said I, "be some place one could go and begin again. This time, untainted."

"The taint," said Dr. Trefusis, "is not a stain upon us, but is, I believe, our primary operation. It is not simply a mark upon our skin."

"As the mark of Cain?" said I.

"Cain, yes. The first slaughter," said he.

"Which accursed and darkened my race, say your theologians."

"They do not belong to me," said Dr. Trefusis. "I simply use them and return them baggy."

"I wish to know if we might begin again somewhere," I said.

"Throw down your spears and such," said Bono. "Break your swords. How long you think before someone swoops into your paradise and makes short work of you? No defenses."

Quoth Dr. Trefusis, "'*Only the dead hath seen the end of war.*'"

"We must persist," said I.

We did not speak after that, save Bono, who said, touching his wife upon the neck, "There must be joy."

[*511*]

So we were agreed; but late at night, lying in our tent, I heard Bono, outside, wrapped in a blanket, whisper his seductions to Nsia. His *douceurs* were nought but such as an artillery marshal might declaim.

"Attention!" (murmured) "Tend the vent! . . . Lower the breech! . . . Advance the worm!" I heard her laugh through the canvas; to each command, she whispered, "Yes, sir."

"Swab the piece," he continued.

"Yes, sir."

We heard the fumbling in the grass. Will we or nil we, we could do no other than hear. "Handle the charge!" said he. "Ram down the charge! . . . Take aim! . . . Prime! . . . Make ready! . . . *Give! Fire!*"

The engagement was not long. Mayhap he turned his sword to ploughshare; but perhaps, too, all was combat now.

Ὅμοιον εἶναι τῇ ἄκρᾳ, ᾗ διηνεκῶς
τὰ κύματα προσρήσσεται·
ἡ δὲ ἕστηκε καὶ περὶ αὐτὴν κοιμίζεται
τὰ φλεγμήναντα τοῦ ὕδατος. [7]

---

7 "Be like the rock against which the waves batter; stand firm and unmoved until the ocean's violence ceases." — Marcus Aurelius, *Meditations* [Editor's note]

♀ The air being thick and oppressive, and all of us tormented with the itch and by abundant fleas which had invaded our quarters, sleep was a stranger to me the night of the 8th. No sooner did welcome rest steal away my waking sense, and I begin dreaming, but a bite would rouse me; and so I lay staring into darkness, breathing the rank, unhealthy vapors of the night, hemmed on one side by Dr. Trefusis, and on the other by Will.

Come the dawn, Dr. Trefusis spake to me, for neither would sleep come to him. We ceased even the pretense of slumber, and he whispered, "The morning star ariseth."

With some bitterness, I replied, "The evening star is barely abed."

"The evening star is also the morning star," Dr. Trefusis informed me. "'Twas Parmenides first noted it. They are both Venus."

I mumbled an assent and complained of my bites; and he avowed his worse; and both of us went so far as to express dissatisfaction at the chorus of the birds, which, with the dawn, had swelled to a great noise.

So were we engaged when the attack began.

With the first blast of the great cannon, all were awake. We heard shouting throughout the camp, and scrambled from the ground and beat at the flap of our tent that we might see what had transpired.

At this came the second blast, louder even than the first, a brisk, sharp blow that rebounded across the whole architecture of the sky, as if the earth itself convulsed.

I had now scrambled outside the tent — and could see others running through the lanes between companies, screaming and making signs of utmost alarm in the gloaming.

From the detonation, 'twas a larger gun than ever the rebels had displayed to us previous; and it had shot two cannonballs through the stern of the *Dunmore,* which tore through the whole length of the ship, shattering window, post, and hull.

Now began the rebels a bombardment of our camp, that eventuality always feared, and through the half-black of night we saw the cannonballs leaping through the tents, tearing them asunder, saw the dark bodies struggling beneath them.

Repeatedly now, we perceived the flares of artillery on the mainland, and the haze of motion in the air — heard the eruptions upon the ships as shot and shell battered them, heard the cries of those waking to disaster.

We knew not what to do; a panic seemed general, and no officer appeared to offer guidance; and still the bombardment fell upon the camp. Now replied our guns from Fort Hamond, and among the ships—I could not see from which—there was steady fire.

We heard the cry of orders, but could not determine who made these demands. Men scurried past us without so much as their muskets, leaping into the ditch we had dug across the promontory, and confusion everywhere reigned supreme.

There was, abruptly, a halt to the fire as both sides prepared their batteries.

"Sweet mercy," said Bono, his arm around his wife.

"They shall land soon," said I. "They shall cross the channel."

"I could wish," said Dr. Trefusis, his hands behind his back, peering down at the fire, scraping at it with his toe, "I could wish that the embers were yet hot enough to boil tea. After a night such as that, there could—"

The grapeshot which killed him took off most of his skull. He spun and his body was thrown forward, so that he lay beside the ashes of our fire.

Nsia's breath was labored; I feared she suffered from some asphyxiation, and went to tend to her; all her attention being fixed on the object behind me. Bono too, as I struggled with his wife's hands to remove them from her mouth, paid me no heed, and did not aid me with my intervention, but rather regarded what lay there with looks bespeaking the greatest agitation; and though I sought to remove Nsia's hands from her mouth, I found they were already at her sides, and she paddled at me, calling my name and resisting the annoyance of my ministrations.

He lay beside the fire and little of his face remained. His hand was in the embers, and smoked.

As I recall it, Bono and I spake for some time, though I cannot recall of what we spake. The light rose. As flight was now general—the breastworks of Fort Hamond being blasted to pieces before us—I did attempt to raise up the body and carry it with me.

He weighed nothing, my tutor, my preceptor; he weighed nothing, and I had carried him across the waters. We fled to Boston once, through the Bay, and all had lain before us, novel and unknown.

I stood with him half-hefted, my arm around his waist.

Then another volley of detonations rang out. With the rising light, I now could see the floating town off the northern shore of the island; the shot fell upon the fleet from the sky, ripping through deck and hull, while warships struggled to come about and return the fire, and tenders towed great ships still crippled without sail, without wind, at low tide.

"Take him," said Pro Bono. "We got—Take him—We—" and neither he nor I could speak, but we ran. The corpse weighed upon my shoulder—light as thrushdown, thought I—light as thought—and yet as I ran from the bombardment he slewed to the side, as if seeking to touch the earth, and Bono lifted him once more so he hung fully upon me.

As the cannonballs fell, before us, over the grass, over uneven beds of moss and stumps where we had sawed down forests to build defenses, fled the King's soldiers and our camp followers: Loyalists in green velvet, children half-dressed, a Negro woman in a stained crewel petticoat, once of the finest, blotched with mud, and soldiers clutching their coats.

They were all shouting there—at the northern tip of the island, where we were mobbed—shouting for transports—the

[517]

crush was unimaginable. The wavelets broke across our feet, and he was in the mud at my side.

Bono insisted that I must leave him; officers now strode among us, calling out for us to form.

I wished to cry, and made some attempts; but found it impossible.

I hunched upon the mud and observed that the transports did not appear like to come for us, the water erupting so frequently with the plumes of detonation. I could not quiet my chest; the pitch of my heart was forward and steep; the arms quivered in fits.

Leave the body, Private, said a lieutenant I did not know. *Come with us. Leave it. He ain't going to dance away.*

"I will put him by a tree."

Yes, be quick.

"Sir, I will lay him against a tree, where the sun will not fall on him."

Famous.

"In the shade," said I. "It is no disrespect, to lay him —"

Soldier! Attend!

"He needs burial."

Set him down there and form.

Bono lifted the feet; the body was dripping with sand.

My breath did not come easily.

Some time later, I was sensible that we marched in columns. We were arrived at the isle's eastern shore; we unloaded cartloads from the stores. I no longer supported Dr. Trefusis.

I said to Bono, "It is noon."

He replied, "You left him. He's against a tree."

The rebel guns had ceased.

They were preparing some new onslaught. I wondered, through my confusion, when we should be removed from the island.

That day, Major Byrd commanded all of us, though he was red with the smallpox; he delivered his orders from a cart pulled by men of our Regiment. His face was scarred with the pox, but he was stern of gesture. We saw him roll past.

I was ordered to stand near the breastworks overlooking the inlet between island and mainland. The rebels were plain to me. The other soldier stationed in the picket, a man unknown to me, asked me when I thought they would put in with their boats and cross over to us for an assault. I could little understand why he believed I should have this intelligence; I shivered throughout the whole of my body.

I wished to see Bono, that we might conduct the burial.

I do not know how I passed the hours, for my mind was in so great a tumult, it scarcely operated.

I wished still to cry, and attempted it again; and once again, my effort failed, all tears occluded.

The afternoon was green; this do I recall; the haze in the atmosphere pregnant with the tinct of leaf and grass, so the water, the sky, all appeared submerged. Looking toward the sick camp, I saw the sufferers gathered outside the huts we had built for them, waving their hands in fear.

I watched them for some while; and then was called away.

In the night, we returned to the encampment on the north-west point. We hauled cannons for an artillery company. This occupied some hours. I was no longer fearful. We rolled tents and retrieved as much as we might.

I came upon our tent, our fire-pit, our blankets. Bono was

there rolling his belongings into a bundle, but his actions were slow and hesitant. He regarded, perplexed, the rocks encircling our dead embers.

I squatted across from him. He looked up, but we exchanged no word.

Dr. Trefusis's blood was on the sand where he had fallen. I reached down and touched it with my fingers. It had dried; and the thought came to me that he had been dead for some twelve hours.

I ran my fingers through the sand; I pressed both of my hands into the dirt and left my impress in the earth.

I still could shed no tears, though calculating for that purpose, I marshaled thoughts of him — memories of that excellent being, gentle and caustic, rocking in the nursery at the College of Lucidity, his knees pulled up against him, regaling me with tales of warriors such as I wished to be, a warrior such as now I was.

My hands were in the dirt, amidst the traces of him — he who was my father, my grandfather — and I lifted that dirt to my face and put his mark upon me. I dragged the ash across my cheeks, the blood over my lips — I ground the dust into my eyes with the heels of my hands — blinding myself with him — and that element stinging — at last, I wept.

And now my heart finally broke, for which, at last, I was grateful. I lay his grave-dirt upon my tongue. It tasted of blood and birth, and of the world upon which we had walked together for a little space.

I cried, and was smeared with the funeral ashes, my tears cutting tracks; Bono came to my side, weeping too, and put his arm around me, and said my name, and we sat in the dark with the rebel watch-fires burning in the air across the water; and we mourned.

We left our tent, as it was too torn from grapeshot for salvage.

Through the night: our torches; the trundling of the wooden trucks through mud; a slave riding past in a phaëton, smoking a pipe; the women weeping on the shore, awaiting the dinghy which should row them to their berth. I carried a child upon my back as her mother walked beside me.

Great crowds still waited for transport at the beach, before the rebels should set out in their boats to conquer the island. It was a scene of utmost confusion.

Pro Bono and I sought out the body of my tutor, where he leaned against a tree. We began to dig a grave, though there was no solemnity there, no rite, no sorrow even, at that chore. We were interrupted by a subaltern, who scolded us and told us to leave the body lie. We protested; but curiously, without vigor, for the body seemed so empty.

We left him once more, called to labor.

At dawn, the firing began again. Bono and I were at the time deployed with a cart upon the northwest point. We ducked at the first blows, then, accustomed to detonation, hurried with our burden toward the embarkation point.

We could not forbear looking backwards, across Milford Haven. A schooner burned in the shallows.

The rebel canoes spilled from the creeks and darted across the inlet, muskets firing. A sloop's crew assayed flight in their long-boat, but they were overtaken. The fleet of canoes passed them by, paddling strong for the isle.

We could see across the Haven, toward the hospital; and there we spied the distant sick struggling out of their huts. Our soldiers ran past them toward our fleet, anxious to escape before the rebels landed and overran them.

We watched sick men crawling upon the ground, holding out their hands in supplication to Redcoats who scurried past; begging to be lifted and carried.

Upon the northern beach, we encountered Captain Mackay, who received each detachment of our Company, and bade us unload our cart into one of the boats. We did so swiftly, and returned to his side.

Over the stumps and rutted tracks of the island, we saw the enemy militia land in their canoes and gain the isle. They swarmed across our emplacements and redoubts, observing us with the temerity of the conqueror.

Captain Mackay did not mark their progress. We gestured at them and he turned. Bono informed him that from the promontory, we had seen the far end of the island, and that none had yet removed the sick; that they were crawling to the water for fear of the enemy.

"Removed?" said the Captain.

"The sick, sir," said I.

"What mean you, 'removed'?"

"We are evacuating," said Bono.

The captain nodded assent. "They have been removed, soldier," he lied.

We began to remonstrate; but he walked away, calling orders, and we heard Olakunde's drum bidding us fall in.

"They can't leave them," said I, and then, emending: "We. We cannot be."

"Jesus have mercy on us," said Bono. "Please have mercy."

"They cannot leave the sick," said I, "to fend."

We were sent forward to wade into the surf and greet our transport. I stood with the water around my legs.

We were soon embarked; they rowed us out toward the *Crepuscule*.

Smoke arose behind us from the island, and with horror, we saw that it issued from the pest-house. The sick lay there still, and the fire burned, and the smoke arose. The rebels had laid torch to the hospital huts, afraid of contagion. They had set them afire with the dying still lain there.

We gained the ship and boarded. Once more, we were within the hold.

Behind us, my tutor lay against a birch, his jaw torn asunder and hanging.

And so we were defeated, and awaited our last, long flight and the end of our campaign.

✠ My recollections of that evacuation are disordered. Let two final memories suffice:

In late afternoon, as we waited to sail, there arrived three boatloads of slaves, newly escaped, having hazarded dangers unimaginable, hearing of Lord Dunmore's promise of freedom and his isle.

My Company were upon the decks, surveying the shore, which prospect was infested with rebels at their work.

The slaves called up to us, "That the island?"

Captain Mackay said to us, "Do not speak." He walked to the gunwales and to those who drifted below, explained, "The rebels have taken the island. We evacuate."

The slaves were distressed, and requested we throw them down a hawser, that they might board us.

"You will have to row on," said our Captain. "You cannot stop here."

A man called, "There ain't noplace to row to."

The Captain said, "We have no water. We have no food."

They paddled to the side of the ship, and one of them made to take hold of the stays.

"You cannot board," said our Captain.

Now a large number of people in our fleet, drawn out by the exclamations and pleas of the refugees, observed the incident from the decks of their ships. To several ships, application was made, but the officers aboard all of them were unbending, and the answer came again and again, "You must row on."

Now the rebels harked to the proceedings; we saw them watching from the shore, though they could not hear. They observed from their canoes; an audience little comforting to those who begged for mercy in the water by our side. To our ears came distant jeering cries of, "Come to us! Come to us, sweeties!"

The slave who had seized upon the stays of our ship stood, and, casting a glance toward the mob awaiting him upon the shore, began to climb, his knees clasped around the cords.

"Back down, man," said our Captain. "We shall fire."

He called his orders, and a file of Marines presented their muskets. The man stalled in his progress, seeking a further handhold. The women in the boat rose and gripped the stays.

"You cannot board," repeated our Captain. "There is no succor here."

"We come this whole way," said one of the women.

"If you do not row on," said the Captain, "we shall fire."

The man said, "Please, sir. Please," and hauled himself up still further.

The Captain called, "Fire." The Marines let loose a volley,

and the slave fell into the waves and sank, then rose again, and sank while the women screamed.

At this sight, this betrayal, there arose from all of us upon the decks of those ships a great moan, protests in all those hundred tongues, as if all the nations of the world cried out in horror.

And yet the women released their grip upon our ship; and the three boats were washed away from us.

The canoes paddled out to greet them.

We saw them try to flee, but they had no art in navigation. We saw them surrounded, and observed as they begged and importuned; we saw them towed to the island and dragged ashore, the mob awaiting them, engorged with victory, armed with brick-bats and bayonets.

And so the Sons of Liberty fell upon them, and they were seen no more.

✣ This I recall, and have learned of the details from Bono: When we fled the beach for our transports, sensible of our hazard, the enemy marching upon us across the fields, we splashed through the shallows—and I saw Better Joe standing desperately upon the shore behind us. He called for assistance.

I saw Charles return for him, despite their quarrel; saw him lift the old man upon his back and charge with him into the foam. Better Joe pushed at the young man's head; seemed to remonstrate; and Charles said something in their tongue. Said Bono later, Better Joe had asked, "Why do you carry me?"—and Charles had replied swiftly, "Because it is an honor for a young man to carry his betters." He held out his hand to be gripped.

And thus, they plunged toward the transport: young man with wise man upon his shoulders, dashing through the waves.

✤ There is no purpose in recalling what then transpired, our long flight, our final defeats. We sailed that day. Then there was, that night, the storm, and ships which had cut their anchor cables to escape the assaults of rebellion were now incapable of mooring, and so were dragged ineluctably toward shore. The *Dunmore's* mizzenmast, cracked by shot, collapsed, and took with it the main topmast. Two ships sank, their crews screaming for aid in their longboats.

At first we starved; the second day, I procured some tallow candles for Bono, Nsia, Olakunde, and myself, and we ate them with thanks. As we ate, we watched two sailors eye Vishnoo, this time with no jest in their appraisal. I recalled Slant's words: "Another thing can't die. Not one more thing."

Days later, I could not find the tortoise, and apprehended that hunger had wrestled custom and comity and triumphed over them both. It was with despair that I related this circumstance to Olakunde, stern Olakunde, who bid me not to weep for the tortoise.

"It is not for the tortoise," said I, "but the remembrance of our friends."

We were, that day, sent ashore on a foraging detail; and while we herded sheep, Olakunde drew me apart from the others to a place where we were embowered, and he lay down his drum and loosed its fastenings. Within lay Vishnoo. "One of us live," quoth Olakunde, and we lifted out the animal. We set him at liberty in the wood.

Vishnoo stood uncertain upon the leaves. We urged him to flee, Olakunde tying the head back upon his drum. That amiable animal stood uncertain of the solid ground, and would not move. We could not longer tarry; he stood.

We abandoned him to a kinder fate and the dictates of nature. None knew how long he hath already lived; he may still thrive a full century more, there upon that isle. He shall perhaps be the last witness to our history, the final creature to have seen Lord Dunmore's Royal Ethiopian Regiment and its deeds.

✤ Two days later, Olakunde himself was taken from my sight. Major Byrd wanted a drummer for actions up the river. Olakunde was plucked from our number. We have not seen him again.

Common report — which I cannot credit — even now, I cannot credit it — common report vows that Lord Dunmore, finished with our number, unable to discover any more utility in our Regiment, sent the other half of us down to the Sugar Isles, that they might be sold to the plantations there, so that there might be some profit from this profitless struggle. If he did so, betrayed them thus, perhaps Olakunde was among them; I still do not know his fate.

The misery which engulfed my senses — even now — Good God, if Dunmore hath committed this — if he hath — there is no pit in Hell too hot, no punishment too searing — my quill will not write of it—too pliant, not iron, not blood—the mind cannot receive the image—*We shall make you proud to serve us, soldier,* said he, *proud to serve us*—then so many of us lost—and yet there is no punishment, no outcome but the profit; and I lay in the dark of our deck; I could not sleep, I could not eat, and there was no room in which to move. I could not be roused, and was as a dirt-eater, a staring eye.

Black hold, the detonations fierce, floor puddled with wet sick; heaving; victory blotched by fog and rain, the wind meddling, ships luffing, stoving up as if careened; and I below. Upon Mr. Gitney's desk: Defeat curls within the body as a mouse's skeleton within the scum of fur and weed left by the owl; for it is infinitely light, and empty of all motivation, and longs in its posture for an impossible sleep.

Some time ago, I fought for the rebel, digging his trenches, mounding his earth; and found myself deceived; and so I fled to the only other power that might protect me, and I pledged myself among these staunch enemies of rebellion, and digged their trenches, and mounded their earth, and killed for them; and yet we were discarded when we were no longer of use.

Rebel or Redcoat, there were none who needed to use us sufficiently to save us.

What more to tell? There were skirmishes; and still we fled upon the ships, and could find no haven. We were pursued on every shore, hunted like foxes, coursed like hares. We were fired upon, and heard shots in the night, signals between rebels on opposite shores, but knew nothing of what these shots might mean, the language of ordnance spoken in the gloom. All were against us. We could not progress; and so we fled.

I prayed that the Lord should destroy utterly the children of men. It seemed to me that we were a race so poisoned in every motive that we should never find happiness; for should felicity appear in one nation, the others must sweep down upon it to destroy it; and it seemed to me that we must be obliterated with a new and profounder deluge, one deep enough to encompass all nations, so that Christ might begin again with a better creature. And as the ship heaved in a storm, I heard the wailing of an infant, which would not cease though the mother proffered her breast. The babe screaming, beating air, I looked upon it, a horror rising in me that there should be still another generation of this verminous race, this piebald mammal, this predator howling for something to batten upon. Its face was empurpled with rage at its limited dominion.

My instinct was to strike it in disgust; to stamp it out; but of course, I stayed my hand. I backed away from its bestial cry and prayed for gentleness, sank to my knees and prayed as best I could.

And so we sailed on.

❦ The day in December upon which Dr. Trefusis, Pro Bono, and I were reunited, before Norfolk was burned, before the plague took us, before Gwynn's Island fell, we crouched together in the rank darkness of the *Crepuscule,* and Bono related to us the tale of his escape; and with childish zany, he and my tutor jested and mocked our surly officer; and, we being once more together, we did not merely rejoice, but in our convergence projected great clash and triumph to come. While they recounted and sported, I pretended study, regimental discipline at that early date not having yet surrendered to the negligence of tactical despair.

That night, Bono talked of flight — and John Locke, beneath my indifferent eye, spoke of place and of motion. Locke wrote that if we have a chess piece — a black king — upon a board, and we remove the chessboard into a different room, we should still say that the black king *had not moved its place,* if it still stood upon the same square; for we judge its place according to locations upon the board. And such would be true of the board as well, said to remain motionless if it stayed upon the same desk in the cabin of a ship, though the ship makes its way along a river, and the river moves against the fixed land, and the Earth hath turned in its revolutions, swinging with it land, and river, and ship, and cabin, and desk, and board, and king, and pawn. Still would the board and the black king be in the same place; for motion is not absolute.

I recall this lesson now, O best of tutors, kindest of wards, philosopher most delighted and most despairing; I recall it as I think upon our travels, upon our fleet's ignominious flight, upon the betrayals offered to my people; as I think of the forests through which Negroes still flee, and the rivers down which they pass in terror and hope of liberty, ignorant of Dunmore's motion and removal. I know not whether there is possibility of change and motion, or whether we are all stranded within one monadic unity; but when I ask *Where doth the black king stand, and where the cabin, and where the ship in motion?* then do change and motion disappear: for what is flight, if you cannot approach safety? What is a sojourn, if you have no home to return to? How doth one conduct a campaign, if there be no hope of victory? For we shall always be human, and always vicious; suspended motionless, yet never at rest; trapped, yet without any solid thing to grasp.

I cannot continue this narrative. A quest must have a final goal, and each campaign its objective, that their success might be judged; but here is no goal which might be obtained, motion toward no succor, a campaign without territory to claim or lose, the field shifting beneath our prow.

There is nothing. And so I make my end.

"*Lo! Thy dread Empire, Chaos, is restored;*
Light dies before thy uncreating word:
Thy hand, great Anarch, lets the curtain fall;
And universal Darkness buries All."

PARTICULAR ACCOUNT OF THE ATTACK
AND ROUT OF LORD DUNMORE, WITH HIS
PIRATICAL CREW, FROM GWIN'S ISLAND.

We got to the Island on *Monday,* the 8th of *July,*
and next morning began a furious attack upon the
enemy's shipping, camp, and fortifications, from two
batteries—one of five six- and nine-pounders, the
other mounting two 18-pounders. . . .

On our arrival upon the island, we found the
enemy had evacuated the place with the greatest precipitation, and were struck with horrour at the number of dead bodies, in a state of putrefaction, strewed
all the way from their battery to *Cherry-Point,* about
two miles in length, without a shovelful of earth
upon them; others gasping for life; and some had
crawled to the water's edge, who could only make
known their distress by beckoning to us. By the
small-pox, and other malignant disorders which have
raged on board the fleet for many months past, it is
clear they have lost, since their arrival at *Gwin's
Island,* near five hundred souls. I myself counted one
hundred and thirty graves, or rather holes, loosely
covered over with earth, close together, many of them
large enough to hold a corporal's guard. One, in the

middle, was neatly done up with turf, and is supposed to contain the remains of the late Lord of *Gosport*. Many were burnt alive in brush huts, which, in their confusion, had got on fire. In short, such a scene of misery, distress, and cruelty, my eyes never beheld; for which the authors, one may reasonably conclude, never can make atonement in this world.

The enemy left behind them, in their battery, a double fortified nine-pounder, a great part of their baggage, with several tents and markees, besides the three tenders, with their cannon, small arms, &c.; also, the anchors and cables of the *Dunmore, Otter,* and many others, to the amount, it is supposed, of twelve or fifteen hundred pounds. On their leaving the Island, they burnt some valuable vessels which had got aground. Mr. *John Grymes's* effects on the Island have fallen into our hands, consisting of thirty-five negroes, horses, cattle, and furniture. Major *Byrd,* on the approach of our canoes to the Island, was huddled into a cart, in a very sick and low condition, it is said, and carried down to *Cherry-Point,* where he embarked. The second shot the *Dunmore* received cut her boat-swain in two, and wounded two or three others; and she had scarcely recovered from the shock, when a nine-pounder from the lower battery entered her quarter, and beat in a large timber, from the splinters of which Lord *Dunmore* got wounded in the legs, and had all his valuable china smashed about his ears. It is said his Lordship was exceedingly alarmed, and roared out, "Good *God,* that ever I should come to this!" We had our information from one of his people that came ashore after the engagement, who was taken by our scouts; he likewise said that many were killed in the fleet, which had sustained some thousand pounds worth of damage. The *Fowey* and *Roebuck* were the lowermost ships; besides which, there were one hundred and large odd sail of vessels, which took their departure on *Thursday* afternoon, and are supposed to have gone into [the] *Potomack.* In this affair we lost not a man but poor Captain *Arundel,* who was killed by the bursting of a mortar of his own invention, although the General and all the officers were against his firing it. His zeal for the service lost him his life.

August 7th, 1776

My dear Mr. Asquith —

There is excellent news from here sir, excellent news. We have drove Lord Dunmore's fleet out from the Chesapeake Bay, it is departed and shall not return, the Lord be praised. After their flight from Gwynn's, they was moored near St. George's Island and was pleased to send a small fleet up the Potomac, we reckon with an aim to sack General Washington's home and take Lady Washington for a prisoner and free his servants, to his great confusion. But the Lord hath delivered us out of our distresses, and a fog came upon them, and we put up a strong fight, and they has gone out of the Bay entire. They head mayhap for New-York or some say one half the fleet to Jamaica for to sell the Ethiopian Reg. now there ain't no use for them.

So sir we see the last of this dog Dunmore, blacker than hell, whose crimes shall be recalled in all ages and he be called cursed by all men. Let us sing the praises of JEHOVAH for He hath given us victory for He hateth the coward and despiseth the slave who seeks to take his master's life. Now there is in all parts rejoicing.

I have made inquiries with those who recovered some few of the papers from the Devil's Own Ethiopian Regiment, among which there is several morning reports with names of such slaves as escaped to Lord Dunmore's side. There is none called Pro Bono nor called *Gitney* nor called *Asquith*. I reckon he never joined with Lord Dunmore, but set out straight for the forests, he is such a rogue.

I mislike to carry no word of him; but I know you shall be rejoiced at the news of our victory. The Lord be praised, and the hymns be led by

Your humble servant,

B. Gray

[IX.]

THE
REASONING
ENGINE

from the Diary of
Mr. *Josiah Gitney*

"I pity
His wretchedness, though he is my enemy,
For the terrible yoke of blindness that is on him.
I think of him, yet also of myself;
For . . . we are dim shapes, no more, and
weightless shadow."
— Sophocles, *Ajax*

[September] 23 [1776] It was my Purpose to investigate the Owl its neck & I am in a Pet for still I have no such Creature. I spake to Aina, saying, Aina yesterday I wishd you would bespeak an Owl for me. She was impert. & now it is Afternoon & no Owl. V. cold this day & the Trembling is vexatious. I hv ceas'd the Course of Lime for the Irruptions only grow, my Arm is all involved with them, & I divine phps twas the Lime. Mr. Clark came today about his Fee & I told Aina inform him I am not at Home. She is an impert. Hussey & tells me he knowth I am here. Well damn his Eyes, knows he the Work in which I am engaged?

24 Still persisting that terrible icy Sensation beneath the Skin of the Arm, as cold Serpents aslither. It is a bad Sensation, it is a v. bad Sensation & I move my Arm but it doth not give over. I consider puncturing the Arm again & disturbing the Muscle.

25 The House is filled with Whispers & Exclamations. I will not believe it haunted but prepare to delve into the Plasticity of Sound. I vow I hear Laughter.

26 Aina says she shall leave me if I carry on thus. I say & a fine Thing too for she is a negligent Slut.

27 A very bad Day, I was under Apprehensions that there was a Trap-Door beneath my Bed, & that my dead Brothers were in a Convocation there, & waited til I slept to creep out and [illegible]. I have soothed myself with nervine bitters. [Illegible sentence.]

28 A Circumst. most startling. Yesterday Rain fell exceeding hard & it is black at all Hours. In the Day, I writ Letters to the French. Come Evening, I am in my Chair & I hear a Tread upon the Stair & I call out Aina, Aina, but tis not her. I am fill'd with Apprehensions. The nervous Particles are in full Operation, & the Spirits agitated, with conspicuous vaporous Disordering in the whole of the Pulmonary Apparatus & the Arm.

   The Door open & it is Octavian, I thought at first it was a Specter & took up the Poker. I demanded whether he had come to deliver me my Bane & he did not speak but closed the Door & sat upon my other Chair. His Countenance it is hard, devilish hard.

   For a long Time we sat & each regarded the other. I could little imagine a subject of Discourse & at last fell asleep. When I awoke this morning he hath builded me a Fire in the Grate.

   He did not speak & I at length gave it out that Mr. Sharpe was receiv'd of his final Reward, to which Oct. saith he had heard thus upon the Road or he should not have come. Then said I, He did not wake from his Slumber, & Oct. saith that he knew that as well. Then said I, You & Dr. Trefusis provided the fatal Dose. You are his Killers, which he was not backward in owning.

   I know not what hath alter'd my Boy, that he be so cruel.

29 The Sabbath come, Oct. inquired did I wish to attend Services, he should assist me. I wisht him not to touch me & told him to remain at a distance.

30 Would I could scrape the Skin off my Arm without prejudice. Continual Pain & today my Palsies barely allow me to eat. The Boy makes v. free use with my Library. He spent the Day by my Fire, reading Volumes. They all must be sold, said I.

October 3. I asked him today How did you come here? to which he says I come from New-York, where a Ship hath [illegible]. Is this House much alter'd I asked him. He saith that the Wood upon the Walls is v. injured from the Redcoats & that the Balustrades be taken for Kindling. This I denied & he said Do you not recall the other Rooms? & I replied, I recall perfectly Boy; but he led me out of my Chamber & twas as he said.

Do you remember this beautiful Place, said I & he replied I recall it sir. Was there not a wonderful Felicity here when we were in our great Days? Your Mother was the Cynosure of all Eyes. He led me back into my Chamber.

He hath spent the Day in writing at my Table.

4 It hath long been a Subject of great Interest
It hath
I have long been concerned in the question, Whether Reason is inherent in the World, & is simply clouded by the Frailties of Mortal Man, or whether Reason is but an imperfect Illusion, & further, whether Man is a Reasonable Creature hamper'd by Passions, or a Passionate Creature hamper'd by

Reason; & whether, if Reason prevailed, that had made him more generous in his Motions. I am sensible that I believed one Way once but I aver that our College's Defeat is due to an imperfect Understanding of this Question.

Today for a space of five Minutes perhaps I became assured that the Answer to this lay in the Sheet upon my Bed, & did I wind it one Way around my Hand, I was sensible of Reason predominating, & the other, Passion was at the Core, I rapidly twined it each Way seeking which was Right, until the Distemper lifted, & I saw my Folly. Returned to my Senses, I lay by the Twist of Sheet. I hope Octav. did not witness my Phrenzy.

5 It hath come before me that Aina hath rented out the Experimental Chambers to a Family of Smiths. This doth explain the ghostly Halloos. Aina — say I — do you believe it is encompassed within your Station to lease portions of this Estate, & she pert as a dog saith It was her Station to buy us Victuals & for such she need Money. Oct. then submitted that the Smith & his Family were respectful & generous & I objected They shall melt down the Silver. Aina saith Sir the Silver is gone Months ago. I said to Octavian, We are a little reduced in our Circs. But our Suffering shall not be indefinite if Aina would only purchase me an Owl & some other Sundries so I might restore our College to its former Glory & win again the Approbation of our Trustees.

The Boy & I shall be once more the Wonder of the World, say I, the Wonder of the World. His Studies continue apace & he reads & writes all day by the Fire. I taught you to read, Boy, say I, & he says, I am sensible of your Generosity.

[546]

He is ever a Blessing as was his dear Mother. In the Evening I remember her.

7 I demanded that I survey the Family of Smiths, wishing that I might observe their Work, to determine what Deficiencies might be found in their Processes that might be rectified by the guiding Hand of rational Inquiry. Oct. demurred, using as his Excuse my Infirmity and the small Distance to their Shop. I spake to him in the strongest possible Terms of my Authority, and he seems much chastened & quieter.

8 I quizzed the Boy on what manner of Smiths. He did not seem to know, and I asked, *viz*. Goldsmiths, Silversmiths, Coppersmiths, Whitesmiths, Brightsmiths, which, Boy? He believes they are pewterers. Said I, Then look ye, do they cast both hollowware & sadware? See? Do they cast in soapstone or brass? That hath silenced him.

9 Today I asked Octavian to fetch me the Natural History of Ælian. He did but I could not read the Greek, something being amiss with my Eyes. He brought the Candle closer but the Letters were repellant & I believe were merely our Letters backward. I fear that it

10 Oct. introduced me to the Table of the Smiths today. They are not of the finest but they met me with Humility & we had an excellent Meal, I regaled them with many Tales of our Successes.

12 Where is Pro Bono? said I. I know not, said Octavian, He & I parted in New-York. I inquired why he & Pro Bono were in New-York. Oct. would not reply.

14 At my importuning, Octavian conveyed me this day to the Smiths' Shop, which is on Hawkins Street, it was not agreeable. They were a dirty, low Sort of People & haughty. They after a Time neglected my Questions entirely & when the Son was burnt by his own Clumsiness accus'd me of Meddling. The Son call'd me many Names I shall not deign to repeat & tho' the Father sought to mollify he did so merely for Fear of their Rent & I informed them to [illegible] & they are to be out in the Morning. My Arm v. troublesome this day & I have asked Octavian to heat it a Bath & administer a pill rolled of camphor & gum asafœtida. Those Scoundrels are below but they shall be out tomorrow.

15 There is Shouting from below-Stairs. I have [illegible] until after Noon. [Next sentence illegible.]

16 I look'd up from my Book, having fall asleep, & found Octavian scratching upon his Writing, an infernal Scratching that tore the Paper & witnessed him take the Book in which he wrote & fling it at the Table & in a childish Fit hurl it to the Floor. I bade him Steady, Steady, but he came to me and stood before me, as he would offer me Violence. I cried out & recalled him to his Duty & the Hazard of a Slave laying Hand upon his Master & he had the impertinence to say he was not this eight Month my Slave & left the Chamber.

He doth not comprehend my full Palsy nor how Agitation inspires its Assaults through the Disequilibrium of the Humors, *viz.* the Superabundance of Bile. He is in a Fury but he doth not consider how such a frightful State might upset the Systems of those around him, he hath no Mind to it. I must hold my Arm against the Bedstead even to write, so great is the Trembling.

In all such Buffets it behooves us to use Patience with the Offenders, that they might be brought back to the Path of Right. Tho' I should use a Switch if I might.

17 I am astonished; Pro Bono hath a Wife, saith Octavian. I inquired why he [illegible]. Then says I, Where is your Fellow Murderer Dr. Trefusis? — He is beyond harm, saith Octavian. — He is in the Grave? — At this, the Boy suffered some Confusion, then to asseverate, My Tutor is deceased, Sir. — Then, said I, he is in Hell, for what he hath done to me and to Dick Sharpe, to which the Boy had no Reply.

Whenever I move — seek to move without Palsy — I curse him who hath brought me low & for he was a Betrayer, an Adder I nursed in my Bosom. I yet recall his simpering Face as he offered us Tea. Sir, you have made me an old Man as you were. In one Stroke you added to me twenty Year, I extremely wish you damned.

18 The Boy is [illegible]. I asked him again of Pro Bono's Bride & their Location. Oct. will not reply, but informs me that it is a hidden Place, & that when he leaves me — mark this! — leaves me — he shall fly to them. You shall not leave, say I. — Says he, I shall, sir. — And again, say I, You shall not. & I demanded to

be told of this Refuge of Slaves. Oct. says only that Others have gone before them, & that it is a considerable Voyage, & that he knows not whether any of them shall reach the Place.—You shall never reach it, say I, for if you stir without this House, you shall be taken by the Watch.—Said he, You have no Power over me, sir.—Said I, No Power, Boy? I have every Power. You shall not in any wise leave.—How may you obstruct me?—I shall tell the Watch! And they shall rush to apprehend you!—He rose and stood.—Tell them, said he. Tell the Watch of me.

He left the Chamber.

I lay in my Bed. He is an ungrateful Wretch. He is returned now, and writing, but he is [illegible] to be hung in a Gibbet, were there equal Justice, he is of so contrary a Temper, he is

22 I for three days have [illegible]. I even now barely can admit Food.

23 I live yet, I live yet. I walked with Oct.'s Aid around the Chamber many Revolutions & that is good. I told Oct. I have suffered illness since his Mother's Death & I avow the procatarctic cause is a Splenetic Vapor released by her Corpse in the Autopsy, for which I have [illegible] all manner of Infusions & Specifics but still cannot rid myself of the Distemper.

24 When I was walking today, I fell and am greatly bruised. I am in some fear, for twas Octavian tripped me. He saith, I did no such Thing, Sir, but I am sensible of his Resentment. He offered

his Foot in my Path, which he denies. He works all Hours at his Writing, copying out some dirty Volume onto fair, & I believe does not sleep.

27 I wish I had an Apparatus with to experiment on Dephlogisticated Air. I requested Octav. to bespeak an Apparatus from a Glazier but he would not & defied me. This Evening, again he tripped me & I fell to the Floor; & again he denied All.

28 Do you recall the Transit of Venus? said I. Those were some fine Times, when Lord Cheldthorpe was among us & this House admitted the first Men among all Nations.—Oct. replied he did recall that circumstance.

30 My Fear of the Boy grows, why has he returned? Tonight he brought me my Soup, & said he had cooked it himself. I tasted it several Bites & then said I would not eat it more. He asked, Why, sir?

He had put Pebbles in it, they were in the Bowl. Octavian, said I, why have you put Stones in it?—I have not, sir.—Then this?—I know not how those appeared there.

31 I cannot sleep for hearing his Breath & I know he is by. I cannot abide how little we know other men's Motive Parts, I speculate might there be a Manner in which we might map the Springs of the Brain & its Excitations? When I was a Child I believed so. We should be happier could we see each other's Thoughts & there should be no Deceit. Perhaps investigate Trepanning.

[November] 4 This Eve Octav. lit us a Fire & sate upon his Chair & moved me to mine. This seemed a pleasant Evening until he announced that he has completed his Work & the Time hath come for his Leaving. — You cannot leave, say I. I have Need of you here. — (As I spake it, sensible of the Spleen Disemboguing nervous Vapors & the whole Frame altering in its chemical Condition.) — I shall leave tomorrow, said he. — What of our Work together? — We have no Work together, sir. — How! I have devoted near Two Decades to you. — To the Study of me. — & I do not wish you disappear from View. — If that is our Work together, then our Work, said he, is complete. — I have Volumes of Data, said I, and you shall in a Stroke render them all useless. — They are gone, sir. — They are in no wise gone, I replied. I preserved them in Canaan against the Occupation. I brought them back to this place. — He shakes his Head. — Lead me, say I, to the Interdicted Room.

He rose & assisted me & we [illegible] into the Hall. It was a melancholy Sight for as he led me, at each Turn I thought I saw our Brethren or his Mother in the Days of our Glory, now the Halls are dark & stain'd where once we

Do you recall the Dragon's Skull? I asked. — I do, sir. — It was broke into a Thousand Pieces by the Redcoats. — I am sorry, sir. — Do you recall your Mother laughing here? Just here — my Jest regarding a Cockerel. — I do not recall the Jest, sir. — I heard you Cry for the first time in that Dining Room, when the Midwife was above. — &c.

We entered the Experimental Chambers to find the wretched Family of Smiths with their Laundry hung over their Sticks of Furniture. A Revelation holding little Surprise.

We came to the Door of the Interdicted Chamber, which had Octavian's Likeness pasted upon it, the Lock was broke open, I was in a Rage. We entered & Octav. lit the Shelves with his Lanthorn & they were empty.

They were here, said I. The Volumes with your Data, your Diet & Excretion &c. I preserved them, I am not mad.

You are not mad, Octavian said, you did preserve them, sir. Every Day this last Month I have kindled your Fire with them.

Aghast—I beat upon him—I beat upon his Chest & called

He would not

17 Years—17 Years—you have burnt 17 Years—all lost—no Record—my God!—you Child!—you fool Intransigent—

He put me by as one would a mewling Infant & without him, I fell—he lifted me, he rested me against the Wall. He went to the highest Shelf and from thence drew down two final Volumes.

Are they your Birth? I asked. You have preserved your Birth?

They are my entire Record, said he. I have writ an History of thy Experiment. He gave the Volumes to me.—There is your Narrative of my Growth, said he. By my own Hand. These Volumes replace yours. I will observe while you read them.

I have not read them, I am too weak, I suffered Fits of Shaking & he & the Smith Father delivered me back to my Chamber & there administered *sal volatile*. Octavian says I shall read them tomorrow.

[553]

5 O my dear Boy. Best of Sons.

6 When I finished, I lay them by & could not speak. Tis a cold & brown day & I can little countenance that I shall be alone this Night. It hath been so pleasant these Months with Octavian offering Company.

For some time we sat without Word or Motion. He asked, What thought you of the Narrative?

I asked, If he would forgive me.

He gave no reply & so we sat. I said, Fain would I alter the Past and keep Dick Sharpe from our Company. By his Silence, I concluded that he was displeased. I asked again if he would forgive me, & this time, he gave me a reply, which I cannot repeat, so heavily does all weigh upon me.

He rose to go, & said farewell & thanked me for all I had done for him. I bid him tarry a time & take his Supper but he would not, I could not detain him longer. Then there is one final Matter, my Boy, said I, & I called Aina & the three of us went into the Nursery where all is stored & I bid them move Pieces until the Case was found & I bade Octavian take it. He inquired as to its Contents & opened it, his Violin. It is yours, said I.

He came to me & shake my Hand & I was sensible I shall never see him more.

18 Years ago came his Mother to this House, a Child herself, & we had such Hopes. All Mankind seemed perfectible & we had Painters & Poets & we were indeed Lords of Matter, all number'd cleanly & meetly. I hear her Step above me as she learn'd the Ways of Hoops & I see him as a Lad disporting himself upon the miniature Fiddle we had wrought for him

& there was never more solemn Poppet. I do not know how, purposed with so high & noble Aims, we end thus in Ruin. You are a Marvel, my Child, you are my best Years.

That said, he was gone, and I watched him depart in the Afternoon, down the Street, away from this House. I assayed to throw up the Sash, that I might longer watch his Progress, who was the great Work of my Hands, but twould not lift. For a while I struggled in vain, then knowing him already gone, retired two Steps to my Bed. I am sure I could not have seen him by then, had I even succeeded; had I even been able to look.

[X.]

TABULA RASA

which concludes the
Manuscript Testimony
of *Octavian Nothing*

"What ought I to do? I see only darkness everywhere. Shall I
believe I am nothing? Shall I believe I am God? 'All things
change and succeed each other.' You are mistaken; there is . . ."
— Blaise Pascal, *Pensées* [uncompleted fragment]

☙ Thus ends my narrative. I cannot say whether it contain wisdom or folly; nor what moral lies therein. I know only that I wished to recount it, and to speak of those whom I have known and who have striven for virtue and have perished.

I sought Rebellion, and found grim Authority engirded there; I mustered in the ranks of Royal Authority, and found there only Chaos fighting in straighter lines. And so when we reached New-York docks in the *Crepuscule,* and were set at liberty there, we determined we must find a new route which should secure us from the ire and indifference of both England and Colony. In a crowded ordinary we found one who spake of a different place, and we returned the next night to receive instructions, that we might be conducted there. When I leave this place, I shall make my way to that fastness, and, God willing, shall there be reunited with several of my Regiment, Pro Bono and Nsia Williams first among them. When I see them again, they shall have taken new names of their own devising.

I fear I shall be apprehended, or they shall; but if we do not meet in that place, then, my brother, my sister, who have voyaged with me upon those great rivers of the South, I shall meet you again beyond that last, that profoundest river, the river of Jordan. A river is not a wall, but a gate through which we might pass to freedom.

O my friends, now gone, who have traveled by my side and dropped away, I have told your tales; let me be thy praise-singer, though I, living last, live least: Morenike, called Cassiopeia, most dazzling of mothers, mistress of the mask; Richard Sharpe, who sought profit even in the skies; Pompey Lewis, called Pomp, gentle teller of horrors; Slant Croak, mild Slant, who witnessed the ravages of kindness; Olakunde, lost, who drummed gods into being; and John Trefusis, who loved mankind so fiercely he could not do other than despise it. I sing your tales so that none of this shall pass from remembrance; so our fleet shall always be sailing, shall always be populated by the brave, anxious for fight; and shall never reach its destination.

Heraclitus saith that *"War is the father of all things,"* for we could not subsist without strife within us and unease. I lament that I can see no flaw in this bitter axiom. I have seen men strive for rectitude, and in the end, take off the vizard of right to discover only self there. And yet Olakunde speaks of *ashe,* and the vow that doth change all of who you are. We have vowed we shall be different from either of these lumbering powers we have witnessed; and setting out thus into a land where we might discover new bonds of amity and social union, perhaps we shall keep those vows. But winter is long, and need is great, and we know not whether we travel to join the ranks of Edenic vision or guilty brigandage. Yet we have made the vow; and though no other human generation hath done other than despoil, perhaps we shall be the first.

There are some who believe that the mind is a blank tablet, on which experience is writ until the page be full, and the cryptic world is known; but I see rather that my own life hath been one long forgetting, the erasure of what was drawn, a terrible redaction; til all that remains is blank white and comfortless.

I know not what we have been; I know not what we are; but I know what we might be.

And so I light out for the unknown regions.

OCTAVIAN NOTHING
November 4th, 1776

If this were the fantasy novel it so much resembles, there would be a third volume. In that book, Octavian, Pro Bono, and Nsia would come forth from their place of hiding; they would orchestrate the desperate clash of these two great nations and engineer the toppling of both governments. There would be gargantuan, cleansing battles, and in their wake, our heroes would found a new realm. All people would be free, shackles would fall from every wrist, and bounty would return to the land.

But of course, this is not what happened. Instead, slavery persisted in this country for another four generations. And a full century after the general emancipation, nearly two hundred years after the Revolution, federal legislation finally ensured legal equality for black and white.

Though the characters are, for the most part, either fabrications or composites, the major events recorded in this novel are real. As an example, the disastrous performance of Lieutenant-General Burgoyne's satirical squib *The Blockade of Boston* was indeed interrupted by news of a canny Patriot attack on Charlestown, exactly as described, though the episode actually happened a few months later than I have set it. On the other hand, the tragic expedition of Lord Dunmore's Royal Ethiopian Regiment occurred very much as it is depicted here. In that instance, I tried to cleave closely to the actual time-line of events. My aim was to see the event from a point of view neglected in the extant sources, a process which of course required speculation as well as the combination of facts and stories usually found in isolation. In the interests of filling in the blanks, I attempted to weave together the military history with tales of escape recorded in the early nineteenth century, with legends of Africa and the Great Dismal Swamp told at the time, and with minutiæ about plantation dress, the employment of tortoises, and reports of the effects of slavery, such as the surprising statistic that roughly one in twenty fugitive slaves was reported as having a stutter, the traumatic effect of servitude and punishment. I wanted to combine these elements to imagine this expedition in its early glory and its later defeat.

It has been estimated that some eight hundred African American men joined the ranks of Lord Dunmore's Royal Ethiopian Regiment, though thousands more, male and female, fled their masters in the midst of Revolutionary chaos. Of the eight hundred who finally reached his fleet and enlisted, an estimated two hundred survived the campaign. Most of those who died succumbed to disease, especially smallpox, which ravaged the African American troops.

Lord Dunmore continued, throughout the rest of the war, to agitate for permission to command an army of freed slaves against the rebels. Even after the final defeat of the British at Yorktown, Dunmore hoped that the tide might still be turned by a more vigorous pursuit of the methods he had implemented in Virginia. As we know, his lobbying came to nothing. He was later made governor of the Bahamas, a post in which he demonstrated exactly the same incompetence and petulance that had made his stint as an embattled governor of Virginia such an abject failure. Eventually, he returned to England. His daughter secretly married one of George III's sons, which enraged the king and lost Dunmore's family considerable favor. Dunmore died in the early years of the nineteenth century.

And what of Octavian? What would have happened to him in the years that followed?

At the end of this volume, he flees to one of the so-called "maroon communities" hidden in the great wilderness expanses of the New World. Following the Revolution, there were many of these outlaw villages, most of them concentrated in the swamps of the South. In the early years of the Republic, the majority were found out and raided, the inhabitants hunted down, killed in battle, imprisoned, or executed. We may hope that we do not hear of Octavian's secret home because it was never discovered.

Others who fought with the Royal Ethiopians continued to fight on the side of the British. When the British finally abandoned their colonies, they took thousands of African Americans with them. Those who were free generally settled in Nova Scotia; many of these, finding the place inhospitable, eventually returned to Africa, where the English government established a repatriation colony in Sierra Leone.

What of the African Americans who fought for the Patriot cause, as Octavian did earlier? There were three exclusively African American units on the Continental side during the conflict: the First Rhode Island Regiment, the Bucks of America, and the Black Brigade of Saint Domingue. Most of the black soldiers in the American forces, however, served side by side with their white brothers-in-arms. Some were decorated for their service to the budding nation, and many were freed. Others remained enslaved.

On the one hand, black freemen in American regiments enjoyed the same pay, the same food, and the same conditions as their white counterparts—the most racially integrated fighting force in the United States until the time of the Korean War. On the other hand, well into the nineteenth century we find African American veterans embroiled in legal battles over their service, their freedom, and their promised pensions. On the American side, as on the British side, policies regarding slavery were more a product of strategy than humanitarian concern. The Americans went so far as to offer slaves as a premium to white men who enlisted in the army toward the end of the war. Thomas Jefferson ratified a bill that granted three hundred acres and a healthy male slave to any Virginian who joined the army and fought for the duration. South Carolina enacted a similar measure. General Thomas Sumter instituted a graduated system of distributing slaves among his officers: Majors received three adults, lieutenant colonels were entitled to three adults and a child, and so on.

The question of which side—the British or the American— offered more to the slave is a complicated one. While, on balance, the British approach to African American allies was generally more consistent, it is clear that neither army's policies were actuated by any concern other than military expediency. The decision to emancipate slaves or leave them in bondage was not based on abstract principles but on strategic interests.

It is startling, perhaps, to consider that the continuance of slavery was so thoroughly interwoven with the politics of freedom. In the course of my research for this book, I have come to believe that the American Republic would not have survived its early years—would not have made it through the War of 1812—if it had not been fueled and funded by two profound acts of ethnic violence: the establishment of slavery and the annexation of Native American land, both of which practices played a major part in the inception and conduct of the Revolution. The freedom—economic, social, and intellectual—enjoyed by the vocal and literate elite of the early Republic would have been impossible if it had not been for the enslavement, displacement, and destruction of others.

As I conducted my research, I watched, appalled, as the term *liberty* proliferated so many meanings that, in the end, it had none: It meant at once the right to declare independence from the Crown and the right to adhere to the Crown; to some, freedom to own slaves, and to others, freedom from slavery. Cast back and forth in relentless cannonades, it became evacuate of meaning.

And thus one of the great paradoxes I encountered while writing: Liberty was at once a quality so abstract as to be insubstantial—and yet so real in its manifestations that it was worth dying for. It is real every time we enjoy the right to a fair trial, judged by a jury of our peers; it is real every time we discuss our government in a newspaper column, a school report, or a historical novel without fear of reprisal, raps on the door in the dead of night. It is a desperately vital reality, worthy of the wars that have been fought for it.

Yes, our Revolutionary forefathers espoused a vexed and even contradictory view of liberty. But it is easy to condemn the dead for their mistakes. Hindsight is cheap, and the dead can't argue. It is harder to examine our own actions and to ask what abuses we commit, what conspicuous cruelties we allow to afford our luxuries, which of our deeds will be condemned by our children's children when they look back upon us. We, too, are making decisions. We, too, have our hypocrisies, our systems of shame.

❋ ❋ ❋

On April 19, in the year 1975, my parents woke me up at four in the morning. They took me down to the river and put me in the canoe. I have only the faintest memory of this. My father and mother paddled us down the Concord River to the Old North Bridge, where, in the rushes, we saw some red-winged blackbirds and the president of the United States. President Gerald Ford was standing on the Old North Bridge, delivering a bicentennial address.

On the one bank was a hill where, exactly two hundred years before I arrived there—down almost to the minute—the men of my town, ordinary citizens, men like my father, had come over the rise and had marched toward the river to engage in battle with the most powerful army in the world.

That time, those people, were not mythic; they had once been real, though now historical—just as the year 1975, the year I bobbed on the waters ten feet below the pants of the president of the United States, is now not real, but historical.

History is not a pageant arrayed for our delectation.

We are all always gathered there. We have come to the riverside to fight or to flee. We are gathered at the river, upon those shores, and the water is always moving, and the president of the United States always gesticulates silently above us, his image on the water. Nothing will cease. Nothing will stop. We ourselves are history.

The moment is always now.

ACKNOWLEDGMENTS

This book could not have happened without the generous support of countless friends and colleagues. I'd like to thank, particularly: Liz Bicknell, my editor; Sherry Fatla, the designer; Hannah Mahoney, the copy editor; Caroline Lawrence, the jacket designer; the Sales and Marketing Department at Candlewick, who were confronted by a book that had missed its audience by two centuries; my parents and sister; Nicole, for reading drafts; my friends and colleagues at Vermont College, for their encouragement. And for their tremendous asistance on a variety of topics: Laura Murphy; J. L. Bell; Peter J. Wrike; Dr. Dana Sutton of the University of California, Irvine; Josh Graml of the Mariners' Museum in Newport News, Virginia; Myles McConnon, Volunteer at Minute Man National Historical Park; Ken Wells of St. Mark's School, Southborough; Robert Howard, former Curator of Technology at the Hagley Museum; Dr. Carmen Giunta, Professor of Chemistry, Le Moyne College; and, as always, the staff of the Boston Athenæum.

I would also like to mention in particular my indebtedness to the two historical studies that cover most fully the actions of Lord Dunmore's Ethiopian Regiment, both of which were invaluable: Ivor Noël Hume's *1775: Another Part of the Field* (Knopf, 1966) and Peter J. Wrike's

The Governor's Island: Gwynn's Island, Virginia, During the Revolution (BrandyLane, The Gwynn's Island Museum, 1993). Other important information came from Percy Burdelle Caley's *Dunmore: Colonial Governor of New York and Virginia, 1770–1782* (PhD Thesis, University of Pittsburgh, 1939).

I am indebted to Brooks Haxton for permission to quote (in slightly adapted form) on page 34 from his gorgeous Heraclitus translation, entitled *Fragments: The Collected Wisdom of Heraclitus* (Viking, 2001). The quotations on pages 295 and 296 are taken from Philip Wheelwright, *The Presocratics* (Macmillan, 1966); that on page 541 is taken from Sophocles' "Ajax" in *Sophocles II* (University of Chicago Press, 1957); and the fragment on page 557 is taken whole from Blaise Pascal, *Pensées* (translated by W. F. Trotter. Modern Library, 1941).

Several of the items in this book are transcriptions of real eighteenth-century documents (slightly edited for length and clarity). These include the documents found on pages 117–120, 264–265, and 536–538. The originals are available in a variety of sources, most notably Peter Force's *American Archives,* Series IV, Volumes 3–6 (Washington: 1837–1853).

A Note on the Type

The font used for the text is a version of Caslon. Modifications have been made to ligatures and kerning pairs. It is based on the original font designed by William Caslon in England in the 1720s. His type designs were highly regarded there and soon set the standard for printing. The use of Caslon spread to the American colonies, where it was the most frequently used font, from printing fine books to newspapers, and was used to typeset the Declaration of Independence.

Archetype is a contemporary font, designed in 2000 by the Hungarian designer Gábor Kóthay. It was chosen for its compatibility with the colonial Caslon and is used for some of the documents and display typography in this book.

A Readers' Guide

1. Many American stories follow the rags-to-riches format made famous by Horatio Alger Jr., in which the main character, living in poverty, works hard and sacrifices to achieve the American dream. By contrast, at the beginning of his story, Octavian appears to have everything — his mother, his health, fine clothes, and a superior education — but at the end, he has little or nothing left. Do you agree? Is this a riches-to-rags story?

2. When Mr. Sharpe takes over the Novanglian College of Lucidity, Octavian is no longer given stories and whole manuscripts to learn from, but rather fragments in isolation, on which he is tested. Might Anderson be making a comment about the current practice of standardized testing in education today? Would you agree with him?

3. When Octavian joins Lord Dunmore's Royal Ethiopian Regiment, he hears the many stories of his fellow Africans and records them in his journal. How does this informal education on the condition of his fellow man compare with the formal classical education he received at the College of Lucidity? Which had more influence on the man that Octavian becomes by the story's end?

4. Late in the story, Dr. Trefusis declares that *"Only the dead hath seen the end of war."* (p. 511). Is a nation that chooses peace and puts down its weapons forever at risk of invasion by another seeking dominion? Or do you believe that Octavian is right in his hope that there must be "some place one could go and begin again. This time, untainted"?

5. A rumination in Josiah Gitney's diary (p. 545) questions "whether Man is a Reasonable Creature hamper'd by Passions, or a Passionate Creature hamper'd by Reason." Which side are you on?

6. For such a serious story, which includes an abundance of grim events, the text is also peppered with humor. Is there a humorous moment or line that stuck out for you? Which character do you find the most humorous?

7. In a story that focuses so intently on identity, names are very important. Cassiopeia is named after a constellation, and astronomy permeates the novels. Some characters are given only numbers for names. Pro Bono takes on many names throughout the books to escape from trouble, and Octavian chooses to take the surname of Nothing. Discuss the implications of these names as they relate to the characters and to the plot.

8. This work was originally published for a teen audience. Some adults think it is too sophisticated for teens to understand. What books were you reading as a teen that adults might suggest were too complicated for you? Were there any that you reread as an adult in order to gain new understanding? Do you think we underestimate teens today?

9. Bravery in the face of uncertainty is a theme throughout the narrative. The rebels rose up against their own powerful British government at great risk and with unknown outcome. What acts of bravery are committed by the book's individual main characters? Octavian? Cassiopeia? Pro Bono? Mr. Trefusis? Mr. Gitney?

10. In his author's note, Anderson says that while researching and writing *Octavian Nothing,* he encountered this paradox of the Revolutionary War era: that "Liberty was at once a quality so abstract so as to be insubstantial — and yet so real in its manifestations that it was worth dying for." What does liberty mean to you? What hypocrisies are at work in our current time for which we may be held accountable in the years to come?

A Conversation with M. T. Anderson

1. This second volume concludes Octavian's story, which you thought of as a single narrative. Did you know everything that was going to happen before you started writing these books?

Like many writers, I usually begin with a messy collection of images and fragments: in this case, the image of Octavian standing in brown gloom; the idea of a pox party; a picture of Octavian's mother playing the harpsichord; the desire to examine the Loyalists during the Revolution; a question about what colonial Boston was like when it was militarized and under siege . . . things like that. So I started doing research and seeing which ideas stuck around and which became less interesting.

It took me about six months before I began writing, and about eight months before I actually knew the whole story. A few months in, the discovery of Lord Dunmore's Ethiopian Regiment — an episode of the war I'd never heard about before — convinced me I needed to change my original ending. By the time I'd written about sixty or so pages of the first volume, I knew pretty much the whole plot. In fact, I ended up working on the two parts simultaneously, revising the first book while I wrote the second book.

2. Both books use a number of different ways to tell the story, such as journal entries and letters. Why did you choose to use a variety of ways to tell Octavian's story?

One of the challenges of writing a historical novel is the question of perspective: People from the past were profoundly different from us in so many ways. The whole way they saw the world was very alien. I find that fascinating. (Who would I have been if I didn't believe in the circulation of the blood, or microorganisms, or outer space, or the equality of women?)

The question is, how do you reproduce that element of difference? How do you make sure your book about the Middle Ages, for example, really feels medieval-ish, and not like a bunch of high-fiving Californians in really stupid hats? The Middle Ages weren't just castles and armor. Ancient Rome wasn't just togas. The Mongol Empire wasn't just *90210* on horses.

Each period, each country, each city has its own constellation of attitudes and beliefs. Some people believe humans to be essentially reasonable. Some people believe humans to be essentially wild and irrational. Some see angels in the stars. Others feel no safety on the earth. For thousands of years, people suffered from diseases we no longer believe could exist and were cured with remedies that seem nonsensical to us. Who's to say they were entirely wrong, or that we're right? They were the ones who hobbled and then could walk.

I decided that the best way to explore the texture of eighteenth-century American thought and life was to try to enter into their language. For example, in the eighteenth century, the word *man* could stand in for all of humankind, male and female. Now that would sound a little weird to us — like leaving out 50 percent of the species. Think of phrases like "the rights of man" or "the rights of all men," which were quite common back in the day. That difference in usage — *all men* versus *all people* — conveys subliminally an important philosophical difference between the eighteenth century and the twenty-first. That's just one example of how trying to write like someone from the past forces you to try to *think* like someone from the past. It conceals certain things from view and reveals others.

So that's why I decided to write the book as a series of documents. I wanted it all to sound like it was coming unfiltered from the period. I wanted to raise the question of who is allowed to describe us and of how those descriptions linger in history and form our understanding of the past.

3. *What was the research process like for this book?*

It took me a long time to do the research and writing — six years in all. I loved doing the research. (Mainly because it allowed me to delay writing for a while. . . . Writing is never easy!) I read as widely as I could in texts of the period: scientific treatises, tactical manuals, Gothic novels, joke books, diaries, ads.

Because I was so incredibly slow, research tools actually changed as I wrote. By the end of the writing, there were these incredible online resources that hadn't existed a few years before — all kinds of obscure books available now on Project Gutenberg and the Internet Archive. You can read them instantaneously, without getting out of your chair (or your tin bathtub). Now, there is something that has improved since the eighteenth century.

4. *Did you have to adjust historical details about the Revolutionary War and Lord Dunmore's regiment in the interest of storytelling?*

In general, I tried to be extremely scrupulous about basing everything in these books firmly on fact — no matter how strange the facts may sound. I was particularly careful about this in the section on Lord Dunmore's Ethiopian Regiment. Not many people have written about this campaign or even know it existed, so I thought it was important to try to reproduce the actual history as closely as possible. I tried to synthesize things that were known rather than making up new events. I did drop several months out of the campaign in the middle. (Pay close attention to the dates and you'll see where this happens.) In my version, they happen, but no one talks about them.

I took more liberties with the timeline of the siege of Boston — but still, the books adhere very closely to the truth, insofar as it can be verified. The skirmish on Hog and Noddle's islands, for example, described in the first volume, is extrapolated from descriptions of the period, and Lieutenant-General Burgoyne's play *The Blockade of Boston*, really was interrupted by an attack on Charlestown, though a few months later than I placed the event.

There are several real documents included among the counterfeits: Dunmore's proclamation, for example, Washington's letter about Dunmore, and the description of the final battle on Gwynn's Island. (A complete list can be found in the acknowledgments.)

5. *The novel ends with Octavian's future unknown. What were your thoughts on leaving the ending open in this way?*

I guess, at the end of this book, I launched him into the world — and I felt that's all he needed from me. He's on his own now! I wanted the reader to feel the ambiguity of Octavian's future. For one thing, this is what looking at history is like: you catch glimpses of these people — sometimes very intimate and intense glimpses — and then they're gone. The record runs out.

The *Astonishing Life of*
OCTAVIAN NOTHING
TRAITOR TO THE NATION
VOLUME I
THE POX PARTY
by M. T. Anderson

A *Los Angeles Times* Book Prize Finalist

A *New York Times Book Review* Notable Book of the Year

"An imaginative and highly intelligent exploration of the horrors of human experimentation and the ambiguous history of America's origins." — *The New York Times Book Review*

★ "Highly accomplished. . . . The novel's questions, which move into today's urgent arguments about . . . what patriotism, freedom, and citizenship mean." — *Booklist* (starred review)

★ "A historical novel of prodigious scope, power, and insight. . . . This is the Revolutionary War seen . . . through a disturbingly original lens." — *Kirkus Reviews* (starred review)

www.candlewick.com